FLIGHT OF
EAGLES

29/7/98

Bought at Stansted Airport on the way to Salzburg.

Also by Jack Higgins

FLIGHT OF EAGLES

JACK HIGGINS

MICHAEL JOSEPH

LONDON

MICHAEL JOSEPH LTD
Published by the Penguin Group
27 Wrights Lane, London w8 5tz, England
Viking Penguin Inc., 375 Hudson Street, New York, New York 10014, USA
Penguin Books Australia Ltd, Ringwood, Victoria, Australia
Penguin Books Canada Ltd, 10 Alcorn Avenue, Toronto, Ontario, Canada m4v 3b2
Penguin Books (NZ) Ltd, 182–190 Wairau Road, Auckland 10, New Zealand

Penguin Books Ltd, Registered Offices: Harmondsworth, Middlesex, England

First published in Great Britain 1998
3 5 7 9 10 8 6 4

Copyright © Jack Higgins, 1998

Set in 11.5/15pt Monotype Bembo
Typeset by Rowland Phototypesetting Ltd,
Bury St Edmunds, Suffolk
Printed in England by Clays Ltd, St Ives plc

A CIP catalogue record for this book is available from the British Library

Hardback ISBN 0 7181 4297 7
Trade paperback ISBN 0 7181 4298 5

The moral right of the author has been asserted

For my wife Denise,
for special help with this one.
Amongst many virtues, pilot
extraordinaire . . .

THE ENGLISH CHANNEL

1997

ONE

When we lost the starboard engine I knew we were in trouble, but then the whole trip was bad news from the start.

My wife had been staying with me for a few days at our house in Jersey in the Channel Islands when a phone message indicated a strong interest from a major Hollywood producer in filming one of my books. It meant getting over to England fast to our house at Chichester, a staging post to London. I phoned the air-taxi firm I usually used, but they had no plane available. However, they'd see what they could do. What they came up with was a Cessna 310 from Granville on the coast of Brittany and a rather ageing pilot called Dupont. Beggars not being choosers, I booked the flight without hesitation because the weather forecast wasn't good and we wanted to get on with it. I sat in the rear, but the 310 having dual controls, my wife, being a highly experienced pilot, chose to occupy the right-hand seat to the pilot. Thank God she did.

The Channel Islands and the English Channel are subject to fogs that appear in an incredibly short time and close down everything fast, and that's exactly what happened that morning. Taking off from Jersey was fine, but within ten minutes, the island was fogged out, and not only the French coast but Guernsey also.

We started for the South Coast of England, Southampton our

destination. Dupont was close to sixty from the look of him, grey-haired, a little overweight. Sitting behind my wife and looking to one side as he worked the plane, I noticed a film of sweat on his face.

Denise was wearing headphones and passed me a spare pair, which I plugged in. At one stage she was piloting the plane as he engaged in conversation with air traffic control. He took over and she turned to me.

'We're at five thousand. Bad fog down there. Southampton's out, including everything to the east. We're trying for Bourne-mouth, but it doesn't look good.'

Having avoided death as a child from IRA bombs in the Shankill in Belfast, and various minor spectaculars in the Army years later, I've learned to take life as it comes. I smiled above the roar of the engine, confident in my wife's abilities, found the half-bottle of Moët et Chandon champagne they'd thoughtfully provided in the bar box, and poured some into a plastic glass. Everything, I've always thought, worked out for the best. In this case, it was for the worst.

It was exactly at that moment that the starboard engine died on us. For a heart-stopping moment, there was a plume of black smoke, and then it faded away.

Dupont seemed to get into a state, wrestling with the controls, frantically making adjustments, but to no avail. We started to go down. In a panic, he started to shout in French to the air traffic control at Bournemouth, but my wife waved a hand at him and took over, calmly, sweetly reasonable.

'We have fuel for perhaps an hour,' she reported. 'Have you a suggestion?'

The air traffic controller happened to be a woman and her voice was just as calm.

'I can't guarantee it, but Cornwall is your best bet. It's not closed in as fully there. Cold Harbour, a small fishing port on the coast near Lizard Point. There's an old RAF landing strip there from the Second World War. Abandoned for years but usable. I'll put out your details to all rescue services. Good luck.'

We were at 3000 for the next twenty minutes and the traffic on the radio was confusing, often blanked out by some kind of static. The fog swirled around us and then it started to rain very hard. Dupont seemed more agitated than ever, the sweat on his face very obvious now. Occasionally he spoke, but again in French and, once more, Denise took over. There were various voices, lots of static and the plane started to rock as a thunderstorm exploded around us.

Denise spoke, very controlled, giving our details. 'Possible Mayday. Attempting a landing at airstrip at Cold Harbour.'

And then the static cleared and a voice echoed strong and true. 'This is Royal National Lifeboat Institution, Cold Harbour, Zec Acland speaking. No way you're going to land here, girl. Can't see my hand in front of my face.'

For Dupont, this was the final straw. He gave a sudden moan, seemed to convulse and his head lolled to one side. The plane lurched down, but Denise took control and gradually levelled it out. I leaned over and felt for a pulse in his neck.

'It's there, but it's weak. Looks like a heart attack.'

I pushed him away from her. She said calmly, 'Take the life-jacket from under his seat and put it on him, then do the same for yourself.'

She put the 310 on automatic and pulled on her own life-jacket. I took care of Dupont and struggled into mine.

'Are we going into the drink?'

'I don't think we've got much choice.' She took manual control again.

I tried to be flippant, a personal weakness. 'But it's March. I mean, far too cold in the water.'

'Just shut up! This is business,' she said and spoke again as we went down. 'RNLI, Cold Harbour. I'll have to ditch. Pilot seems to have had a heart attack.'

That strong voice sounded again. 'Do you know what you're doing, girl?'

'Oh, yes. One other passenger.'

'I've already notified Royal Navy air sea rescue, but not much they can do in this pea-souper. The Cold Harbour lifeboat is already at sea and I'm on board. Give me a position as accurately as you can.'

Fortunately the plane was fitted with a Global Positional System, satellite linked, and she read it off. 'I'll go straight down,' she said.

'By God, you've got guts, girl. We'll be there, never fear.'

My wife often discusses her flying with me, so I was aware of the problems in landing a fixed wing light twin aircraft in the sea. You had to approach with landing gear retracted and full flaps and reasonable power, a problem with one engine dead.

Light winds and small waves, land into the wind, heavy wind and big waves, land parallel to the crests. But we didn't know what waited down there. We couldn't see.

Denise throttled back and we descended and I watched the altimeter. One thousand, then five hundred. Nothing – not a damn thing – and then at a couple of hundred feet, broken fog, the sea below, small waves and she dropped us into the wind.

For those few moments, I think she became a truly great pilot. We bounced, skidded along the waves and came to a halt. The shock was considerable, but she had the cabin door open in an instant.

'Bring him with you,' she called and went out fast on to the wing.

I leaned over, unfastened Dupont's seat-belt, then shoved him head first through the door. She reached for him, slid off the wing into the water and pulled him after her. I went then and slipped off the wing. I remembered some statistics she'd shown me on landings at sea. Ninety seconds seemed to be about par for the course before the plane sank.

Denise was hanging on to Dupont as they floated away in their yellow life-jackets. As I followed, the plane sinking, she shouted, 'Oh God, Tarquin's in there.'

This requires a word of explanation. Tarquin was a bear, but a unique bear. When we found him sitting on a shelf in a Brighton antique shop, he was wearing the leather flying helmet, flying boots and blue flying overalls of the Second World War's Royal Air Force. He also wore Royal Flying Corps Wings from the First World War. He had had an enigmatic look on his face, which was not surprising, the dealer informed us, because he had flown repeatedly in the Battle of Britain with his former owner, a fighter pilot. It was a romantic story, but I tended to believe it, and I know my wife did, because he had the appearance of a bear who'd done things and been places. In any case, he'd become her mascot and flew with her frequently. There was no question of leaving him behind.

We'd placed him in the rear of the cabin, in a supermarket shopping bag, and I didn't hesitate. I turned, reached for the handle of the rear cabin door, got it open and dragged out Tarquin in his bag.

'Come on, old lad, we're going for a swim,' I said.

God, but it was cold, like acid eating into the bones and that, I knew, was the killer. You didn't have long in the English

Channel, as many RAF and Luftwaffe pilots had found to their cost.

I held on to Dupont and Tarquin, and she held on to me. 'Great landing,' I said. 'Very impressive.'

'Are we going to die?' she demanded, in between gagging on sea water.

'I don't think so,' I told her. 'Not if you look over your shoulder.'

Which she did, and found an RNLI Tyne Class lifeboat emerging from the fog like some strange ghost. The crew were at the rail in yellow oilskins and orange life-jackets, as the boat coasted to a halt beside us and three men jumped into the water.

One old man stood out, as he leaned over the rail. He was in his eighties obviously, white-haired and bearded, and when he spoke, it was that same strong voice that we'd heard on the radio. Zec Acland. 'By God, you brought it off, girl.'

'So it would appear,' Denise called.

They hauled us into the boat – and then the strangest thing happened. Acland looked at the soaked bear in my arms, a look of bewilderment on his face. 'Dear God, Tarquin. Where did you get *him*?'

Denise and I sat on a bench in the main cabin, blankets around us, and drank tea from a thermos flask while two crew members worked on Dupont, who lay on the floor. Zec Acland sat on the bench opposite, watching. He took out an old silver flask, reached over and poured it into our mugs.

'Rum,' he said. 'Do you good.' At that moment, another man entered, black-haired, energetic, a younger version of Acland. 'This is my boy, Simeon, cox of this boat, the *Lady Carter*.'

Simeon said, 'It's good to see you people in one piece. Makes it worthwhile.'

RNLI crews being unpaid volunteers, I could imagine how he felt. One of the two crew members kneeling beside Dupont fastened an oxygen mask over the Frenchman's face and looked up. 'He's still with us, but it's not good.'

'There's a Navy Sea King helicopter landing at Cold Harbour right about now,' Simeon Acland said. 'Take you people to civilization in no time.'

I glanced at Denise, who made a face, so I said, 'Frankly, it's been one hell of a day. Our friend Dupont needs a hospital, that's obvious, but do you think there's a chance my wife and I could stay overnight?'

Simeon laughed. 'Well, you've come to the right place. My Dad, here, is publican at the Hanged Man in the village. Usually has a room or two available.' He turned and saw the very wet bear on the bench beside his father. 'What's that?'

'It's Tarquin,' Zec Acland said.

A strange expression settled on Simeon's face. 'You mean –? Dear God, you weren't lying, you old bugger. He really existed. All these years, I thought you just made it up.' He picked Tarquin up and water poured out. 'He's soaked.'

'Not to worry,' Zec Acland said. 'He'll dry out. He's been wet before.'

It was all very intriguing, and I was just about to take it further when my wife had a severe bout of seasickness, due to swallowing so much water. I followed her example only minutes later, but we were both back to normal by the time we rounded a promontory and saw an inlet on the bay beyond, a wooded valley above.

There was a grey stone manor house in the trees, no more than two or three dozen cottages, a quay, a few fishing boats moored. The *Lady Carter* eased into the quay, two or three fishermen came forward and caught the thrown lines, the engines stopped and then there was only the quiet, the fog and pouring rain.

In the near distance, we heard a sudden roaring, and Simeon said, 'That'll be the helicopter. Better get him up there.' He nodded at Dupont.

His father said, 'Good lad. I'll see to these two. Hot baths in order. Decent dinner.' He picked up Tarquin.

I said, 'And an explanation. We'd love that.'

'You'll have it,' he said, 'I promise you.'

They had Dupont on a stretcher by then, carried him out and we followed.

The whole place had been put together in the mid eighteenth century by a Sir William Chevely, we were told later, the cottages, harbour, quay, everything. By repute, Chevely had been a smuggler, and the port had been a front for other things. The pub, the Hanged Man, had mullioned windows and timber inserts. It certainly didn't look Georgian.

Zec took us in and found a motherly sort of woman behind the bar who answered to the name of Betsy and who fussed around Denise immediately, taking her off upstairs. I stayed in the old, beamed bar with Zec and sat in front of the roaring log fire and enjoyed a very large Bushmills Whiskey.

He sat Tarquin on a ledge near the fire. 'Let him dry natural.'

He took out a tin of cigarettes and selected one. I said, 'The bear is important to you?'

'Oh, yes.' He nodded. 'And to another. More than you'll ever know.'

'Tell me.'

He shook his head. 'Later, when that wife of yours is with us. Quite a girl, that one. Got a few years on you.'

'Twenty-five,' I said. 'But after fifteen years together, we must have got something right.'

'Take it day by day,' he said. 'I learned that in the war. A lot of dying in those days.'

'Were you in the Navy?'

'Only for the first year, then they pulled me back to be coxswain of the lifeboat. It was like a full-time occupation in those days. Ships torpedoed, pilots down in the Channel. No, I missed out on the real naval war.'

As I discovered later, this was a totally false impression of a man who had earned the Distinguished Service Medal during his year with the Navy, then the George Cross, the MBE and four gold medals from the RNLI during his extraordinary service to that fine institution.

I said, 'The sign outside the inn shows a young man hanging upside down suspended by his ankle. That's a tarot image, isn't it? I think it means regeneration.'

'Ah, well, it was Julie Legrande painted that back in the big war. Housekeeper of the manor and ran the pub. We've had to have it freshened over the years, but it's still what Julie painted.'

'French?' I asked.

'Refugee from the Nazis.' He stood. 'Time you had a bath too. What business would you be in?'

'I'm a novelist,' I said.

'Would I know you?' I told him and he laughed. 'Well, I guess I do. You've helped me get through a bad night or two. It's a pleasure to meet you. Now, if you'll excuse me . . .' He stood and walked out.

I sat there thinking about it. Mystery piled on mystery here. The solution should be interesting.

★

We had dinner in the corner of the bar – sea bass, new potatoes, and a salad – and shared an ice-cold bottle of Chablis with Zec and Simeon. Denise and I both wore jeans and sweaters provided by the management. There were perhaps eight or more fishermen at the bar, three of them crew members of the lifeboat. The log fire burned brightly, rain rattled against the windows, and Tarquin steamed gently.

'My dad used to tell me about Tarquin, the flying bear, when I was a kid,' Simeon said. 'I always thought it was a fairy story.'

'So now you've finally learned the truth,' Zec said. 'You listen to me in future, boy.' He turned to Denise. 'Tell me where you got him.'

'Antique shop in Brighton the other year,' she said. 'They told us he'd flown in the Battle of Britain with his owner, but they didn't have any proof. I was always intrigued by the fact that besides RAF wings, he also wears Royal Flying Corps wings, and that was the First World War.'

'Yes, well he would,' Zec said. 'That's when he first went to war with the boys' father.'

There was silence. Denise said carefully, 'The boys' father?'

'A long time ago, 1917 in France, but never mind that right now.' He nodded to Simeon. 'Another bottle.' Simeon went obediently to the bar and Zec said, 'I last saw Tarquin in 1944. On his way to occupied France. Then all these years later, he turns up on a shelf in an antique shop in Brighton.'

He opened his tin, took out a cigarette and my wife said, 'Could I join you?' He gave her one and a light, and she leaned back. 'Tarquin is an old friend, I think?'

'You could say that. I took him out of the Channel once before. Nineteen forty-three. Went down in a Hurricane. Great fighters, those. Shot down more of the Luftwaffe than Spitfires did.' He seemed to brood and as Simeon returned with the new bottle of Chablis, the old man said, 'Harry, that was, or was it Max? We could never be sure.'

Simeon put the tray down. 'You all right, Dad?' There was concern in his voice.

'Who, me?' Zec Acland smiled. 'Wasn't there a book about some Frenchman who smelled or tasted something and the past all came flooding back?'

'Marcel Proust,' Denise said.

'Well, that's what that damned bear's done for me. Brought it all back.' There were tears in his eyes.

Simeon poured the wine. 'Come on, Dad, drink up. Don't upset yourself.'

'My bedroom. The red box in the third drawer. Get it for me, boy.'

Simeon went obediently.

Zec put another log on the fire, and when Simeon returned with the box, Zec placed it on the table and opened it, revealing papers and photos.

'Some of these you've seen, boy,' he told Simeon. 'And some you haven't.'

He passed one of the pictures to Denise: the quay at Cold Harbour, a lifeboat moored, a much older model, Simeon on deck, a naval cap on the back of his head. Simeon and yet not Simeon.

'I looked good then,' Zec said.

Denise leaned across and kissed his cheek. 'You still do.'

'Now don't you start what you can't finish, girl.' He fell about laughing, then passed photos across, one after another, all black and white.

The pub looked the same. There was a shot of an Army officer, engagingly ugly, about sixty-five from the look of him, steel-rimmed spectacles, white hair.

'Brigadier Munro,' Zec said. 'Dougal Munro, Oxford professor before the war, then he joined the intelligence service. What was called Special Operations Executive. SOE. Churchill cooked that up. Set Europe ablaze, he said, and they did. Put secret agents into France, that sort of thing. They moved the local population out of Cold Harbour. Turned it into a secret base.'

He poured more wine and Simeon said, 'You never told me that, Dad.'

'Because we and everyone else here had to sign the Official Secrets Act.' He shook out some more photos. A woman with Brigadier Munro. 'That was Julie Legrande. As I said, housekeeper at the manor and ran the pub.' There was another picture with Munro and an officer, a captain with a ribbon for the MC, a stick in one hand. 'That was Jack Carter, Munro's aide. Left his leg at Dunkirk.'

There were others, and then he came to a large brown envelope. He hesitated, then opened it. 'Official Secrets Act. What the hell. I'm eighty-eight years old.'

If the photos before had been interesting, these were astonishing. One of them showed an airstrip with a Junkers 88S night fighter, the German cross plain on the fuselage, a swastika on the tailplane. The mechanic wore black Luftwaffe overalls. To one side was a Fieseler Storch spotter plane. There were two hangars behind.

'What on earth is this?' I asked.

'The airstrip up the road. Yes, Cold Harbour. Night flights to France, that sort of thing. You foxed the enemy by being the enemy.'

'Not too healthy if they caught you, I should have thought,' Denise observed.

'Firing-squad time if they did. Of course, they also operated

RAF stuff like this.' He passed her another photo. 'Lysander. Ugly beast, but they could land and take off in a ploughed field.'

Another photo showed the Lysander, an officer and a young woman. He wore an American uniform, the bars of a lieutenant-colonel, and a string of medal ribbons. I could make out the DSO and the DFC, but the really fascinating fact was that on the right breast of his battledress blouse were RAF wings.

'Who was he?' I asked.

His reply was strange as he examined the photo. 'Harry, I think, or maybe Max, I could never be sure.'

There it was again, that same comment. Simeon looked as bewildered as I did. I was about to ask what he meant, when Denise said, 'And the young woman?'

'Oh, that's Molly – Molly Sobel, Munro's niece. Her mother was English, her father an American general. Clever girl. A doctor. Trained in England before the war and worked in London during the Blitz. Used to fly down from London with Munro when a doctor was needed. It was all secret, you see.'

He seemed to have gone away to some private place of his own. We said nothing. The fire crackled, rain battered the window, the men at the bar talked in a low murmur.

Simeon said, 'You all right, Dad?'

'Never better, but better I'll be with a large rum in me. I'm cutting loose a burden tonight, a secret nurtured over the years.' He shook a fist at Tarquin. 'All your fault, you damn bear.'

Simeon got up and went to the bar. Tarquin, still slightly steaming, sat there, enigmatic to the end.

Simeon, obviously concerned said, 'Look, Dad, I don't know what this is about, but maybe it's a bit much for you.'

Again, it was Denise who cut in, leaning forward and putting her hand on Zec's. 'No, leave him, Simeon, he needs to talk, I think.'

He clasped her hand strongly and smiled. 'By God, I said you were a woman of parts.' He seemed to straighten.

'Right,' she said. 'The pilot, the American, Harry or Max, you said?'

'That's right.'

'Which doesn't make sense.'

'Dear God, girl, all the sense in the world.' He leaned back, laughing, then opened another envelope from the box. 'Special these. Very, very special.'

They were large prints and once again in black and white. The first was of an R A F flight lieutenant standing against a Hurricane fighter. It was the same man we'd seen earlier in American uniform.

'Yank in the R A F,' Zec said. 'There were a few hundred before America joined the war at the end of '41, after Pearl Harbor.'

'He looks tired,' Denise said and handed the photo back.

'Well, he would. That was taken in September 1940 during the Battle of Britain just after he got his second D F C. He flew for the Finns in their war with the Russians. Got some fancy medal from them and when that caved in, he got to England and joined the R A F. They were funny about Yanks at that time, America being neutral, but some clerk put Harry down as a Finn, so they took him.'

'Harry?' Denise said gently.

'Harry Kelso. He was from Boston.' He took another large print out, Kelso in American uniform again. 'Nineteen forty-four, that.'

The medals were astonishing. A D S O and bar, a D F C and two bars, the French Croix de Guerre, the Legion of Honour, the Finnish Gold Cross of Valour.

I said, 'This is incredible. I mean, I've a special interest in the Second World War and I've never even heard of him.'

'You wouldn't. Thanks to that clerk, he was in the records as a Finn for quite some time and, as I said, there were reasons. The Official Secrets Act.'

'But why?' Denise demanded.

Zec Acland took another photo from the envelope and put it on the table, the show-stopper of all time.

'Because of this,' he said.

The photo was in colour and showed Kelso once again in uniform, only this time, that of the Luftwaffe. He wore flying boots and baggy, comfortable trousers in blue-grey with large map pockets. The short flying blouse with yellow collar patches gave him a dashing look. He wore his silver pilot's badge on the left side, an Iron Cross First Class above it, a Knight's Cross with Oak Leaves at his throat.

'But I don't understand,' Denise said.

'It's quite simple,' Zec Acland told her. 'Munro gave me that. The other photos, the Yank in the RAF? That was Harry. This is the Yank in the Luftwaffe, his twin brother, Max. American father and German mother, a baroness. So Max, being the eldest by ten minutes, was Baron Max von Halder. The Black Baron, the Luftwaffe called him.' He put the photos away. 'I'll tell you what I can, if you like.' He smiled. 'Make a good story for you.' He smiled again. 'Not that anyone would believe it.'

By the time he'd finished, the bar was empty, Betsy locking the door after the last customers and bringing us tea on a tray without a word. Simeon, I think, was as astonished as Denise and I were.

Again, it was Denise who said, 'Is that it?'

'Of course not, girl.' He smiled. 'Lots of pieces in the jigsaw missing. I mean, the German end of things. Top secret there too. Can't help you there.' He turned to me. 'Still, a smart chap like you might know where to pull a few strings.'

'A possibility,' I said.

'Well, then.' He stood up. 'I'm for bed and Simeon's wife will wonder what he's about.' He kissed Denise on the cheek. 'Sleep well, girl, you deserve it.'

He went out. Simeon nodded and followed. We sat there by the fire, not speaking, and then Denise said, 'I've just thought. You served in Germany for a while in the Army. You mentioned those German relatives from years ago. Didn't you say one of them was in the police or something?'

'In a manner of speaking. He was Gestapo.'

She wasn't particularly shocked. The war, after all, had been half a century before, well before her time. 'There you are, then.'

'I'll see,' I said, and pulled her up. 'Time for bed.'

The room was small, with twin beds, and I lay there, unable to sleep, aware only of her gentle breathing as I stared up through the darkness and remembered. A long time ago – a hell of a long time ago.

TWO

The German connection for me was simple enough. National Service with the old Royal Horse Guards, a little time with the Army of Occupation in Berlin, a lot more patrolling the East German border in Dingo scout cars and Jeeps in the days when the so-called Cold War was hotting up.

The area we patrolled was so like the Yorkshire moors that I always expected Heathcliff and Cathy to run out of the mist or the snow or the torrential rain for I can honestly say that inclement was a mild word to describe the weather in those parts.

The border at that time was completely open and, as a kind of police action, we were supposed to stem the tide of refugees trying to flee to the West as well as the gangs of black marketeers, usually ex-SS, who operated out of East Germany, using it as a refuge.

Our opponents were Siberian infantry regiments, hard men of the first order and occasionally the odd angry shot was fired. We called it World War Two and a Half, but when your time was up, you went home to demobilization. American troops doing the same work in their sector got three medals. We got nothing!

Back home in Leeds, as I started a succession of rather dreary jobs, I received a buff envelope from the authorities reminding me that I was a reservist for the next ten years. It suggested that I join the Territorial Army, become a weekend soldier and, when I discovered there was money to be earned, I took them up on it, particularly as I was considering going to work in London. There was a Territorial Army Regiment there, called the Artists Rifles, which the War Office turned into 21 SAS. When the Malayan Emergency started many members volunteered for the Malayan Scouts, which in 1952 became a Regular Army Unit, 22 SAS.

When in London job-hunting, I reported to 21 SAS with my papers and was enthusiastically received as an ex-Guards NCO. I filled in various papers, had the usual medical and found myself finally in front of a Major Wilson, although in view of what happened later, I doubt it was his real name.

'Just sign here, Corporal,' he said and pushed a form across the desk.

'And just what am I signing, sir?' I asked.

'The Official Secrets Act.' He smiled beatifically. 'This is that kind of unit, you see.'

I hesitated, then signed.

'Good.' He took the form and blotted my signature carefully.

'Shall I report Saturday, sir?' I asked.

'No, not yet. A few formalities to be gone through. We'll be in touch.'

He smiled again, so I left it at that and departed.

I had a phone call from him about two weeks later at the insurance office in Leeds where I worked at that time, suggesting a meeting at Yates' Wine Bar near City Square at lunchtime. We sat in a corner enjoying pie and peas and a light ale while he broke the bad news. I was surprised to find him in Yorkshire, but he didn't explain.

'The thing is, old son, the SAS can't use you. The medical shows a rather indifferent left eye. Although you don't advertise the fact, you wear glasses.'

'Well, the Horse Guards didn't object. I fired for the regimental team at Bisley. I was a crack shot. I had a sharpshooter's badge.'

'Yes, we know about that. At least two Russians on the East German side of the border could confirm your skill, or their corpses could. On the other hand, you only got in the Guards because some stupid clerk forgot to fill in the eye section on your records and, of course, the Guards never admit mistakes.'

'So that's it?'

'Afraid so. Pity, really. Such an interesting background. That uncle of yours, staff sergeant at Hamburg headquarters. Remark-able record. Captured before Dunkirk, escaped from prison camp four times, sent to Auschwitz to the enclave for Allied prisoners considered bad boys. Two-thirds of them died.'

'Yes, I know.'

'Of course they've kept him at HQ Hamburg because of his excellent German. He married a German war widow, I see.'

'Well, love knows no frontiers,' I told him.

'I suppose so. Interesting family though, just like you. Born in England, Irish-Scot, raised in the Shankill in Belfast. What they call an Orange Prod.'

'So?'

'But also raised by your mother's Catholic cousin in Crossmaglen. Very republican down there, those people. You must have fascinating contacts.'

'Look, sir,' I said carefully. 'Is there anything you don't know about me?'

'No.' He smiled that beatific smile. 'We're very thorough.' He stood up. 'Must go. Sorry it turned out this way.' He picked up his raincoat. 'Just one thing. Do remember you signed the Official Secrets Act. Prison term for forgetting that.'

I was genuinely bewildered. 'But what does it matter now? I mean, your regiment doesn't need me.'

He started away then turned again. 'And don't forget you're a serving member of the Army Reserve. You could be recalled at any time.'

What was interesting was a German connection he hadn't mentioned, but then I didn't know about it myself until 1952. My uncle's wife had a nephew named Konrad Strasser, or at least that was one of several names he used over the years. I was introduced to him in Hamburg at a party in St Pauli for my uncle's German relatives.

Konrad was small and dark and full of energy, always smiling. He was thirty-two, a Chief Inspector in the Hamburg Criminal Investigation Department. We stood in the corner in the midst of a noisy throng.

'Was it fun on the border?' he asked.

'Not when it snowed.'

'Russia was worse.'

'You were in the Army there?'

'No, the Gestapo. Only briefly, thank God, hunting down some crooks stealing Army supplies.'

To say I was shaken is to put it mildly. 'Gestapo?'

He grinned. 'Let me complete your education. The Gestapo needed skilled and experienced detectives so they descended on police forces all over Germany and commandeered what they wanted. That's why more than fifty per cent of Gestapo operatives weren't even members of the Nazi party and that included me. I was about twenty in 1940 when they hijacked me. I didn't have a choice.'

I believed him instantly and later, things that happened in my life proved that he was telling the truth. In any case, I liked him.

★

It was 1954 when Wilson re-entered my life. I was working in Leeds, as a civil servant at the time, still writing rather indifferent novels that nobody wanted. I had a backlog of four weeks' holiday and decided to spend a couple in Berlin because my uncle had been moved there on a temporary basis to Army headquarters.

The phone call from Wilson was a shock. Yates' Wine Bar again, downstairs, a booth. This time he had ham sandwiches, Yorkshire, naturally, and off the bone.

'Bit boring for you, the Electricity Generating Authority.'

'True,' I said. 'But only an hour's work a day. I sit at my desk and write.'

'Yes, but not much success there,' he informed me brutally. There was a pause. 'Berlin should make a nice break.'

I said, 'Look, what the hell is this about?'

'Berlin,' he said. 'You're going to stay with your uncle a week next Tuesday. We'd like you to do something for us.'

Sitting there in the normality of Yates' Wine Bar in Leeds with the muted roar of City Square traffic outside, this seemed the most bizarre proposition I'd ever had.

'Look,' I said. 'I tried to join 21 SAS, you said my bad eye ruled me out, so I never joined, did I?'

'Not quite as simple as that, old boy. Let me remind you, you did sign the Official Secrets Act and you are still a member of the Army Reserve.'

'You mean I've no choice?'

'I mean we own you, my son.' He took an envelope from his briefcase. 'When you're in Berlin, you'll take a trip into the Eastern Zone by bus. All the details are in there. You go to the address indicated, pick up an envelope and bring it back.'

'This is crazy,' I said. 'For one thing, I remember from my service in Berlin that to go through on a British passport is impossible.'

'But, my dear chap, your Irish antecedents earn you an Irish passport as well as a British one. You'll find it in the envelope. People with Irish passports can go anywhere, even China, without a visa.' He stood up and smiled. 'It's all in there. Quite explicit.'

'And when I come out?'

'All taken care of.'

He moved away through the lunchtime crowd and I suddenly realized that what I was thinking wasn't '*When I come out.*' It was '*Will I come out?*'

The first surprise in Berlin was that my uncle had been posted back to Hamburg, or so I was informed by the caretaker of the flat he lived in.

She was an old, careworn woman, who said, 'You're the nephew. He told me to let you in,' which she did.

It was a neutral, grey sort of place. I dropped my bag, had a look round and answered a ring at the door to find Konrad Strasser standing there.

'You're looking good,' he said.

He found a bottle of schnapps and poured a couple. 'So, you're doing the tourist bit into the Eastern Zone, boy?'

'You seem well-informed.'

'Yes, you could say that.'

I swallowed my schnapps. 'What's a Hamburg detective doing in Berlin?'

'I moved over last year. I worked for the BND, West German Intelligence. An outfit called the Office for the Protection of the Constitution. Our main task is to combat Communist infiltration into our part of the country.'

'So?'

He poured himself another schnapps. 'You're going over this

afternoon with Germanic Tours in their bus. Leave your Brit passport here, only take the Irish.'

'Look, what is this?' I demanded. 'And how are you involved?'

'That doesn't matter. What does is that you're a bagman for 21 SAS.'

'For God's sake, they turned me down.'

'Well, not really. It's more complicated than that. Have you ever heard the old IRA saying? Once in, never out?'

I was stunned but managed to say, 'What have you got to do with all this?'

He took a piece of paper from his wallet and passed it over. 'There's a crude map for you and a bar called Heini's. If things go wrong, go there and tell the barman that your accommodation is unsatisfactory and you must move at once. Use English.'

'And what's that supposed to mean?'

'That someone will come for you. Of course, if everything works, you come back on the tour bus, but that would imply a perfect world.'

I said, 'You're part of this. Me, Wilson. My uncle's not here, yet you are. What the hell goes on?'

I suddenly thought of my desk at the office in Leeds, the Astoria ballroom on a Friday night, girls in cotton frocks. *What was I doing here?*

'You're a fly in the web, just like me in the Gestapo. You got pulled in. All so casual, but no way back.' He finished his schnapps and moved to the door. 'I'm on your side, boy, remember that.' He closed the door and was gone.

The tour bus took us through Checkpoint Charlie, everything nice and easy. There were tourists from all over the world on board. On the other side, the border police inspected us. In my case, my tourist visas and Irish passport. No problems at all.

Later, at lunch at a very old-fashioned hotel, the guides stressed that if anyone got lost on any of the tours, they should make for the hotel, where the coach would leave at five.

In my case, the instructions in the brown envelope told me to be at my destination at four. I hung in there for two boring hours and dropped out at three-thirty, catching a taxi at just the right moment.

The East Germans had a funny rule at the time. The Christian church was allowed, but you couldn't be a member of the Communist Party and go to church – it would obviously damage your job prospects. The result was that the congregations were rather small.

The Church of the Holy Name had obviously seen better days. It was cold, it was damp, it was shabby. There was even a shortage of candles. There were three old women sitting waiting at the confessional box, a man in a brown raincoat praying in a pew close by. I obeyed my instructions and waited. Finally, my turn came and I entered the confessional box.

There was a movement on the other side of the grille. I said, 'Forgive me, Father, for I have sinned,' and I said it in English.

'In what way, my son?'

I replied as the instructions in the envelope had told me. 'I am here only as God's messenger.'

'Then do God's work.'

An envelope was pushed under the grille. There was silence, the light switched off on the other side. I picked up the envelope and left.

I don't know how long it took me to realize that the man in the brown raincoat was following me. The afternoon was darkening fast, rain starting to fall and I looked desperately for a taxi with no success. I started to walk fast, moving from street to street, aiming for the River Spree, trying to remember the city from the old days, but at every corner, looking back, there he was.

Turning into one unexpected alley, I ran like hell and suddenly saw the river. I turned along past a line of decaying warehouses and ducked into an entrance. He ran past a few moments later. I waited – silence, only the heavy rain – then stepped out, moving to the edge of the wharf.

'Halt! Stay exactly where you are.'

He came round the corner, a Walther PPK in his left hand, and approached.

I said, in English, sounding outraged, 'I say, what on earth is this?'

He came close. 'Don't try that stuff with me. We both know you've been up to no good. I've been watching that old bastard at the church for weeks.'

He made his one mistake then, coming close enough to slap my face. I grabbed his right wrist, knocked the left arm to one side and caught that wrist as well. He discharged the pistol once and we came together as we lurched to the edge of the wharf. I turned the Walther against him. It discharged again and he cried out, still clutching his weapon, and went over the edge into the river. I turned and ran as if the hounds of hell were at my heels. When I reached the hotel, the coach had departed.

I found Heini's bar an hour later. It was really dark by then. The bar, as was to be expected so early in the evening, was empty. The barman was old and villainous, with iron-grey hair and a scar bisecting his left cheek up to an empty eye socket. I ordered a cognac.

'Look,' I said in English. 'My accommodation is unsatisfactory and I must move at once.'

It seemed wildly crazy, but to my surprise, he nodded and

replied in English. 'Okay, sit by the window. We've got a lamb stew tonight. I'll bring you some. When it's time to go, I'll let you know.'

I had the stew, a couple more drinks, then he suddenly appeared to take the plates. There were half a dozen other customers by then.

'Cross the street to the wharf where the cranes are beside the river. Black Volkswagen limousine. No charge, just go.'

I did as I was told, crossed the road through the rain and found the Volkswagen. In a strange way, it was no surprise to find Konrad Strasser at the wheel.

'Let's go,' he said.

I climbed in. 'What's this, special treatment?'

'Decided to come myself. What was your score on the border? Two Russians? Well, you're now an Ace. A Stasi agent went into the Spree tonight.'

Stasis were members of the East German State Security Police.

I said, 'He didn't give me a choice.'

'I don't imagine he would.'

We drove through a maze of streets. I said, 'Coming yourself, was that in the plan?'

'Not really.'

'Risky, I'd have thought.'

'Yes, well, you are family in a way. Look, the whole thing's been family. You, the border, your uncle, me, the old Gestapo hand. Sometimes we still have choices. I did tonight and came for you. Anyway, we're returning through a backstreet border post. I know the sergeant. Just lie back and go to sleep.' He passed me a half-bottle. 'Cognac. Pour it over yourself.'

The rain was torrential as, minutes later, we drove through an area where every house had been demolished, creating a no-man's-land protected from the West by barbed-wire fences.

Of course, the Berlin Wall had not been built in those days. There was a red and white barricade, two Vopos in old Wehrmacht raincoats, rifles slung. I lay back in the seat and closed my eyes.

Konrad braked to a halt and one of the men, a sergeant, came forward. 'In and out, Konrad,' he said. 'Who's your friend?'

'My cousin from Ireland.' Konrad offered my Irish passport. 'Pissed out of his mind.' The aroma of good cognac proved it. 'I've got those American cigarettes you wanted. Marlboros. I could only manage a thousand, I'm afraid.'

The sergeant said, 'My God!', thrust my passport back and took the five cartons Konrad offered. 'Come again.'

The bar lifted and we drove forward into the bright lights of West Berlin.

In my uncle's flat, Konrad helped himself to whisky and held out a hand. 'Give me the envelope.'

I did as I was told. 'What is it?'

'You don't need to know.'

I started to get indignant but then decided he was right.

'Look,' I said. 'I've been meaning to ask. You told me I was a bagman for the SAS. I was given the job by a Major Wilson, but by a strange coincidence, you're involved. Why is that?'

'It's no coincidence – grow up! Everything fits like a jigsaw. Let me fill you in on the facts of life. Twenty-one SAS is comprised of weekend soldiers, everything from lawyers to cab drivers and most things in between. A hell of a range of languages. Twenty-two Regiment, the regulars, spends its time shooting Chinese in Malaya and Arabs in the Oman and things like that. People in Twenty-one are odd-job men like you. You were coming to Berlin, it was noted. You were useful.'

'And expendable?'

'Exactly, and a coincidence that I was lurking in the family background.'

'You probably saved my life.'

'Oh, you managed.' He laughed. 'You'll be back at that favourite ballroom of yours in a few days, picking up girls, and none of them will know what a desperate fellow you are.'

'So that's it,' I said. 'I just go back?'

'That's about the size of it. Wilson will be quite pleased.' He finished his Scotch. 'But do me a favour. Don't come back to Berlin. They'll be waiting for you next time.'

He moved to the door and opened it. I said, 'Will there be a next time?'

'As I said, Twenty-one uses people for special situations where they fit in. Who knows?' For a moment he looked serious. 'They turned you down, but that was from the flashy bit. The uniform, the beret, the badge that says: *Who Dares Wins.*'

'But they won't let me go?'

'I'm afraid not. Take care,' and he went out.

He was accurate enough. I went through a totally sterile period, then numerous jobs, college, university, marriage, a successful teaching career and an equally successful writing career. It was only when the Irish Troubles in Ulster really got seriously going in the early seventies that I heard from Wilson again after I'd written a successful novel about the situation. He was by then a full colonel, ostensibly in the Royal Engineers when I met him in uniform, although I doubted it.

We sat in the bar of an exclusive hotel outside Leeds and he toasted my success in champagne. 'You've done very well, old chap. Great book and so authentic.'

'I'm glad you liked it.'

'Not like these things written by television reporters and the like. Very superficial, whereas you – well, you really understand the Irish, but then you would. I mean, an Orange Prod, but with Catholic connections. Very useful that.'

I was aware of a sense of déjà vu, Berlin all over again.

I said carefully, 'What do you want?'

'Nothing too much. You're doing an appearance in Dublin next week, book signings, television?'

'So?'

'It would be very useful if you would meet one or two people for us.'

I said, 'Nearly twenty years ago, I met someone for you in Berlin and nearly got my head blown off.'

'Another side to that. As I recall, it was the other chap who took the flak.' He smiled. 'Interesting that. It never gave you a problem, just like the Russians.'

'They'd have done worse to me,' I said. 'They shouldn't have joined.' I took out a cigarette and lit it. 'What am I supposed to do, repeat the performance, only in the Liffey this time instead of the Spree?'

'Not at all. No rough stuff. Intermediary, that's you, old chap. Just speak to a few people, that's all.'

I thought about it, aware of a certain sense of excitement. 'You've forgotten that I did my ten years in the Army Reserve and that ended some time ago.'

'Of course it did, but you did sign the Official Secrets Act when you joined Twenty-one.'

'Which threw me out.'

'Yes, well, as I said to you a long time ago, it's more complicated than that.'

'You mean, once in, never out?' I stubbed out my cigarette. 'Konrad said that to me in Berlin. How is he, by the way? I haven't seen him for some time.'

'Fine,' he said. 'Very active. So, I can take it you'll co-operate?'

'I don't seem to have much choice, do I?'

He emptied his champagne glass. 'No need to worry. Easy one, this.'

No rough stuff? Easy one, this? Five trips for the bastard, bombs, shooting, glass on the streets, too many bad Saturday nights in Belfast until that eventful day when men with guns in their pockets escorted me to the airport with the suggestion that I not come back. I didn't, not for years, and interestingly enough, I didn't hear again from Wilson, although in a manner of speaking, I did, through the obituary page in the *Daily Telegraph*, his photo staring out at me, only he was a brigadier, not a colonel and his name wasn't Wilson.

Dawn came over the Cornish coast with a lot of mist, as I stood on the little balcony of the bedroom at the Hanged Man. A long night remembering. My wife still slept as I dressed quietly and went downstairs to the lounge bar. She'd been right, of course. The German connection was what I needed on this one and that meant Konrad Strasser. I hadn't spoken to him for a few years. My uncle's death, and my German aunt's, had tended to sever the connection, but I had his number on what I called my essential card in my wallet. Damp but usable. I got it out and just then the kitchen door opened and Zec Acland looked in.

'Up early.'

'And you.'

'Don't sleep much at my age. Just made a pot of tea.'

'I'll be in shortly. I'd like to make a phone call. Hamburg. Don't worry, I'll put it on the bill.'

'Hamburg. That's interesting. Early there too.'

'Another older man. He probably doesn't sleep much either.'

Acland returned to the kitchen, I sat on a stool at the bar, found my card and dialled the number. As I remembered, Konrad had been born in 1920, which made him seventy-seven. His wife was dead, I knew that. A daughter in Australia.

The phone was picked up and a harsh voice said in German, 'Now who in the hell is that?'

I said in English, 'Your Irish cousin. How's Hamburg this morning?'

He lived at Blankenese on the Elbe. 'Fog on the river, a couple of boats moving out.' He laughed, still calling me boy as he always had. 'Good to hear from you, boy. No more of that damned Irish nonsense, I hope.'

'No way. I'm an older guy, now, remember.'

'Yes, I do and I also remember that when you first met your present wife and told me she was twenty-five years younger, I gave you a year.'

'And that was fifteen years ago.'

'So, even an old Gestapo hand can't be right all the time.'

He broke into a terrible fit of coughing. I waited for him to stop, then said, 'Are you okay?'

'Of course. Blood and iron, that's us Germans. Is your wife still Wonder Woman? Formula One, diving, flying planes?'

'She was Wonder Woman yesterday,' I said. 'Saved our lives.'

'Tell me.'

Which I did.

When I was finished he said, 'My God, what a woman.'

'An understatement. She can be infuriating, mind you.'

'And the rest of the time?'

'Absolutely marvellous.'

He was coughing again and finally said, 'So, what's it all about? A phone call out of the blue at the crack of dawn.'

'I need your expertise. A rather astonishing story has come

my way. I've got brothers, twins, born 1918, named Harry and Max Kelso. Father American, mother Baroness Elsa von Halder.'

He grunted. 'Top Prussian aristocrats, the von Halders.'

'The twins were split. Harry, the youngest, stayed in the States with his rich grandfather, who bankrolled the Baroness to return to Germany in 1930 with Max after her husband was killed in a car crash. Max, as the eldest, was automatically Baron von Halder.'

'I've heard that name.'

'You would. The Black Baron, a top Luftwaffe ace. The brother, Harry, was also a flyer. He flew for the Finns against Russia, then was a Yank in the RAF. Battle of Britain, the lot. More medals than you could shake a stick at.'

There was a silence, then, 'What a story, so why isn't it one of the legends of the Second World War?'

'Because for some reason, it's classified.'

'After all these years?'

'I've been talking to an old boy who's past caring at eighty-eight so he's given me a lot of facts, but the German side is virtually missing. I thought an old Gestapo hand might still have access to classified records. Of course, I'll understand if you can't.'

'What do you mean if I can't?' He started to cough again. 'I like it, I love it. It could give me a new lease of life, not that it matters. I'm on limited time. Lung cancer.'

God, but that hurt, for he was a man I'd liked more than most. I said, 'Jesus, Konrad, leave it.'

'Why should I? I'll have such fun. I'm old, I'm dying, so I don't care about classified information. What a joy. For once in a lengthy career in Intelligence, I can turn over the dirt and not give a damn. You've done me a favour. Now just let's go over a few facts, whatever you know about the Black Baron, and then I'll get on with it.'

★

A little while later, the aroma of frying bacon took me to the kitchen, where Zec had made sandwiches. I sat at one end of the table, drank tea you could have stood a spoon up in and ate the sandwiches and felt on top of the world.

'Phone call okay?' he asked.

'Oh, yes,' I told him. 'A relative of mine. If anyone can find out the German side of things as regards Max Kelso, he can.'

'You seem pretty certain.'

'Oh, I am. He's a lot like you, Zec. Seventy-seven, seen it all, has the right connections.' I poured another cup of tea. 'He was in the Gestapo during the war.'

He almost fell out of his chair laughing. 'Dear God.'

I said, 'You've told me everything you can?'

'Of course not. Let's see what you come up with, then we'll look at any missing pieces.' He got up. 'Must check the beer kegs. I'll see you later.'

After breakfast, I went to the end of the jetty, lit a cigarette and stared out into the fog, thinking about it all. Denise turned up about ten minutes later, in a huge sweater and jeans obviously intended for a man. She was holding two mugs of tea.

'I thought you might like a wet. I've been on to Goodwood Aero Club. Bernie Smith's flying down to pick us up.'

'That's good.' I drank a little and put an arm about her waist. 'Thanks!'

'Bad night?'

'The German connection. Things you never knew about. The border a long, long time ago. Ireland, the Troubles. It all went round and round.' I hesitated. 'You mentioned that cousin of mine in Hamburg, the one who'd been in the Gestapo.'

'So?'

'I phoned him earlier. He's still in Hamburg. He has the kind of past that gives him access to things.'

'Was he willing to help?'

I gave a deep sigh. 'Absolutely delighted. Turns out he's got lung cancer. He said the problem would give him a new lease on life, but not for long, I should imagine.'

She held me tight. 'How rotten for you.'

How rotten for me? I said, 'Let's go back to the pub. You could do with some breakfast. Konrad will come up with something. Hot stuff, the Gestapo.'

He did, of course, performed magnificently and also died six months later. Pieced together from what he uncovered, and from what Zec told me, and from some researches of my own, this is what we found out: the true and remarkable story of the brothers Kelso.

THE BEGINNING

1917

THREE

August 1917. At 10,000 feet over the lines in France, Jack Kelso was as happy as any human being could be. Twenty-two years of age, and the scion of one of Boston's finest and richest families, he could have been doing his final year at Harvard, but instead, he was working through his second year with the British Royal Flying Corps.

The aircraft he was flying was a Bristol fighter, one of the great combat aircraft of the war, a two-seater with an observer-gunner in the rear. Kelso's sergeant, who had taken shrapnel the day before in a dogfight, had been hospitalized and Kelso, a hotshot pilot with a Military Cross and fifteen German planes to his credit, had illegally taken off on his own. Well, not quite on his own, for sitting in the bottom of his cockpit was a bear called Tarquin in leather helmet and flying jacket.

Kelso tapped him on the head. 'Good boy,' he said. 'Don't let me down.'

At that period, the British War Office still banned parachutes on the argument that their use made cowards out of pilots. Jack Kelso, a realist and a rich young man, sat on the very latest model, his private possession.

He was a realist about other things as well: *Always watch for attacks out of the sun. Never cross the line under 10,000 feet on your own.*

The great von Richthofen once shot down four Bristols in one day and there were reasons. The pilot had a fixed machine-gun up front, a Vickers. The observer carried two free-mounting Lewis guns in the rear, which meant the man in the back did all the shooting. After a series of disasters, it had been pilots like Kelso who'd discovered that the plane was so manoeuvrable that she could be handled like a single-seater.

The weather was bad that morning, wind and rain, thick storm clouds and in the noise and confusion, Kelso wasn't even aware what kind of plane it was that made his luck run out. There was a roaring, a shadow to port, machine-gunfire ripping the Bristol apart, a bullet tearing into his left leg and then he descended into the safety of heavy cloud.

He turned back towards the British lines, to 7000 then 5000 and was aware of a burning smell. He made 3000, flames flickering around his engine. There was the briefest glimpse of the trenches below, the battlefields of Flanders. Time to go. He unbuckled his seat-belt, picked up Tarquin and stuffed him inside his heavy leather coat then turned the Bristol over and dropped out. He fell for 1000 feet, pulled his ripcord and floated down.

He landed in a shell hole half filled with water, unsure of whether he was on the British or German side of the trenches, but his luck was good. A khaki-clad patrol half plastered in mud reached him in a matter of minutes, clutching rifles.

'Don't shoot, I'm Flying Corps,' Kelso shouted.

There was a burst of machine-gunfire in the vicinity. As two soldiers unbuckled Kelso's parachute, a sergeant lit a cigarette and put it between his lips.

'Funny accent you got there, Captain,' he said in ripest Cockney.

'American,' Kelso told him.

'Well, you've taken your time getting here,' the sergeant told him. 'We've been waiting since 1914.'

The field hospital was in an old French château which stood in glorious parkland. The trip out of the war zone had been hazardous and Jack Kelso had lapsed into unconsciousness thanks to the morphine the infantry patrol had administered. He awakened to a fantasy world: a small room, white sheets, French windows open to a terrace. He tried to sit up and cried out at the pain in his leg, pulled the sheets to one side and saw the heavy bandaging. The door opened and a young nurse in a Red Cross uniform entered. She had blonde hair, a strong face and green eyes and looked to be in her early twenties. She was the most beautiful thing he had ever seen in his life and Jack Kelso fell instantly in love.

'No, lie back,' she said, pushed him down against the pillows and adjusted his sheets.

An Army colonel entered the room wearing Medical Corps insignia. 'Problems, Baroness?'

'Not really. He's just confused.'

'Can't have that,' the colonel said. 'Taken a rather large bullet out of that leg, old son, so you must behave. A little more morphine, I think.'

He went out and she charged a hypodermic and reached for Kelso's right arm. 'Your accent,' he said. 'You're German and he called you Baroness.'

'So useful when I deal with Luftwaffe pilots.'

She started to go and he reached for her hand. 'I don't care what you are as long as you promise to marry only me, Baroness,' he said drowsily. 'Where's Tarquin?'

'Would that be the bear?' she asked.

'No ordinary bear. I've shot down fifteen planes and Tarquin was always there. He's my good luck.'

'Well, there he is, on the dressing-table.'

And so he was. Jack Kelso got one clear look. 'Hi there, old buddy,' he called then drifted into sleep.

Baroness Elsa von Halder had been trapped in Paris with her mother when the war began. At twenty-two, her father an infantry general killed on the Somme, she was from fine old Prussian stock with a decaying mansion and estate, and absolutely no money at all. As the days passed, Kelso filled her with tales of his privileged life back in the States, and they found they had something in common: both had lost their mothers in 1916, in each case to cancer.

Three weeks after he arrived at the hospital, sitting in a deck-chair on the terrace looking out over a lawn with many wounded officers taking the sun, Kelso watched her approach, exchanging a word here and there. She carried a package which she held out to him.

'Field post.'

'Open it for me,' he said, and she did.

There was a leather box and a letter. 'Why, Jack, it's from headquarters. You've been awarded the Distinguished Service Order.' She took it out and held it up. 'Aren't you pleased?'

'Sure. But I already have a medal,' he said. 'What I don't have is you.' He took her hand. 'Marry me, Elsa. You know I'll keep asking until you give in.'

She did, and this time she heard herself asking, 'What about your father? Shouldn't you speak to him first?'

'Oh, it'll take too long to get a letter to the States and back. Besides, amongst his many other qualities, my father is a snob. He'll love you, and so will Boston society, so let's get on with it. There's a resident chaplain here. He can tie the knot any time we want.'

'Oh, Jack, you're a nice man – such a nice man.'

'Germany is going to lose the war, Elsa. All you have to go back to is a decaying estate and no money. I'll take care of you, I promise.' He took her hand. 'Come on, it'll be good. Trust me.'

So, she did, and they were married two days later. After all, he was right: she *did* have nothing to go back to.

The honeymoon in Paris was fine, not the greatest romance in the world, but then he was always aware that she hadn't married him for love. His wound had left him with a pronounced limp, which needed therapy, and she transferred to a Red Cross hospital in Paris. She became pregnant very quickly and Kelso insisted that she go to the States.

'Any child we have must be born at home, I won't hear any argument.'

'You could come, too, Jack. Your leg still isn't good, and I asked Colonel Carstairs. He said they'd give you a discharge if you asked for it.'

'You did *what*? Elsa, you must never do anything like that ever again.' For a moment, he looked a different man, the warrior who'd shot down fifteen German fighters . . . and then he smiled and was dashing Jack Kelso again. 'There's still a war to win, my love, and now that America's joined in, it won't take long. You'll be fine. And my old man will be ecstatic.'

So, she did as she was told and sailed for America, where Abe Kelso did indeed receive her with considerable enthusiasm. She was a big success on the social scene, and nothing was too good for her, especially when she went into labour and produced twin boys. The eldest she named Max after her father; the other Harry, after Abe's.

On the Western Front, Jack Kelso received the news by telegraph. Still in the Royal Flying Corps, where he had decided to stay instead of joining the Americans, he was by now a lieutenant-colonel, one of the few old hands still around, for losses on both sides had been appalling in what proved to be the last year of the war. And then suddenly, it was all over.

Gaunt, careworn, old before his time, Jack Kelso, still in his uniform, stood in the boys' bedroom shortly after his arrival in Boston, and looked at them sleeping. Elsa stood at the door, a little afraid, gazing at a stranger.

'Fine,' he said. 'They look fine. Let's go down.'

Abe Kelso stood by the fire in the magnificent drawing room. He was taller than Jack, with darker hair, but had the same features.

'By God, Jack.' He picked up two glasses of champagne and handed one to each of them. 'I've never seen so many medals.'

'Loads of tin.' His son drank the champagne down in a single swallow.

'It was bad this past year?' Abe inquired, as he gave him a refill.

'Bad enough, though I never managed to get killed. Everyone but me.' Jack Kelso smiled terribly.

'That's an awful thing to say,' his wife told him.

'True, though.' He lit a cigarette. 'I see the boys have fair hair. Almost white.' He blew out smoke.

'They *are* half German.'

'Not their fault,' he said. 'By the way, my personal score there at the end? It was forty-eight.'

She saw then, of course, just how damaged he was, but it was Abe who spoke with forced cheerfulness. 'Now then, Jack, what are you going to do with yourself? Back to Harvard to finish that law degree? You can join the firm then.'

'You must be joking. I'm twenty-three years old, and if you include my time machine-gunning the trenches, I've killed hundreds of men. Harvard is out, the firm is out. I've got the trust fund my mother left me. I'm going to enjoy myself.' He emptied the glass. 'Excuse me, I need the bathroom.'

He limped out. Abe Kelso poured a little champagne into her glass. 'Look, my dear, he's been through a lot. We must make allowances.'

'Don't apologize for him.' She put down her glass. 'That isn't the man I married. He's back there in those Godforsaken trenches. He never got out.'

Which wasn't far from the truth, for in the years that followed, Jack Kelso acted as if he didn't care if he lived or died. His exploits on automobile-racing circuits were notorious. He still flew, and crash-landed on three occasions. He even used his motor yacht to run booze during Prohibition, and his capacity for drink was enormous.

One thing that could be said for him, however, was that he treated his wife with grave courtesy. For her part, Elsa played the good wife, the elegant hostess, the affectionate mother. She was always Mutti to Max and Harry, taught them French and German, and they loved her greatly, and yet their affection for their drunken war-hero father was even greater.

He'd managed to buy a Bristol fighter and kept it at a small flying club outside of Boston that was owned by another old air ace from RFC days, named Rocky Farson. The boys were ten the day Jack strapped them into the rear cockpit and took them for a flight. Their birthday treat, he called it. The boys loved it and Elsa threatened to leave him if he ever did such a thing again.

Abe, as usual, was the man in the middle, trying to keep the peace, on her side because Jack had been drunk, but since Jack was rich in his own right, there was no controlling him.

Nineteen twenty-eight and 1929 came. Disillusioned not only with her marriage but with America, Elsa had only her sincere friendship with Abe and her love of the boys to sustain her. They were, of course, totally alike: their straw-blond hair and green eyes, their high German cheekbones, their voices, their mannerisms. No individual blemishes or birthmarks set them apart. Most times, even she couldn't tell them apart, and neither could Abe. It was a constant sport for them to change roles and make fools of everyone. Totally bonded, the only thing they ever argued about was who owned Tarquin. The fact that Max, as the eldest by ten minutes, was legally Baron von Halder never bothered them.

It was the summer of 1930 when the tragedy happened. Jack Kelso was killed when his Bentley spun off a mountain road in Colorado and fireballed. What was left of him was brought back to Boston, where Abe, now a Congressman, presided over the funeral. The great and the good were there, even the President, the twins in black suits on either side of their mother. They seemed strangely still, frozen almost, and older than their twelve years.

Afterwards, at the big house when everyone had left, Elsa sat by the open French window in the drawing room, elegant in black, and sipped a brandy. Abe stood by the fire.

'Now what?' he asked. 'It's a bleak prospect.'

'Not for me,' she replied. 'I've done my bit. I was a good wife for years, Abe, and put up with a hell of a lot. I want to go back to Germany.'

'And live on what? Most of the fortune his mother left is gone. Sad to say, there's not much coming to you in his will, Elsa, you know that.'

'Yes, I know,' she said. 'But you've got millions. More than you know what to do with. You could help me, Abe.'

'I see.'

'Abe, we've always been good friends. Let me go home. I'll restore the estate, I'll restore the family name.'

'And take my grandsons with you?' He shook his head. 'I couldn't bear that.'

'But they're my sons, too, they belong with their mother. And Max – Max is the Baron von Halder. You can't make him give that up, Abe, it wouldn't be right, it wouldn't be just. *Please*, Abe, I'm begging you.'

Abe Kelso sat for several long moments, the air thick with regret and loss. Finally, he spoke.

'I've often worried about it, you know – what would happen when Max was old enough to appreciate the title. Would he move away to claim it, leave us all here? I always thought I'd have at least a few more years before it came to that, but –' He stopped and sighed. 'But with Jack dead, and you wanting to leave, there's not much of *us* left, is there?' He smiled sadly. 'You're right, Elsa. Max does deserve that chance. And so do you. But on one condition.' Here his voice became firm and strong. 'Harry stays here. I won't give up both my grandsons, I couldn't possibly agree to that. I'll give you what you need to restore the von Halder estate – but Harry stays with me. Are we agreed?'

She didn't even argue. 'Agreed, Abe.'

'Okay. We can sort out the details later about visitation, schooling and the rest. The only thing that worries me is how the boys will feel about this.'

'I'll talk to them.'

'No, let me first. Ask them to come to my study, would you?'

Later that evening before dinner, when she went back to the drawing room, Max and Harry were surprisingly calm, but then they'd always been like that: alone, cool, detached, on the outside looking in. Although they loved their mother, they were aware of her inner selfishness, so the latest turn of events came as no real surprise. She kissed them in turn.

'Your grandfather has told you?'

'Of course. They understand,' Abe said. 'Took it surprisingly well. The only problem, it seems, was who was to take possession of Tarquin, but he stays here. That bear sat in the bottom of the cockpit on every flight Jack made.' For a moment, he seemed lost in thought then he straightened up. 'Champagne,' he said. 'Half a glass each. You're old enough. Let's drink to each other. We'll always be together one way or another.'

The boys said nothing, simply drank their champagne, old beyond their years, as usual, as enigmatic as Tarquin the bear.

The Germany to which Elsa von Halder returned was very different from what she remembered – unemployment, street riots, the Nazi party beginning to rear its head – but she had Abe's money, so she put Max into school and set about regenerating the von Halder estate. There was Berlin society, of course. One of her father's oldest friends, the fighter ace from the war, Hermann Goering, was a coming man in the Nazi party, a friend of Hitler's. As an aristocrat, all doors were open to him and Elsa, beautiful and rich and an undeniable aristocrat herself, was an absolute asset to the party. She met them all – Hitler, Goebbels, Ribbentrop – and was the toast of café society.

Hitler assumed power in 1933, and Elsa allowed Max to go to America for six months in 1934 to stay with his grandfather and brother, who was a day student at prep school. Abe was overjoyed to see him. As for the brothers, it was as if they'd never been apart, and on their birthday Abe gave them a special present. He took them out to the airfield their father used to fly from, and there was Rocky Farson, older, a little heavier, but still the old fighter ace from the Western Front.

'Rocky's going to give you a few lessons,' Abe said. 'I know you're only sixteen, but what the hell. Just don't tell your mother.'

Rocky Farson taught them in an old Gresham biplane. Someone had enlarged the rear cockpit to take mail sacks, which meant there was room to squeeze them both in. Of course, he also flew with them individually, and discovered that they were natural-born pilots, just like their father. And, just like their father, whoever was flying always had Tarquin in the cockpit.

Rocky took them way beyond normal private pilot skills. He gave them classroom lessons on dogfighting. *Always look for the Hun in the sun,* was a favourite. *Never fly below 10,000 feet on your own. Never fly straight and level for more than thirty seconds.*

Abe, watching one day, said to Rocky after they'd landed, 'Hell, Rocky, it's as if you're preparing them for war.'

'Who knows, Senator?' Rocky said, for indeed that was what Abe Kelso was now. 'Who knows?'

So brilliant were they that Rocky used the Senator's money to purchase two Curtis training biplanes, and flew with each of them in turn to take them to new heights of experience.

During the First World War, the great German ace Max Immelmann had come up with a brilliant ploy that had given him two shots at an enemy in a dogfight for the price of one. It was the famous Immelmann turn, once practically biblical knowledge on the Western Front, now already virtually forgotten by both the US Air Corps and the RAF.

You dived in on the opponent, pulled up in a half-loop, rolled out on top and came back over his head at fifty feet. By the time he'd finished with them, the boys were experts at it.

'They're amazing – truly amazing,' Abe said to Rocky in the canteen at the airfield.

'In the old days, they would have been aces. A young man's game, Senator. I knew guys in the Flying Corps who'd been decorated four times and were majors at twenty-one. It's like being a great sportsman. You either have it or you don't, that touch of genius, and the twins have it, believe me.'

The boys stood at the bar talking quietly, drinking orange juice. Abe, watching them, said, 'I think you're right, but to what purpose? I know there are rumbles, but there won't be another war. We'll see to that.'

'I hope so, Senator,' Rocky said, but in the end, it wasn't to matter to him. He had the old Bristol refurbished, took it up for a proving flight one day, and lost the engine at 500 feet.

At the funeral, Abe, standing to one side, looked at the boys and was reminded, with a chill, that they looked as they had at their father's funeral: enigmatic, remote, their thoughts tightly contained. It filled him with a strange foreboding. But there was nothing to be done about it and the following week, he and Harry took Max down to New York and saw him off on the *Queen Mary*, bound for Southampton in England, the first stage of his return to the Third Reich.

EUROPE

1934–1941

FOUR

Max sat on the terrace of their country house with his mother, and told her all about it – the flying, everything – and produced photos of himself and Harry in flying clothes, the aircraft standing behind.

'I'm going to fly, Mutti, it's what I do well.'

Looking into his face, she saw her husband, yet, sick at heart, did the only thing she could. 'Sixteen, Max, that's young.'

'I could join the Berlin Aero Club. You know Goering. He could swing it.'

Which was true. Max appeared by appointment with Goering and the Baroness in attendance, and in spite of the commandant's doubts, a Heinkel biplane was provided. A twenty-three-year-old Luftwaffe lieutenant who would one day become a Luftwaffe general was there, named Adolf Galland.

'Can you handle this, boy?' he asked.

'Well, my father knocked down at least forty-eight of ours with the Flying Corps. I think I can manage.'

Galland laughed out loud and stuck a small cigar between his teeth. 'I'll follow you up. Let's see.'

The display that followed had even Goering breathless. Galland could not shake Max for a moment, and it was the Immelmann turn which finished him off. He turned in to land, and Max followed.

Standing beside the Mercedes, Goering nodded to a valet, who provided caviar and champagne. 'Took me back to my youth, Baroness, the boy is a genius.'

This wasn't false modesty, for Goering was a great pilot in his own right, and had no need to make excuses to anybody.

Galland and Max approached, Galland obviously tremendously excited. 'Fantastic. Where did you learn all that, boy?'

Max told him and Galland could only shake his head.

That night, he joined Goering, von Ribbentrop, Elsa and Max at dinner at the Adlon Hotel. The champagne flowed. Goering said to Galland, 'So what do we do with this one?'

'He isn't seventeen until next year,' Galland said. 'May I make a suggestion?'

'Of course.'

'Put him in an infantry cadet school here in Berlin, just to make it official. Arrange for him to fly at the Aero Club. Next year, at seventeen, grant him a lieutenant's commission in the Luftwaffe.'

'I like that.' Goering nodded and turned to Max. 'And do you, Baron?'

'My pleasure,' Max Kelso said, in English, his American half rising to the surface easily.

'There is no problem with the fact that my son had an American father?' Elsa asked.

'None at all. Haven't you seen the Führer's new ruling?' Goering said. 'The Baron can't be anything else but a citizen of the Third Reich.'

'There's only one problem,' Galland put in.

'And what's that?' Goering asked.

'I insist that he be kind enough to teach me a few tricks, *especially* that Immelmann turn.'

'Well, *I* could teach you that,' Goering told him. 'But I'm sure the Baron wouldn't mind.' He turned. 'Max?' addressing him that way for the first time.

Max Kelso said, 'A pity my twin brother, Harry, isn't here, Lieutenant Galland. We'd give you hell.'

'No,' Galland said. 'Information is experience. You are special, Baron, believe me. And please call me Dolfo.'

It was to be the beginning of a unique friendship.

In America, Harry went to Groton for a while, and had problems with the discipline, for flying was his obsession and he refused to sacrifice his weekends in the air. Abe Kelso's influence helped, of course, so Harry survived school and went to Harvard at the same time his brother was commissioned as a lieutenant in the Luftwaffe.

The Third Reich continued its remorseless rise and the entire balance of power in Europe changed. No one in Britain wanted conflict, the incredible casualties of the Great War were too close to home. Harry ground through university, Europe ground onwards into Fascism, the world stood by.

And then came the Spanish Civil War and they all went, Galland and Max, taking HE51 biplanes over the front, Max flying 280 combat missions. He returned home in 1938 with the Iron Cross Second Class and was promoted to Oberleutnant.

For some time he worked on the staff in Berlin, and was much sought after on the social circuit in Berlin, where he was frequently seen as his mother's escort, and was a favourite of Goering, now become all-powerful. *And then came Poland.*

During the twenty-seven-day Blitzkrieg that destroyed that country, Max Kelso consolidated his legend, shot down twenty planes, received the Iron Cross First Class and was promoted to captain. During the phoney war with Britain and France that followed, he found himself once again on the staff in Berlin.

In those euphoric days, with Europe in its grasp, everything seemed possible to Germany. Max's mother was at the very peak of society and Max had his own image. No white dress jackets, nothing fancy. He would always appear in combat dress: baggy pants, flying blouse, a side cap, called a *Schiff*, and all those medals. Goebbels, the tiny, crippled Nazi propaganda minister, loved it. Max appeared at top functions with Goering, even with Hitler and his glamorous mother. They christened him the Black Baron. There was the occasional woman in his life, no more than that. He seemed to stand apart, with that saturnine face and the pale straw hair, and he didn't take sides, was no Nazi. He was a fighter pilot, that was it.

As for Harry, just finishing at Harvard, life was a bore. Abe had tried to steer him towards interesting relationships with the daughters of the right families, but, like his brother, he seemed to stand apart. The war in Europe had started in September. It was November 1939 when Harry went into the drawing room and found Abe sitting by the fire with a couple of magazines.

'Get yourself a drink,' Abe said. 'You're going to need it.'

Harry, at that time twenty-one, poured a Scotch and water and joined his grandfather. 'What's the fuss?'

Abe passed him the first magazine, a close-up of a dark taciturn face under a Luftwaffe *Schiff*, then the other, a copy of *Signal*, the German forces magazine. 'The Black Baron,' Abe said.

Max stood beside an ME 109 in flying gear, a cigarette in one hand, talking to a Luftwaffe mechanic in black overalls.

'Medals already,' Harry said. 'Isn't that great? Just like Dad.'

'That's Spain and Poland,' Abe said. 'Jesus, Harry, thank God they call him Baron von Halder instead of Max Kelso. Can you imagine how this would look on the front page of *Life* magazine? My grandson the Nazi?'

'He's no Nazi,' Harry said. 'He's a pilot. He's there and we're here.' He put the magazine down. Abe wondered what he was thinking, but as usual, Harry kept his thoughts to himself – though there was *something* going on behind those eyes, Abe could tell that. 'We haven't heard from Mutti lately,' Harry said.

'And we won't. I speak to people in the State Department all the time. The Third Reich is closed up tight.'

'I expect it would be. You want another drink?'

'Sure, why not?' Abe reached for a cigar. 'What a goddamn mess, Harry. They'll run all over France and Britain. What's the solution?'

'Oh, there always is one,' Harry Kelso said and poured the whisky.

Abe said, 'Harry, it's time we talked seriously. You graduated *magna cum laude* last spring, and since then all you do is fly and race cars, just like your father. What are you going to do? What about law school?'

Harry smiled and shook his head. 'Law school? Did you hear Russia invaded Finland this morning?' He took a long drink. 'The Finns need pilots badly, and they're asking for foreign volunteers. I've already booked a flight to Sweden.'

Abe was horrified. 'But you can't. Dammit, Harry, it's not your war.'

'It is now,' Harry Kelso told him and finished his whisky.

The war between the Finns and the Russians was hopeless from the start. The weather was atrocious and the entire country snowbound. The Army, particularly the ski troops, fought valiantly against overwhelming enemy forces but were pushed back relentlessly.

On both sides, the fighters were outdated. The most modern planes the Russians could come up with were a few FW190s Hitler had presented to Stalin as a gesture of friendship between Germany and Russia.

Harry Kelso soon made a name for himself flying the British Gloucester Gladiator, a biplane with open cockpit just like in the First World War. A poor match for what he was up against, but his superior flying skills always brought him through and as always, just like his father in the First World War, Tarquin sat in the bottom of the cockpit in a waterproof zip bag Harry had purchased in Stockholm.

His luck changed dramatically when the Finnish Air Force managed to get hold of half a dozen Hurricane fighters from Britain, a considerable coup in view of the demand for the aircraft by the Royal Air Force. Already an ace, Harry was assigned to one of the two Hurricanes his squadron was given. A week later, they received a couple of ME109s from a Swedish source.

He alternated between the two types of aircraft, flying in atrocious conditions of snowstorms and high winds, was promoted to captain and decorated, his score mounting rapidly.

A photo journalist for *Life* magazine turned up to cover the air war, and was astonished to discover Senator Abe Kelso's grandson and hear of his exploits. This was news indeed, for Abe was now very much a coming man, a member of Franklin D. Roosevelt's kitchen cabinet.

So, Abe once again found a grandson on the cover of a magazine, Harry in a padded flying suit standing beside one of the ME109s in the snow, looking ten years older than when Abe had last seen him and holding Tarquin.

Abe read the account of Harry's exploits with pride, but also sadness. 'I told you, Harry, not your war,' he said softly. 'I mean, where is it all going to end?' And yet, in his heart of hearts, he knew. America was going to go to war. Not today, not tomorrow, but that day would come.

Elsa von Halder was having coffee in the small drawing room at her country mansion, when Max arrived. He strode in, wearing his flying uniform as usual, in one hand a holdall, which he dropped on the floor.

'Mutti, you look wonderful.'

She stood up and embraced him. 'What a lovely surprise. How long?'

'Three days.'

'And then?'

'We'll see.'

She went to a drinks table and poured dry sherry. 'Do you think the British and French will really fight if we invade?'

'You mean when we invade?' He toasted her. 'Of course, I have infinite faith in the inspired leadership of our glorious Führer.'

'For God's sake, Max, watch your tongue. It could be the death of you. You aren't even a member of the Nazi party.'

'Why, Mutti, I always thought you were a true believer.'

'Of course I'm not. They're all bastards. The Führer, that horrible little creep Himmler. Oh, Goering's all right and most of the generals, but – Anyway, what about you?'

'Politics bore me, Mutti. I'm a fighter pilot, just like this fellow.' He unzipped his holdall, produced a copy of *Life* magazine and passed it to her. 'I saw Goering in Berlin yesterday. He gave that to me.'

Elsa sat down and examined the cover. 'He looks old. What have they done to him?'

'Read the article, Mutti. It was a hell of a war, however short. A miracle he came through. Mind you, Tarquin looks good on it. Goering heard from our Intelligence people that Harry got out to Sweden in a Hurricane. The word is he turned up in London and joined the RAF.'

She looked up from the article, her words unconsciously echoing Abe Kelso's. 'How will it all end?'

'Badly, I expect. If you'll excuse me, I'll have a bath before dinner.' He picked up his bag and went to the door and turned. 'Twenty-eight Russkies he shot down over Finland, Mutti. The dog. I only got twenty in Poland. Can't have that, can we?'

There were at least thirteen American volunteers flying in the Battle of Britain in the spring and summer of 1940, possibly more. Some were accepted as Canadians – Red Tobin, Andy Mamedoff, Vernon Keogh, for example, who joined the RAF in July 1940. The great Billy Fiske was one, son of a millionaire and probably the first American killed in combat in the Second World War, later to be commemorated by a tablet in St Paul's Cathedral in London. And others bound for glory like Pete Peterson, a DSO and DFC with the RAF, and a lieutenant-colonel at twenty-two when he transferred to his own people.

Finland surrendered on 12 March 1940. Harry flew out illegally in a Hurricane, as Max had told his mother, landed at an aero club outside Stockholm, went into the city and was in possession of a ticket on a plane to England before the authorities knew he was there.

When he reported to the Air Ministry in London, an ageing squadron leader examined his credentials. 'Very impressive, old boy. There's just one problem. You are an American and that means you'll have to go to Canada and join the RCAF.'

'I shot down twenty-eight Russians, twelve of them while flying a Hurricane. I know my stuff. You need people like me.'

'A Hurricane?' The squadron leader examined Harry's credentials again. 'I see they gave you the Finnish Gold Cross of Valour.'

Harry took a small leather box from his pocket and opened it. The squadron leader, who had a Military Cross from the First War, said, 'Nice piece of tin.'

'Aren't they all?' Harry told him.

The other man pushed a form across. 'All right. Fill this in. Country of origin, America. I suppose you must have returned to Finland to defend your ancestral home against the Russians?'

'Exactly.'

'Ah, well, that makes you a Finn and that's what we'll put on your records.' The squadron leader smiled. 'Damn clerks. Always making mistakes.'

Operational Training Unit was a damp and miserable place on the edge of an Essex marsh. The CO was a wing commander called West with a wooden leg from 1918. He examined Pilot Officer Kelso's documents and looked up, noticing the medal ribbon under the wings.

'And what would that be?'

Harry told him.

'How many did you get over there?'

'Twenty-eight.'

'It says here you've had considerable experience with Hurricanes?'

'Yes, the Finns got hold of a few during the last couple of months of the war.'

'All right, let's see what you can do.'

West pressed a bell and the station warrant officer entered. 'I'm going for a spin with this pilot officer, Mr Quigley. Set up my plane and one of the other Hurricanes. Twenty minutes.'

The warrant officer, without a flicker of emotion, said, 'Right away, sir.'

West got up and reached for his walking stick. 'Don't let my leg put you out. I know a man called Douglas Bader who lost both in a crash and still flies.' He paused, opening the door. 'I got twenty-two myself in the old Flying Corps before the final crash so don't mess about. Let's see if you can take me.'

Those in the curious crowd which assembled to stare up through the rain were never to forget it. At 5000 feet, West chased Harry Kelso. They climbed, banked, so close that some in the crowd gasped in horror but Harry evaded West, looped and settled on his tail.

'Very nice,' West called over the radio, then banked to port and rolled and Harry, overshooting and finding him once again on his tail, dropped his flaps and slowed with shuddering force.

'Christ Almighty,' West cried, heaved back on the control column and narrowly missed him.

Harry, on his tail again, called, 'Bang, you're dead.' Then, as West tried to get away, Harry pulled up in a half-loop, rolled out on top of the Immelmann turn and roared back over West's head at fifty feet. 'And bang, you're dead again, sir.'

The ground crews actually applauded as the two of them walked back. Quigley took West's parachute and gave him his walking stick, then gestured towards Kelso.

'Who in the hell is he, sir?'

'Oh, a lot of men I knew in the Flying Corps all rolled into one,' West said.

In his office, West sat down, reached for a form and quickly filled it in. 'I'm posting you immediately to 607 Squadron in France. They've been converted from Gladiators to Hurricanes. They should be able to use you.'

'I flew Gladiators in Finland, sir. Damn cold, those open cockpits in the snow.'

West took a bottle of brandy from a drawer and two glasses. As he poured, he said, 'Kelso – an unusual name, and you're no Finn. I knew a Yank in the Flying Corps called Kelso.'

'My father, sir.'

'Good God. How is he?'

'Dead. Killed in a motor accident years ago.'

'That fits. Didn't he use to fly with a bear?'

'That's right, sir. Tarquin.' Harry picked up the bag that he'd carried out to his plane and back, took Tarquin out and sat him on the desk.

West's face softened. 'Well, hello, old lad. Nice to see you again.' He raised his glass. 'To your father and you and brave pilots everywhere.'

'And my twin brother, sir.'

West frowned. 'He's a pilot?'

'Oberleutnant in the Luftwaffe, sir.'

'Is he now? Then all I can say is that you're in for a very interesting war, Pilot Officer,' and West drank his brandy.

607 Squadron was only half-way through its conversion pro-gramme when the Blitzkrieg broke on the Western Front on 10 May. In the savage and confused air war that followed, it was badly mauled and took many casualties, the old Gladiator biplanes being particularly vulnerable.

Harry, flying a Hurricane, put down two ME109s above Abbeville at 15,000 feet and although neither of them was aware of it, his brother shot down a Hurricane and a Spitfire on the same day.

The squadron was pulled back, what was left of it, to England and Dunkirk followed. Harry, awarded a DFC and promoted to Flying Officer, was posted to a special pursuit squadron code-named Hawk, near Chichester in West Sussex, only there was nothing to pursue. The sun shone, the sky was incredibly blue and everyone was bored to death.

On the other side of the English Channel, Max and his comrades sat in similar airfields on the same deck-chairs and were just as bored.

And then, starting in July, came attacks on British convoys in the Channel: dive-bombing by Stukas, heavier stuff from the Dorniers and Junkers, protected by the finest fighter planes the Luftwaffe could supply. The object of the exercise was to close down the English Channel and the RAF went up to meet it.

So Harry Kelso and his brother, the Black Baron, went to war.

The air battles over the Channel lasted through July and then came the true Battle of Britain, starting on Eagle Day, 12 August.

Hawk Squadron was based at a pre-war flying club called Farley Field in West Sussex – grass runways, Nissen huts, only four hangars – and it was hot, very hot as Harry and the other pilots lounged in deck-chairs, smoking, chatting or reading books and magazines. Two weeks of boredom, no action, had introduced a certain apathy and even the ground crews working on the dispersed Hurricanes seemed jaded.

The squadron leader, a man called Hornby, dropped down beside Harry. 'Personally, I think the buggers aren't coming.'

'They'll come,' Harry said and offered him a cigarette.

Some of the pilots wore flying overalls, others ordinary uniform; it was too hot for anything else. On his right shoulder, Harry wore an embroidered insignia that said Finland. Beneath it was a shoulder flash of an American eagle with British and American flags clutched in its claws.

'Very pretty,' Hornby said.

'Got a tailor in Savile Row to run them up for me.'

'What it is to be rich, my Yankee friend.' Hornby tapped the jump bag at Harry's feet. 'Tarquin in good fettle?'

'Always. He's seen it all,' Harry told him.

'Wish you'd lend him to me,' Hornby said, just as they heard a loud roaring noise nearby. 'Bloody tractor.'

'That's no tractor.' Harry Kelso was on his feet, bag in hand and running for his plane as the Stukas, high in the sky above, banked and dived.

His flight sergeant tossed in his parachute. Kelso climbed into the cockpit, dropped the bag into the bottom, gunned his engine and, roaring away, lifted off as the first bombs hit the runway. A Hurricane exploded to one side, smoke billowing, and he broke through it, banking to port, carnage below, four Hurricanes on fire.

Harry banked again, found a Stuka in his sights and blew it out of the sky. There were four more, but they turned away, obviously considering their work done, and he went after them. One by one he shot them down over the sea – no anger, no rage, just using all his skill, everything calculated.

He returned to Farley Field, a scene of devastation, and managed to land on the one intact runway. He found Hornby lying on a stretcher, his left arm and his face bandaged.

'Did you get anything?'

Harry gave him a cigarette as an ambulance drew up. 'Five.'

'Five?' Hornby was astonished.

'Stukas.' Harry shrugged. 'Slow and cumbersome. Like shooting fish in a barrel. They won't last long over here. It's ME109s we need to watch for.'

There were several bodies on stretchers, covered with blankets. Hornby said, 'Six pilots dead. Didn't get off the ground. You were the only one who did. Was it this bad in Finland?'

'Just the same, only in Finland it snowed.'

The stretcher bearers picked Hornby up. 'I'll notify Group and suggest they promote you to flight lieutenant. They'll get replacements down here fast. Let's have a look at Tarquin.'

Harry opened the bag and took Tarquin out. Hornby managed to undo a small gilt badge from his bloody shirt and handed it over. 'Nineteen Squadron. That's where I started. Let Tarquin wear it.'

'I sure will.'

Hornby smiled weakly. 'Those Stukas? Were they over land or the Channel?'

'One over land.'

'What a pity. The bastards will never credit you.'

'Who cares? It's going to be a long war,' Harry Kelso told him and closed the ambulance doors.

On the same day, Max and his squadron, flying ME109s, provided cover for Stukas attacking radar stations near Bognor Regis. Attacked by Spitfires, he found himself in an impressive dogfight, during which he downed one and damaged another, but nearly all the Stukas were shot down and three 109s. It was hurried work, with no drop tanks, so that their time over the English mainland was limited, and they had to scramble to get back across the Channel before running out of fuel. He made it in one piece, and was back over Kent again an hour and a half later, part of the sustained attacks on RAF airfields in the coastal areas.

That was the pattern, day after day, a war of attrition, the Luftwaffe strategy to destroy the RAF by making its airfields unusable. Max and his comrades flew in, providing cover to Dornier bombers and Harry and his friends rising to meet them. On both sides, young men died but there was one problem: the Luftwaffe had more pilots. As Air Chief Marshal Sir Hugh Dowding, commander-in-chief of Fighter Command once observed, it would be necessary for the RAF's young men to shoot the Luftwaffe's young men at the ratio of four to one to keep any kind of balance and that wasn't likely.

So it ground on until 30 August, when Biggin Hill, the pride of Fighter Command, was attacked by a large force of Dorniers with great success and Max was one of the escorts. On the return, many Spitfires rose to intercept them and since the 109s needed to protect the bombers, too much time and too much precious fuel were used up over England. By the time Max finally turned out to the Channel, his low fuel warning light was already on.

At that same moment over the sea near Folkestone Harry Kelso shot down two Dornier bombers, but a lucky burst from one of the rear gunners hit him in the engine. He sent out a Mayday and dropped his flaps, aware of a burning smell and calmly wrestled with the canopy. He'd lost an engine over the Isle of Wight the previous week and parachuted in from 2000 feet, landing in the garden of a vicarage where he'd been regaled with tea and biscuits and dry sherry by the vicar's two sisters.

This was different. That was the Channel down there, already the grave of hundreds of airmen, the English coast ten miles away. He reached for Tarquin in the jump bag. He'd arranged a strap with a special clip that snapped on to his belt against just such an eventuality, stood up and went out head first.

He fell to a thousand feet before opening his chute, then, the sea reasonably calm, he went under, inflated his Mae West and got rid of his parachute. Tarquin floated by him in his waterproof bag. Harry looked up into a cloudless sky. There was no dinghy to inflate – that had gone down with the Hurricane. He wasn't even sure if his Mayday had got through.

He floated there, thinking about it, remembering comrades who'd gone missing in the past week alone. Is this it? he thought calmly and then a klaxon sounded and he turned to see an RAF crash boat coming up fast. The crew were dressed like sailors, in heavy sweaters, denims and boots. They slowed and dropped a ladder.

The warrant officer in charge looked down. 'Flight Lieutenant Kelso, is it, sir?'

'That's me.'

'Your luck is good, sir. We were only a mile away when we got your message.'

Two crew members reached down and hauled him up. Harry crouched, oozing sea water. 'I never thought a deck could feel so good.'

'You American, sir?' the warrant officer asked.

'I surely am.'

'Well, that's bloody marvellous. Our first Yank.'

'No, two actually.'

'Two, sir?' The warrant officer was puzzled.

Harry indicated his bag. 'Take me below, find me a drink and I'll show you.'

Max, down to 500 feet, raced towards the French coast. On his left knee was a linen bag containing a dye. If you went into the sea, it spread in a huge yellow patch. He'd seen several such patches on his way across and then he saw the coast east of Boulogne. No need to do a crash landing. The tide was out, a huge expanse of sand spread before him. As his engine died, he turned into the wind and dropped down.

He called in his position on the radio, with a brief explanation, pulled back the canopy and got out, lit a cigarette and started to walk towards the sand dunes. When he got there, he sat down, looked out to sea and lit another cigarette.

An hour later, a Luftwaffe recovery crew arrived in two trucks, followed by a yellow Peugeot sports car driven by Adolf Galland. He got out and hurried forward.

'I thought we'd lost you.'

'No such luck.' Galland slapped him on the shoulder and Max added, 'The plane looks fine. Only needs fuel.'

'Good. I brought a sergeant pilot. He can fly her back. You and I will drive. Stop off for dinner.'

'Sounds good to me.'

Galland called to the burly Feldwebel in charge. 'Get on with it. You know what to do.'

Later, driving towards Le Touquet, he said, 'Biggin Hill worked out fine. We really plastered them.'

Max said, 'Oh, sure, but how many fighters did we lose, Dolfo – not bombers, fighters?'

'All right, it isn't good, but what's your point?'

'Too many mistakes. First, the Stukas – useless against Spitfires and Hurricanes. Second, the bombing policy. Fine – so we destroy their airfields if possible, but fighters are meant to fight, Dolfo, not to spend the whole time protecting the Dorniers. That's like having a racehorse pulling a milk cart. The strategy is flawed.'

'Then God help you when we turn against London.'

'London?' Max was aghast. 'All right, I know we've raided Liverpool and other places, but London? Dolfo, we must destroy the RAF on the South Coast, fighter to fighter. That's where we win or lose.' He shrugged. 'Unless Goering and the Führer have a death wish.'

'Saying that to me is one thing, Max, but never to anyone else, do you understand?'

'That we're all going down the same road to hell?' Max nodded. 'I understand that all right,' and he leaned back and lit another cigarette.

★

Harry was delivered back to Farley Field by a naval staff driver from Folkestone. Several pilots and a number of ground crew crowded round.

'Heard you were in the drink, sir. Good to see you back,' a pilot officer called Hartley said. 'There's a group captain waiting to see you.'

Harry opened the door to his small office and found West of the false leg sitting behind his desk. 'What a surprise, sir. Congratulations on your promotion.'

'You've done well, Kelso. Anxious couple of hours when we heard where you were, but all's well that ends well. Congratulations to you too. Your promotion to flight lieutenant has been confirmed. Also, another DFC.'

Harry went to the cupboard, found whisky and two glasses. 'Shall we toast each other, sir?'

'Excellent idea.'

Harry poured. 'Are we winning?'

'Not at the moment.' West swallowed his drink. 'We will in the end. America will have to come in, but we must hang on. I need you for a day or so. I see you've only got five Hurricanes operational. Flying Officer Kenny can hold the fort. You'll be back tomorrow night.'

'May I ask what this is about, sir?'

'I remembered from your records that you flew an ME109 in Finland. Well, we've got one at Downfield north of London. Pilot had a bad oil leak and decided to land instead of jump. Tried to set fire to the thing, but a Home Guard unit was close by.'

'That's quite a catch, sir.'

'Yes, well, be a good chap. Have a quick shower and change and we'll be on our way.'

Downfield was another installation that had been a flying club before the war. There was only one landing strip, a control tower, two hangars. The place was surrounded by barbed wire, RAF guards on the gate. The 109 was on the apron outside one of the hangars. Two staff cars were parked nearby and three RAF and two Army officers were examining the plane. A Luftwaffe lieutenant, no more than twenty, stood close by, his uniform crumpled. Two RAF guards with rifles watched him.

Harry walked straight up to the lieutenant and held out his hand. 'Rotten luck,' he said in German. 'Lucky you got down in one piece.'

'Good God, are you German?'

'My mother is.' Harry gave him a cigarette and a light and took one himself.

The older army officer was a brigadier with the red tabs of staff. He had an engagingly ugly face, white hair and wore steel-rimmed spectacles. He looked about sixty-five.

'Dougal Munro. What excellent German, Flight Lieutenant.'

'Well, it would be,' Harry told him.

'My aide, Jack Carter.'

Carter was a captain in the Green Howards and wore a ribbon for the Military Cross. He leaned on a walking stick, for, as Harry discovered a long time later, he'd left a leg at Dunkirk.

The senior of the three Air Force officers was, like West, a group captain. 'Look, I don't know what's going on, Teddy,' he said to West. 'Who on earth is this officer? I mean, why the delay? Dowding wants an evaluation of this plane as soon as possible.'

'He'll get it. Flight Lieutenant Kelso has flown it in combat.'

'Good God, where?'

'He flew for the Finns. Gladiators, Hurricanes and 109s.' West turned to Harry. 'Give your opinion to Group Captain Green.'

71

'Excellent plane, sir. Marginally better than a Hurricane and certainly as good as a Spitfire.'

'Show them,' West said. 'Five minutes only. We don't want to get you shot down.'

Kelso went up to 3000 feet, banked, looped, beat up the airfield at 300 feet, turned into the wind and landed. He taxied towards them and got out.

'As I said, sir,' he told Green. 'Excellent plane. Mind you, the Hurricane is the best gun platform in the business and, at the end of the day, it usually comes down to the pilot.'

Green turned and said lamely to West, 'Very interesting, Teddy. I think I'd like a written evaluation from this officer.'

'Consider it done.'

Green and his two officers went to their staff car and drove away. Munro held out his hand. 'You're a very interesting young man.' He nodded to West. 'Many thanks, Group Captain.'

He went to his car, Carter limping after him. As they settled in the back, he said, 'Everything you can find out about him, everything, Jack.'

'Leave it to me, sir.'

Harry gave the German pilot a packet of cigarettes. 'Good luck.'

The guards took the boy away and West said, 'I know a country pub near here where we can get a great black-market meal and you can write that report for me.'

'Sounds good to me.' They got in the car and as the driver drove away, Harry lit a cigarette from his spare pack. 'I asked you were we winning and you said not at the moment. What do we need?'

'A miracle.'

'They're a bit hard to find these days.'

But then it happened. London was accidentally bombed by a

single Dornier, the RAF retaliated against Berlin, and from 7 September, Hitler ordered the Luftwaffe to turn on London. It was the beginning of the Blitz and gave the RAF time to repair its damaged fighter bases in the South of England.

In a café in Le Touquet, Dolfo Galland was playing jazz on the piano and smoking a cigar when Max came in and sat at the end of the bar.

'That's it, Dolfo. The rest is just a matter of time. We had the Tommies beaten and our glorious Führer has just thrown it all away. So what happens now?'

'We get drunk,' Dolfo Galland told him. 'And then we go back to work, play the game to the end.'

FIVE

The Blitz on London, the carnage it caused, was so terrible that the red glow in the sky at night could be seen by Luftwaffe planes taking off in France, and by day, the sky seemed full of bombers, the contrails crisscrossing the horizon of hundreds of RAF and Luftwaffe planes fighting it out.

The Knight's Cross was awarded to those who shot down more than twenty planes. Galland already had it, plus the Oak Leaves for a second award. Max got the Cross on 10 September, although by then he'd taken care of at least thirty planes.

Harry and Hawk Squadron engaged in all the battles, six or seven sorties a day, flying to the point of exhaustion and taking heavy losses. It finally reached a point where he was the only surviving member of the original squadron. And then came the final huge battles of 15 September: 400 Luftwaffe fighters over the South of England and London against 300 Spitfires and Hurricanes.

In a strange way, nobody won. The Channel was still disputed territory and the Blitz on London and other cities continued, although mainly by night. Hitler's grandiose scheme for the invasion of England, Operation Sealion, had to be scrapped, but Britain was still left standing alone, and the Führer could now turn his attention to Russia.

★

In Berlin in early November, it was raining hard as Heinrich Himmler got out of his car and entered Gestapo headquarters in Prinz Albrechtstrasse. A flurry of movement from guards and office staff followed him as he passed through to his office dressed in his black Reichsführer SS dress uniform. He wore his usual silver pince-nez and his face was as enigmatic as ever, as he went up the marble stairs to his suite of offices, where his secretary, a middle-aged woman in the uniform of an SS auxiliary, stood up.

'Good morning, Reichsführer.'

'Find Sturmbannführer Hartmann for me.'

'Certainly, Reichsführer.'

Himmler went into his palatial office, put his briefcase on the desk, opened it, then extracted some papers, sat down and looked them over. There was a knock at the door and it opened.

'Ah. Hartmann.'

'Reichsführer.'

Hartmann wore an unusual uniform, consisting of flying blouse and baggy pants Luftwaffe-style, but in field grey. His collar tabs were those of a major in the SS, although he wore the Luftwaffe's pilot's badge and sported an Iron Cross First and Second Class. He also wore the German Cross in gold. The silver cuff title on his sleeve said RFSS: Reichsführer SS. This was the cuff title of Himmler's personal staff. Above it was the SD badge indicating that he was also a member of Sicherheitsdienst, SS Intelligence, a formidable combination.

'In what way can I be of service, Reichsführer?'

At that time, Hartmann was thirty, almost six feet with a handsome, craggy face, his broken nose – the relic of an air crash – giving him a definite attraction. He wore his hair, more red than brown, in close-cropped Prussian style. A Luftwaffe fighter pilot who had been badly injured in a crash in France before the Battle of Britain, he'd been posted to the Air Courier Service, to transport high-ranking officers in Fieseler Storch spotter planes, when a strange incident had occurred.

Himmler's visit to Abbeville had been curtailed and, due to bad weather, the Junkers which had been due to pick him up had been unable to get in. As it happened, Hartmann was at the airfield with his Storch, having dropped off a general, and Himmler had commandeered him.

What had happened then was like a bad dream. Rising above low cloud and rain, Hartmann had been bounced by a Spitfire. Bullets shredding his wings, he'd had the courage to go back to the mess below, with the Spitfire in on his tail. A further salvo had shattered his windscreen and rocked the aircraft.

Himmler, incredibly calm, had said, 'Have we had it?'

'Not if you like a gamble, Reichsführer.'

'By all means,' Himmler told him.

Hartmann had gone down into the mist and rain, 2000, 1000, broken into open country at 500 feet, and hauled back on the control column. Behind him, the Spitfire pilot, losing his nerve, had backed away.

Himmler, a notoriously superstitious man, had always asserted that he believed in God and was immediately convinced that Hartmann was an instrument of divine intervention. Having him thoroughly investigated, he was enchanted to discover that the young man had a doctorate in law from the University of Vienna, and the upshot was that Hartmann was transferred to the SS on Himmler's personal staff to be his pilot and good-luck charm, but, in view of his legal background, he was also to serve with SS intelligence as the Reichsführer's personal aide.

Himmler said, 'The Blitz on London continues. I've been with the Führer. We will overcome in the end, of course. Panzers will yet roll up to Buckingham Palace.'

With personal reservations, Hartmann said, 'Undeniably, Reichsführer.'

'Yes, well, we let the English stew for the time being and turn to Russia. The Füher has an almost divine inspiration here. At most, six weeks should see the Red Menace overcome once and for all.'

Hartmann, in spite of serious doubts, agreed. 'Of course.'

'However,' Himmler said, 'I've spoken to Admiral Canaris about the intelligence situation in England and frankly, it's not good.' Canaris headed the Abwehr, German Military Intelligence. 'As far as I can judge, all our Abwehr agents in Britain have been taken.'

'So it would appear.'

'And we can do nothing.' Himmler was angry. 'It's disgraceful!'

'Not quite, Reichsführer,' Hartmann said. 'As you know, I've taken over Department 13, after Major Klein died of cancer last year. And I've discovered that he recruited a few deep cover agents before the war.'

'Really? Who would these people be?'

'Irish mostly, disaffected with the British establishment. Even the Abwehr has had dealings with the Irish Republican Army.'

'Ach, those people are totally unreliable,' Himmler told him.

'With respect, not all, Reichsführer. And Klein also recruited to his payrolls various neutrals — some Spanish and Portuguese diplomats.'

Himmler got up and went to the window. He stood, hands behind his back, then turned. 'You are telling me we have, in the files, deep cover agents the Abwehr doesn't know about?'

'Exactly.'

Himmler nodded. 'Yes. Yes, this is good. I want you to pursue this matter, Hartmann, in addition to your usual duties, of course. Make sure they are still in place and ready when needed. Do you understand me?'

'At your command, Reichsführer.'

'You may go.'

Hartmann returned to his own office, where his secretary, Trudi Braun, forty and already a war widow, looked up from her desk. She was devoted to Hartmann – such a hero, and a tragic figure besides, his wife killed in the first RAF raid on Berlin. She was unaware that Hartmann had almost heaved a sigh of relief when it happened; his wife had chased everything in trousers from the start of their marriage.

'Trouble, Major?' she asked.

'You could say that, Trudi. Come in and bring coffee.'

He sat behind his desk and lit a cigarette, and she joined him two minutes later, a cup for her and a cup for him. She sat in the spare chair.

'So?'

Hartmann took a bottle of brandy from a drawer and poured some in his coffee, mainly because his left leg hurt, another legacy of that plane crash.

'Trudi, I know our esteemed Reichsführer believes God is on our side, but he now also believes Operation Sealion will still take place.'

'Really, sir?' Trudi had no opinion on such matters.

'So, that list of Klein's you told me about. You worked for him – give me a full rundown on it, particularly the Spanish or Portuguese that were on his payroll.'

'They still are, Major.'

'Well, now it's pay-up time. Come on, Trudi.'

She said, 'Well, one of the contacts, a Portuguese man in London named Fernando Rodrigues, has actually passed on low-grade information from time to time. He works at their London embassy.'

'Really,' Hartmann said. 'And who else?'

'Some woman called Dixon – Sarah Dixon. She's a clerk at the War Office in London.'

Hartmann sat up straight. 'Are you serious? We have a clerk in the War Office and she's still in place?'

'Well, she was never Abwehr. You see, if I may talk about how things were before your arrival, Major, only the Abwehr were supposed to run agents abroad. Major Klein's operation for SD was really illegal. So, when the Brits penetrated the Abwehr and lifted all their agents in England, ours were left intact. They were never compromised.'

'I see.' Hartmann was excited. 'Get me the files.'

Fernando Rodrigues was a commercial attaché at the Portuguese London embassy and his brother, Joel, was a commercial attaché at the Berlin embassy. Very convenient. Hartmann read the files and recognized the two of them for what they were: greedy men with their hands out. So be it. At least you knew where you were with people like that and you could always cut the hand off.

Sarah Dixon was different. She was forty-five, the widow of George Dixon, a bank clerk who'd died of war wounds from 1917. Originally Sarah Brown, she'd been born in London of an English father and Irish mother. Her grandfather, an IRA activist in the Easter Rising in Dublin against the British, had been shot.

She lived alone in Bayswater in London, had worked as a clerk at the War Office since 1938. She had originally been recruited as an IRA sympathizer by an IRA activist named Patrick Murphy in 1938 during the bombing campaign in London and

Birmingham and Murphy had worked for Klein and the SD. She'd agreed to co-operate and then Murphy had been shot dead in a gun fight with Special Branch policemen.

Hartmann looked up. 'So, she's still waiting?'

'So it would appear, Major.'

'Good. Get this Joel Rodrigues at the Portuguese embassy here. You handle it. Tell him to contact his brother in London by diplomatic pouch. He's to link up with this Mrs Dixon, make sure she's still available if we need her. Any trouble with these Rodrigues brothers, let me know and we'll put the fear of God in them.'

'Very well, Major.'

Trudi went out and Hartmann lit another cigarette. 'What a way to run a war,' he said, softly.

'So you see,' Trudi Braun said to Joel Rodrigues as he sat across the desk from her, 'it's quite simple. Your brother contacts this woman and cultivates her. Her work at the War Office in London should be worth something, plenty of juicy information to be obtained there. Nothing too heavy, mind you. He can keep it low key. We don't want her compromised. There may come a time when she's going to be really useful.'

Rodrigues was upset and it showed. 'I don't know, Frau Braun. Perhaps my brother, Fernando, won't be happy about this.'

Hartmann, listening in the adjacent room, door ajar, entered at once. Joel Rodrigues took one look at that magnificent uniform and started to sweat.

'Your brother has no option and when you write to him, care of your embassy's diplomatic pouch,' Hartmann said, 'you will remind him that he has been on a monthly retainer for three years now and has done little to earn it.'

Rodrigues was on his feet. 'Please, Major, I didn't mean to imply there would be a difficulty here.'

'I'm glad to hear it. I would remind you that you also have been well paid for rather minuscule services to the Reich, so get on with it.'

'Of course. You may rely on me.'

Rodrigues got to the door fast. As he opened it Hartmann said, 'I know everything about you, Rodrigues. Personally, I consider your sexual orientation your own affair, but I would remind you that in the Third Reich homosexuality is an offence punishable by a term in a labour camp.'

Rodrigues was trembling. 'Yes, Major.'

'Of course, if you behave yourself . . .' Hartmann shrugged.

'I'm very grateful, Major.'

'Good. That was a nice villa you bought your parents in Estoril. They must be very happy in their retirement. A pity to disturb them.' He smiled coldly. 'I have a long arm, my friend. Now get out.'

Rodrigues exited and Trudi said, 'Sometimes I don't recognize you.'

'Sometimes I don't recognize myself, my love, but if I hadn't been as hard as I was, he wouldn't have been scared out of his wits. It's all play-acting, Trudi, in this wonderful production we call the Third Reich.'

He turned and went back to his office.

Later that evening, he accompanied Himmler to a reception at the Adlon, held in the ballroom. The Führer held court, with his entourage hovering. There was Josef Goebbels, Reich Minister of Propaganda and Minister of State for Total War, Admiral Wilhelm Canaris, Chief of Military Intelligence, von Ribbentrop, Foreign Minister.

'The only one missing appears to be that fat fool Goering,'

Himmler said acidly, waving away a waiter with glasses of champagne on a tray, much to Hartmann's regret. 'Although he should be ashamed to show his face after the failure of his fighters over Britain.'

Truly angry, Hartmann contained himself by lighting a cigarette because he knew Himmler could not abide smoking. Before Himmler could comment, however, Goering entered.

'The woman on his arm,' Himmler said. 'Isn't that the Baroness von Halder?'

'I believe so,' Hartmann said.

'Is she his mistress?'

'My information is that she is not, Reichsführer.'

'She had an American husband, did she not?'

'Died years ago.'

'Interesting. So are her diamonds. How does she manage?'

'Her late husband's father is an American Senator, a millionaire many times over. He set up a trust for her in Sweden. She receives substantial sums from there.'

'You are singularly well-informed.'

'We have a file on her.'

'And who are the two Luftwaffe officers with Goering?'

'The one in the white dress jacket is Major Adolf Galland, the highest scorer in the Battle of Britain – and that includes both sides.'

'And the Captain?'

'Baron von Halder, her son. They call him the Black Baron.'

'How theatrical.'

'A brilliant flyer. Spain, Poland. He shot down twenty there and twenty-nine over the Channel. He received the Knight's Cross back in September. He's one of those who's been flying against London. His total score as of last week was sixty.'

'Impressive. You like him?'

'We flew together for a while before my crash.'

'Friends, then?'

Hartmann shrugged. 'In a way, but Max Kelso is a strange man and difficult to get close to.'

'Kelso?'

'His father's name. And one thing more. He has a twin brother – who flies with the RAF.'

'Good God.' Himmler frowned. 'Is that true?' He stared across the room for a moment. 'Make sure you keep the file on the von Halders open. I smell something I don't like here.'

At that moment, Goering called for silence and turned to Hitler. 'My Führer, you have decorated Major Galland twice and you know Baroness von Halder well. But her son here, Baron von Halder, received his Knight's Cross from me in France during the attacks on England. Only two days ago he was flying over London helping to protect our gallant bomber crews. I had him flown here for a special reason. His score of enemy planes now stands at sixty and for this, he has been awarded the Oak Leaves for the Knight's Cross.' Goering nodded to Galland, who passed a red leather box to him. 'I beg you, my Führer, to honour this brave officer personally.'

There was silence while Hitler gazed at Max with that strange penetrating look and then he nodded gravely and held out his hand.

'You are wrong, Reichsmarschall. The honour is mine.' Goering handed him the medal and Hitler in turn presented it to Max. He shook his hand. 'The Reich is proud of you, Baron.' He turned to Elsa. 'And you, too, Baroness, like all mothers, honour the Reich.'

The entire crowd burst into applause. The Führer nodded then, seeing Himmler, beckoned and the Reichsführer moved to join him. Hartmann seized his chance and reached for a glass of champagne.

★

'Well, that went well,' Elsa von Halder said.

'Yes, you must be proud of your boy here,' Goering told her. 'I only wish he'd dress up. Look at him. Straight out of a cockpit.' He thumped Max on the shoulder. 'Mind you, the public loves it.' He took a glass of champagne from a waiter and then Hitler beckoned him also. 'Duty calls,' he said, put his glass on the nearest tray and left them.

Hartmann appeared, slightly diffident. 'Dolfo – Max,' he said.

'My God, it's Bubi.' Galland laughed.

Max shook Hartmann's hand. 'You old bastard. We thought you were finished after the crash.'

'They made me a courier pilot in a Storch. I had to pick up the Reichsführer one day in France, a Spitfire tried to bounce us. I bounced him instead – and here I am.'

'In a Storch?' Galland said. 'A considerable feat.'

'Anyway, Himmler decided I was lucky and made me his personal pilot, only he insisted I be transferred to the SS.'

'Well, you can't have everything.' Max turned to his mother. 'Mutti, this is an old comrade, Bubi Hartmann.'

'Sturmbannführer,' she said. 'What a pretty uniform.'

'I am, alas, Baroness, but a poor player.' He kissed her hand. 'May I add to your pride in your son here? I am told that your other boy was awarded his second Distinguished Flying Cross last week.'

'My God,' she said.

'Are you sure about this?' Galland demanded.

'Oh, yes. The Reichsführer makes me spend my spare time helping out in the SD. Our intelligence sources are very good.' He turned to Max. 'The Biggin Hill attack, 30 August? He had to bail out over the Channel off Folkestone.'

Max turned to Galland. 'The day I made my beach landing.'

'He was picked up by an RAF crash boat. The week before,

he bailed out over the Isle of Wight. He was awarded his first DFC flying over France before the Battle.'

'And the second?'

'As I said, last week. It was in the *London Gazette*. We get it regularly courtesy of the Portuguese embassy. "Sustained and gallant action" and shooting down an ME 109 and four Dorniers on the same day, all confirmed kills.'

Elsa turned to Max. 'He's as bad as you, as bad as your father. You all have the same death wish.'

'Never mind, Mutti.' Max waved to a waiter. 'Champagne for all of us and let's drink to Harry.'

'And gallant pilots everywhere,' Adolf Galland said. 'Whoever they are.'

On the following day, Harry Kelso had an appointment in London. It was raining, St James's Park shrouded in mist as his taxi drove up Pall Mall to Buckingham Palace. Harry smoked a cigarette, his cheeks hollow, his face pale.

'Here, guv, you up for a medal or something?' the cabby demanded. 'I mean, that's the DFC you got there already, isn't it?'

'Yeah, well they're giving them away at the moment,' Harry said. 'It's that sort of day.'

'Christ, you're a Yank, guvnor. What are you doing in the RAF?'

'Oh, there are a few of us around,' Harry told him.

A policeman waved them through the gates into the courtyard of the Palace. Harry got out his wallet and the cabby waved it away. 'You must be bleeding mad, guvnor. You don't even have to be here.'

'Oh, yes, I do,' Harry Kelso said.

He went through the main entrance and mounted the stairs to the picture gallery, following the crowd. Court officials seated people, a military band played light music. After a while they struck up 'God Save the King' and King George and Queen Elizabeth came in and sat in chairs up on the dais.

Awards were called in ascending order. There hadn't been time in the midst of the Battle of Britain for Kelso to go through this for the first award. He was not nervous, but tense and then his name was called.

'Flight Lieutenant Harry Kelso, Finland.'

Somehow he was there, the King in front of him. He pinned on the DFC. 'Finland by way of Boston, I believe, Flight Lieutenant? We're very grateful.'

'My privilege, your Majesty.'

Later, he walked rather aimlessly through the crowd, strangely lonely. He had no one because there was no one. He turned out of the gate and was immediately hailed.

'Harry. Over here,' and there was an RAF staff car, West leaning out of it.

'Air Commodore now, I see,' Harry said.

'Fast promotion, Harry, it's a fast war. I knew you were up for your gong today. Thought I'd take you to my old club, the Garrick. They still do a decent lunch. Basic, but sustaining.'

'Sounds good to me.'

'Off we go then.'

At the Garrick, they sat in the corner of the bar and enjoyed a whisky and soda and Dougal Munro and Jack Carter came in wearing uniform.

'Dougal,' West called. 'Join us.' They came over and he added, 'You remember Brigadier Munro and Captain Carter, Harry? They were at Downfield when you tested the 109 for us.' He smiled. 'Harry's just been to the Palace for a bar to his DFC.'

'Splendid,' Munro said. 'Let's split a bottle of champagne on it.' He called to the barman. 'Veuve Cliquot, 31 and don't say no. I know you've got some.' He offered Harry a cigarette. 'Actually, you could do me a favour, old boy.'

'And what would that be, sir?'

'Oh, don't call me sir. I was a professor of archaeology before the war. They made me a brigadier so that I can, what I believe you Americans describe as, kick ass.'

Harry laughed. 'Pretty succinct, Brigadier. What can I do for you?'

'Same as last time only this time a Fieseler Storch spotter plane. Are you familiar with it?'

'Certainly. We used them in Finland. How did you get it?'

'The compass malfunctioned. Flying by night from Holland, the pilot landed in Kent and thought he was in France. Would tomorrow morning suit you? Downfield again?'

'My pleasure.'

'Good. I've got a treat for you. My niece is joining us. Molly – Molly Sobel. American actually. Her father's a colonel at the War Department. The parents parted, so she came here in '35 when she was seventeen to live with her mother and go to medical school.'

'Did she qualify?'

'Oh, yes. In 1939. Brilliant girl, a surgeon at the Cromwell Hospital at the moment. Sad though, her mother was killed in the bombing two months ago.'

'I'm sorry,' Harry Kelso told him.

'Aren't we all,' Dougal Munro said and then Molly Sobel entered the bar, hesitantly, for by tradition, it was men only. Munro ignored that and got up.

'Molly, my love, let's go to the dining room.'

She was, at that time, twenty-three, three months older than Harry. She was a small girl, around five feet four or five, with fair hair, blue eyes and a determined and rather stubborn face.

87

Introductions were made and they all had shepherd's pie with a bottle of hock.

'A German wine. That's ironic,' she commented.

'Nothing wrong with a good German wine,' Harry said.

'I thought you were a Yank in the RAF,' she replied.

'Sure I am, by way of Boston. But I also have a German mother in Berlin right now, and a twin brother who's a captain in the Luftwaffe.' He grinned when he saw he'd left her speechless. That was the usual reaction.

'Doing very well, the Baron,' Munro told him. 'Just awarded Oak Leaves to his Knight's Cross. They've certainly made him wait. His score is sixty at the moment, I understand.'

'And how would you know that?'

'Oh, I run that kind of department.' He stood up. 'Got to go. Got a place to stay tonight?'

Harry shook his head no.

'I have a flat in Haston Place, only two minutes' walk from my headquarters. Molly stays there when she's not at the hospital. Plenty of room. You can stay overnight, if you like.' Munro patted her on the shoulder. 'Take care of him, my dear.' He turned to West. 'Lift, Teddy?'

'No, got my own car.'

Off they went, and West lit a cigarette. 'Listen to me. With more of you Yanks arriving and the numbers already in the RAF, the powers that be are forming what's going to be known as the Eagle Squadron. All Yanks together. You'll want to transfer, I imagine.'

'Not particularly.' Harry stood and said to Molly, 'I'm sure you're busy. If you give me the address, I'll turn up this evening.'

'I haven't had a break in forty-eight hours, so I've got the rest of the day off. What do you want to do? Go dancing at the Lyceum? They have an afternoon session.'

'Walk,' Harry Kelso told her. 'I'd just like to walk.' He turned to West. 'I'll see you in the morning, sir.' He walked to the door with Molly and turned. 'And do me a favour. Keep me out of this Eagle Squadron thing. I started RAF and I'll finish RAF.'

'Actually, Harry, you started Finnish.'

'Same difference,' Kelso told him and went out with Molly.

They walked through the city, smoke hanging in the air from the bombing. After a while it started to rain and she put up the umbrella she was carrying.

'It must have been rough for you, all this,' he said. 'Thousands killed, death, destruction. Your hospital must be overflowing.'

'Most nights are pretty rough, but we get by. People are wonderful. London pride, Noël Coward called it in that song of his.'

'Your father. Munro told me he was a colonel at the War Department.'

'That's right. A flyer like you, bombers.'

'And your mother was killed in the Blitz two months ago? That was rough.'

'I didn't have time to mourn. Too busy in the casualty department.'

They reached the Embankment and looked out at the river, the boats passing up and down, then the rain got heavier and they made for a small shelter. He took out his cigarettes.

'Do you use these?'

'The only thing that gets me by.' She took one, he lit it for her and they sat on a bench. 'What's all this about your brother in the Luftwaffe?'

'My brother Max. Our father was American. Died years ago, but then, Munro being what he is, I'm sure he's given you all the gory details about my mother, the baroness.'

'And your brother, the baron.'

'The Black Baron. A real ace, Max.'

'But so are you. Doesn't it bother you?'

'Max over there and me over here? Same difference. If I'd been born ten minutes earlier, I'd have been over there and he'd have been over here.'

'No, it's not the same. Your brother was in Germany. He didn't have a chance, but you did. You're an American, but you chose to be here. There's a difference.'

'Don't imply noble motives. I fly, that's what I do. I flew for the Finns. Now I fly for the Brits. Look, most of those Luftwaffe pilots are just like the young guys back in my squadron at Farley Field. Flyers are flyers.' He stood up. 'Anyway, let's go. I like walking in the rain.'

She took his arm. 'You look tired.'

'Tired?' he laughed. 'I'm exhausted. We all are. Those left, anyway.'

'What's your casualty rate then?'

'Fighter Command as a whole, fifty per cent. My squadron? I'm the only one left from what we started with at the beginning of the Battle. You're walking with a ghost, doctor. Look, there's a pub across the road. I hear they've varied the opening hours because of the Blitz. Let's grab a drink.'

'You'll find Scotch in short supply.'

'Anything for our gallant heroes.' He smiled, took her arm and they ran across the road.

Later in the afternoon they walked up and had a look at the bomb damage in the West End and generally wandered around. It was early evening when they reached Haston Place. It was a pleasant old square with a central garden.

'Nice,' Harry said. 'Munro told me it's only a ten-minute walk from his headquarters.'

'That's right. S O E in Baker Street.'

'And who might they be?'

'Oh, some sort of intelligence unit.'

The house was Georgian, the flat spacious and pleasant. A fire burned in the grate in the sitting room and there were a great many antiques on display, most of them Egyptian.

'Your uncle was an archaeologist?'

'Egyptologist, to be exact. Let me get you a drink.' She poured whisky from a decanter into two glasses. 'A small one for me. I'm supposed to have a break, but I'm on call if things get rough tonight.' She toasted him. 'I'd like to say one thing. You told me your brother was an ace. Well, so are you and, one half Yank to another half Yank, I'm damn proud of you.'

She swallowed her whisky, tears in her eyes and Harry put down his glass and put his hands on her shoulders. 'Molly, my love, don't let that shell crack that's kept you whole. Death night after night, then your dear mother. You've been to hell and back.'

'Still there.'

'Not you. A soldier's daughter and a real trouper. You'll survive, only don't waste good living time on me. I shouldn't be here.'

'That's a terrible thing to say.'

'But true. Could I see my room? I'd really appreciate a shower.'

She was sitting by the fire reading *The Times* when Munro appeared, Jack Carter limping behind. 'There you are, my dear. Interesting afternoon?'

'You could say that.' She folded the newspaper. 'How are you, Jack?' She kissed his cheek warmly.

'All right, old girl.'

'Any problems with the leg?'

'Well, it hurts like hell on occasion, but so what?'

'You're a lovely man, Jack Carter.'

'All right, enough of all this mild erotic by-play and give me a Scotch, Jack,' Munro said and sat down. 'Find out anything that we didn't know, Molly?'

'Not much and I wish you wouldn't pull me into these devious schemes of yours, Dougal. We spoke about his past, his brother. If you want a doctor's opinion, he loves his brother, admires him. A real ace, he called him. He didn't refer to himself that way.'

'What rubbish,' Carter said. 'Don't believe what you read in the papers. There are so-called aces getting not only the DFC but the DSO as well and believe me, some of the highest scorers are men the public haven't even heard of. We've checked Kelso out. Half the time, he doesn't even claim a plane down, even lets some youngster in his squadron claim it.'

'Youngster?' she said. 'He's only twenty-two himself.'

'Don't get worked up. All I'm saying is he must be close to top scorer in the Battle. Dammit all, my love, he does have two DFCs.'

'A man who thinks he shouldn't be here.'

'Rather melodramatic, but perhaps apt.'

Harry, having heard most of this on the stairs, came in smiling. 'Well, here we are. What delights have you got for me tonight, Brigadier?'

'The River Room at the Savoy. Decent meal, though expensive.'

'You do have influence.'

'Not me, Jack. Tell me, if your brother died in action, would you become Baron von Halder?'

'That's right.'

'Well, you and Jack have something in common. Jack's father is not only a major-general of artillery, he's also Sir William

Carter, Baronet and filthy rich. So, in the right unfortunate circumstances, Jack becomes Sir Jack.'

'Okay, so he pays for dinner tonight,' Harry said.

The dinner at the River Room was superb. Smoked salmon, Dover sole, salad, champagne.

'You wouldn't know there was a war on,' Jack said.

The band was playing, Carrol Gibbons and the Orpheans. Molly said, 'Well, isn't anyone going to ask me to dance?'

'I'm too old and Jack's not up to it any more. Your turn, Flight Lieutenant,' Munro said.

So Harry took her to the floor and they danced to 'A Foggy Day in London Town'. 'Very apt,' he said. 'Only make it smoky for foggy.'

'God, but this is good,' she said. 'I feel alive for the first time in weeks. Do you feel alive, Kelso?'

Before he could reply, the head waiter moved towards her through the dancers. 'I'm sorry, Doctor Sobel. The Cromwell have been on. They want you back as soon as possible.'

They returned to the table. 'The hospital?' Munro asked.

'I'm afraid so.'

He nodded to Carter. 'Send her in my staff car and tell him to get back as soon as possible.'

She picked up her purse and Carter helped her into her coat. She smiled. 'Take care, Kelso.'

He didn't reply, and she turned and went out, Carter limping after her.

Harry and Munro had a brandy, and the Brigadier said, 'Seventy-one will be the first Eagle Squadron and I believe they want to have two more. They'll be after you, Harry.'

'Not if I can help it.'

'May I ask why?'

'I told West. I started RAF and I'll finish RAF. It's what my old man did in the First World War, but then you know that.'

'Yes . . . Harry? I don't suppose you know, but I handle an outfit that's putting agents into France by air, usually by Lysander. I don't suppose you'd be interested?'

'I'm a fighter pilot.'

'Fair enough, but there's a lot of protection in a special duties squadron. Especially from . . . hungry Eagles, shall we say?'

Harry smiled, but shook his head again.

'No? Well, all right. Still, you know where I am.'

'Yes, you could say that,' Harry told him. 'Anyway, I'll fly the Storch for you tomorrow, but I can tell you now. The Lysander is good, but the Storch is better.'

Munro smiled. 'You know, somehow I thought you'd say that.'

SIX

It was two weeks later that Sarah Dixon left the War Office and walked quickly through the winter sleet. Christmas wasn't too far away, not that it meant much these days. She caught the tube at the nearest station. It was overcrowded, everyone tired and wet, and she was unaware that she was being followed.

Fernando Rodrigues was darkly handsome, thirty-five, of medium height and wore a trilby hat and trench coat. The details his brother had forwarded in the diplomatic pouch had been comprehensive and included a photo. He'd checked her address, a flat in a block off Westbourne Grove. Her name was listed clearly with many others.

That morning, he'd waited at the end of the road at half past seven. It was eight when she'd walked down the street and he'd recognized her at once from the photo, had followed her up Queensway to Bayswater tube station, in fact, all the way to the War Office.

He was back there at five o'clock and she emerged with a crowd of other office workers at five-thirty. He could have simply pressed the buzzer at the front door of the flats and spoken directly to her, but he was cautious by nature. Strangely enough, it was not that he was afraid. He'd worked for the SD in Berlin for long enough to have faith in the fact that his diplomatic immunity would always cover his tracks. In any case, he'd never been involved in anything big. Reports on the war situation, bombing damage, troop movements, no more than that.

He got out of the tube with her at Bayswater station and followed her down Queensway, turned into Westbourne Grove and finally arrived at the block of flats in the side street. She was still unaware of his presence, and as she took out her key for the front door, he loomed behind her.

She turned, and to his surprise, seemed not alarmed in the slightest. He said, 'Mrs Sarah Dixon?'

'Yes, what do you want?' Impatient. Had she been expecting someone?

'I have a message for you. *The day of reckoning is here.*' It was the code the Irishman, Patrick Murphy, had given her in 1938 and her response was astonishing. 'Good Lord, you have been a long time. You'd better come in.'

The flat was very small, just a bathroom, kitchen, sitting room and bedroom. She took off her coat. 'Sit down, I'll make some tea. Who are you?'

She went into the kitchen and he followed her to the door. 'Before I answer, tell me one thing. When Patrick Murphy recruited you in '38, he said you were very anti-British. Are you still of that mind?'

'Of course.'

'But your father was English.'

'He meant nothing to me. He died when I was two.' She spoke matter-of-factly as she busied herself making the tea. 'They murdered my grandfather in 1916, shot him like a dog. I'll have my revenge for that. Let's sit down.'

Rodrigues was astonished at her control and also strangely excited. So middle class, so neat and orderly in her tweed skirt and twin set, a single row of pearls at her throat. Her hair was fair rather than blonde and well kept, her face plain and yet not plain. It was very confusing.

'So, what is this about?'

'When Murphy recruited you it was not for the Abwehr. It was for the SD, that's the Secret Intelligence Service.'

'I know what it is. You work for them?'

'Only in a manner of speaking. Look, there must be some small restaurants near here. Let me give you a meal.'

'What an excellent idea. You might even get around to telling me your name.'

'Fernando Rodrigues,' he said as he helped her into her coat.

'Portuguese? Now that *is* interesting.'

They found a small Italian family sort of place on Westbourne Grove, deserted so early in the evening. In spite of the war, there were candles on the tables. They sat in a secluded corner and he ordered a bottle of red wine and lasagna for both of them. It was incredible how he warmed to her, ended up telling her everything.

'Most Abwehr agents in Britain have been lifted.'

'British Intelligence claims all of them have. I'm a very unimportant cog in the War Office machine, but I know that,' she said.

'That may be true, but the SD connection has never been broken. It was set up by a genius called Klein, now dead. His successor is a Major Hartmann who works directly for Himmler.'

'Exalted company. Where do you fit in?'

'I'm a commercial attaché at the Portuguese embassy. I communicate by diplomatic pouch, which is, of course, inviolate, with my brother, Joel, who has a similar post at our embassy in Berlin. It's all very convenient and foolproof.'

'And very lucrative.'

'A man must eat.'

'A nice suit you're wearing and the watch looks like gold to me.'

'Life should be for pleasure, Senhora.' He smiled.

'I think you're a rogue, Mr Rodrigues, but I like you,' she said.

'Fernando – please. Tell me, are you in or out?'

'Of course I'm in. I'm a secretary cum clerk in accounts at the War Office. Very boring and I don't have access to anything of great interest.'

'Who knows? Things change.' He took a card from his wallet. 'The embassy is in the book, but there's my address and phone number. The other side of Kensington Gardens. Ennismore Mews.'

'You *are* doing well.'

The sirens started in the distance. 'Here they come again.' She jumped up. 'Let's get out of it while the going's good.'

He paid the bill and got their coats. 'Where to?' he asked. 'I suppose the nearest shelter is Bayswater underground station.'

'Good God, I'd never go down there in a raid, never go down anywhere. Over a hundred people killed at Holborn the other week when the station received a direct hit. Come on.'

She took his hand and half ran along Westbourne Grove, as bombs fell in the distance. They reached the flats, she got the front door open and they moved into darkness.

'The electricity's off again. That means the lift's not working. Hold my hand and follow me up the stairs. I know the way blindfold.'

Rodrigues stumbled once and she laughed and pulled him up and then they were at the flat door and she got it open and they went in.

She got her coat off and opened the blackout curtains. A

certain amount of light flooded in, there was a glow of flames in the distance and the rumble of bombs exploding.

'I don't think you'll be getting back to Ennismore Mews tonight,' she said.

'Tell me,' he said. 'Is there a man in your life?'

'Would it matter?'

'Not in the slightest.'

'I said you were a rogue. As it happens, there isn't.'

He moved behind her, slipped his arms around her waist and kissed her neck.

'Lovely,' she said. 'But so much nicer in bed, don't you think?'

It was the start of an extraordinary friendship. She had a strange nature, part extreme passion, part complete control. He saw her regularly. There were other women, of course, it was his nature. She knew that and was content.

In Sussex it snowed in January, reminding Harry of Finland as he took off on routine patrols. It snowed in France also, where Galland and Max and the Luftwaffe in general kept up the relentless pressure of the night raids on London.

It was in one of those raids at the end of January, the tube closed because of damage, that Sarah Dixon walked home from the War Office in the early evening with many others. It was already dark, a light powdering of snow over everything. She moved with care along streets littered with rubble, and then the sirens sounded.

People panicked, started to run, with already the odd scream, some sobbing with fear. Bombs fell nearby, there was the sound of glass shattering and then a bomb fell at the end of the street. Sarah Dixon knew only of the force of the blast that seemed to blow her away.

★

There was a great deal of pain, she was aware of that, as she surfaced. Time to take stock. She tried to sit up, and became aware that she was in the end bed in a hospital ward. A nurse ran forward.

'Now then, none of that, lie back.' She eased her down and called, 'Doctor Sobel!'

A young ward surgeon came in wearing a crumpled white coat. She took Sarah's pulse and checked her heart.

'Where am I?'

'The Cromwell Hospital. You've been here two days. German bomb. You're lucky to be here.'

Sarah was aware of the cradle under the sheets on the right side. 'Oh, God, I've lost my leg.'

'No, some damage only, you're going to be fine.' Molly Sobel turned to the nurse. 'Ring that number again. It's in the case file.'

'What number?' Sarah asked weakly.

'A Mr Rodrigues. We found his card in your wallet yesterday. He came at once.'

He was there within the hour, full of concern, had even managed to find a bunch of grapes. 'The best the black market could offer,' he said, and kissed her. 'You look as if someone's punched you several times, but it could be worse.'

'It's the leg I'm worried about.'

'You'll be fine. Let me get you a drink.' He went into the ward office. Molly Sobel was writing notes at the desk, but there was a nurse there. 'Could she have a cup of tea?' he asked.

'Of course, I'll see to it.'

The nurse went out. Rodrigues said, 'She's worried about the leg. What do you think?'

'Not good.' Molly lit a cigarette. 'The chief surgeon put a

stainless steel plate in and some pins. The bone was shattered. Frankly, she came close to needing amputation.'

'Mother of God.' He was shocked. 'But she'll be all right?'

'With time, but to be frank, I think she'll always need a walking stick. Sorry I can't be more helpful.'

'Not your fault, Doctor.'

He found Sarah sitting drinking the cup of tea. 'So, you're up already,' he said cheerfully and sat on the edge of the bed.

'What did the doctor say?'

'Doctor?'

'Come on, Fernando, I can read you like a book. It's not good, is it, the leg?'

'You almost lost it.'

'And what have I got left?' He hesitated and she nodded almost in satisfaction. 'I'm crippled, that's about the size of it. Good job you didn't throw away all those young girlfriends.'

He lit a cigarette and stuck it between her lips. 'Have a smoke and shut up.' In the distance, the sirens started again. 'Christ Almighty, don't they ever stop?'

She coughed and as he took the cigarette, she smiled and whispered, 'Don't be silly, Fernando. After all, they're on our side.'

During March, West turned up unexpectedly at Farley Field and once again sat in Harry Kelso's office and talked. 'You look tired, Harry, you've done too much. I could rotate you as an instructor.'

'No, thanks. Certain way to get killed.'

West said, 'Look, this Eagle Squadron thing is really taking off and it's definite now that eventually they'll form second and third squadrons. All Yanks together. They want you, Harry. You're the top scorer.'

'Don't be silly. That's got to be Peterson or someone else.'

'You know you don't claim your kills half the time. You're famous for it, Harry.'

'Look, I told everyone before. I'm not going and that's final. There are Americans in other squadrons who haven't joined, some in Bomber Command.'

'But gradually, they're being pulled in.' West saw he was making no headway, sighed and shook his head. 'What am I going to do with you?'

'Lose me,' Harry told him. 'Somewhere they can't find me.'

'All right,' West said. 'The Italians have made a mess of their attack in Egypt from Libya. Hitler has sent a General Rommel to take over an outfit they've called the Afrika Korps. We've got two Hurricane squadrons in Egypt. I'll post you.'

'Many thanks.'

'Unfortunately, it means your promotion won't go through. I was putting you up for squadron leader.'

'Stuff the promotion,' Harry Kelso said.

In Adolf Galland's office, Max sat on the window-sill and smoked. 'Libya? What in the hell for?'

'The Italians have cocked up this campaign against Egypt. The British gave them a bloody nose – a very bloody nose. The Führer's created an Afrika Korps under Rommel.'

'Rommel's a coming man.'

'Yes, well if you stay with me there's a slight chance you might make major. If you go to Libya you stay a captain for the time being. The choice is yours.'

'What choice, Dolfo? It's snowing out there. How can I turn down all that sun and sand?'

'Silly bastard!' Galland said. 'Still, so be it.'

★

Bubi Hartmann was going over some papers at his office in Prinz Albrechtstrasse, when Trudi looked in.

'He's here.'

'Show him in.'

Joel Rodrigues brushed snow from his hat. 'Herr Major.' He laid an envelope on Hartmann's desk. 'My brother's latest report.'

'Tell me.'

'The woman is back at work at the War Office. Her leg isn't good. She walks with a stick.'

'Anything else?'

'Some details of troop movements to Egypt, also RAF squadrons.'

'Good. Every little bit helps. Off you go.'

Rodrigues left and Trudi said, 'Shall I transcribe the report?'

'Yes, do that.'

'Copy for the Reichsführer?'

'Low-grade stuff, Trudi, too low for the Reichsführer.' He turned and smiled. 'Don't worry. Our day will come.'

INTERIM

1941–1943

SEVEN

Harry now found a different kind of war: desert, baking heat, sandstorms and an Afrika Korps under Rommel that took everything before it. Rommel's charisma was so powerful that when a prominent English newspaper held a poll of its readers to choose the most outstanding general, it was Rommel they picked. The War Office didn't care for that and sent General Montgomery to take command of desert forces that included not only British but French, Australian and South African troops. Montgomery not only turned things around but soon was as famous as Rommel.

The battles in North Africa waged back and forth. Harry, flying Hurricanes as usual, took out another sixteen German and Italian planes, and in September 1942 was awarded his third DFC and the French Croix de Guerre for air support at the Free French outpost, Bir Hacheim. El Alamein followed only days later, the turning point of the war in North Africa.

Max, flying 109s, fought much the same battles. His score rose another dozen. It wasn't as easy as it had once been, though, for most of the Spitfire and Hurricane pilots were veterans from the Channel war and knew their stuff.

In June 1941, the German Army invaded Russia in Operation Barbarossa, and the Luftwaffe destroyed half of the Russian air force on the ground on the first day. Anything seemed possible now, Africa a sideshow, and Max and his comrades chafed at the bit, feeling that they were missing out on more important things. The feeling only grew stronger after the Japanese attack at Pearl Harbor brought America into the conflict. The desert war dragged on. And then in September 1942, a week before El Alamein, Max had his closest call so far.

Attacking fuel dumps on an oasis called Gila, south of the Sahara, with only a wingman, a boy called Goertz, Max had clear skies and no worries, when a momentary lapse of concentration slowed his reaction to three Hurricanes coming in from the sun. Goertz cried out in alarm and fireballed.

Max broke away, but not quite fast enough, as fire from one of the Hurricanes' four Hispano cannons gave his 109 huge punishment. He rolled into a dive and they followed, caught by surprise as he suddenly climbed, then looped, then fired at one in passing: another fireball.

It was no good, though. He was losing power and height, his engine smoking, the 109 shuddering at the sustained pounding of the cannon. With nothing else to do, he pulled back the canopy at 10,000 feet, flipped over and tumbled out, taking his survival bag with him.

He dropped to 5000 feet before opening the chute. Only the desert was below, the dunes stretching to infinity. He hadn't even had a chance to radio in. At 3000 feet, two Hurricanes swept past, waggling their wings, and turned away and by the happenstance of war, one of them was his brother.

In Max's survival bag were iron rations, a canteen of water, a first aid pack, a compass and various bits and pieces. Also, a Mauser pistol and an MP40 machine-pistol, the famous Schmeisser. On the ground Max drank a little water, set his course by compass and started to walk.

Things were not good, of course, it was far too hot, but it was late afternoon, and evening was falling. Soon it was dusk and then dark, but plenty of light still shone from a full moon. But cold. My God, how cold it was.

The rescue, when it came, was miraculous. Max heard the clanking of bells, and then a line of camels came over a sand dune, three laden with goods, three with riders. The men looked like typical desert Bedouins. The leader raised his hand, and the columns stopped. He rode forward, and Max took the Schmeisser from his bag and cocked it. The clip it contained had another taped to it. His Arabic was basic, to put it mildly.

The Bedouin called in his own language, 'Heh, effendi, which side?'

'*Ich bin Deutsch*,' Max told them.

'No good.' The Bedouin tried English. 'You understand English, effendi?'

'Sure I do!'

'Who are you?'

'Pilot. Shot down. You take me to the German lines and there will be a great reward for you.' One of the others called out in Arabic and the leader shouted back at him. 'What does he say?' Max asked.

'That we should kill you, effendi.'

'You don't like Germans?'

The man shrugged. 'We don't take sides. You come here, you, the English, the French, and war over our land. What we would like is for you to go away.'

'At the right time we will, but let me reply to your friend.' Max fired a burst from the Schmeisser, which kicked up sand.

'Very impressive, effendi.'

'What's your name?'

'Rashid.'

'I can be even more impressive.' Max reached into the survival bag and took out a leather pouch which he tossed across. 'Twenty-five English gold sovereigns. You wouldn't earn that in a year.'

Rashid held it in his hand. 'You are right.'

Max produced a further pouch. 'Another twenty-five when you deliver me to the German lines or a German patrol.'

Rashid smiled. 'I think that could be arranged. We are closer than you think. First, we must change the supply camels' load to make room for you. Two hours then we camp.'

'Let's get on with it then.'

Later, at about two in the morning, lying by a fire of dried camel dung, Max was aware of movement in the shadows and reached for the Schmeisser as a shadow rushed him, one of the camel drivers, as it turned out. Another shadow was behind him, however, and Rashid put a hand over the mouth as the man groaned and Rashid wiped his knife on the man's robe and let him fall.

'My apologies, effendi. He was from the Hakim tribe. It serves me right for giving him work. No honour, those dogs.'

'So it would seem,' Max said drily.

Rashid stirred the fire, sat down and produced dates and camel's milk. The remaining Bedouins joined them, ignoring the body.

'Honour,' Rashid said as he ate. 'If a man doesn't have that, he has nothing. It is what he is. It is how he judges himself.'

'You're right,' Max said. 'Absolutely bloody right. It isn't what others think. It's what you think. Here, have a cigarette. In fact, keep the packet.'

Rashid and his friends lit up and Max took a half bottle of cognac from his bag, opened it and drank. 'I'd offer you some, but I know Arabs don't drink.'

Rashid reached for the bottle. 'The night is cold, effendi, and Allah is merciful.'

It was six o'clock the following morning when they came across a Panzer patrol of armoured scout cars. The young lieutenant in charge was ecstatic.

'Your luck is good, Herr Hauptmann. What do we do with the Arab scum, shoot them?'

'You do and I'll shoot you,' Max said pleasantly. 'And it isn't Herr Hauptmann, it's Baron von Halder.'

'The Black Baron? My God.' The lieutenant was aghast.

Max took the second pouch of sovereigns from his bag and the Schmeisser plus the spare magazine. 'My gift to you,' he said to Rashid.

'May you have a dozen sons, effendi.'

'Not likely. I shouldn't be here now. My time is long gone.'

'Then go to a good death, my friend.' Rashid mounted his camel, nodded to the other Bedouins and they moved away, bells clanking.

At Galeila base hospital, Max was in the colonel's office having a personal check-up when the door opened and Erwin Rommel strode in.

'You must excuse me, Hardt,' he said to the surgeon colonel. 'I paused for lunch on the way through and was told of Baron von Halder's amazing escape.' He held out his hand to Max. 'We have never met, but your mother is a dear friend of mine. I have already authorized a priority message to Berlin confirming your survival.'

Max was standing now. 'Field Marshal, an honour.'

'No, it is you who honour us.' Rommel smiled. 'So, I must leave you. The final battle. El Alamein, then Cairo. Gentlemen.' He saluted and went out.

'What a man,' Colonel Hardt said. 'How can we lose?'

But the Battle of El Alamein destroyed the German Panzers,

driving them back relentlessly and in November British and American forces landed in Morocco and Algeria. Not that it bothered Max. Promoted to major, he'd already been sent to the Russian front.

As for Harry, a serious shortage of pilots had seen him transferred to Halifax bombers, engaged on flights across the Mediterranean to Italy. In January 1943, he was supposed to have attacked installations at Taranto but extremely bad weather had dispersed the squadron. Going down hard through mist, he'd come across the Italian cruiser *Orsini*, had changed plans on his own initiative and attacked from 1000 feet, scoring two direct hits that caused the cruiser to break up and sink.

Badly damaged, with one engine out and two of his crew dead, he'd managed to nurse the Halifax back to a base on the Egyptian coast where he'd had to crash land. He received an immediate award of the Distinguished Service Order and promotion to squadron leader.

Afterwards, he had a rest, serving on staff in Cairo, finally returning to Hurricanes for the final retreat of the Afrika Korps, culminating in the surrender of 150,000 Germans and Italians in May 1943 in Tunisia. Only Rommel and a small number escaped.

In Russia things were no better. At first, there were great victories, then came the hell of war in the winter and the defeats began. Though the German armies ground to a halt in the snow, on the whole, the Russian pilots were no match for their adversaries of the Luftwaffe, men honed to a fine edge by experience in Spain, Poland, and the Battle of Britain. Max's score rose rapidly until he'd downed sixty on the Eastern Front and was awarded the Swords, particularly for his work out of the battered airfield at Stalingrad, which he finally left a week before von Paulus surrendered to the Russians. It was the greatest disaster in the history of the Germany Army, 300,000 men down the drain.

In the British and American systems, pilots flew a fixed number of operations and were then rested. The Luftwaffe had no such system. You just kept going. Fortunately for Max, Goering, back in Berlin, decided he'd done enough, particularly after the award of the Swords to his Knight's Cross, and pulled him out in May.

In Berlin, his mother waited for him in a suite at the Adlon. She looked well, not a day older, but she was shocked at his appearance.

'Max, you look terrible.'

'So would you, Mutti. Russia was the bottom of the heap. A terrible place. What in hell the Führer wants it for I'll never know.'

There was a knock at the door and her personal maid, Rosa Stein, came in. 'A message, Baroness. General Galland will meet you for dinner at seven.'

Galland had been promoted to major-general in November 1942, at the age of thirty-one the youngest in the German armed forces, and was now in command of all fighter aircraft.

'So we're meeting Dolfo?' Max said. 'That's good.'

'You need a decent dinner,' she said. 'So let's just enjoy ourselves for a change and forget our beloved Führer and his damned Nazi party.'

'You *have* changed,' Max observed. 'There was a time you thought they were rejuvenating Germany.'

'That time is long gone, Max. You know the old joke about who's running the lunatic asylum? I think I know.'

'Don't say it out loud, Mutti. Come on, let's find Dolfo.'

As they went downstairs, he said, 'Rosa looked worried.'

'She has a right to. Her husband, Heini, is Jewish. They haven't sent him to one of their damn camps because he's an electronics wizard and works here at a factory in Berlin like many other Jews, but lately.' She shrugged. 'The SS have been making noises.'

'Isn't it ever going to end?' Max asked wearily.

'Only in victory.'

'Mutti, if you believe that you'll believe anything.'

'I didn't specify whose victory, Max.'

They went into the bar, which was still as magnificent as in pre-war days and the head waiter rushed in from the restaurant.

'Baroness.'

'Thank you, Paul. You'll remember my son.'

'Of course. An honour, Baron. General Galland telephoned. He'll be thirty minutes late and sends his regrets.'

'Thank you. Champagne cocktails, I think,' she told him.

'At once.'

They sat on a couch in the corner and Max gave her a cigarette. 'Any news of Harry?'

'Not really. There was the sinking of that Italian cruiser in January when he got the DSO. Goering told me about that, but of course I wrote to you.'

'I wonder how he is. I'd love to see him,' Max said.

A waiter hurried over. 'Standartenführer Hartmann presents his compliments. Would it be convenient for him to say hello?'

Elsa turned her head and saw Hartmann at the bar. 'Full colonel. He has done well.' She inclined her head and Hartmann came across.

'Baroness, as always, a delight.' He turned to Max, genuinely enthusiastic. 'You look about a hundred years old, my friend, but then you would. I'm not sure what to congratulate you on first – getting out of Stalingrad or winning the Swords.'

Max shook his head and waved to the waiter. 'A glass of

champagne for the colonel. We're waiting for Dolfo. What about you?'

'The Reichsführer is with the Swedish ambassador upstairs. I'm killing time.' He lit a cigarette. 'May I also congratulate you on your brother's magnificent feat in sinking the *Orsini*.'

'Magnificent? But it hurt our side.'

'Of course. But an airman can admire another airman's ability, can't he? I understand that your brother flew Hurricanes in the desert. Maybe you and he bounced each other, Max.'

'Maybe we did.' Max lit another cigarette, uncomfortable.

'Alas, since the Afrika Korps surrendered last week, my information on your squadron leader is now rather limited, I'm afraid.'

'I would have thought it pretty comprehensive,' Max told him.

'Good intelligence, that's all, Max.'

Himmler appeared in the archway and Hartmann stood up, kissed Elsa's hand and nodded to Max. 'My master calls and like a good dog I obey.'

He approached the Reichsführer and they went out. A moment later, Galland entered. Max jumped up and embraced him.

'You've done well, Dolfo.' He touched the Knight's Cross. 'The Diamonds as well.'

'*I've done well?*' Galland held him at arm's length. 'You look terrible. Some time on staff is what you need, good food, young women. Yes, Colonel, that's what you need.'

'Colonel?' Elsa said.

'Lieutenant-Colonel will do for a start,' Galland told her. 'He was offered the appointment in Russia and tore the order up.'

'I fly for a living, Dolfo,' Max told him. 'And I can't fly a desk.'

'All right, staff for a while and then I'll let you return to flying.

France, if you like, the Channel, just like the old days, but an Oberstleutnant you are, old friend, whether you like it or not. I command our country's fighter force and what I say goes.'

'Good,' Elsa said. 'Now that's settled. Shall we eat?'

As they moved into the restaurant, Max said, 'But what about Harry? According to Bubi he's still a squadron leader. The equivalent rank is Major.'

'What comes next?' she asked as the head waiter showed them to their table.

'Wing commander,' Galland told her. 'So Bubi was here?'

'He's behind you in the corner with Himmler,' Elsa said. 'North Africa's down the drain and Russia doesn't look too good. Are we still winning, Dolfo?'

Galland said, 'We've still got a few things up the sleeve. There's a weapons programme involving rockets which could give them a headache in England.' He turned to Max. 'And there's a great new plane in hand – the ME262 jet. Heavy rockets, cannons. It could decimate bomber streams, only the Führer wants it developed into a Blitz bomber for a new attack on England.'

'The Führer again,' Elsa said.

'Enough, Mutti,' Max told her. 'Let's eat.'

In the corner, Himmler looked across. 'What an arrogant young man Galland is. They should never have promoted him.'

'A fine pilot,' Bubi said.

'Pilots are two a penny,' Himmler observed. 'He should choose his companions more carefully.'

'Reichsführer?'

'The Baroness, my dear Colonel. She cultivates entirely the wrong people, those who are not friends of the Nazi party. What I might describe as a conspiracy of generals. Even you don't know the details, Hartmann. Generals like Steiff, Wagner, von Hase. Even Rommel, the people's hero in spite of failure in

Africa. When the moment comes, I shall strike. No firing squad – it's too good for traitors. The noose is all they deserve, wouldn't you agree?'

'Of course, Reichsführer,' Hartmann said lamely.

'Strange, the fact that the Baroness is a friend of all of them. Still.' Himmler adjusted his pince-nez. 'Now we eat.'

In London that evening, Sarah Dixon limped along Westbourne Grove, leaning heavily on her walking stick and entered the little Italian restaurant where she and Rodrigues had had their first meal. He was sitting at a corner table reading a newspaper and rose to meet her, kissing her affectionately on the mouth.

'How are you?'

'Could be worse.' She sat down.

He already had a bottle of red wine open and poured her a glass. 'The leg?'

'I'm trying a new painkiller. One of those things, love. It won't get any better. Anyway, I've got some rather startling news. I'm being transferred.'

'To where?'

'Special Operation Executive in Baker Street.'

'My God,' he said. 'That's hot stuff. SOE handle all this undercover work in Europe, parachute agents in, isn't that it?'

'So it would appear. Mind you, I'm not being posted to anything special. My boss called me in and said a senior clerk in administration at Baker Street had died of a heart attack. It's the same old boring office routine, but it's more money and I start Monday.'

'The possibilities could be limitless.'

'Well, it would be nice to come up with something important for a change, after all the low-grade rubbish of the past couple of years.' She squeezed his arm. 'I'm so excited, Fernando.'

'You should be.'

'Are you coming back to the flat afterwards?'

'Of course.' He leaned over and kissed her with genuine warmth. The affection which had developed between them was very real.

'Good,' she said. 'Then let's order. I'm starving.'

When Trudi Braun went into Hartmann's office she had the latest communication from London which Joel Rodrigues had brought. Hartmann read it and passed it to her.

'Have a look.'

Which she did. 'Interesting.'

'More than that. This could be a hell of a breakthrough. SOE are giving us considerable problems in France, dropping in agents by parachute or Lysander, stirring up French Resistance. Get me the file.'

'I know it by heart, Colonel, just as I know the heart of our problem there. Brigadier Dougal Munro, head of Section D, commonly called the Dirty Tricks Department.'

'Exactly. Has Joel Rodrigues left?'

'No, he's in the outer office. Do you wish to see him?'

'No, you can handle it. Tell him from now on he and his brother are on double wages.'

'Very well.'

'The Dixon woman isn't in it for money, of course. A pity in a way. Still, it must be impressed on her how important any information about SOE is, particularly concerning Munro.'

She went out and Hartmann got up, went to the window and lit a cigarette. Limitless possibilities. How interesting.

In August Sicily was occupied and in September Allied troops landed on the Italian mainland. In Cairo, Harry Kelso, pulled back from his squadron, reported to a transportation officer based at Shepheard's Hotel.

'England for you, sir,' he said. 'Dakota to Malta to refuel and then Gibraltar. The thing is they usually take two pilots, but we've heard one of them's sick or something. Not available. Would you mind being back-up?'

'My pleasure,' Harry told him.

At the airport, he met the pilot in the crew room, a flying officer called Johnson, who was all over him. 'My God, you sank the *Orsini*, sir, what a job that was.'

Harry ignored that. 'Do you envisage any problems?'

'The Luftwaffe's based on their part of the Italian mainland now. Milk run really and we're flying by night. Two supply sergeants and half a dozen passengers.'

'Anyone special?'

'Oh, some brigadier or other. They're all in the lounge. Sandwiches and tea laid on there, sir. I suggest you join them. We leave in two hours.'

Harry went into the lounge, a bag in each hand. There was a half-colonel, a couple of majors, two men in civilian clothes, all drinking and laughing. They turned to look as he entered, took in the side-cap, the straw hair, the tanned face, finely drawn, and all those medals on the khaki shirt. There was a silence.

Harry said, 'Kelso.'

The colonel said, 'Good Lord, my dear chap, you sank the *Orsini*.' He stood up to shake hands so that Harry had to place one bag on the floor.

A voice said, 'So there you are. Would that be the famous Tarquin in the jump bag?'

Harry turned and found Dougal Munro standing there.

They sat in the corner and drank whisky and soda. 'Would there be anything devious behind this meeting, Brigadier?'

'Now do I look like that sort of chap?' Munro asked.

'Actually, you do.'

'Well, you're wrong. You have been covering yourself with glory since we last met, as has that brother of yours.'

'Max? What about him?'

'Got out of Stalingrad by the skin of his teeth. Shot down God knows how many Russian planes. Let's see, Knight's Cross, Oak Leaves and Swords. Goering's pulled him out and he's on staff in Berlin. Moved up one, lieutenant-colonel.'

'Good for Max.'

'What are they going to do with you back in England?'

'No idea.'

'Did you know Teddy West is now Air Vice Marshal?'

'I didn't.' Harry was genuinely pleased. 'He's a great man. He deserves it. How's your Jack Carter?'

'Holding the fort in London.'

'And your niece, the good doctor?'

'Molly? Worked off her feet. She's developed into a fine surgeon though. She liked you, Harry.'

'I'm no good for her, Brigadier. I'm no good for anybody. It's a miracle I'm here at all and that can't last for ever.' He stood up. 'I'm going to go and catch a quick shower before we leave.'

There was a full moon when Johnson took off, Harry in the right-hand seat. They rose to 10,000 and levelled out.

'Would you like to take over, sir?' Johnson asked.

'Not necessary,' Harry said. 'I'll be in the cabin if you need me.'

He joined Munro at the rear. The two supply sergeants were

supplying drinks and sandwiches. Harry asked for tea and a Scotch whisky.

'Not coffee?' Munro commented.

'No, it's been a long war, Brigadier, so I'm a tea man now. In any case, you Brits make the worst coffee in the world.'

'Filthy stuff,' Munro said cheerfully and accepted a whisky himself from one of the sergeants. 'All right, Harry. You remember I told you not to call me sir.'

'Yes.' Harry hesitated. 'Sir.'

'Never mind. I've just been with Eisenhower. Your name came up.'

'Is that so.'

'Your grandfather, Senator Abe Kelso? President Roosevelt has made him a sort of roving ambassador.'

'Good for Abe.'

'Naturally the President knows of your existence. Eisenhower was surprised you haven't switched to your own people.'

'And who would my own people be?'

'Let me explain, in case you don't have the full facts. Three Eagle Squadrons in the RAF, American volunteers. In September '42, they were transferred and became Squadrons of Number Four Pursuit Group, 8th US Air Force.'

'I know about that.'

'Well, there were many Yanks like you, even in Bomber Command, people who didn't join the Eagle Squadron. There was no pressure to transfer. It was taken for granted that they would, but men like you who'd served at least two years in the RAF preferred to hang on.'

'Particularly as those who transferred were often rotated to America as instructors,' Harry said. 'Who needs that?'

'But understandable. The American Air Force is filled with greenhorns, Harry, they know nothing. You shot down twenty-eight planes in Finland, at least twenty-five in the Battle, God knows how many in North Africa and you sank the *Orsini*.'

'Stuff them,' Harry said. 'Where were they when we were fighting the Battle of Britain? Roosevelt, the War Department, my grandfather – all playing games while Britain stood tall.' Harry shook his head. 'No soft soap, Brigadier. The simple truth.'

'All right.' Munro waved to one of the sergeants. 'Two more Scotches. Listen to me, Harry, we all know about you and your famous habit of not claiming your kills, sometimes letting them go to others. You're probably the top scorer on the Allied side although the general public don't know it.'

'Thank God.'

'They want you, Harry. Eisenhower was troubled that you haven't transferred and he and Monty are returning to the UK soon to prepare for the invasion of Europe. They seem to think you're letting the side down.'

'Well, tough,' Harry said – just as the Dakota rocked violently under cannon fire.

There were cries of alarm and Harry felt the aircraft start to go down as he made it up the aisle into the cockpit. The windscreen was shattered and Johnson had blood on his face, his mouth agape. He was slumped forward and Harry scrambled into the right-hand seat and grabbed the control column.

Munro appeared in the doorway behind him. 'What is it?'

A dark shadow banked away. Harry recognized it at once. It was a Junkers 88S twin-engined night fighter, festooned with strange aerials, an aircraft which had created havoc amongst Allied bombers in night raids.

'Junkers,' Harry said.

'Good God, we've got nothing to fight him off with,' Munro cried.

'Maybe – maybe not. Let's see.'

Harry took the Dakota down, aware of the Junkers turning, coming in fast, too fast, so that he had to pull up to avoid a collision. Which was exactly what Harry was counting on. He took the Dakota all the way down to 600 feet. The Junkers came in again and fired his cannon. The Dakota seemed to shake itself in mid-air as the Junkers banked and one of the supply sergeants appeared at Munro's shoulder.

'Four dead back there, sir.'

Harry ignored him. 'Right, you bastard, let's be having you.'

He kept his course straight and true at 500. The Junkers came in to finish him off, the Dakota shuddered under more cannon fire and then Harry chose one of his favourite tricks, one of the first things Rocky had taught him and Max. He dropped flaps, the Dakota almost came to a stop, the Junkers banked steeply to port to avoid him and carried on down into the sea.

Harry climbed to 3000, levelled off and spoke to air traffic control at Malta. A moment later Munro appeared at his shoulder again.

'Bloodbath back there, five in all.'

Harry nodded to Johnson, slumped to one side in his seat. 'He's gone too. That makes six.'

'I wouldn't have believed it if I hadn't been here. You had no weaponry and yet you took him out.'

'It's called knowing your business, Brigadier.'

'No,' Munro said. 'It's more than that. Must be.'

'Malta in thirty minutes,' Harry Kelso said and eased back the column.

They flew in a Liberator to Gibraltar the following day, refuelled and continued to England. Somewhere over Biscay, Munro said, 'We must talk.'

'About what?'

'The American air force business. As I said, there was no pressure to force Americans in the RAF to transfer, not at first, but when it became apparent that a number wouldn't, the War Department struck a deal with the RAF. By September last year, all Americans had to transfer. Equivalent rank, American uniforms. Oh, and one privilege – the right to wear their RAF wings on the right breast.'

'How thoughtful,' Harry said.

'There was one dispensation, although it was mainly intended for bomber pilots. Any pilot who had started a tour of thirty operations, let's say on a Lancaster bomber and with an RAF crew, would be allowed to finish that tour, but had to transfer, adopt equivalent rank and wear American uniform.'

Harry considered it. 'Are you telling me there aren't any guys out there evading this?'

'Some, but the Americans are trawling all the time.'

'So let them trawl.'

'You could make things awkward for them.'

'Flying Lysanders for you?'

'Flying many things for me, Harry. I rate as a Special Duties Squadron, remember? The rules are different. You don't do a thirty-trip tour, it's sixty. Under that ruling, they'd have to let you finish the tour.'

'In American uniform?'

'If they catch up with you.'

'Let's see if they can and let's see what Teddy West has to say.'

'Oh, I think you could be surprised,' Munro told him, lay back and dozed.

In England, Harry had two weeks' leave and went back to the small cottage he'd bought near Farley Field. He kept away from the squadron. They would all be new boys anyway and he knew that his presence would make the station commander nervous.

He walked on the shingle beach, threw pebbles in the water and remembered the air battles in the Channel and his parachute drop into the sea off Folkestone. When he was hungry, he ate at the Smugglers Inn, not far from the cottage, never in uniform, always in a sweater and pants.

Sometimes pilots from Hawk Squadron came in, fresh-faced kids, their youth making them loud and arrogant. Jessy Arnold, the publican, was an old friend of Harry's from Battle days; she'd gone through it, the constant dogfights high above, the deaths.

One day Harry was sitting at the end of the bar eating a meat and potato pie when half a dozen young pilots came in. She gave them beer and returned to Harry.

'Got something special for you, Harry. It's American. Bourbon whiskey,' she whispered.

'Dear God, I've forgotten how it tastes.'

She poured it and a young pilot officer named Green said indignantly, 'What have you got there, Jessy, something special? Bit thick wasting it on the civilians.'

She was angry and opened her mouth to reply but Harry put a hand on her arm. 'Let it go, Jess.' He swallowed the bourbon and walked out.

Green laughed. 'Bloody man should be doing his bit like everyone else.'

'Mr Green,' Jessy said. 'Has anyone ever told you you're a prick, because you are. You've just made the biggest mistake of your life and one day you'll know, but never mind that. If you ever do anything like that again, I'll bar you from this pub.'

Green gazed at her in astonishment and she turned and went into the kitchen.

★

On one day of cold rain in late September, Harry was throwing pebbles into the sea, when he heard the noise of a vehicle drawing up above the beach. He turned and found an RAF staff car. A sergeant jumped out, put up an umbrella and opened the rear door. Teddy West emerged resplendent in Air Vice Marshal's uniform.

'Harry!' He waved. 'Good to see you.'

Harry hurried up the beach and shook hands. 'Great to see you, sir.'

'Dougal Munro told me you looked a bit rough. You seem fine to me.'

'Sea air, pub grub, lots of sleep.'

'Good. Get in and let's go to this cottage of yours. Lots to discuss.'

'Work, sir?' Harry asked as he joined him in the rear seat.

'Yes, I think you could call it that.'

The driver parked the staff car in the shed beside the MG two-seater sports car. West got a bag from the front seat and followed Harry into the cottage. Harry tossed some more logs on the fire.

'Can I get you anything, sir?'

'I thought we could eat at the local pub, but business first.'

'Yes, sir.'

'The Americans would still love to get their hands on you, Harry. I've tried to lose you in the files. You're still officially Finnish, of course, but it can't last for ever. I do have a suggestion.'

'What would that be, sir?'

'We have 138 Special Duties Squadron at Tempsford. Better known as the Moon Squadron. They drop agents into France, pick people up and so on.'

'You'd like me to join?'

'Not exactly. There are many links to Tempsford in the

Special Duties area of things. Tangmere, for example, which you remember from the Battle.'

'And Munro has an interest.'

'Yes, a secret base at a place called Cold Harbour in Cornwall. He operates all sorts from there. Not only Lysanders, but Fieseler Storchs, even a Junkers 88S in Luftwaffe insignia. Let's wait until your compatriots run you to earth, then we'll see.'

'So what would my duties be?'

'A run to France by night if I want it. More test-flying of captured enemy planes. Plenty of odd jobs. Would that suit?'

'Sounds interesting.'

'A sort of aide to me, in a way, but that means appropriate rank for the times when you need a little muscle.' He opened the bag he'd brought in and took out a brand new uniform. 'Forgive me, Harry. I went to that Savile Row tailor of yours. He's put it on your account. You notice that you are now a wing commander. That makes you equivalent to your brother. A lieutenant-colonel I hear.'

'Good God,' Harry Kelso said.

'The tailor's put all your medal ribbons on and that interesting American eagle with the two flags on your shoulder.'

'I don't know what to say.'

'Just get dressed, there's a good chap and we'll go to the pub and have lunch.'

It was early when they went into the pub. Jessy Arnold was putting logs on the fire in the bar, turned and gaped in astonishment. 'Oh, my word, Harry Kelso. Wing commander now.' She kissed his cheek impulsively.

'Air Vice Marshal West, Jessy. We've come for one of those pies of yours. No use asking for Scotch in these hard times.'

'Oh, yes, there is.' Jessy smiled. 'For you two gentlemen anyway.'

They sat at the end of the bar and as she walked back with the bottle, Green and three other pilots burst in. Green saw the bottle and reached over the bar and tried to take it from her.

'Come on, Jessy, saving it for the civilians again?'

West called, 'Young man! Try to behave with some sort of manners. You are, after all, supposed to be an officer and a gentleman.'

Green turned, his anger replaced by total astonishment at the sight of such a senior officer and West stood up. At that moment a flight lieutenant came in.

'Ah, if you're Hawk Squadron you'll be Varley,' West said.

Varley managed to stammer, 'Yes, sir.'

'Air Vice Marshal West. Wing Commander Kelso here commanded Hawk during the Battle of Britain.'

The sudden silence was breathtaking as they all turned to Harry. 'Good Lord, sir,' Varley said. 'You're a legend in this squadron – a legend.'

'Then let's all have a drink on it.' Harry turned to Jessy. 'Whatever you can manage, my love, but no bourbon for Mr Green.'

END-GAME

1943—1944

EIGHT

During October, Harry worked for West, visiting various squadrons throughout the country and assessing readiness for what everyone knew was bound to be ahead during 1944, the invasion of Europe. It was boring, but necessary work. Strangely enough Max was doing similar things for Galland, mainly in France although he spent a great deal of time in Berlin. Like Harry, he chafed at the bit, but Galland urged him to be patient.

One person who wasn't patient was Elsa. Earlier in the year there had been a Gestapo round-up of Jewish men with German wives, men employed in important war work. Not all of them had been taken, but at the end of October, SS soldiers and Gestapo agents marched into laboratories, offices and engineering plants and arrested Jews on the spot. Those involved in mixed marriages were held at the Jewish community administration building in Rosenstrasse.

What happened then was extraordinary. Over three hundred German women gathered in protest outside Gestapo headquarters in Prinz Albrechtstrasse and at the very front stood Baroness Elsa von Halder, beside her maid, Rosa Stein, whose husband, Heini, had been arrested. Himmler, looking from his window inside with Bubi Hartmann, was not amused.

'Decent German women making such an exhibition and

supported by a baroness of one of our oldest families. Disgraceful. Even more so that they married Jews in the first place.'

Bubi Hartmann had absolutely nothing against Jews. In fact his dark secret was that his maternal great-grandmother had been Jewish and had married out, as it was called. Thankfully, it was so far back that it had never come out.

'Of course the industrialists have all protested at the arrest of such men,' Bubi said. 'All highly skilled and an asset to the Reich. I believe you pointed out their usefulness to the Führer some months ago, Reichsführer.'

Himmler nodded gravely. 'You're right. Animals, but if we have a use for them . . .' He shrugged.

'A great pity that the Minister of Propaganda didn't listen,' Bubi said smoothly. 'This is the direct result of his order.'

'That fool Goebbels. Always the stupid thing,' Himmler said.

'The Führer won't be pleased. If I may suggest, Reichsführer, a word from you. Good sense as usual? It would leave Goebbels with egg on his face.'

'You're right, Hartmann, and it's an excuse to see the Führer. I have other matters to discuss as well.'

'Of course, Reichsführer.'

Hartmann turned to go and Himmler said, 'One more thing. The presence of the Baroness von Halder out there puts another nail in her coffin. I told you she's been mixing with the wrong company. The fact that her son is one of our great war heroes won't save her.'

Bubi's mouth was dry. 'I understand.'

'I have, as you know, a special unit dealing with these traitors, these generals. It's not your business, Colonel, but I make a point. Valuable as your services are to me, everyone is expendable. I know you count Baron von Halder as a friend, but I advise caution.'

'I'm very grateful, Reichsführer.'

Bubi got out fast, returned to his office, walked straight past Trudi, sat down at his desk, took a bottle of cognac from a drawer and poured a large one.

Trudi came in. 'Trouble?'

So he told her.

'What do you think will happen?' she asked.

'That little idiot Goebbels will have to rescind the order.'

'You think so?'

'Definitely. It suits Himmler to make him look like the fool he is, especially in the eyes of the Führer.'

'And the Baroness?'

He shrugged. 'She was always strong-willed and the von Halders have been used to getting their own way for centuries.'

'Times have changed.'

'Try telling her that.'

'But Max von Halder is your friend.'

'So what do you want me to do, put my head on the block?' he asked her with some violence. 'Go on, get on with your work.'

She shook her head. 'You're a good man, Bubi, in entirely the wrong job.'

That same evening, at the White House in Washington, Abe Kelso's limousine delivered him to the west basement entrance. The Secret Service agents knew him, of course, but with respect for protocol he produced his pass.

'The President is expecting you, Senator,' one of them told him. 'I'll show you up.'

The Oval Office was in half-darkness, with only a table light on the desk and there seemed to be papers everywhere. The air was heavy with smoke and Roosevelt sat behind the desk in his wheelchair, a cigarette in his usual long holder.

'There you are, Abe.'

'Mr President.'

'How do you think the war's going?'

'Up and down. Poorly in Italy.'

'That was a slick one, the way that SS guy Scorzeny and those paratroopers grabbed Mussolini from the mountaintop where he was being held prisoner. Shows the world Hitler still has a long arm.'

'Churchill told the House of Commons that it was the most outstanding commando raid of the war.'

'Winston was always generous, but he was right.'

'What can I do for you, Mr President?'

'Well, Abe, top secret, but the Allies will land at Anzio, south of Rome, in January.'

'The German army in Italy is one of their best and Kesselring is arguably the most successful general they've got. It could be tough,' Abe said.

'I expect it will. Eisenhower and Montgomery will move to London in January to prepare for the invasion of France. I want you to go over, Abe, as my private fact-finder. I'm telling you now so you can have plenty of time to clear your desk.'

'At your command as always, Mr President.'

'Good, and remember, the reason I gave you unofficial ambassador status is so you have muscle. I know you don't have a specific function, but it makes you Priority One at all times for travel or whatever.' Roosevelt pushed an envelope across. 'You'll find a presidential warrant in there, signed by me. That should impress even Eisenhower.'

Abe put it in his pocket. 'Anything else, Mr President?'

'I don't think so. What about your grandsons? How are they?'

'Well, the one we don't mention is now a half-colonel in the Luftwaffe. Medals up to his eyes.'

'And the other? Harry, isn't it?'

'A wing commander, also medals up to his eyes.'

Roosevelt frowned. 'You mean he's still in the RAF? Abe, we've been in the war quite some time. Don't you think he should be with the Air Force?'

'Quite a number of people have suggested it, but he doesn't seem to see it that way.'

'Then I think you should change his mind, Abe. Speak to him when you're over there. Tell him it's the Presidential wish.'

'As you command, Mr President.'

'Excellent. Now push me into the sitting room and I'll mix you one of my celebrated Martinis before you go.'

In Berlin, Goebbels gave in and ordered the release of intermarried Jews, so Rosa was reunited with her Heini. Elsa was ecstatic the day Max, in Berlin for a staff meeting, joined her.

'Isn't it wonderful? We've beaten that little Nazi bastard.'

'For now, Mutti, only for now. You must take care.'

'I'm not afraid of these swine.'

The telephone rang. She answered, then held it out. 'For you.'

'Max, it's Bubi. I knew you were here to have dinner with Galland. Can you spare five minutes?'

'Of course.'

Max replaced the phone and turned to his mother. 'Bubi. He's in the bar and wants a word.'

'I'll join you when I've changed my frock,' she said and went into the dressing room, where Rosa waited.

Max sat in the corner booth and sampled the champagne cocktail Bubi had ordered. 'What can I do for you?'

'Max, you're my friend. We flew together in France before Dunkirk. You saved my life on at least one occasion.'

'So?'

'So I'm putting my career in your hands and very probably also my life.'

Max frowned. 'What is this?'

'Your mother. Her involvement in the Jewish protest has gone down like a lead weight in the wrong quarters.'

'You mean the Reichsführer?'

'There's more. I don't know all the details, but there's an investigation of disaffected army officers, people who wouldn't shed tears if the Führer met with an accident. There have already been two failed bomb attempts, I'm told.'

'But how does this affect my mother?'

'She's keeping the wrong company. Look, Max, I'm sure she's not involved personally, but friends of hers are. She could go down with the ship.'

He was agitated and Max said, 'All right, Bubi. I take the point and I'm grateful.'

'Do me one favour. If you try to warn her, don't tell her the tip-off came from me. When the Baroness talks, she talks loudly and if you want to punch me in the mouth for saying that, do it quickly because I've got to go.'

Max grinned. 'You're perfectly right, Bubi, and I'm still grateful.'

'I'll see you soon,' Bubi told him and left.

Max ordered another glass of champagne and thought about it. There was no sense in locking horns with her. He'd have to be more subtle.

A moment later Galland came in and sat down. 'Is your mother joining us?'

'Yes.' Max waved to the barman. 'But I want a word before she does. All this staff work, all these inspections in France. I'm bored, Dolfo.'

'Listen, you dog, I'm well aware that you've been flying

136

yourself down to the French coast. ME109s, a Junkers 88S last week. No crew, just a delivery pilot and you took over.'

'I have to keep my hand in.'

'So do I.' Galland grinned. 'Be patient, Max, after Christmas. Let's say January and I'll put you back on fighters, night or day, your choice.'

'Now you're talking.' Max jumped to his feet as his mother entered the room.

Later, on the balcony of her suite, the French windows open to the cold night air, he smoked a cigarette and looked out.

'No RAF tonight,' Elsa said as she joined him.

'I saw the met report for England. The Lancasters wouldn't be able to land when they got back. Heavy fog.'

'Thank God. It's good to have a night off. It's been bad lately. Are you going back to France soon?'

'In the morning.' He hesitated. 'Mutti, there's a lot of loose talk going around these days, suggestions of plots by staff officers against the Führer.'

'How pleasant if one of them succeeded.'

'Don't be silly, Mutti. Just be careful who your friends are and, please, no more performances like the Jewish protest. That's really asking for it.'

'I'm Elsa von Halder and I do as I please.'

'That's such arrogance,' he said, angry now. 'Don't you realize what these bastards are like? They'd string you up without a thought.'

'Don't be absurd,' she said, yet there was something new in her eyes.

'When they arrest one they arrest all,' Max said. 'That means the staff at the estate, good old Rosa and the Black Baron, hero of the Luftwaffe. We all go down the same road to hell because of your stupidity.'

'Max, you're exaggerating.'

He went and picked up his *Schiff* and pulled it on. 'I'll stay at the air base tonight. I've got an early start.' He walked to the door.

'Max!' she called.

He opened the door and went out.

Sarah Dixon found life considerably more interesting at Baker Street with SOE than at the War Office. For one thing and in spite of the fact that her duties were administrative, she did get to see who was who. Munro for example, Jack Carter and others. One day West came in with Harry Kelso.

'That wing commander,' she said to a woman called Madge Smith in the canteen. 'I heard him speak and he sounded American, but the flash on his uniform says Finland.'

'Oh, that's Kelso, Harry Kelso. A real ace. He sank that Italian cruiser, the *Orsini*, and you're right, he is a Yank.'

'Then why isn't he in the American Air Force?'

'I don't really know. He's Air Vice Marshal West's aide, I know that and he does courier work for Munro.'

'Courier work?'

'Special Duties flights out of Tangmere and Croydon or down to Cold Harbour. That's a base we have in Cornwall.'

'How interesting,' Sarah said.

Even more interesting were the events of Tuesday afternoon. Madge Smith said, 'Be a love, take this file to Nelly in the copying room. Five copies. It's on the chit.'

On her way through the downstairs corridor, Sarah had a quick look. There was a covering letter to some War Office department, a map of Cold Harbour, details of aircraft normally there, flights on two levels. Lysander drops to France and flights by Lysander from London's Croydon base to Cold Harbour, with pilots listed. Harry Kelso was mentioned.

She couldn't believe it, went into the copying room and found Nelly, a middle-aged grey-haired woman, stacking sheets.

'They want this fast, Nelly. Five copies.'

'God, what a morning I've had. Run off my feet. I haven't even had a chance to go you-know-where.'

'Well, go now. I'll start this lot for you.'

'What a dear you are.'

She rushed out and Sarah ran the sheets through one after another, placed them together, folded them and put them in the inside pocket of the jacket. Then she started on the five copies, was almost done when Nelly appeared.

'Just about through.'

'Bless you, I had a smoke while I could.' The final sheet went through and she stapled the copies. 'There you are, dear, and give Madge my love.'

It was four days later that Joel Rodrigues delivered the report to Trudi, who took it in to Hartmann at once. Bubi read it with awe on his face and held it out to her.

'We've struck gold. Read that.'

She went through it quickly. 'Good heavens, what a coup and did you note the name of one of those Special Duties pilots?'

'Harry Kelso.'

'Will you tell the Baron?'

'Of course not, but Himmler, yes, if only to show what great work we do. Tell Rodrigues to send a signal back to his brother in London. Tell him to inform Mrs Dixon we must have all information possible.'

'Of course,' Trudi said and went out.

Max was flying a Junkers 88S from Berlin to a coastal base called Fermanville. The Junkers usually had a crew of three – a pilot, navigator and rear gunner – but on delivery jobs it was just the pilot. He shouldn't have been doing it, but like Galland, he couldn't resist the chance to fly.

Near Le Touquet at 0200 hours, he crossed the coast in scattered cloud with a half moon. Visibility was fair as he called the night fighter base at Fermanville and gave his position.

'Who are you?' the ground controller's voice crackled in Max's headphones.

'Colonel von Halder delivering a new black bird for you.'

'Have you a crew?'

'No.'

'What a pity, Baron. I have a target.'

'Give me the position and I'll take a look.'

'Steer nought-six-seven degrees. Target range five kilometres.'

The Junkers moved out of the cloud and Max saw the prey up ahead, a Lancaster bomber, smoke feathering from one of the starboard engines.

He called in, 'I have visual sighting.' Then he closed.

It was very badly damaged, so badly that the rear gunner's turret had disappeared. He went down five or six hundred feet into cloud and came up at the rear, but below the stricken bomber. As he closed, he moved underneath. The JU88S had a pair of twenty-millimetre cannon mounted to aim upwards at an angle. When fired, it would rip out the belly of the target.

Max looked up, aware of the immense damage, and thought of the carnage he would cause in there, the cold wind whistling through the gaping holes in the fuselage, the dead and the dying. And for some reason, surprising even to himself, he thought: No. It was enough. He banked across, aware of the pilot over there, clear in the moonlight. He raised a hand in salute, then flew away.

He landed at Fermanville, taxied to dispersal and got out as the ground crew came forward. The intelligence officer, a major named Schultz, stood there smoking a cigarette.

'What happened, Baron, what was it?'

'A Lancaster and trailing smoke. I caught a glimpse, but then he was into heavy cloud. With no navigator and no one to operate the Lichtenstein set, there was no way I could follow him.'

'Better luck next time.'

Max walked towards the officers' mess, his boots drubbing the tarmac, depressed, weary and disturbed. A sitting duck and he'd let it go. Why? He'd never done such a thing before, always gone for the kill.

'What's happening to you, old boy?' he asked himself softly in English.

The mess was empty except for the group commander, a colonel named Haupt. They went back a long way. He was drinking coffee at the bar.

'Here we are again, Max. What happened up there?'

Max gave him the same explanation and ordered coffee and a schnapps.

Haupt said, 'Not much you could do with no navigator or rear gunner.'

'Yes, that Tommy's luck was good. I hope he makes it back.'

'From bombing the Reich?'

'All right, I take your point.'

'Galland isn't going to be pleased when he hears you've made another flight like this.'

'You'll tell him, of course.'

'I have to.'

Max shrugged. 'He's got broad shoulders. I saw him in Berlin. He's promised me fighters again in January.'

Haupt frowned. 'Max, you've done enough and more than enough. Dammit, man, it's a miracle . . .'

He hesitated and Max smiled. 'A miracle that I'm here at all? True enough. Not many left from the old days. Someone told me only twenty per cent of those who flew in the Battle of Britain are still around.' He smiled again at Haupt. 'And you and I are two of them and Dolfo makes three. There's also my brother, of course, but we don't mention him.'

He ordered another schnapps and Haupt said, 'Why do you still want to carry on, Max? With your record, your title, you could have a permanent staff job.'

'It's what I do,' Max said. 'Flying is what I am. My father flew Bristols for the Royal Flying Corps. Back home in Boston after the war, he bought one and kept it at a local airfield. When Harry and I were ten, he strapped us into the rear cockpit and took us for a flight. Nothing was ever the same after that. When we were sixteen and I went back to the States to spend time with my brother, we learned to fly with another old RFC pilot and we were good, Colonel, damn good from the start.' He shrugged. 'Nothing else but flying was important to me after that.'

Haupt nodded. 'I understand, but do you know what's really interesting about your story, Max? The fact that your father, an ace over the Western Front in 1917, was still flying the same fighter plane years after the war. Why was that?'

'Come in, Doctor Freud.' Max nodded. 'I take your drift. The high spot in his life and he couldn't let it go.'

'So it would seem. I'd let go now, Max, if I were you, while there's still time.'

Max thought about it. 'Maybe you're right. Anyway, I'm due at Abbeville tomorrow. I'll get some sleep.' At the door he hesitated. 'Tell me, do you ever feel tired? I mean, really deep down tired? As if you were at the end of something?'

'Yes, we can all feel like that. It's been a long war,' Haupt said gravely. 'Go on, go to bed, Max.'

The door closed. Haupt sat there, an expression of gloom on his face and said to the barman, 'Give me a cognac, I could do with it.'

The first time Munro asked Harry to fly him and Carter down to Cold Harbour by Lysander, it was a bad flight. The New Year was starting, and there was heavy cloud and slate-grey rain slicing across the Cornish landscape. They went in at a thousand feet and below was the Cornish coast, the inlet of Cold Harbour, the quay with a naval craft moored beside it.

'Isn't that a Kriegsmarine E-boat?' Harry said as he circled.

'That's right,' Munro told him cheerfully. 'Secret project and nothing to do with you. It's a mind-your-own-business sort of place this, Harry. You'll see.'

'What about the villagers?' Harry asked as he started to go down.

'Moved them all out, old boy,' Carter told him. 'Still use the pub, that's the Hanged Man, for base personnel. A lady called Julie Legrande runs it for us. She's also housekeeper at the manor. Ah, you've got a good view. Grancester Manor.'

Grey stone, a couple of towers, all very imposing with a walled garden running down to the river. A lake.

'Nice,' Harry said.

'We keep the Joes there overnight. That's what we call the agents we deliver to France. Julie looks after them. She used to be in that line of work herself.'

Harry concentrated on landing, as he skimmed across the manor with its lake and dropped down on to a grass runway with a wind-sock at one end.

There were two hangars and several huts. Two aircraft were on the apron, one a JU88S and the other a Fieseler Storch, both with Luftwaffe insignia. The mechanics working on them wore

Luftwaffe overalls. Harry switched off, opened the door and he and Carter and Munro got out. It was raining slightly.

Munro said, 'Recognize the Storch? That's the one you checked out for us. To assuage your curiosity, dear boy, it's useful on occasion in our line of work to use enemy aircraft.'

'And the E-boat?'

'Just the thing for jobs off the French coast, but not your business.'

A Jeep appeared, driven by a woman in her early thirties. She wore a sheepskin coat and her blonde hair was tied back. She had a calm and rather sweet face.

'There you are, Brigadier,' she smiled. 'Jack, how are you?'

'Julie Legrande, Harry Kelso, Air Vice Marshal West's aide, so show some respect. However, his rather special talents mean he can be useful to us on occasion.'

'Oh, the wing commander's reputation goes before him.'

'Enough of that. We'll take the Jeep.' He turned to Harry. 'Straight back to Croydon for you. Just wanted you to see the place. Jack and I might be here for a couple of days. Get him a sandwich or something in the canteen, Julie, then see him off.'

The canteen was simple enough: a few tables and chairs, a bar counter, a kitchen.

'Coffee?' she said.

'No, tea.'

Just now the place was empty. He sat down and waited and she appeared with a tray containing a pot of tea, crockery and a plate of cheese sandwiches. As he ate, she lit a cigarette and watched.

'The great Harry Kelso. That Italian cruiser was something.'

'Luck,' he said. 'One of the handful of times I was flying a bomber. I'm a fighter pilot.'

'What's that mean?' she said. 'If someone claims to be an artist, or an author or an actor.' She frowned and scratched her head. 'What do I mean? I'm suddenly at a loss.'

'I get your drift,' Harry said. 'You don't think flying fighter planes is an art form.'

'I accept that it can be done superbly well. You and your brother are prime examples.' She nodded. 'Yes, Munro told me about you both. In our line of work, he thinks I should be kept informed.'

'So, it can be done superbly well. What's your point?'

'What happens after? It's a temporary condition. Wars come and go, but they always end sometime, isn't this true?'

'French philosophy on a wet morning in Cornwall? I don't think I'm up to that.' He finished the last sandwich and got up. 'Time to go.'

'I'll see you off.'

As they walked to the Lysander he said, 'Munro's niece, Molly. Do you know her? She's a doctor.'

'Yes, she comes down here from London in the Lysander if there is an emergency.'

'What kind of emergency?'

'Oh, sometimes people arrive from the other side in a poor condition.'

'I see.' He took her hand. 'Nice to meet you.'

'And more often in the future,' she said.

He climbed into the Lysander, closed the door, switched on and taxied away. As he rose up through the heavy overcast, he was thinking about what she had said and she was right. What was he going to do when it was all over? It suddenly came to him, with a sense of shock, that he'd never thought it *would* be over, not in his heart.

★

Eisenhower and Montgomery reached London in January. Ike stayed in Grosvenor Square, sometimes walking down to the Connaught Hotel where General de Gaulle had lived in some splendour for two years or more.

In that month the Luftwaffe started to bomb London again. The Little Blitz, it was called. It wasn't as bad as the first time around, but bad enough and much more skilful this time. JU88s pathfinders operating out of Chartres and Rennes led the way in and pinpointed the targets and Max, having finally persuaded Galland to return him to duty, flew one of them.

It was the end of February when Munro presented himself at Hayes Lodge, Eisenhower's temporary headquarters in London. He found the General in the library enjoying coffee and doughnuts.

'Join me, Brigadier.'

'Just tea if you don't mind, sir.'

'Help yourself at the sideboard. That report on Rommel's intentions about the invasion was a real coup. I know it took some getting and I know some of your people at your Cold Harbour project suffered. I'm sorry.'

'It's the name of the game, General.'

'Anyway, I'll be using Southwick as soon as we get more involved in preparation for D-Day.'

Southwick House north of Portsmouth had been taken over by the Royal Navy Navigation School and selected as headquarters for Operation Overlord, the invasion of France. Ike and Montgomery were to have caravans in the grounds although Montgomery was also a resident at nearby Broomfield House.

'I've been thinking,' Ike said. 'Backwards and forwards from London to Southwick by road will eat up my time. Is there an airstrip at Southwick?'

'Grass runway. Small but suitable for a Lysander. You could fly from Croydon in half an hour.'

'Perfect. Your Special Duties people can handle it.'

'Certainly, General. Anything else?'

'Not at the moment. Our greatest secret will be the landing beaches. If Rommel gets that information we're sunk because they'll be able to concentrate everything they've got in just the right spots.'

'It's hardly likely he would find out, General. We wrapped up every Abwehr agent in England in 1940. Most of them we turned and they send false information to the Reich.'

'Let's keep it that way.' Ike shook hands. 'Now, if you'll excuse me. I've got a pile of work.'

Harry once again found himself flying Munro, on his own this trip, down to Cold Harbour. The weather was even worse this time, with very low cloud and as he swept in at five hundred feet, he realized that the E-boat had gone. Instead, a Royal National Lifeboat Institution boat was tied up at the quay. When they landed, there was no sign of the Junkers although the Storch was still there.

As he opened the door, he said, 'There seems to have been some changes here.'

'As I told you before, it's none of your affair, Harry,' Munro said, as Julie Legrande appeared in the Jeep.

'Fine by me.'

'You may be required for some essential courier work soon. You could even find yourself flying Ike down from London to Southwick House.'

'Is that so?'

'Yes, it is. Remember rank has no meaning in a Special Duties Squadron. A pilot is a pilot.'

'I'm suitably reprimanded, Brigadier.'

'Back to Croydon. I'll send for you when I need you. Morning, Julie. I'll take the Jeep. See to the wing commander,' and he climbed behind the wheel and drove away.

In the canteen, drinking tea and smoking a cigarette, Harry said to Julie, 'What happened here? Munro wouldn't tell me.'

'The Junkers and the E-boat were lost in action,' she told him. 'That's all I can say.'

'Isn't war hell?' Harry got up. 'I'd better get going.'

'It's pretty foggy. Shouldn't you wait?'

'I walk on water, Julie, didn't you know that?' He got into the Lysander and switched on, took off fast and climbed out of sight.

She stood there for quite some time before she turned and walked away.

NINE

It was a day or two later that Abe Kelso found himself back in the Oval Office with the President. It was a fine sunny morning this time, the atmosphere totally different.

'Time to go, Abe,' Roosevelt told him. 'A week, no more. Winston's agreed to see you. Listen to what he has to say, listen to all of them – Ike, Montgomery, Patton, the lot. All I'm seeking is your opinion, honest and unbiased, about the way they all see the invasion of Europe.'

'I'll do my best, Mr President.'

Roosevelt fitted another cigarette into his holder. 'This bombing of London, the Little Blitz. It seems to have run its course.'

'That would appear to be so. There was never more than sixty or seventy planes at a time according to the War Department,' Abe said. 'Plenty of damage and people killed, but not on the old scale.'

'That may be, but one report I had from our intelligence people suggests that the good citizens of London are getting rather impatient. They want to see some action. Always remember, the British have been at this war since 1939. Another thing – this Nazi rocket programme, the missiles we know they've been constructing. Get me a profile on that. I need to know what people are saying, but it's your opinion I need.'

Abe smiled. 'In other words, what the politicians and top brass over there are really thinking.'

'Exactly.' The President smiled. 'On your way, Abe. I know I can rely on you.'

Crossing the coast of New England later that night in a Flying Fortress on its way to join the 8th Air Force in England, Abe made himself comfortable with the army blankets and pillows the crew had given him and accepted coffee from the young sergeant waist-gunner.

He went over again his conversation with Roosevelt. In fact, he went over it several times. He had to get it right, it was as simple as that. In any event, the prospect of meeting some of the most important people in the Allied war effort face-to-face filled him with joy, but also a kind of fear.

After a couple of hours, one of the pilots, a young lieutenant named Miller, came back with a thermos of coffee and sat beside him. The lieutenant filled two cups and gave him one.

'Sorry, it's not comfortable, Senator. You won't be too familiar with military flying.'

Almost without thinking, Abe replied, 'Maybe not me, but it's in the family. My son was a fighter pilot with the British in the First War.' He hesitated, then left Max out of the equation. 'And my grandson's a fighter pilot with the RAF now.'

'With the RAF? Shouldn't he be flying with us by now?'

'Yes, he should, is the answer to that,' Abe told him. 'But he seems to be a fairly stubborn fellow.'

Miller laughed. 'Fighter pilots are like that – a funny breed. Know what they call bomber pilots? Truck drivers!'

'Actually, he flew bombers for a little while, too, in the Middle East. Sank an Italian cruiser.'

It didn't register with Miller, who simply nodded and got up.

'Good for him. Well, I've got work to do now, Senator. I'll see you later.'

Abe sat there thinking about it as the Fortress droned on into the night, then hitched a blanket around his shoulders and went to sleep.

In Berlin, Max reported to Galland at Luftwaffe headquarters and found him in the canteen having sandwiches and beer. He looked up, genuinely pleased. 'Good to see you, Max.'

'I thought we should talk.' Max sat down. 'Now that our latest escapade over London has run its course, I'd like to return to 109s. The Junkers is all very well, but it's not my cup of tea.'

'Well, you took one to London fifteen times and brought it back in one piece.'

'That's not the point. Come on, Dolfo.'

Galland sat there looking at him, frowning slightly and then nodded. 'I'll make you my personal aide in the general area of the French coast. You'll have your own ME109. What you do with it when my back is turned is your business. Is that acceptable?'

'Perfectly.'

'Good. I must go. By the way, I hear the Gestapo lifted Generals Prien and Krebs the other day, also Prien's aide, Colonel Lindemann and some junior people.'

'Why?'

'The whisper is there was a failed bomb plot against the Führer. They were all members of that bridge club at the old Adler Hotel.'

'So?' Max said.

'Doesn't your mother play there?'

Max was thunderstruck. 'I'm not certain.'

'I think she'd be advised to go to another club,' Galland said. 'These are troubled times,' and he turned and went out.

Max immediately tried Bubi at his office, but he was out, Trudi Braun said. He told her he wanted to meet him and would be in the Adlon Bar at six. She put the phone down and Bubi, the extension in his hand, replaced it.

'Is this bad?' she said.

'It could be.'

'Should you get involved?'

'He's my friend.' He straightened his uniform. 'I'm going to sound out the Reichsführer. Give me that report on French Resistance activity on the West Wall. It will give me an excuse to talk.'

She was worried now. 'Be careful.'

Himmler examined the report and nodded. 'Very thorough. All these terrorists will be instantly shot when rounded up. No exceptions.'

'Certainly, Reichsführer.'

'And now, I have to meet with the Führer in the Bunker. I just got the call.'

'Anything in particular?' Bubi Hartmann asked carefully.

'I'm not sure although he is hardly pleased by that abortive attempt on his life the other day. Naturally my special unit arrested all involved. A bridge club, would you credit such a thing? They were all executed at once – Prien, Krebs, Lindemann and some junior officers and a couple of women.'

Bubi turned pale. 'Firing squad, Reichsführer?'

'Too honourable a way out for such scum. No, the Führer's orders were clear. Execution with piano wire, the whole process to be filmed. Such a record has its uses,' Himmler added. 'And no, Colonel, your friend's mother, the good Baroness, was not among them. At the moment, there isn't enough proof.'

'I see, Reichsführer.'

Bubi made for the door and Himmler called, 'I'd advise you to consider your friendship with the Baron, Hartmann. You are valuable to me, but no one is indispensable.'

In the bar at the Adlon Max sat at his usual table, drinking cognac to steady his nerves. He was afraid, but not for himself, only his mother. How stupid she had been, how incredibly stupid. Hartmann came in and joined him, waving the waiter away.

'Thank God you came,' Max said.

'The last time, Max. I can't take chances any more. This is a very bad scene.'

'Tell me.'

Which Bubi did in graphic detail. 'So now you know.'

'God in heaven, that they can do such things.'

'They can, believe me. So, your mother must walk very carefully.' He stood up. 'We won't meet like this again, Max. Himmler himself has warned me off.'

Elsa was in her suite, sitting on the couch by the fireplace enjoying a drink, when Rosa opened the door for Max.

'My darling boy, how marvellous. Just in time for a cocktail.'

'Never mind that. I've news for you. Your friends Generals Prien and Krebs? Colonel Lindemann and the others plus a couple of women, all members of your Adler bridge club? Does any of this mean anything to you?'

She was almost petulant. 'I heard a whisper that there had been some difficulty.'

'That's one way of putting it. The difficulty was an attempt to blow up the Führer which, of course, failed. Your friends, the people I've mentioned, are all dead, Mutti, hung by the neck by piano wire and their sorry end filmed for Himmler's files.'

She was visibly shaken. 'That can't be true.'

'My good friend Bubi Hartmann has risked his own neck to

warn me. The only reason Himmler hasn't had you arrested is that he lacks solid proof.'

'God damn him!' Elsa said and there were angry tears in her eyes. 'They can't do this to me.'

The dressing-room door flew open and Rosa appeared. 'Is everything all right, Baroness?'

Rosa's eyes were swollen with weeping and Max said, 'What's wrong?'

'They've arrested Heini again and sent him to Auschwitz,' Elsa said.

'Is that so? How could that be, Mutti? You just told me "they can't do that to me", wasn't that your phrase?'

'Damn you, Max.'

She hammered at his chest and he took her wrists. 'Stupid, arrogant, vain. You think being Baroness von Halder is important? Not in the Third Reich. You think Goering will help you when you're in a mess like this? Not in the Third Reich. You were always window dressing, Mutti, just like me. The Black Baron in flying clothes with all the medals.'

'Max – please.'

'I've had it. You carry on down this road, as I've said before, and you'll take everyone with you.' He turned to Rosa. 'So they took your Heini? Never mind. The way my mother's behaving, they'll have you too before long. Perhaps even me.'

He walked to the door. Elsa called, 'Max – listen.'

He turned. 'And it was for this that we left Boston? It was to support the arrogance of a von Halder that I lost my brother?'

He opened the door and went out and she collapsed on the couch in tears.

Himmler's Mercedes turned out of Wilhelmplatz and into Vosstrasse and drove towards the Reich Chancellery. Beneath that incredible building the Führer had had a bunker constructed. It was his underground headquarters protected by thirty metres of concrete, proof against any bomb the Allies could drop on Berlin.

The Mercedes drew into a car ramp and an SS sentry approached. That it was the Reichsführer, he knew full well, but Himmler had rigid standards so the sentry demanded his identification papers. He examined them and saluted and Himmler got out and went below.

Through dim lighting, endless corridors, the gentle droning of electric fans in the ventilating system, he finally came to a door manned by another SS sentry. He nodded, the sentry opened it and Himmler passed inside, to find Goebbels, von Ribbentrop, Martin Bormann and Admiral Canaris standing at what was called the General Map Table. He could hear the angry sound of the Führer's voice from his private study.

'What's going on?' Himmler asked Bormann.

'He isn't pleased.'

The door opened and Field Marshal von Rundstedt, Rommel and Field Marshal von Kluge emerged, the Führer behind them.

'Go on, get out. Come back to me with common sense or not at all.'

They went out in confusion, Rommel looking grim, and Hitler turned to the others. 'This map,' he said. 'The Channel, France. All they can talk about is where will the enemy land. Pas de Calais or Normandy, who cares? We will crush them on the beaches, isn't this so?'

'Naturally, my Führer,' Bormann told him.

'So, where the enemy will land, as I say, is irrelevant. Why can't they come up with something useful, these clowns?' He slapped his thigh and laughed. 'Do you know what would be useful, gentlemen, really useful?'

They all stared nervously. It was Himmler who said, 'What would that be, my Führer?'

'For a bomb to fall on Eisenhower! He's the leader, he's the brain, good German stock, a worthy adversary. With him out of the way, they'd be in total disarray. Montgomery is a clown.'

'You are right as always,' Himmler said. 'There are, of course, many ways to skin a cat. What a pity the Abwehr's secret intelligence organization in England was totally destroyed.' He glanced at Canaris. 'There could have been an obvious solution, a simple assassination, but of course there's nobody left to do it.'

Canaris looked haggard and Hitler said in an almost kindly tone, 'Not your fault. The fortunes of war, Admiral.' He turned to Himmler. 'But what a pleasing prospect, Reichsführer. It lifts my heart to think of it.'

Later in his office, Himmler said to Bubi Hartmann, 'So, I've told you what the Führer said. Tell me, is there anyone amongst your English agents who could accomplish such a task?'

'I regret to say no one, Reichsführer. Can you imagine the security around Eisenhower? There is always the IRA, of course. We could approach them to arrange a contract killing.'

'Nonsense,' Himmler said. 'They bungle everything, those Irish clodhoppers. Still, bear it in mind, Colonel.'

Back in his own office, he reached for the cognac again as he told Trudi all.

'Kill Eisenhower?' she said.

'The ultimate fantasy.' He toasted her. 'To you and me, Trudi, the only sane people in a crazy world.'

In London, Abe moved into a suite at the Savoy. One of the first things he did was to trace Harry, which led him to a phone conversation with West.

'I understand my grandson is your aide?' Abe said.

'In a manner of speaking, Senator, but it's more complicated. He operates with a Special Duties Squadron, mainly because he has extensive experience flying enemy aircraft. Sometimes they fall into our hands and he's our chief test pilot when that happens.'

Abe said, 'Are you telling me I can't see him?'

'It's not that. The fact is he isn't here. He's in Scotland. A Junkers 88S operating out of Norway put down there by mistake. Harry's gone up to supervise the inspection. He'll fly it down to what we call the Enemy Aircraft Flight at a special base, but it could be several days. I wish we'd known you were coming.'

'Top secret. I flew over in a Fortress. Trouble is, I'm due back in six days. I've plenty to do. I'm seeing Winston and Ike and others, but Harry was a priority. I last saw him in November '39, when he left for Finland.'

'I know and it's a damn shame. I'll speak to him and see if we can hurry things along.'

'One more thing. He still hasn't transferred to the US Air Force.'

'He doesn't want to, Senator.'

'Well, the President of the United States wants him to. There are those who take it as a slap in the face.'

West was angry and took a deep breath. 'That annoys me considerably, Senator. Your grandson is famous for not claiming all his kills. He is, in my opinion, the RAF's top scorer and the finest pilot I've ever known. You'll have to excuse my anger, but the pressure comes from people in your Air Force, usually at high rank, who've done damn all. Your grandson is what, twenty-six years of age? Five years of combat flying. He shouldn't be here, but he is.'

'Thank God for it,' Abe told him. 'And get as angry as you like. I'll have to go. I've an immediate meeting with Ike at Hayes Lodge.'

'I hope we get a chance to meet,' West said.

'Oh, we will, you can count on it.'

The JU88S in Scotland had experienced bad luck. Bounced by a Mosquito over the North Sea, its instruments damaged and the navigator and rear gunner dead, the wounded pilot had gone down into heavy cloud cover and escaped. As he couldn't see the Pole Star, he couldn't navigate that way and in any event, his left arm was so badly wounded that it took everything he had to hang on to the column. When the coast came and he saw the lights of an airfield, he went down fast and landed on an RAF bomber station called Kinross. When they took him from the aircraft he was unconscious.

There was no question of flying the aircraft down to the south of England until at least minimum repairs had been made to the cockpit and instruments. An engineering officer and a top crew were supplied and Harry made a close inspection and told them what was needed.

He was in the mess that evening when West called. 'How soon can you bring that thing down?'

'Three days, maybe four.'

'Could you make it sooner? Your grandfather's here.'

It was quite a shock. Harry said, 'Do you know for how long?'

'Six days, which includes today. Look, Harry, just leave it. Fly back. I'll find someone else.'

'There is no one who has the expertise I have, you know that.'

'He raised the question of you transferring to your Yankee friends, says Roosevelt thinks you should.'

'Well to hell with him too,' Harry said. 'I'll be back when I'm back, sir. I'll be in touch.'

He stood at the bar in the officers' mess, had a whisky and water and thought about it. The other officers tended to keep away, awed by the medals, the legend. Harry was oblivious to all that. He could have rushed back to London, so why not? The answer was simple. He was deliberately avoiding his grandfather. It was as if the old man was from another life, a life that had included Max and Mutti, but that life was in the past, a distant dream. Still, he would have to see him, no way round it.

He called to Jervis, the flight lieutenant in charge of engine repairs. 'Come and have a drink, we need to talk.'

'Thank you, sir.' Jervis, touched with glory, was delighted.

'You said three or four days on the JU. Thing is, there's a flap on. I've had Air Vice Marshal West on the phone and he wants it yesterday. Could you manage two days?'

'Well, I'd need two teams and work nights, sir.'

'I'm sure the Air Vice Marshal would appreciate it. By the way, once they see what you've accomplished when we deliver it to the Enemy Aircraft Flight, they'll probably refuse to let you go. You're a first class aircraft engineer and I'm sure West will appreciate that when he sees my report.'

It was enough. Jervis couldn't have been more pleased. 'I say, sir, coming from you!' He pushed his drink away. 'If you'll excuse me, I think I'll go and get things moving. Two days you said, sir. Consider it done.'

'And you'll enjoy the Enemy Aircraft Flight,' Harry said. 'Consider that done.'

Abe worked his way through Churchill, Anthony Eden, Eisenhower, listening patiently. Even when generals like Patton and Omar Bradley were disagreeing they were worth listening to as well. He had an uncomfortable lunch with Montgomery at Broomfield House, when the Field Marshal made no secret of his belief that he and not Ike should be in supreme command.

He was even driven up to Norfolk to visit an American base

from which B17s were engaged in daylight raids on Germany. The carnage had been terrible already, almost non-sustainable. Abe witnessed for himself some planes returning in the middle of the afternoon, one of them so badly damaged it had to pancake, skidding to the end of the runway and then exploding into fire. It was one of the most shocking experiences of his life and not improved by being told that five planes hadn't made it back.

He had a drink in the officers' mess before leaving and said to his host, a brigadier general named Read, 'So young, those boys. I'll tell the President what I've seen, you may be sure, but in a way I feel ashamed.'

A young major moved to the bar, his face strained and tired. On his left breast he had the usual wings and ribbons, but on his right he wore RAF wings.

'This is Major Wood,' Read said. 'He was on the raid.'

'RAF wings,' Abe said.

'Oh, sure. Woodsy flew Wellingtons and then Lancasters with RAF Bomber Command. Senator Abe Kelso, Major.'

Wood shook hands, then frowned. 'Kelso? Would you by any chance know Harry Kelso?'

'My grandson.'

The young man pumped his hand vigorously. 'He's the best. Right through the Battle of Britain, then Africa and sinking that Italian cruiser. He *is* still around, I hope?'

'Wing commander now. Some sort of special duties.'

'That's wonderful. I mean, when a guy like that is still here, it gives us all hope.' Wood smiled and moved away.

Read said, 'I hadn't realized, Senator. I'm surprised he hasn't moved over.'

'A long story, General.' Abe smiled. 'And now, I think I'd better get back to London.'

★

The following morning, Harry flew down to Surrey escorted by two Spitfires just in case anyone tried to shoot him down. Jervis took the navigator's seat and Tarquin sat on the floor in his jump bag, Harry unzipping it so the bear's head showed through.

'He looks thoughtful,' Jervis said.

'So would you if you'd seen what he's seen. He's been flying since 1916.'

'My God.'

The flight was uneventful. At the last moment, the Spitfires banked away and Harry landed, listened to the controller then taxied to a row of hangars and switched off. He and Jervis got out. Inside the hangars were a selection of Luftwaffe planes: an Arado, two ME109s, a couple of Storchs.

'Plenty for you to get your teeth stuck into here,' he told Jervis.

An RAF staff car rolled up and West got out. 'Thought I'd pick you up.'

'That's good of you, sir. May I introduce Flight Lieutenant Jervis? I mentioned him in my daily dispatch yesterday.'

'Excellent work, Jervis.' West shook his hand. 'I'm having you transferred to Special Duties. I'm putting you up to acting squadron leader. Do a good job and maybe we'll make it permanent.'

Jervis stammered, 'Thank you, sir.' Harry waved at him and followed West into the car.

'Your grandfather's at the Savoy. I thought I'd drop you off.'

'Very kind of you, sir. Have you met?'

'Oh, yes. Nice man.' West offered Harry a cigarette. 'It's getting more difficult to hang on to you, Harry, and the Air Ministry don't want any trouble.'

'I couldn't care less,' Harry said.

'Awkward sod. Anyway, I'll drop you off. Oh, and by the

way, I've got a courier flight for you tomorrow. Kill two birds with one stone.'

'And what would that be?'

West told him, then dropped him at the Savoy and Harry walked in with a bag in each hand. The concierge himself took them and handed them to a boy.

'I think we're full, Wing Commander.'

'My grandfather's here, Senator Kelso.'

The concierge beamed. 'Of course, sir. Two-bedroomed suite, on the first floor. No problem.'

Abe, standing by the window of the sitting room of his suite, was enjoying a cigar and looking out over the Thames. There was a knock at the door.

'Porter, sir.'

'Come in, it's not locked,' Abe bellowed.

The door opened and the porter entered with the bags. 'What's this?' Abe demanded and then Harry stepped in.

'Hello, Abe,' he said, just like the old days and it was as if the years had melted away.

Abe, overcome by emotion, flung his arms round him and wept.

A few minutes later, sitting by the window, he drank brandy to settle his nerves. 'Dammit, Harry, this is unbelievable. My God, all those medals.'

'Remember what Dad used to say? Nice bit of tin. Any news of Max and Mutti?'

'No, my Swedish connection has dried up.'

'I might be able to find something out.'

'How could you?'

'I work for a Brigadier Munro. He's with SOE and very clued up in the intelligence field.'

'I've heard of him. He's heavily involved with Ike.'

'He would be,' Harry said. 'The invasion. Munro drops agents into France all the time. I do flights for him. I'll see what I can do.'

Abe nodded. 'We've got a problem. The President wants you in the US Air Force and so does Ike.'

'Oh, for heaven's sake!' Harry exploded. 'I've had just about enough of this! What are they going to do, court-martial me?'

'Harry, you're being stupid.'

'How come? I mean, do they think Max should transfer in from the Luftwaffe?' He got up and took a deep breath. 'Enough. I need a bath. What are you doing tonight?'

'I've booked a table in the River Room.'

'Excellent.' Harry opened the jump bag and put Tarquin on the table. 'There you go, Abe, doesn't that take you back? Every flight I've done, he's been there.' He picked up his other bag. 'I'll use the spare room.' As he opened the door he added, 'I hear you're flying down from Croydon to Southwick House with Ike tomorrow.'

'How do you know that?'

'Because I'm the courier pilot.'

The River Room was busy early, but then everywhere in London was these days and when Abe and Harry arrived the head waiter came up at once.

'I have a nice table for you at the window, Senator. For four, you said?'

'That's fine,' Abe told him.

They were seated, he ordered champagne cocktails and Harry said, 'Who are the others?'

'Oh, I decided to check out your Brigadier Munro while you were in the bath. I told him you were dining with me and asked him to join us. He suggested bringing his niece, a Doctor Sobel. I understand you know her?'

'Yes, we've met, but it was some time ago. Her mother was Munro's sister, English. The girl's father was an air force colonel last I heard.'

'Not any more. He's a major-general now and he's been here for a month. He's around Ike quite a lot.'

'Well, good for him.' Harry frowned. 'I wonder what Munro's up to?'

'Does he have to be up to something?'

'Oh, yes, it's meat and drink to him.'

At that moment Munro arrived with Molly. He was in uniform, she wore an evening suit of a jacket and short skirt in some sort of brown crêpe. She had little make-up and her hair was tied back with a brown velvet bow.

Harry and Abe stood up and Munro said, 'My niece Molly, Senator.'

Abe looked at her with considerable approval. 'I know your father, and you, I understand, know my grandson.'

She smiled at Harry and shook hands. 'How are you?'

'In my prime.'

'You always were.'

'Last time I saw you, you looked tired,' he said.

'And now?'

'Good enough to . . .' he hesitated, 'dance with and let's do just that and leave the older generation to talk.'

The Orpheans were playing a slow foxtrot, 'Night and Day', and she moved into his arms. 'Here we are again,' he said.

'And here you are covered in glory as usual.'

'What about you? You were at the Cromwell, as I remember. Still there?'

'Now and then. I'm a senior surgeon now.'

'That's great. You must be good.'

'Oh, the war helps, you know how it is. I operate from a central unit and service several hospitals.'

'Do you still work for Munro? Julie Legrande told me you were a sort of flying doctor to Cold Harbour.'

'Now and then.' She frowned. 'You mean something more.'

'That time you and I took a walk through town after lunch at the Garrick. I overheard dear old Dougal talking to you afterwards at the flat. He'd asked you to see what you could get out of me.'

'Oh, damn,' she said. 'I'd make a rotten spy.'

'That's okay. I enjoyed the walk. Are you supposed to do the same thing tonight?'

'If you must know, my uncle told me he was seeing you and your grandfather for dinner and I asked if I could come.'

'Did you now? I wonder why?'

'Don't be a pig, Harry Kelso. You know damn well why.'

For a moment, she was close to tears and he was immediately contrite. 'Okay, I'm sorry and I am a pig.'

The orchestra moved into 'A Foggy Day in London Town' and Molly inched closer. 'How's Jack Carter?' he asked.

'He's fine. Major Carter now.'

'Any man in your life?'

'Yes, but he isn't doing much about it.'

He held her even closer and at the table, Munro said to Abe, 'I might as well tell you, Senator, the poor girl fell for the wretch the first time she met him.'

'And I might as well tell you that suits me just fine,' Abe said.

Molly and Harry sat down, the wine waiter poured champagne and the head waiter suggested the evening's main dish, a haddock, potato and onion pie. They all took it.

'That's war for you, real food.' Munro raised his glass. 'To us and to hell with Hitler.'

'Speaking of the Führer,' Harry said, 'do you have any news of Max?'

'None that you'd like to hear. During the Little Blitz, he was a pathfinder flying a JU 88S out of Chartres and also Rennes. I believe he made something like fifteen or sixteen raids.'

'That must have been tough,' Harry said calmly. 'The South of England is no place for the Luftwaffe these days.'

There was a slight pause. Molly said, 'Tough? Harry, he was bombing London. Did you know that over a hundred people died in a single tube station that was hit?'

'The cruiser *Orsini* had a crew of eight hundred and twenty men,' Harry replied quietly. 'After I sank her, do you know how many they picked up?'

'No,' she said, in a small voice, and there was something close to fear on his face.

'Seventy-two. So I killed seven hundred and forty-eight people.' He shrugged. 'Like they say, war is hell. A tube station, a cruiser . . . People die, Molly. We kill them. That's what we do.'

Silence reigned for a few uncomfortable moments, before Munro hastily changed the subject. 'You're going down to Southwick tomorrow with Ike?' he said to Abe.

'That's right, and Harry's the courier pilot.'

'Have you met Ike yet, Harry?' Munro asked.

'You know I haven't, you old fox.'

'Watch out. He'll try to get you to join up.' At that moment, the head waiter came over. 'I'm terribly sorry, but they've phoned from Guy's Hospital, Doctor Sobel. You're wanted immediately.'

'Oh, dear, here we go again. May I use your staff car, uncle?'

'Of course.'

'I'll see you to the door,' Harry said.

They went out of the entrance and the porter on duty said, 'Brigadier Munro's driver went across the road for a sandwich and a cup of tea, Wing Commander. I'll go and get him.'

He hurried away and Harry and Molly walked after him and stood on the pavement in the main road. A camera shop was next door, and a photographer stood outside accosting passers-by in the fading light.

'Isn't it too dark?' Molly asked.

The photographer heard and shook his head. 'I use flashlight. Ready in twenty-four hours. One pound.'

'I could be dead in twenty-four hours,' Harry said.

'That's a terrible thing to say,' Molly told him.

Harry took a white five-pound note from his wallet and unfolded it. 'Two copies. One for the lady and one for me delivered at the reception desk of the Savoy within two hours. Name of Kelso. If you let me down, I'll get my brother to bomb your shop.'

'You're a card, guv, and no mistake, but you're on.' They walked back to the Savoy and stood in the entrance and he took the picture once and again for luck. 'I won't let you down, guv.'

The staff car drew up and Harry opened the door for her. 'It was nice seeing you again.'

'Oh, you fool.' She reached up and kissed him on the mouth. 'I suppose you'll go to hell your own way,' and she got into the staff car.

Harry found Munro and Abe deep in conversation when he rejoined them. 'What are you two up to?' he said as he sat down. 'Winning the war?'

'No, the war *is* won, Harry,' Abe told him. 'Just a matter of time.'

'What about the Führer's secret weapons? The rockets and so

on? We all hear the whispers. They've even got a great jet plane in development.'

'Our estimate is that none of it will matter,' Munro said. 'We will win, there's no doubt about that. Bloody battles to come both in Russia and Europe, but at the end stands victory.'

'That's a German slogan.'

'Yes, I'm aware of that. More champagne?'

'Better not. I'm flying in the morning.'

Abe said, 'Brigadier Munro's mentioned one item of news out of Berlin that isn't too comforting. There was a bungled attempt on Hitler's life. A number of officers and two women were arrested and executed. They were all members of the same bridge club.'

'So what?'

'The thing is, Elsa was a member of the same club.'

Harry turned very pale, his face like stone then snapped his fingers at the wine waiter. 'I will have that other glass of champagne.' He lit a cigarette and turned to Munro. 'Tell me.'

When Munro was finished, there was a silence. Finally, Harry said, 'Your contacts in Berlin are good?'

'Very good. We even have people within the armed services who do what they can.'

'And you're sure my mother hasn't been arrested?'

'Definitely. Harry, she has a very high profile socially. She's frequently in Goering's company.' He shook his head. 'However, her association with the wrong people won't go down well at Gestapo headquarters. From what I'm told, she's no friend to the Nazis, but so far, her privileged position has protected her.'

'But not for ever?'

'I'd say she needs to take care.'

'Well, let's hope the shock of what's happened gives her pause for thought,' Abe said.

'Yes, well, the only trouble with that is she never paused for a thought in her life.' Harry was angry.

'Just like you?' Munro observed.

Harry laughed reluctantly. 'Okay, Brigadier, okay. Still, I hope she's learned a lesson.'

'So do we all,' Abe said.

At that moment, the head waiter appeared with a large envelope. 'The photographer from the shop round the corner has delivered this, Wing Commander.'

'Thanks.' Harry opened the envelope and took out four prints. 'He's done me proud. I asked for two.'

It was a nice shot, the two of them with the entrance of the Savoy behind. 'Take one for Molly, another for yourself. You can have the spare, Abe.' Harry took out his wallet, measured the photo and called the head waiter again. 'I'm sure you have some scissors. Cut that for me so it fits in the wallet.'

'A pleasure, sir.'

Harry finished his champagne. 'And so to bed. We've got to be up and ready for Croydon pretty early, Abe.'

'I'm with you.'

The head waiter returned with the wallet and photo. 'Many thanks.' Harry fitted the photo inside. 'You can tell Molly I'm wearing her over my heart, Brigadier. See you soon,' and he got up and walked out.

In the little café in Westbourne Grove, Sarah and Fernando sat at the usual table.

'Nothing much to report really,' she said. 'I've got a duty roster here for Special Duties pilots flying Eisenhower from Croydon to Southwick House. He's using the landing strip there a lot these days. Backwards and forwards from London.'

'This Wing Commander Kelso who flies him tomorrow,'

Fernando said. 'Berlin wanted any mention of him, am I right?'

'That's so. You'll see he's permanently attached to the Courier Service, but there's more to him than that. Special Duties stuff. As we've mentioned before, it all ties in with Tempsford and Tangmere and, of course, Cold Harbour.'

'Good.' He folded the papers and put them in his pocket. 'So, now we eat.'

Croydon was thick with mist and heavy rain was falling as Abe waited in a rather bare Nissen hut and drank bad coffee. The Lysander, that squat and ugly high-wing monoplane, was on the apron being checked by two mechanics. Harry, in raincoat and boots, rather incongruously held an umbrella over his head as he talked to them. He turned and came in as a staff car drew up. The driver got out and opened the door for Eisenhower and a young major ran round from the other side. Harry went forward with the umbrella.

'Well, thank you, son,' Ike said and they walked to the Nissen hut.

'Morning Abe,' Ike said. 'Is that coffee?'

'The worst in the world but it's hot.'

'That'll do me.' He took the cup that a sergeant offered him. 'One of my aides, Major Hill.'

Hill had pilot's wings, a DFC and a Purple Heart. 'A pleasure, Senator.'

'Are we going anywhere?' Ike asked, peering out at all that mist and rain. 'What do you think, Major?'

'I'm not sure. Better ask the pilot.' Harry came out of the map room at that moment and Hill said, 'Are we going? It looks like a wipe-out to me.'

Harry peered out. 'No problem. Fog doesn't mean a thing on taking off, Major, you should know that.'

Hill was annoyed. 'Listen, we're talking the Supreme Commander here. I don't want some transport driver trying to make a name.'

'Well, we'll just have to do our best, Major, and adopt a more appropriate tone. I outrank you.'

Harry removed his raincoat and took a flying jacket from a peg. Ike turned, frowning, and Hill took in all the medals, the shoulder tabs and stammered, 'I'm sorry, Wing Commander. I didn't realize.'

'Well, now you do.'

Harry pulled on his flying jacket and Ike said, 'You're American?'

'Harry Kelso, sir.'

Ike held out his hand. 'So at last we meet, Wing Commander, and it's a privilege.' He turned to Hill. 'Senator Kelso's grandson.'

Again, there was that look of awe on Hill's face that people in the same trade so often showed on meeting Kelso. 'You were in the Battle of Britain. You sank the *Orsini*.'

'All in the day's work, Major.' Harry turned to Ike. 'Heavy rain, but otherwise clear in the Southwick House area. A little bumpy, but I'll have you there in forty minutes.'

'That's fine by me,' General Eisenhower said.

It wasn't a good trip. It was noisy, the heavy rain drumming against the canopy, and they dropped alarmingly in air pockets, but then there was Portsmouth over to the left, swallowed in rain, and Harry, as good as his word, landed at the airstrip right on time. A staff car was waiting.

As they walked to it, Ike said to Harry, 'Back at four. That suit you, Wing Commander?'

'Fine. They're already putting a crew on the engine and we'll refuel, though we don't need it. Comes of being important, General. I'll be here.'

'No, you won't. Come up to the house with us.' Ike got into the staff car.

Fort Southwick was of nineteenth-century construction, with a maze of tunnels, and it was being utilized as Combined Underground Operations headquarters for Overlord. All signal traffic concerned with the coming invasion passed through it, and at its heart was the Naval Plotting Room. It was one of the best-kept secrets of the war.

Southwick House had been chosen as Overlord HQ because of its proximity to the Fort, and the Navy had subsequently been turned out and SHAEF had taken over. There were tents and caravans all over the ground to accommodate the vast numbers of personnel. Montgomery had a caravan, although he wasn't there that day. Eisenhower had an enormous one alongside Pitymoor Lane. It was incredibly spacious, complete with a communications room, sitting and bedrooms and bathroom facilities.

He said to Abe, 'We've got to talk,' and turned to Hill. 'Take the wing commander for a walk. Show him everything. We'll see you for something to eat. Let's say one o'clock.'

Hill did show Harry everything, one place of particular interest being what Hill called the Map Room. Two workmen were starting to put up in sections what was obviously going to be a vast wall map.

'The French coast and general invasion area.' Hill shook his head. 'Poor devils.'

'Why do you say that?'

'Those workmen don't know it, but when they finish, they won't be allowed to leave here until after the great day.'

Harry laughed out loud. 'They'll be wondering which side they're on.'

Later, in the canteen, they sat in the corner, had a cigarette and Harry drank tea. 'See what a Brit I've become? Can't stand coffee.'

'You've been at it a long time.'

'Finland, November '39.'

'Christ, five years.'

'What about you?'

'B17 pilot. Eleven missions, then took cannon fire in the cockpit. My left arm is only half-strength. I'll never fly again. I'm lucky this job came along.'

'What will you do when it's over?'

'I was in publicity in Hollywood before it started. I'll go back and rejoin the work of fantasy. Maybe they'll do flying movies, like they did after the First War. What about you?'

'I never consider it. A long way to go yet.'

'I understand.'

A moment later, an orderly appeared and asked them to join General Eisenhower and Abe in the dining room.

Over roast beef and Yorkshire pudding, Eisenhower said, 'Wing Commander, I've got to be frank with you. The time has come for you to move to our air force, with the equivalent rank of lieutenant-colonel, naturally.'

Harry suppressed his impatience – this was Eisenhower, after all. 'I'm very happy as I am, General. I'd like to finish what I started.'

'I believe your grandfather has told you it's the President's wish, and it is also mine as your Supreme Commander. Now let's finish our meal in harmony. The beef is really excellent.'

Later that night back at the Savoy, Munro phoned him. 'How did it go with Ike?'

'To use a grand old English phrase, he put the boot in. He's given me a week to decide to transfer of my own choice. After that, I don't have a choice. Do you know if Teddy West is around?'

'I'll see, but I can offer you something to take your mind off it for the next two days.'

'Anything. What is it?'

'I've someone very important to be picked up in France by Lysander operating from Cold Harbour. I don't need you to fly the Lysander, but I do need you to shadow the mission in a Hurricane. The client is really very important. A big man in de Gaulle's organization. Will you do it?'

'My God, yes.'

'If West approves, such a mission means you will be starting an official tour with my Special Duties Squadron and I think you are aware that such tours extend to sixty operations.'

'I know that.'

'I may just have saved your bacon.' Munro rang off.

'Everything okay?' Abe asked.

'I'm back on duty tomorrow. Special job. Sorry, but that's the way it is.'

'Will it be rough?'

'I'll be flying over there, but what the hell, I've been doing that for years. You'll be going back the day after tomorrow anyway.'

'True.' Abe nodded. 'I can't tell you how much it's meant to me to see you.' He was very emotional. 'I think I'll go to bed.'

Harry switched off the lamps, lit a cigarette and looked out over the Thames in the half-light then turned and saw Tarquin peering at him out of the gloom.

'Well, here we go again, old buddy,' he said.

TEN

Harry reported to Croydon at ten the following morning and found a Hurricane waiting for him which had been delivered from Duxford by a Czech pilot named Hess with heavily accented English.

'Wing Commander Kelso. Is pleasure to meet you.' He had some Czech decoration plus a DFC.

'I know you lot,' Harry said. 'Are you sure you're not palming me off with second-hand goods?'

Hess grinned. 'How would we do that to you? I was in the Battle too, you know.'

'That's all right then.'

'I don't know what this is about, but good luck, my friend. I'll get off. A car's waiting to take me back to Duxford.'

He walked away through the rain and the flight sergeant who was checking the Hurricane with a crew turned to Harry. 'Looks good to me, Wing Commander. We'll refuel, do a final check and then you can go whenever you're ready.'

Harry changed into flying jacket and boots, then drank tea and ate a bacon sandwich while looking out of the window at the Lysander parked on the other side of the Hurricane. A pilot in flying dress was doing something inside. The sky was overcast and it looked as if a front was coming in. He went into the Ops Room and checked conditions for Cornwall. Clear at the moment, but the news wasn't all that good. As he went back into the other room, he saw a staff car drive up outside. Munro and Jack Carter emerged. The surprise was Molly Sobel.

They came in and the Lysander pilot got out and followed. Munro said cheerfully, 'Ah, there you are.'

Harry said to Molly, 'Are you coming with us?'

'So it would appear.'

'Just a precaution,' Munro told him. 'A hazardous mission could lead to casualties. Better to have Molly on hand.'

Harry turned to Jack Carter. 'Major now? Congratulations.'

'And you.'

They shook hands and the Lysander pilot came in.

'Flight Lieutenant Grant,' Munro said. 'He flew in from Tangmere last night. He's done umpteen drops in France for me. Really knows his business.'

Grant was twenty-two or three and had a ginger moustache. 'I say, this is a first, meeting you, sir.' He turned to Munro. 'I'll check the weather reports.'

'I already have,' Harry told him. 'We'll get there all right, but there's a front moving in. It's not good for tonight.'

Grant made a face and went off to the Ops Room. The orderly sergeant provided tea and Harry unzipped his holdall and found a carton of cigarettes. His Swedish jump bag was on the table beside the holdall and Molly said, 'Is the famous Tarquin in there?'

'Oh, you know about him?'

'Of course. May I look?'

'If you like.'

He lit a cigarette and she unzipped the bag and took Tarquin out. Munro and Jack stopped talking. 'My word,' Jack said.

'Oh, he's wonderful.' Molly held Tarquin close.

'He did every flight over Flanders with my dad when he flew

for the Royal Flying Corps, that's why he wears RFC wings. The RAF wings come from me. He's earned them.'

'Every flight?' Munro asked.

'Every flight.'

Molly replaced Tarquin in his bag and closed it, as Grant came back. 'Wing Commander Kelso was spot on, Brigadier. It's going to make it rather uncertain this evening.'

'Ah, well, let's get on with it then.' Munro turned to Harry. 'We'll see you at Cold Harbour.'

The flight was perfectly straightforward, but rain was already driving in from the sea as Harry took the Hurricane down for a perfect landing at Cold Harbour and taxied towards the hangars. A flight crew came out to meet him, still wearing Luftwaffe overalls, but this time with RAF sidecaps. He pushed back the canopy and tossed his bags to a corporal. As he got down, he noticed that the Fieseler Storch was still in one of the hangars.

He stretched and lit a cigarette and Julie Legrande drove up in the Jeep. 'Hello there, jump in quickly,' she said as the rain started. 'It doesn't look good, does it, for the mission?'

'Lousy met report.'

'The forward forecast was good.'

'It might change later tonight. How are you anyway?'

'Fine. I hear the Yanks are after you.'

'So they tell me.' He was totally indifferent.

'You're stubborn, aren't you?'

'No, just bloody-minded, as you say.' She turned into the top of the village High Street and Harry added, 'Where are we going?'

'You can settle in at the manor later. The Lysander won't be here for an hour. I just heard. I'm needed at the pub. Lunch for the lifeboat crew and I'm sure you could do with something to eat.'

'That suits me. How do you manage about the lifeboat crew? I thought all the villagers were turfed out of here?'

'They were, but things have changed. It's still top secret, but the crew live in the cottages and their families are dispersed locally. Farms, villages, that sort of thing. The men take turns seeing them at weekends.'

'Isn't that risky from a security point of view?'

'You obviously don't know lifeboatmen. They're probably the most disciplined men you could find anywhere. Usually they're unpaid volunteers. In this case, they get paid, because they can't follow their usual occupation.'

She pulled up outside the Hanged Man and Harry got out and looked up at the sign. 'That's nice. A Tarot symbol. Where did you get that?'

'I painted it myself.'

'Is Tarot a hobby of yours?'

'Tarot isn't a hobby, Wing Commander.'

'Maybe you could give me a reading,' Harry said and tossed his flying jacket into the Jeep.

'It's not possible. I know too much about you,' she said and she turned and led the way in.

A log fire burned brightly in the open fireplace. There were eight men in there, four playing cards, one by the fire reading a newspaper, the others drinking beer at the bar.

'Come on, Julie, we're starving,' someone called.

'Don't fuss. I was down earlier. The pies are in the oven and the potatoes and cabbage. Satisfied?'

The man reading the newspaper called, 'You leave her be or I'll belt you one.' The rest of the crew laughed.

Someone said, 'You tell him Zec, that's the way.'

They all looked curiously at Harry and Julie took him over to the fire. 'Zec Acland, the coxswain.'

Acland was thirty-five, an intensely attractive human being, full of energy and with a tanned seaman's face. He looked what he was, a fisherman bred to the sea since childhood.

'Wing Commander Harry Kelso,' Julie said.

'Ah, the Hurricane pilot.' Zec held out a hand as hard as granite. 'By God, boy, is there any medal you're missing there?'

'I bought them as a job lot in Camden Market in London,' Harry told him.

'Ah, well, you would, wouldn't you?' The rest of the crew laughed and Harry put the jump bag carefully on the table and sat down.

Zec was immediately curious. 'Something special in there?'

'A bear,' Harry told him and lit a cigarette.

Everyone stopped talking and then someone laughed. 'A bear?'

'I see, a mascot?' Zec said.

'No, more than that. He flew with my father in the First War and he's flown with me every mission in this.'

Again, someone laughed and Julie went behind the bar and pulled two pints. 'I was a Navy man myself,' Zec said. 'No room for mascots on torpedo boats.'

Julie put the two pints on the table. 'The wing commander sank the *Orsini*.'

The room went quiet and it seemed as if everyone was looking at Harry. Zec said, 'You did that?'

'That's right.'

'A lot of sailors went down in that one.'

'Seven hundred and forty-eight.' Harry tasted his pint. 'That's good. Did I do something wrong?'

'We're all sailors here and most of us have done time in the

Navy. Sailors are sailors, Wing Commander, irrespective of their country, it's always that way. The sea has always been the common enemy.'

'The war, the war, the bloody war,' Julie said.

'That's about it. Not your doing, Wing Commander, the war's doing. Was the bear with you?'

'Oh, yes.'

'Let's have a look then.'

Harry took Tarquin out and got up and put him on the bar. No one laughed. There was silence and then one of the sailors, built like a brick wall with tangled hair and beard, spoke for all of them.

'Why, you marvellous old bugger. I declare, I've never seen the like.'

They crowded round and Julie leaned across the bar. 'What a darling. Can we leave him here for a while?'

'Sure,' Harry said. 'As long as he's back in the bag for the flight tonight.'

'Nowhere you're going tonight, boy,' Zec told him. 'It's going to get worse before it gets better.'

'Munro isn't going to like that,' Harry said and at that moment the door opened and Munro, Molly, Jack Carter and Grant entered.

'Wonderful smell, Julie my love,' Munro said. 'Just in time for the pies, are we?'

Late that evening, with the rain drumming against the windows of the manor, they gathered round the map table in the library. There was a large chart before them of the Cornish coast stretching across the Channel to France.

Munro said, 'There's the target, two miles outside this village, Grouville. As you know, Grant, one pick-up, a Colonel Jobert, immensely important to General de Gaulle. The Gestapo have dogged his heels for weeks. We must get him out.'

'Yes, but the original plan as I understood it, envisaged bright moonlight so that Wing Commander Kelso could shadow me with no trouble around midnight and the met forecast now shows no hope of any improvement.'

Zec Acland turned from the fire, lighting a pipe. 'Wrong as usual. I'd say winds four to five and driving rain will kill the fog around three-thirty to four o'clock. Forty-five minutes' flight for you over there, in and out. You'll have a clear moon fading into dawn. As long as your passenger can wait, you'll be able to get him.'

'The voice of experience,' Munro said. 'We have radio contact. I can move the pick-up time forward, no problem.' He turned to Harry. 'That suit you?'

'Absolutely,' Harry said. 'But I would point out that it will be dawn which means we'll be highly visible.'

'That's what you're there for,' Munro told him. 'Now that's settled, let's have dinner.'

Zec was absolutely right, for there was rain with the wind and the fog cleared, then the rain stopped and a half moon was plainly visible in a clear sky. At the airfield, Grant took off first, the Lysander lifting up into the sky and turning out to sea.

Originally these planes had housed two 20mm Hispano cannons on each side of the undercarriage and the fairings on the wheels had housed a .303 Browning machine-gun, but that had been in the days when it was a reconnaissance aircraft. Modified for Special Duties, it was now unarmed and usually flew so low that it followed its course by landmarks on the ground, often flying below radar height.

Harry gave Grant fifteen minutes then took off, levelled at 2000 feet and went after the Lysander at 300 miles an hour, closing upon it in no time at all. He found the Lysander way below, went down himself and swept by, rose again to 2000 and then took up station.

They passed the French coast, moved inland and there was the target, bicycle torches laid out in an L-shape in the usual Resistance manner. Harry circled and Grant went down, the dawn already coming up.

At the airfield at Fermanville twenty miles away, Max and two others, duty pilots on the night shift, were playing cards when the alarm sounded.

The controller said calmly, 'We have traffic, we have traffic. Two targets. Scramble at once and I'll give you the co-ordinates.'

Max and his friends, already dressed for flying, were out of the door and running across the apron to where their three ME 109s were waiting. Max took his parachute from the sergeant, pulled it on and then his flying helmet. A moment later as flight leader he took off first and the others followed fast.

As the day dawned, grey clouds swept in and rain hammered against the canopy. At 3000 feet Harry flew through broken cloud, turning in wide curves, aware of Grant far, far below and then a couple of miles away, an ME 109 emerged from low cloud and pounced on the Lysander.

Harry went down. The Hurricane could do four hundred miles an hour in a dive. He was aware of movement to starboard, knew that meant another 109, but couldn't afford to play games. The Lysander was of primary importance. He came up behind the first ME, his four Hispano cannons thundered and he blew most of the tail off the other plane. At the same time, a second ME came in from starboard and fired cannons that raked the Hurricane from stem to stern. Part of the cockpit and the windscreen disintegrated and a splinter ripped Harry's left cheek. He banked, rolled as the second ME flashed past, fired his cannon instinctively and the Luftwaffe plane simply blew up.

The Cornish coast was fifteen miles away, the Lysander at 800 feet making for home. Grant, looking up, had seen it all. He also saw two other things. That the Hurricane was trailing smoke and that a third ME had appeared from the clouds.

'A miracle,' Colonel Jobert cried. 'I've never seen such a thing.'

'He'll need more than a miracle now,' Grant told him and called Cold Harbour over the radio. 'Estimated time of arrival fifteen minutes, but Hurricane badly damaged. Suggest you launch lifeboat.'

Max, on the outer edge of the sweep, had seen the action from afar, and knew great flying when he saw it. He watched one, then two, go down, then he swept round, rolled and came in for the kill, aware of the Hurricane trailing heavy black smoke. He came up behind to finish it off and it was the Lancaster all over again.

As the Hurricane slowed, Max throttled back and took up station to port. He had a secondary channel designed to eavesdrop on the RAF frequency and used it now.

'Hey, Tommy, you fought a great fight, but it's time to go or you'll end up like burnt steak at a barbecue.'

Harry, hanging in there, didn't need to recognize the voice, although he did. Every instinct in his entire being told him who it was.

'Hello, Max, it's been a long time.'

'Dear God, Harry, it's you,' Max said and the Hurricane started down.

'Do you think you can make the coast?' said Max.

'It's not likely, but I'll give it a try.' Harry's face was hurting. 'Hard to hold this lovely bitch. How's Mutti?'

'For God's sake, Harry.'

'Tell her to take care. The way I hear it, Himmler's just waiting for his chance.'

'Watch it, Harry, watch it! Pieces of your fuselage are breaking away.'

Zec Acland's voice came over the radio. 'This is lifeboat *Lively Jane* out of Cold Harbour. We're on our way, Kelso. Give me your position.'

At that moment the radio started to smoke and went dead.

The sea was heaving, the wind, force four and freshening, as the *Lively Jane* pressed on at top speed, bouncing over the waves. She was a forty-one-foot Watson type boat, weighed fifteen tons and was powered by two thirty-five horsepower petrol engines. She carried a crew of eight and in rough weather could take fifty people on board. She was also of the self-righting type, which meant that when she capsized, she was supposed to come up again. The men were all at their stations and Zec was at the wheel in the rear cockpit. Molly stood beside him in oilskins and a yellow life-jacket, a medical kit beside her on the deck.

'Is there a chance, Zec?' she cried.

The *Lively Jane* veered sharply to port, taking a mountain of green water and she fell to her knees. He hauled her up with one hand. 'I've enough to do here without having to look out for you. Get below with that box of yours, girl, and pray.'

She did as she was told and Zec varied the speed and fought on.

'Flames, Harry, I can see flames.' Max had throttled right back and kept station. 'You've got to go, old boy, or you'll burn.'

That was always the fighter pilot's worst nightmare. Harry was at 1500 now. 'I guess you're right. It's been nice talking to you, Max. Let's try to make it not so long next time.'

Folkestone all over again. He snapped the link on the jump bag, pulled back his canopy and unfastened his seat-belt. The smell of burning was terrible, the flames licking around his flying boots. He flipped the Hurricane over and fell out.

Zec Acland's voice came over the channel again. 'Are you there? Can you give me your position, Wing Commander?'

Max cut in. 'Listen to me. This is your friendly local Luftwaffe pilot here. He's just jumped. Now take down his position.' He gave it and went into a steep dive, following the parachute as it descended to port.

It was raining again now, blowing in from the Atlantic and the carpet of waves and foam below was terrible to see. My God, he thought, he's had it. They'll never see him. And then it came to him, the one chance, and he reached for the dye bag on his left knee and pulled it free. He yanked back his canopy and went down.

Harry plunged into the waves, went under, inflated his Mae West, surfaced and fought to get rid of his parachute. He went into a trough, the waves so high that he couldn't see beyond, then rose in a crest to see a bleak dawn landscape under dark storm clouds.

The ME 109 was over to the left several hundred yards away and only a few hundred feet up. He wondered what his brother was playing at and then Max throttled back to virtually stalling speed and came in incredibly at a hundred feet. Obviously judging his moment, Max leaned out of the cockpit and dropped the dye bag. It fell only fifty feet to one side of Harry and the yellow stain started to spread.

Harry struggled towards it and Max increased speed, pulled back the column and climbed to a thousand and there, only a mile away to the north, was the *Lively Jane*.

Some of the crew shouted in dismay as the black plane with the Luftwaffe crosses and the swastika tailplane flew over.

Max called over the radio. '*Lively Jane*, listen to me. He's a mile due south of you. I dropped my dye bag, so look for the yellow stain. I'll circle him till you get there, and get it right or I'll blow you out of the water.'

'All right, you bastard. I don't know what your game is, but we'll be there,' Zec replied and Max turned away. Zec was so involved in the hunt that it took a moment for the penny to drop: was that Luftwaffe pilot speaking *English*?

God, it was cold, colder than Folkestone in water all the way from America. Harry went down in the troughs, bounced up on the waves like a cork, the jump bag on its strap following him.

'Not good, old buddy, not good at all,' he said, pulling the jump bag close, and then he was aware of the roaring of the engine and looked up.

Max came in low and waggled his wings, then circled and came in again.

'Silly damn fool,' Harry whispered. 'Go on, get the hell out of it, Max, while you still have enough juice.'

The yellow stain was enormous now, dispersed by the motion of the waves and he floated almost in the centre and then, as he was tossed high again, he saw the *Lively Jane* a hundred yards to his left. He went down, was thrown high and the lifeboat was suddenly there, turning broadside.

God, but he was tired. He tried to strike out and then it was on top of him. Two of the crew tied to lifelines jumped into the water and got him between them, a ladder was thrown over the side and hands reached down and hauled him over the rail. A moment later he was on his knees in the rear cockpit, vomiting salt water.

Molly was there, crouched beside him. 'Your face, it's bad. Let's get you below.'

A voice crackled over the speaker of the radio. 'Hey, you got him?'

'Yes, thanks to you,' Zec said, 'whoever you are.'

Harry put up a shaking hand. 'Give me the mike.' He grabbed it. 'Max, it's me.'

'I love you, Harry.'

'And I love you. Remember what I said. Tell Mutti to take care.'

The ME 109 turned away, climbed high into the sombre sky and fled like a departing spirit.

One of the crew pulled Harry up and Molly had an arm around his shoulders. 'Who in the hell was that?' Zec demanded. 'What was he playing at? He sounded American.' He frowned. 'Hell, he sounded like you.'

'Well, he would,' Harry said. 'That was my brother Max, my twin brother.'

In the medical room at the manor at breakfast time, Harry, in a robe, sat back, the morphine injection Molly had given him taking satisfactory effect as she examined his left cheek.

'How bad is it?'

'Could be worse.'

'Hospital?'

'Show a little faith. I'm a truly great surgeon. Anyway, this is just Casualty Department stuff. Now keep still while I stitch you up. Ten should do it. You're going to end up with a really interesting scar, Harry, the girls will love it.'

'Get lost,' he told her.

'I've no intention of getting lost. Now shut up and keep still.'

After a while the door opened and Munro looked in. 'Can I join you?'

'Look and learn,' Harry said. 'Obviously Grant and the colonel made it back.'

'They certainly did and proceeded onwards to London after refuelling. Jack went with them. The colonel was ecstatic. Said you were a hero extraordinaire and intends to ask de Gaulle to make you a Chevalier of the Legion of Honour.'

'Oh, no,' Harry groaned.

'Brace yourself. I've just spoken to Teddy West and gave him the full details of the entire operation. He told me he's recommending you for the immediate award of a bar to your DSO.'

'That makes it worse.'

'He's proud of you, Harry, you were his protégé in a way. Also he's your friend.' He went to the door and opened it. 'And so am I. We're on your side. I'll see you later.'

'You see?' Molly said as she placed the final stitch. 'You always act as if you're alone. It's not true. Today you had Max and Zec, Munro and Air Vice Marshal West.'

'And you.'

'Oh, that goes without saying. Poor old me, hanging around with the wrong kind of stars in her eyes.'

Before he could reply, the door opened and Julie came in. 'How's the boy wonder?'

'A touch of morphine and ten stitches and he's as good as new. He's going to come down for a meal.'

'One problem.' Harry stood up. 'I didn't bring a spare uniform. I imagine what I was wearing is ruined.'

'Let's see what we've got in the supply room,' Julie said. 'We've most things in there.'

Harry and Molly followed her out, they went along the corridor and she opened a door at the far end and entered. It was an Aladdin's cave, handguns and automatic weapons laid out in rows on a huge table. Garments of every description, British and German uniforms and civilian clothes both male and female.

'These are all French,' Julie told him. 'We fit the agents out when they overnight here before flying to France. Let's see what we have for a flyer. Oberstleutnant, Luftwaffe. Not quite the thing. Here we are, RAF and looks your size. Flight lieutenant, I'm afraid.'

'Just give him a nice comfortable sweater and some slacks,' Molly said. 'A decent late breakfast and two glasses of red wine, then I'll tuck him up in bed.'

Julie shrugged. 'Help yourself, Harry. There's everything you could want here. Underwear, shirts, shoes and socks.'

'I'll see you in the library.' Molly followed the other woman out.

They went down to the kitchen, where Julie busied herself with the meal. Molly said, 'Can I help?'

'Not really.' Julie checked the chicken in the oven. 'He's not for you, *chérie*,' she said, without turning.

'He's not for anyone,' Molly said.

'Then why bother? He's always been on borrowed time.'

'There's a war on, Julie, you take what you can.'

'It's your choice, *chérie*.'

'Not really. I don't have a choice, you see.'

At the impromptu meal Julie provided, Munro was all avuncular bonhomie. 'And how's your father?' he asked Molly. He turned to Harry. 'Major General Sobel is on Ike's staff, responsible for Navy and Air Force co-ordination.'

'Well that's nice,' Harry said. 'How long has he been here?'

'A month,' Molly said.

'Wasn't he at the War Department?'

'That's right.'

'Well, he surely must know a lot about Navy and Air Force co-operation.'

She was good and angry. 'My father is fifty years old, rather long in the tooth for combat flying. As it happens, he did what your father did, only in his case he was flying fighter planes for the French in 1916. The Lafayette Escadrille. I think he was twenty-one at one time.'

'So I got it wrong.'

'You get a lot of things wrong, Harry.' She got up and walked out.

'You certainly blew that one,' Julie said as she cleared the plates.

'Oh, to hell with it. I feel lousy.' Harry announced, 'I'm going to bed,' and he walked out too.

Later, in bed, the curtains drawn against the light, he lay propped up against a pillow and smoked a cigarette. The door clicked open and a moment later Molly slipped into bed beside him.

'Grant will be back with the Lysander late afternoon.'

'Good.' He slipped an arm around her.

'What's going to happen to us, Harry?'

'God knows,' he said and held her close in the soundless dark.

ELEVEN

In London two days later, and staying with Munro again, Harry caught a taxi to Guy's Hospital to keep an appointment which Molly had arranged at the casualty department. He reported to reception and sat on one of the benches. It was busy, most places taken, but within a few minutes a nurse came for him.

'This way, Wing Commander.'

He followed her along a corridor and into a surgical theatre. Molly, in a white coat, was seated at a bench.

'There you are. Let's take a look. Tell Professor Joseph I'm ready for him,' she said to the nurse.

Harry said, 'Is it going to hurt?'

'Always, so the best way is the quick way.' She ripped the surgical tape away in one deft movement. 'That wasn't so bad, was it?'

'Like hell it wasn't.'

The door opened and a grey-bearded and pleasant-looking man in a white surgical coat entered. 'Right, Molly, what have we here?'

'Wing Commander Kelso got slightly damaged in aerial combat,' she said. 'Came down in the sea, so the wound received a very satisfactory cleansing.'

'Let's take a look.' He examined Harry's face and nodded. 'Very nice, Molly, you should take up embroidery. You are, of course, going to have a rather permanent scar, Wing Commander.'

'I can stand it if Molly can.'

'Like that, is it? Excellent.' Joseph put an arm around her shoulders. 'But don't take her away just yet, Wing Commander. There is a war on, remember.'

He went out and Molly said, 'I'm not going to tape you up again. Especially after all that salt water. It's healing already so we'll leave it open to the air.' She picked up a can. 'A little antiseptic spray and you'll be fine.'

When she was finished he said, 'What now? Do you have time for lunch?'

'I'm free now, actually, but I had a phone call from my uncle. He wants you back at Haston Place. Air Vice Marshal West wants words with you.'

'Okay. Maybe we can have lunch later.'

'We'll see. I'll be back in a moment,' and she went out.

At Haston Place, they went upstairs to the flat and when Molly rang the bell, it was Jack Carter who opened the door. He kissed her on the cheek and turned to Harry and shook hands.

'It's wonderful to see you in one piece.'

'I think it's wonderful too,' Harry said.

Laughter came from the sitting room and Carter led the way in. There was Munro and West and an American major-general with pilot's wings. The big surprise was General Eisenhower sitting on the window seat.

'What is this, a conspiracy?' Harry asked Molly.

'Not at all,' Munro said. 'Molly had no idea the Supreme Commander would be here.'

'I'm sorry, Harry,' she murmured and moved to the major-general and kissed him. 'Hello, Dad.'

Eisenhower got up and held out his hand. 'Wing Commander, you're an extraordinary man. I don't think you've met Molly's father, Tom Sobel.'

Sobel was of medium height with a black moustache and hair, no sign of grey there at all. He had the sort of face that most military men of high rank had, the kind that didn't take kindly to interference. His handshake was firm.

'It's an honour to meet you, son.'

'Fine, so now we've got the pleasantries over, to business,' Eisenhower said. 'I gave you a week.'

'I told you how I feel, General.'

'Listen to me,' Sobel told him. 'I was in the Lafayette Squadron in the first war and when our people came in I didn't want to transfer, but I did because I was needed. The same with you. You've served magnificently with the RAF, but it's time to put on your country's uniform.'

There was a silence. Eisenhower said, 'I can make it a direct order.'

It was West who said smoothly, 'The agreement between our two air forces is that American personnel would transfer, American uniform and equivalent rank, but anyone into a tour with the RAF would finish that tour. I believe that Wing Commander Kelso has a wee bit of tour left to go.'

Eisenhower gave him a sharp look. 'Okay, tell me the worst.'

'Wing Commander Kelso has just started a tour with our most important Special Duties Squadron.'

'How many missions?' Sobel demanded.

'One, actually, and as Special Duties Squadrons do sixty missions in a tour he has fifty-nine to go.' He turned to Ike. 'Of course, some of these missions are flying you, sir, for the Courier Service.'

Eisenhower stared at West for a long moment, then he burst

out laughing and even Sobel smiled. 'You sly fox,' Ike said. 'And you, Brigadier. Okay, you win, but I want him in American uniform today.' He turned to Harry. 'That's an order, Colonel.'

Munro smiled. 'Actually, it's all taken care of, General. Air Vice Marshal West and I spoke to Wing Commander Kelso's tailor in Savile Row yesterday. They agreed to do a rush job.'

Eisenhower grinned. 'You two really go to town when you start, don't you?'

'Well, we want him to look right. As the General knows, he's due at the Connaught Hotel at three to receive the Legion of Honour from General de Gaulle.'

'My God,' Harry groaned.

'Tomorrow morning at eleven, Buckingham Palace for his second award of the DSO.'

Eisenhower grinned again and said to Harry, 'That just about takes care of you, I'd say.'

Munro said to Molly, 'If you've got time before going back to the hospital, go to Savile Row with him and make sure they've done a good job. We want him to look good for de Gaulle, he's very particular.'

'You can all go to hell,' Harry said and walked out, Molly hurrying after him.

Ike called, 'Keep an eye on him, Doctor.'

At the tailors' in Savile Row, old Crossley and his assistant, George, laid everything out.

'I'm afraid most of what we've put together for you is from stock, Wing Commander.' Crossley laughed. 'I do apologize. Lieutenant-Colonel.'

'That's quite all right,' Harry said.

'Anyway, two uniforms with tunic, but knowing how you've always liked the battledress during RAF service, I've provided two similar outfits as favoured by many American pilots. Oh, and we've had your medal ribbons made up for you, patch style with simple safety-pin fasteners.'

Harry took a look. 'You're a little premature. I see you've added the Legion of Honour and the bar to the DSO.'

'Same difference, sir, and it saves time.'

'Go on,' Molly said. 'Let's see how you look,' so he went off with George.

When he returned, he was wearing cream slacks and the brown battledress type of tunic which, as Crossley had said, was favoured by many officers in the US Air Force. The silver wings of a pilot were over his left breast above the medals. RAF wings were on his right breast.

Crossley said, 'Very nice. Peaked cap or side cap, Colonel?'

'I suppose I'd better take both.'

Harry adjusted the side cap over his straw hair and looked in the mirror morosely. 'It isn't me.'

'Nonsense, you look lovely,' Molly said. 'Terribly dashing.'

'Just one thing, Colonel, there should be some American campaign ribbons there which you're entitled to now you're with your own people. I'm checking on that. We'll sort it out.'

Molly glanced at her watch. 'We must get a move on. General de Gaulle awaits. Send everything to Haston Place, Mr Crossley.'

'I will, Doctor. George, the door.'

They walked out into pale sunlight and she took his arm. 'As the English would say, you look absolutely smashing, so buck up,' and she flagged down a taxi.

General de Gaulle had left Suite 103 at the Connaught Hotel in 1943, but facilities were always available for high-ranking members of his staff.

'I'll wait,' Molly said as they approached reception.

'Like hell you will. The Supreme Commander told you to keep an eye on me, so you can do just that.' Harry nodded to the desk clerk. 'Colonel Kelso and Doctor Sobel for General de Gaulle. We're expected.'

'Yes, I know, Colonel.' The clerk picked up the phone.

Harry and Molly waited. 'I love this place,' she said. 'It used to be known as the Coburg – something to do with Queen Victoria's Prince Albert, then towards the end of the Great War, King George did away with all the royal family's German names, so the hotel changed Coburg to Connaught.'

'You learn something new every day.'

A young French captain appeared. 'Colonel Kelso?' He looked uncertainly at Molly. 'The young lady is with you?'

'Yes, on General Eisenhower's orders. This is Doctor Sobel.'

'Ah, I see.' The captain gave her his most charming smile. 'If you would follow me.' As they went upstairs, he added, 'Colonel Jobert is waiting in the General's old suite. He wishes to thank you personally.'

They reached the door marked 103, he opened it and led the way in. General de Gaulle was seated next to a coffee table by the window and there was a box in Moroccan leather on the table. Colonel Jobert, now in uniform, stood close by and he rushed forward and embraced Harry.

'No longer wing commander, but lieutenant-colonel, I see. You are a remarkable man. I will remember your heroism all my life, for it was my life you saved.'

'May I introduce Doctor Sobel? She's here at the Supreme Commander's request.'

'As the Colonel was so recently wounded, we thought it prudent,' Molly added.

'The doctor's father is Major-General Sobel on Eisenhower's staff,' Harry told Jobert.

'Excellent.' The Frenchman turned to de Gaulle, who was

lighting a cigarette and seemed indifferent to the whole business. 'With your permission, General?'

General de Gaulle nodded and Jobert opened the box, took out the insignia of Chevalier of the Legion of Honour and pinned it on Harry's tunic. He kissed both cheeks, stepped back and saluted.

General de Gaulle spoke for the first time. 'The Republic thanks you, Colonel, but now you will excuse us. There is much to do.'

Harry gave him a perfunctory salute, turned to Molly and nodded. The captain opened the door, they exited, made it to the top of the stairs and collapsed into laughter.

'The Republic thanks you,' she said in a deep voice. 'He doesn't like anybody, that man, he's not even grateful. He gives Winston and Eisenhower terrible problems.'

Harry was trying to unpin the medal. 'Damn thing is stuck.'

'Here, let me. It's very nice. Give me the box.'

As they went downstairs, she replaced the medal, snapped the lid of the box shut and offered it to him.

'No, you keep it,' he said. 'Souvenir.'

'Don't be silly.'

'I insist. After all, I'm getting another. Eleven o'clock at the Palace in the morning. Will you come? Guests are allowed.'

'Harry, I'd love to.' She was obviously very moved and took his arm as they stood on the pavement. 'But I'm going to have to leave you.' A cab pulled up at that moment to drop somebody off and she waved to the driver. 'I'm due on the evening shift at Guy's and it often drags on very late.'

'Don't worry, we've got the Palace. Eleven o'clock. Don't forget.'

'How could I?' She kissed his cheek, got in the cab and was driven away.

★

It was too much to expect, of course. She did three operations, worked until midnight and fell into one of the beds kept for medical staff, utterly exhausted. At eight she got up, showered, had breakfast in the canteen, was about to leave when her name was called over the Tannoy.

'Doctor Sobel. Emergency in casualty.'

A young soldier knocked down by a bus when drunk. Left lung punctured by a broken rib.

'Theatre Three. Get him ready and I'll be right along.'

The soldier was trundled away and she grabbed the nearest phone and rang the flat. It was her uncle who answered. 'Munro.'

'It's me and I'm on the run. Emergencies all over the place. Tell Harry I'm sorry.'

'I will, don't worry.'

Harry came into the sitting room at that moment, perfectly dressed for the occasion. 'My, you do look pretty,' Munro said. 'But bad news from the medical front, she can't make it.'

'Really?' Harry shrugged. 'Serves me right for falling for a doctor. I might as well get going. I feel like a walk anyway.'

He found the military Burberry trenchcoat Crossley had supplied with the uniforms, put it on and went out. It wasn't raining, although the sky was the kind that seemed to threaten rain any moment. He smoked a cigarette and wandered about rather aimlessly, aware of being alone and that made him think of Max and the dogfight over the sea off Cornwall, his voice. What was it Zec Acland had said? *He sounded like you.* But then he would. Max must have told his mother by now. He was certain to have done that, which made Harry think of Elsa. She'd have loved to turn up at the palace this morning, nothing was more certain.

He flagged down a cab. 'Buckingham Palace,' he told the driver.

He lit a cigarette and the driver said, 'Are you getting a medal or something, guv?'

'No, nothing like that.'

'Well, you wouldn't, would you? I mean you being a Yank.'

'You're absolutely right,' Harry told him and sat back.

It was raining hard when he came back out through the Palace gates again. The policeman on duty saluted. Harry saluted back and hesitated at the people milling around and then, just as before, the staff car drew up and Munro leaned out of the window.

'Come on, let's be having you.'

Harry scrambled in and closed the door. 'Why do I have a feeling of déjà vu?'

'Tried to get here earlier. Wanted to go in with you, but I got held up at the War House. Come on, let's see it.'

Harry took out the box and opened it. 'Same as before.'

'It's never the same, Harry. What did the King say?'

'He said, "This is getting to be a habit", and then Queen Elizabeth said, "I see you've changed sides".'

'Well that was nice.' Munro tapped his sergeant driver on the shoulder. 'Find a decent pub, Jack, and the wing commander, damn, the colonel and I will celebrate. Sorry you can't join us, but you're driving.'

Harry took a fiver out of his wallet, reached over and slipped it in the sergeant's breast pocket. 'Make up for it tonight, Jack.'

'God help me, Colonel, with that I'll be drunk for a week.'

'Does Eisenhower know how Max saved me? I mean, how many people know?' Harry demanded.

'Only my people, dear boy. I prefer to keep it that way. It isn't even mentioned in my official report. You parachuted down and the *Lively Jane* saved your bacon. End of story.'

Jack pulled up outside a pub called the Grenadier near St James's Palace. It was pleasant enough and not very busy, just before lunch. Munro, in uniform himself, went to the bar. The landlord, sleeves rolled up, exhibited many tattoos.

'What can I get you, Brigadier?'

Munro, quite shameless, said, 'The colonel here having just transferred to his own people from the RAF, has had his second DSO pinned on his manly chest by His Majesty only forty minutes ago. We'd like to celebrate. I know champagne would be out of the question, but . . .'

'Not for you, it isn't. I happen to have one in my fridge right now, promised to a major of the Grenadiers at Kensington Palace. He'll have to wait. Navy man myself, sir, chief petty officer gunner in the first lot. You gentlemen sit down then.'

They took a booth near the window and Munro offered Harry a cigarette. 'Well, here we are. You finally ended up in that Yankee uniform after all.'

'So it would appear.'

The landlord arrived with a bucket of ice, the bottle and two glasses. 'Moët, gentlemen, I hope it will do.'

'No, it won't,' Harry said. 'Not unless you get a third glass and join us.'

'I don't know about that, Colonel.'

'We'd appreciate it if you would,' Munro told him. 'So be a good chap and let me do the uncorking while you find that glass.'

He thumbed off the cork expertly and had started pouring when the landlord returned. Munro charged his glass and raised his own. 'To Colonel Harry Kelso, to you, Chief Petty Officer, and may I include myself? Brave men who put duty before all.'

The landlord was flushed with pleasure. 'Why, thank you, Brigadier. I'll leave you to it.' He hesitated. 'If you fancy a bite, my wife does a very nice meat and potato pie. They all come in for that.'

'That sounds excellent,' Munro said. He turned. 'All right with you, Harry?'

'Sure.'

The landlord disappeared behind the bar into the kitchen, four soldiers came in, saw Munro and Harry and beat a hasty retreat.

Munro refilled the champagne glasses. 'After you left yesterday, Ike said he felt you'd really done your bit, that combat flying should be out. Courier work over the southern counties is fine, chauffeuring him in a Lysander is fine, but escapades like the other day are out.'

'Are you saying that's it? No more Special Duties?'

'Let's keep him happy. Good God, man, don't you ever sit still? Take it easy for a while.'

The landlord came in with the pies and cutlery on a tray. 'There you are, gentlemen.'

Munro cut into the crust and tried a mouthful. 'Ecstasy. Takes me back to Eton as a boy.'

Harry followed suit and nodded. 'You know, in the four and a half years I've been here, some of my best meals have been pub grub. So, I'm stuck on the courier run?'

'I didn't say that, Harry. You're very, very good. You can fly anything, even most Luftwaffe hardware. You're very special.'

'So you wouldn't rule me out?'

Munro refilled their glasses, emptying the bottle. 'My dear boy, there's a war on.'

The destruction of the two ME 109s by Harry in the Hurricane had been so instantaneous that the controller back at Fermanville had no idea what had happened and the secondary channel wasn't monitored, which meant that Max's two-way conversation with Harry and, later, Zec Acland, had gone unrecorded. On his return, his story had been simple. They had undertaken a sweep search, his two comrades had made first contact. He'd seen them go down and also the Hurricane. He made no mention of the Lysander. The story was accepted totally. After all, who would think to query the Black Baron?

Back in Berlin, he discovered that Elsa was at the country house and he drove out there. As usual, she was overjoyed to see him and fussed a great deal.

'No, Mutti, just shut up. I've something to tell you.'

When he was finished, she sat there looking astounded. 'Oh, my God, Harry, what a miracle.'

'Yes, he came out of it in one piece and that's all that matters, but what he said about Himmler . . . What do you think?'

'How would he know?'

'I can only guess. He was covering a plane called a Lysander that drops and picks up Allied agents in France. That means a Special Duties Squadron and that means Intelligence. It's all I can think of.'

For the first time, she actually showed panic. 'What do I do?'

'You take care, Mutti, very great care. See Goering, be charming to the others and if the Führer speaks to you at any function, show how much you're dazzled by his greatness. That's all I can say.'

There were tears in her eyes. 'I'm sorry, Max, so sorry.'

'That's all right, Mutti, we all get it wrong, it's as simple as that. We helped create the beast and now it threatens to devour us.'

It was dark three days later when Bubi Hartmann flew down to Wewelsburg in a Storch, piloting himself. He put down at the Luftwaffe feeder station ten miles away, where a Mercedes and driver were waiting for him.

He didn't even know why Himmler wanted to see him. The

Reichsführer had been in retreat at Wewelsburg for almost a week. He'd had the castle developed into a centre for all true SS values, a round table with chairs for his twelve most trusted aides, all based on the legend of King Arthur and the Knights of the Round Table, with which Himmler was obsessed. It was also a centre for racial research.

As the Mercedes approached, the towers and battlements became clear, there was no blackout, lights shone at the windows and flaring torches at the drawbridge. It looked like a set for a historical movie. Bubi loathed it.

In the entrance hall, the sergeant of the guard took his coat and relieved him of his Walther pistol. 'The Reichsführer is in his sitting room in the south wing, Colonel. Do you need an escort?'

Bubi shook his head and went up the stairs. The place was festooned with Nazi flags, there were even swastikas on the ceilings. He walked through the shadows and came to the sitting room, hesitated, knocked and went in.

Before him there was a log fire, more flags and Himmler, in a tweed suit, behind the desk. He looked up. 'So you finally got here?'

'Fog and rain in Berlin, Reichsführer. How may I be of service?'

'I've gone through the mail bag you sent me yesterday. Of particular interest was your most recent report from London from the Dixon woman. I refer to Brigadier Munro and his Cold Harbour base.'

'Yes, Reichsführer.'

'The information about the Baron von Halder's brother shooting down two of our planes while on some covert mission for Munro, then parachuting into the sea where a convenient lifeboat saved him, is melodrama of the finest quality.'

'I agree,' Bubi said, because he couldn't think of anything else to say.

'And now Kelso becomes a lieutenant-colonel in the US Air Force and is a Special Duties pilot often employed to ferry Eisenhower. Quite bizarre, isn't it?'

'I suppose so,' Bubi said lamely.

'Even more bizarre, I've discovered something you missed, Colonel. The third plane, the one that survived? Would you be interested to know who the pilot was?'

Bubi felt cold, very cold indeed and swallowed hard, appalled if what he feared should prove to be true. 'Reichsführer?'

'It was Baron von Halder, a remarkable coincidence, but then I understand life to be full of them.'

Bubi managed to control his breathing. 'What would the Reichsführer like me to do?'

'Why nothing, Colonel, nothing at all, except for extra surveillance on the good Baroness. Her day will come. However, there is another matter I wish to discuss. You'll recall the Führer raised the question of a possible assassination of Eisenhower. I asked you if you had anyone in England capable of such work.'

'And I suggested the IRA.'

'Useless,' Himmler said. 'Totally useless. Would there be no chance of us putting in one of our own people? A trained specialist?'

'I don't think so, Reichsführer, not at this stage of the war. I have a few people in England, such as Rodrigues and Sarah Dixon, and they do good work, but they don't constitute a network. To drop such an agent in by parachute would be very hazardous.'

'What if he went in another way? The Portuguese as neutrals operate shipping to England, also passenger planes. Perhaps we could infiltrate a suitable agent that way. I have remarkable contacts in Lisbon. Nunes da Silva, a minister in their Foreign Office, has been in my pocket for years. He helped with the abortive attempt to kidnap the Duke of Windsor in Estoril in 1940. He's had a great deal of money from us. Hopelessly compromised. Besides, his fondness for boys is his undoing. The photos are particularly disgusting.'

Bubi said, 'It just wouldn't work, Reichsführer.'

'Really? Well, try and think of something, Colonel. I don't want to disappoint the Führer. You can return to Berlin now. I'll be back at the weekend.'

Bubi couldn't get out of the room fast enough.

For Harry, things took a kind of steady turn. He did general courier work and frequently flew Eisenhower on the Croydon-to-Southwick run. Just as frequently, he flew to Cold Harbour with Munro and Jack and Molly sometimes came. Things were hotting up as everything converged towards D-Day in Europe, Munro putting in more and more agents and sometimes OSS and SAS operatives.

The weather was good and when Molly was at Cold Harbour, she and Harry would walk on the beach, eat at the Hanged Man and fool with Zec Acland and the crew of the lifeboat.

'It's as if the war has ceased to exist,' Molly said to Harry, as they sat on the rocks by the beach one day.

'Oh, it's still there,' Harry said. 'Don't kid yourself.' He gazed out to sea and thunder rumbled on the horizon. 'There you are, guns.'

'You devil,' she said, pushed him off his rock and ran away. Harry picked himself up and went after her.

It couldn't last of course and, landing at Croydon after bringing a couple of returning agents back to London, he found a message asking him to report to SOE Headquarters in Baker Street and a staff car waiting to transport him and the two agents.

When they got there, a young captain appeared, who spirited the agents away and Harry went upstairs and found Jack Carter coming to meet him.

'He's in the map room, Harry.'

'A big flap on or something?'

'Or something. I'll let him tell you.'

Munro had on the table a large-scale map of the Channel from Cornwall across to the French coast. He was making rough measurements with a ruler.

'What's it all about?' Harry asked.

'Morlaix, twenty miles in from the French coast on a direct line from Cold Harbour. Grant plotted a course. He said forty-five minutes in the Lysander, maybe an hour. Would you agree?'

Harry had a quick look. 'Depending on weather, I wouldn't argue with that.'

'I've a major agent to drop in over there at midnight. An in-and-out job, no one to bring back. It's vitally important. It's a Frenchman named Jacaud, the leader of the Resistance in that whole area. There's a lot happening and he must be there.'

'So what's the problem?'

'Grant was doing the flight, Grant put it all together. Now the silly sod's fallen off his motor cycle and broken his left arm.'

'And you'd like me to do it.'

'Harry, at such short notice it needs somebody of your calibre.'

'No need for soft soap. When do I leave?'

'Let's say two hours. Jack and I will come with you. Jacaud as well.'

'Gives me time to go to the flat, get a shower and change my clothes.'

'I'll have a staff car take you.'

'See you later then,' Harry said and went out.

He showered, found clean underwear and a shirt and had just finished dressing and was going downstairs, when Molly came in.

'Wonderful, you're back.'

'And on my way out again. Did you know Grant broke his arm?'

'No.'

'He was due to drop a Joe over the other side tonight from Cold Harbour. Munro's asked me to do the flight.'

'Harry?' She was alarmed and grabbed his arm.

'In and out, drop-off, no pick-up. I'll be back before you know it. Hey, trust me.' He kissed her lightly on the mouth. 'Got to go. I'll see you soon.'

He picked up Tarquin in his jump bag, and his holdall and went out. She stood there staring at the door and for some reason knew fear.

In his office, Bubi Hartmann sat at his desk, drinking brandy, and Trudi leaned against the wall. 'Crazy, Trudi, absolute madness, all this talk about putting an assassin into England via Lisbon or anywhere else.'

'Well, don't even hint at your true feelings,' Trudi said. 'Look as if you agree, tell him how we're exploring every avenue. Just string it out until he moves on to something else.'

'All right, I'll be a good boy.' He poured another brandy. 'But really, an assassin into England. What do they *expect* of me?'

'Don't worry, they'll forget about it after a while. I'll make some coffee. You'll need it with all that brandy,' and she went into her office.

They were both wrong, of course, for just around the corner, a series of events was waiting, the consequences of which would be extraordinary for all of them.

TWELVE

Jacaud was not what Harry had expected at all. He was no more than five feet six in height, wore round steel spectacles, a tweed suit, raincoat and trilby hat and looked more like a schoolmaster than anything else. At Croydon, they spoke in French.

Jacaud said, 'Your rather special status has been explained to me, Colonel, by Brigadier Munro. If I may say so, like something out of a novel this story of you and your brother.'

'I think it was Oscar Wilde who said that life at its most remarkable resembled a bad novel,' Harry told him.

'Interesting, though terms such as bad and good mean very little in the life I lead.' Jacaud lit a Gitane cigarette. 'Is the weather prospect okay from Cold Harbour?'

'Excellent. You've been there before?'

'Oh, yes, the Brigadier and I go back a long time and Julie Legrande and her husband were comrades in the early days of the Resistance in Paris.'

At that moment, a staff car drew up outside and Munro and Jack Carter got out.

'There you are,' Munro said. 'Sorry about the delay. We'll get straight off if that suits you, Harry.'

'Certainly, Brigadier, ready to go.'

Munro and Jacaud went first and Harry and Carter followed. The major said, 'Message from Molly. She wanted to see you off, but there's the usual emergencies at Guy's. You know how it is.'

'She worries too much,' Harry said. 'I'll take her to the River Room tomorrow night. A decent meal, Carrol Gibbons and the band playing the right kind of music – who could ask for anything more?'

'Molly could,' Carter said.

'Yes, well, the ways of women are a mystery to me. Let's get moving.'

He'd been right about the weather prospect. There was broken cloud, a quarter moon: excellent conditions for low flying. In the library, they went over the map and Harry drew a red circle around Morlaix.

'Five miles outside the village on a heath. You'll know it, of course.'

'Like the back of my hand,' Jacaud said.

'Good. Usual ground signals. Straight in, you get out and I take off instantly.'

'Be confident, Colonel, I've done this six times before,' Jacaud told him.

'That's it then.' Harry checked his watch and turned to Munro. 'Twenty minutes, Brigadier?'

'You're in charge,' Munro told him, picked up his cap and made for the door.

Lysander pilots varied between those who preferred flying at several thousand feet and those who opted for a flight close to sea level, which made them impervious to enemy radar. It also made them an easy target for naval gunfire when they came across vessels of both sides. But in the case of a comparatively short flight of extreme hazard with the intention of off-loading a cargo as important as Jacaud, there wasn't really much choice.

The flight across to France from Cornwall in such excellent weather conditions posed few problems and at four to five hundred feet Harry was below enemy radar. It was all really quite pleasant, Tarquin as usual in the bottom of the cockpit, and then the unexpected happened.

Suddenly there to port were two motor torpedo boats of the Royal Dutch Navy operating out of Falmouth naval base. They opened up with everything at once, machine-gun bullets hitting the Lysander close to the tail and a couple of cannon shells puncturing the port wing.

Harry went up fast into broken cloud, climbed to a thousand feet and lost them.

He turned to Jacaud and shouted, 'You okay?'

'Fine.'

'Sorry about that. The bastards don't know which side they're on. We've taken a few hits, but no problem. ETA in fifteen minutes.'

At Fermanville, air traffic control picked them up at the greater height and the controller scrambled the night patrol. Max, not on duty that night, was enjoying a three-day leave in St Malo when the three ME 109s rose into the night sky in search of his brother.

The dropping zone at Morlaix was clearly marked on the heath and Harry made a perfect landing, taxied to the far end and turned into the wind. Jacaud patted him on the shoulder, scrambled out to meet the people running towards him and slammed the door behind him. Harry gunned the engine, roared down the heath and started to rise and at 800 feet, disaster struck.

Two MEs, one after the other, came in low and shot up the heath where the landing lights were still visible, the sound of it filling the night and, as Harry lifted, a third ME chased him, cannon fire tearing his wings apart. His nose dipped and he went down. At the far end of the heath were trees and he pulled back on the column in an effort to rise, but his wheels clipped the top branches and he disappeared on the other side. A moment later, flames erupted into the night.

Jacaud, five of his men grouped around him, said, 'God in heaven, come on,' and started to run towards the fire.

They came to the wood and started through and then, outlined against the flames, they saw two armoured personnel carriers. One of the men, a local farmer named Jules, grabbed Jacaud's arm.

'SS. We had a Panzer unit move in only yesterday. They were supposed to be resting. Nothing we can do. They may be bastards, but they know what they're doing.'

'All right,' Jacaud said. 'But let's see what happens.'

He crawled to the edge of the wood with the others and watched.

Harry had managed to get the door open, reached for Tarquin in the jump bag and scrambled to the ground, his flying jacket on fire. When he tried to stand, though, he fell down again, his left ankle refusing to support the weight. He started crawling, dragging the jump bag with him, but the pain in his ankle was so intense that he released his grip. And then one of the personnel carriers was beside him and several soldiers jumped out and tore the burning flying jacket off him.

All this Jacaud saw from the wood. The SS carried Harry to the personnel carrier, put him inside and a moment later they drove away. There was little of the Lysander left now, as it burned fiercely, then the flames subsided. The men in Jacaud's group got up and moved close, examining the area.

Jacaud lit a cigarette and said to Jules, 'What a bastard. He was a really top man, Legion of Honour, everything.'

One of the men came back with the jump bag. 'I found this near the plane.'

'What is it?'

'Well, that's the crazy thing. It's a bear in flying clothes.'

'Really?' Jacaud said. 'Well, that's okay, because after tonight I'll believe anything. Bring it with you and let's get to the mill. I need to radio my people in Cornwall.'

The loft in the old mill was comfortable enough, sacks of grain stacked everywhere, but a secret door in the wooden wall opened into a back room, the control centre for the Resistance in the Morlaix area for two years now. A young woman stirred coffee over a stove.

Jacaud said, 'It's Cold Harbour I need, Marie, you can leave that.'

'I can't contact them for another thirty minutes,' she said. 'We're on a fixed time schedule. In the meantime, coffee and maybe a cognac will do you good.'

'Right, as usual.' He took the mug she handed him. 'Where would they take Colonel Kelso?'

'Château Morlaix, just outside the village. The count and his family fled to Britain and left a caretaker in charge. The SS have appropriated it as their headquarters.'

'No way of getting to him?'

'Only if you're intent on committing suicide.'

He nodded, sat back and Jules came in, put the jump bag on the table, opened it and sat Tarquin on the table. 'There's a label inside. It says: Tarquin's bag.'

Jacaud said, 'It must have been some kind of mascot.'

'Daft I call it,' Jules said. 'A bear with wings.'

'Oh, no.' Marie picked Tarquin up. 'He's special, you can tell.' She turned to Jacaud. 'Can I have him? My five-year-old daughter would fall instantly in love.'

'Why not?' Jacaud looked at his watch. 'But get me Cold Harbour now.'

Munro left the radio room, went downstairs, got into a Jeep and drove himself down to the Hanged Man. When he went in, all the lifeboat crew were there, Jack having a beer with Zec Acland by the fire, Julie behind the bar.

Munro stood just inside the bar, his face saying it all. As people glanced at him, they stopped talking one by one. It was Julie who said, 'What is it, Brigadier?'

Later, sitting by the fire with Jack and Zec, he said, 'At least Jacaud made it safely. Yes, I know that sounds callous, but it's the name of the game. Jacaud is of primary importance. You agree, Jack?'

'I suppose so, Brigadier, but to be frank, what seems of primary importance to me is who's going to break this to Molly?'

Munro took a deep breath. 'Well, Jack, you are very close to her . . .'

'And you, Brigadier, are her uncle.'

'All right, point taken. Leave it with me,' and Munro got up, went out and left them.

In the doctors' rest room at Guy's Hospital, Molly was snatching a coffee and sandwich. A young surgeon captain named Holly who worked with Army patients sat in the corner reading a newspaper. There was a knock at the door. He got up and opened it to find Major General Tom Sobel standing there.

'Would my daughter be here?'

Holly, who had met him once before, was suddenly all military. 'Yes, here she is, General.'

Molly turned, smiling. 'Why Dad, what brings you here?' and then her smile disappeared totally.

'I wonder if you'd give us a few minutes, Captain?'

'Of course, sir.'

Holly went out. As the door closed Molly said, 'Just tell me the worst, don't dress it up.'

Sitting there minutes later, smoking a cigarette, her face haggard, she said, 'So he could still be alive?'

'From what this Resistance leader Jacaud says, yes. His flying jacket was on fire when the SS got to him, then they bundled him into a personnel carrier and took him away, but from all accounts it was a very bad crash.'

'But he survived.' She nodded and stubbed out her cigarette.

'Molly, he must have sustained heavy injuries at least.'

'Perhaps, but he's alive.'

'How on earth can you be certain?'

'Because I'd know, Dad.' She smiled a strange, cold smile. 'If Harry Kelso was dead I'd know it, it's as simple as that.'

The door opened and Holly looked in. 'I'm terribly sorry, but that leg amputation you did on that young mine disposal chap? He's had a relapse.'

'I'll come at once.' She stood and kissed her father on the cheek. 'Work to do, Dad, and thank God for it. Uncle Dougal knows where I am. He'll keep me posted. I must go.'

Tom Sobel stood there for a moment then followed her with a heavy heart.

At Châteaux Morlaix Kelso was very much alive as he lay on a single bed in a room on the ground floor which the SS Panzer unit now occupying the château had turned into a surgery. He lay propped up against pillows smoking a cigarette. No burns, that was the incredible thing, though he had been knocked about a bit, his face bruised and the left ankle hurt like hell. The SS guard on the door wore a black Panzer uniform and carried a Schmeisser. He showed no emotion at all, didn't even look at Harry, but stared in front of him.

The door opened and the young SS Hauptsturmführer called Schroeder who'd introduced himself as the unit doctor came in, holding an X-ray.

'As I feared, Colonel, the ankle is badly broken, but the break is clean. I've spoken to my commanding officer, Major Müller. He was in Dinard for the evening. He's on his way.'

'Thank you, Captain,' Harry said. 'Very efficient of you.'

'We pride ourselves on our medical facility, Colonel. A portable X-ray machine, operating facilities. Our men expect the best. We are, after all, SS.'

'Your English is excellent.'

'I spent a year at Southampton General Hospital just before the war.'

At that moment, the door opened and a Sturmbannführer in black uniform festooned with awards entered. Schroeder got his heels together.

'Major Müller.'

'What's the story here?' Müller asked in German.

'This officer is a lieutenant-colonel of the US Air Force, a Colonel Kelso. He gave me his name, rank and number. His ankle is broken.'

'Yes, but what was he up to?'

'Flying one of those Lysander planes the English use to bring secret agents in. ME 109s from Fermanville shot him down.'

'Landing or taking off?'

'Our patrols saw him land. The MEs got him when he took off again.'

'Which means he dropped somebody off. Didn't they do anything about it?'

'I suppose they concentrated on the crash, Major.'

'You suppose?' Müller shook his head. 'God help me. Anyway, you'll have to translate for me.'

It might have been the clever thing to stay quiet, but Harry's ankle was hurting like hell now so he said in German, 'That's not necessary, Major, but what is necessary is that I get a shot of morphine right now and something done about this ankle.'

Both of the SS officers were astonished. Müller said, 'I congratulate you on the excellence of your grasp of our language, Colonel.'

'Thank you, but what about the ankle? I've complied with the Geneva Convention. Name, rank and serial number.'

Müller frowned, then walked across the room to where Harry's tunic had been hung on a chair. He noted the medals, the RAF wings.

'Good God, Colonel, you have had an interesting war.' He took out a silver cigarette case, offered Harry one and gave him a light. 'Captain Schroeder will see to you at once. We are all soldiers here, after all. I'll speak with you later.'

He beckoned to Schroeder and went out. Schroeder said, 'It's a bad break, but I can fix it. A little minor surgery and then a plaster of Paris cast.'

'Anything he needs,' Müller said.

'One thing, sir,' Schroeder said. 'We haven't informed Luftwaffe headquarters at St Malo or the night fighter base at Fermanville that he survived.'

'And we won't,' Müller was excited. 'The colonel's medals are extraordinary, and did you notice the RAF wings on his right breast? That means he was an American volunteer in the

RAF before the US entered the war. This man is a big fish, Schroeder, very big.'

'But Major,' Schroeder stammered. 'Regulations stipulate that we inform the Luftwaffe of his presence.'

'Stuff the Luftwaffe,' Müller said. 'I'm sending a signal to SD Headquarters in Berlin right away. I'm going to the top.' He slapped Schroeder on the back. 'Your best work, that's what I expect on this one,' and he hurried away.

Like most people these days at Prinz Albrechtstrasse, Bubi Hartmann didn't bother going home because of the regularity of RAF Lancaster raids. He had a cot made up in the corner of the office. He'd slept well until three in the morning, when the RAF had struck. Half an hour of hell and then they were gone. He got up, went to the toilet, splashed cold water on his face, then went to his desk, found the brandy and poured one. He started to go through some papers and a moment later, the door opened and Trudi came in. Like Bubi, she'd had a cot installed in the outer office. She was holding a signal flimsy in one hand.

'Are you all right?' he asked.

'Yes, but I'm not sure how you'll feel about this. It's a report from a major commanding a Panzer unit at a place called Morlaix in Brittany. The signals unit received it twenty minutes ago.'

'What's so special about it?'

'You put a red flag out on anything to do with Lieutenant-Colonel Harry Kelso the other week.' She held out the flimsy. 'Read it.'

Afterwards, as he sat there smoking a cigarette and thinking about it, she said, 'Are you going to notify the Baron?'

He shook his head. 'I can't afford to, Trudi. This goes to the Reichsführer. Is he overnighting?'

'Yes, I believe so.'

He reached for a sheet of paper and a pen. 'Get me an orderly.'

She turned at the door. 'Kelso is a prisoner of war, isn't he? I mean, that's a fact.'

'Don't be stupid, Trudi, he's no ordinary prisoner of war and you know it. Now fetch the orderly.'

She went out, he wrote a brief note to Himmler, put it in an envelope with the signal flimsy and sealed it.

It was nine o'clock in the morning when the Reichsführer summoned him. Himmler was in uniform, standing at the window looking out. He spoke without turning round.

'Another night of terror bombing, Colonel, and that fat fool, Goering, swore that if a single bomb fell on Berlin you could call him Meyer.'

'I believe so, Reichsführer.'

'So much for the Luftwaffe helping us win the war. They can't even protect Berlin.' He turned. 'So, it is left to the rest of us to help the Führer fulfil his glorious mission.' He walked to the desk and picked up the signal flimsy. 'And this, Colonel, presents us with our opportunity.'

Bubi was totally mystified. 'Reichsführer?'

Himmler sat. 'God sometimes looks down through the clouds, Colonel, and he has this morning. I've found your assassin for you.'

Bubi was bewildered. 'I'm afraid I don't understand, Reichsführer.'

'It's simple enough. We have in our hands one rather damaged Lieutenant-Colonel Kelso of the US Air Force. According to your reports, he does special operations flights and frequently flies Eisenhower.'

'That's correct.'

'So we allow him to escape and fly back to England, where, at the first opportunity, he disposes of Eisenhower.'

For a moment, Bubi was convinced that he was going mad. 'But, Reichsführer, why should he? And in any case, he has a broken ankle.'

'But his brother doesn't.' Himmler smiled at Bubi's astonished expression. 'They can't be told apart, or so I'm informed. A simple change of uniform is all that's needed. We arrange for him to conveniently escape from Château Morlaix, then steal a Storch or some such plane from the feeder station outside the town. There is one, I've checked. Anyway, he flies back to Cold Harbour and Brigadier Munro. Even if he doesn't get to fly Eisenhower, the good general is certain to want to see him.'

Bubi Hartmann struggled to come to terms with all this. 'But, Reichsführer, for Baron von Halder to impersonate his brother, he would need to know everything about him, which presupposes that Colonel Kelso would be willing to go along with the plan. It also presupposes that the Baron would also agree.'

'Oh, but he will, they both will, especially after you've arrested their mother, which you will this morning. Very discreetly, of course. I've already spoken personally to Major Müller at Château Morlaix, informing him that he is now under my direct command. The Château will be sealed up tight and perfect for our purposes.'

'But Reichsführer, how will this persuade the Baron and his brother to co-operate?'

Himmler told him in graphic detail. When he was finished, Bubi felt sick.

'You seem upset,' Himmler said. 'I would have thought you would have welcomed this chance to serve the Reich, Colonel, for it has served you well, in fact given you unequal opportunities for one with Jewish antecedents.' Bubi was numb with horror and Himmler smiled gently. 'How could you imagine that I wouldn't know? And the taint affects your whole family. Your father is still alive, I believe, and his sister? Your wife, as I recall, was killed in a car crash at twenty-two, so there's no children, but there is, of course, the question of your secretary. Frau Braun, an intimate relationship.'

Bubi took a deep breath. 'What does the Reichsführer require of me?'

'Good. I've always admired your pragmatism. I've been on the telephone to Nunes da Silva, the minister I told you about in the Portuguese Foreign Office. This man at their embassy here, Joel Rodrigues, will be transferred to Lisbon today. You will see him this morning, write a report for his brother and the Dixon woman in London outlining the operation and telling them to expect the Baron in a matter of days.'

'But Joel Rodrigues in London, Reichsführer? I don't understand?'

'It's simple. Nunes da Silva will transfer Joel Rodrigues to courier duties. You will have him flown to Lisbon today. Tomorrow, he'll fly to London with the usual embassy bag. That's what couriers do, Colonel. So, we have the Baron in London, the back-up of the Dixon woman and the Rodrigues brothers. I don't see how we can fail, do you?'

Bubi's mouth was so dry that he couldn't swallow. He coughed. 'I agree, Reichsführer.'

'Excellent, Colonel. Now that I would appear to have done all your work for you, please oblige me by getting on with it.'

The first thing Hartmann did was to tell Trudi to get hold of Joel Rodrigues and order him to report at once. Then he told her to come with her shorthand book. He poured brandy again.

'Should you be doing that?' she asked.

'It's all that's holding me together. You'll understand when I've finished dictating.'

What he gave her was a letter of instruction for Fernando

Rodrigues and Sarah Dixon, the project in complete detail as Himmler had outlined it.

When he finished, Trudi said, 'He's crazy. He must be. Why would Kelso and the Baron agree to this thing?'

Bubi told her. She sat there, her face white, then ran into his washroom. He heard her vomiting in the basin, then the water running. After a while, she returned, her face still pale.

'What a swine. And you'll go through with it?'

'I have no choice. There's Jewish blood in my family, Trudi. I didn't think anyone knew, but he did. My father's under threat, my old aunt. Even you as my secretary.'

'Oh, my God.'

'So, I don't have much choice, do I?'

She sat there staring at him and the bell rang in the outer office. She got up without a word, went out and returned with Joel Rodrigues.

'Type up the letter,' he said. 'And as quickly as possible.'

She went out. Joel wore a raincoat and fingered his hat anxiously. 'I have rather startling news, Colonel.'

'I know,' Bubi said. 'You've been summoned to Lisbon at once and I've been asked to facilitate your transport by air to that fair city as soon as possible. You were probably informed of the move by Nunes da Silva of your foreign office.'

'How did you know that, Colonel?'

'I know everything. Did he tell you what he wants you for?'

'No.'

'Well, I will. You're joining the Courier Service, carrying diplomatic bags by air to London. You won't be in Lisbon more than a few hours.'

Joel looked immediately alarmed. 'But, Colonel, this wasn't in our agreement.'

'It is now. Of course, you could discuss it with the Reichsführer or da Silva when you get to Lisbon, but I wouldn't advise it. You're a small man, Rodrigues, caught up in big things. Come to think of it, so am I. We don't have choices, they're made for us.' Trudi came in with the letter of instruction. Bubi read it, then folded it and put it in an envelope unsigned. He handed the envelope to Joel Rodrigues. 'For your brother. Be at the airport in two hours.'

'Yes, Colonel.'

Joel went out and Bubi lit a cigarette. 'Find out where Max is then order a plane for me to leave in, say, three hours. A Storch will do. I'll fly myself.'

'Any passengers?'

'Why, the Baroness, of course.' He stood up and as she reached the door, said, 'And Trudi?'

She turned. 'Yes?'

'Any chance you get to do a disappearing act, take advantage of it. Just in case things go wrong. You understand?'

'Perfectly, but I'd rather wait and see.' She was strangely calm as she went out.

Handling Elsa von Halder was extraordinarily easy. He stuck as far as possible with the truth, it was as simple as that. When he knocked on the door of the suite at the Adlon, he was admitted by Rosa Stein. Elsa was seated by the fire, reading a magazine, which she put down. She held out her hand and Bubi kissed it.

'What a surprise, Colonel.'

'I bring you rather momentous news, Baroness. I might as well get it over with. Your son, Colonel Kelso, was shot down on a mission to Brittany last night. He is now in our hands.'

She said calmly, 'Is he well?'

'A broken ankle. He's at a place called Château Morlaix. I'm under orders to fly down there to interrogate him.'

'Does Max know of this?'

'No, but he'll be informed. I'm acting on behalf of the SD, which means the Reichsführer, but he has given me permission to take you with me if you should desire.'

'May I bring my maid?'

'Naturally.'

She stood up. 'Then how long have I got, Colonel?'

'I'll have a car pick you up in an hour.' He put on his cap and saluted. 'Please excuse me. I've things to do.'

As Rosa hurriedly packed, Elsa told her of her conversation with Bubi Hartmann.

'It would be strange, Baroness,' Rosa said, 'to perhaps see both of your sons together.'

'A long time since that happened, a long time.' Elsa put her jewellery in its usual box and passed it to Rosa. 'Put that in my large handbag. Oh, and this.'

She produced a Walther PPK pistol from a drawer, took out the magazine, checked the weapon expertly and reloaded.

Rosa put it in the handbag. 'You think you might need this, Baroness?'

'Who knows?' Elsa von Halder smiled serenely. 'It's as well to be prepared.'

THIRTEEN

At Fermanville, Max was enjoying a drink in the mess in the early evening when Bubi Hartmann walked in. Max excused himself from a group of officers and went to greet him.

'Bubi, what brings you here?' and then he frowned. 'Is there a problem? My mother?'

'In the corner,' Bubi said. 'We need privacy.'

The other officers stared for a moment, then turned from Bubi's frown.

Max said, 'What is this?'

Bubi waved the mess waiter away. 'Do you know a place called Château Morlaix about forty miles from here?'

'Of course. There's a Luftwaffe feeder station there. We often use the emergency strip.'

'I landed there early this afternoon. Flew down from Berlin in a Storch with your mother and her maid.'

Max looked anxious. 'Is she under arrest?'

'Not in the way you mean. Read this, Max.' He took an envelope from his pocket, extracted a letter and passed it over. It was quality paper and the heading was embossed in black.

Berlin, April 1944

DER REICHSFÜHRER – SS

The bearer acts under my personal orders on business of the utmost importance to the Reich. All personnel, civil and military must assist him in any way he sees fit.

Heinrich Himmler.

It was countersigned by the Führer.

Max handed it back. 'Your credentials would appear to be impeccable. In the circumstances, I really would appreciate a drink.' He waved to the waiter. 'Cognac – large ones.' He turned back to Bubi. 'Dolfo Galland's at Abbeville tomorrow. He wanted me to fly up there.'

'I know and he's been informed that as of now you are detached from Fighter Command.'

'As bad as that?' The waiter appeared with the cognac. Max took his down in one long swallow. 'So, Bubi, what do we have here? I heard an SS Panzer unit had taken over Château Morlaix?'

'Yes, and they are now under my direct orders. A ring of steel around the place.'

'Because my mother is there? Come on, Bubi.'

'No, because your brother is there.' Bubi swallowed his cognac. 'If you could collect your kit, we'll be off.'

'Harry at Château Morlaix?' Max was very pale. 'Tell me.'

'On the way, Max. Please hurry and remember, this is top secret.'

Max didn't bother calling his orderly, but packed himself. As he was finishing, the door opened and Major Berger, the station adjutant, came in. 'Hartmann flourished an order from Himmler himself that chilled my bones. You've been posted to the SS command at Morlaix.'

'So it would appear.'

'But what goes on there? I've been ordered to detach an ME 109 to the Morlaix feeder station. Again, it will be under Hartmann's command.'

Max zipped up a bag. 'Who are you sending?'

'I thought young Freiburg.'

'Not a bad choice. He's got potential.' Max picked up a bag in each hand. 'I must get off.'

'Max,' Berger said. 'We've been friends for a long time. Are you in trouble?'

'No more than we've all been since the Führer took over in '33.' Max smiled. 'Watch your back,' and he went out.

The car was a Citroën, long and black, and Bubi drove it himself. Max sat beside him, smoking a cigarette.

'So what happened to Harry?' he asked.

'He was dropping an agent off in a Lysander from Cold Harbour in Cornwall. I expect you recall the name.'

'Why should I?'

'Max, your brother was shot down in a Hurricane some weeks ago, while covering a Lysander on its way back to Cold Harbour with a very important French officer. He took out two ME 109s and went into the drink. It was Himmler who pointed out to me that the pilot of the third ME on the scene was you. What happened, Max?'

'All right, Bubi.' Max laughed. 'I'll tell you then you tell me.'

'Agreed.'

When Max was finished, Bubi said, 'Remarkable and I'm not condemning you. I hope I'd have done the same.'

'So what about Harry?'

'It would seem he was dropping one of those Resistance leaders off, an in-and-out job, bicycle lamps on the heath. He went too high into the radar level after being fired at by Allied naval forces. Can you believe that?'

'Oh, I can believe anything.'

'Anyway, boys from your base strafed the landing area and brought him down. He got out as the Lysander fireballed.

Strangely enough he was saved by a Panzer patrol which just happened to be in the area. They got his burning flying jacket off him before it did more than singe him, but his left ankle was badly broken.'

'But otherwise, he's all right?'

'Yes.'

'Does he know I'm coming? Does my mother know?'

'Not at the moment.'

'I understand you've asked for an ME 109. They've allocated young Freiburg. Why?'

'A precaution only, in case we get unauthorized aircraft in the area and that's common enough these days.'

Max lit two cigarettes and passed one to Bubi. 'Look, what is this? The Reichsführer isn't into happy families. What does he want?'

'Later, Max, later. That's all I can say for now,' and Bubi concentrated on the driving.

At Morlaix, Elsa and Rosa had been installed in an apartment suite, Major Müller all courtesy. As with everyone else, the sight of Bubi's letter from Himmler had had a salutary effect.

'Colonel Hartmann has gone to Fermanville to pick up Baron von Halder, Baroness,' he told her. 'He has left instructions that, when you are ready, you may see your son.'

'Ah, you know about that,' she said.

'Of course. As an officer of the SS I swore a holy oath of obedience. In this matter I am under orders from the Reichsführer himself.'

'Say no more,' Elsa told him sweetly. 'In the circumstances, I would appreciate seeing my son as soon as possible.'

'Of course, Baroness.'

★

Harry was propped up in bed, his left leg in a plaster cast across a pillow, flicking through a copy of *Signal*, which showed in graphic detail how Germany was still winning the war. The door clicked open and Müller stepped in.

'Colonel Kelso, I have your mother here.'

Elsa stepped into the room and Müller withdrew, closing the door. Harry looked at her and smiled. 'My God, Mutti, you haven't aged at all. It's incredible.' He dropped the magazine and held out his arms and she ran to him.

Later, she sat beside the bed. 'So you've no idea what's going on here?' he said.

She shook her head. 'I've told you all I know. Bubi Hartmann, Himmler. Max, of course, told me of your warning when you went down in the sea and he saved you. Where did you get your information?'

'I do special flights for British Intelligence. The people I deal with have contacts in Berlin.'

'I see. So, you haven't married?'

'Mutti, I'm still only twenty-six years old.'

'Your father was twenty-two when he married me.'

'Well, I have been rather busy.'

She lit a cigarette. 'So, I don't know what's going on here and neither do you?'

'So it would appear.'

She nodded. 'Is there a girl in your life, a proper girl?'

'Perhaps. Her mother was English, killed in the Blitz. Her father's an American general.'

'She sounds promising.'

'She's a few months older than me and a brilliant surgeon.'

'Couldn't be better. I'm impressed.'

'Don't be, Mutti, she deserves better.'

Before she could reply, the door opened and Bubi appeared.

'Another guest for you, Colonel.' He stepped back and Max moved into the room.

Dinner was served in the château's magnificent dining room. Harry was carried down in a chair by two SS orderlies. Müller, Schroeder and two young lieutenants joined the party. The food was excellent: turtle soup, mutton roasted to perfection, an excellent salad, good champagne and a fine claret, a pre-war Château Palmer.

Elsa said, 'I must say the SS do know how to do things well, Major Müller.'

'Anything else for you would be totally unacceptable, Baroness,' he replied gallantly and raised his glass. 'To brave men everywhere and to Colonel Kelso and the Baron von Halder, brothers in arms.'

Everyone stood, except Elsa and Harry, and drank the toast. Bubi said, 'And now, Major, if you could excuse us.'

'Of course, Colonel.'

As Müller and his officers made for the door, Schroeder turned and said, 'I've been in touch with the local doctor, Colonel Kelso. He'll have crutches for you here tomorrow.'

'That's kind of you,' Harry said.

The door closed, Bubi got up and reached for the claret and went round the table topping up the glasses.

Max said, 'All right, Bubi, what's the game?'

Bubi stood by the fire. 'Everyone thinks the important question about the invasion is where the Allies are going to land. The Führer doesn't agree. He thinks we should put our efforts into something really worthwhile.' He paused. 'Such as assassinating General Eisenhower.'

There was total astonishment on every face.

'But that's crazy,' Max said.

'It is, but unfortunately Himmler agrees with him. I have agents in London, separate from the Abwehr and still at large. Through them, Colonel Kelso, I know all about Brigadier Dougal Munro, Major Carter, Cold Harbour and SOE in Baker Street. I know you have a lady friend, a Doctor Sobel, whose father is a general on Eisenhower's staff. I know you often fly him as a courier pilot. I told the Reichsführer that we couldn't oblige the Führer, that I had no one in London capable of such a task and that at this stage in the war, I didn't think one of our own people, however capable, would ever get near Eisenhower, even if we managed to get someone into England.'

'So?' Kelso asked.

'Things have changed, however, with you falling into our hands, and this has led to the Reichsführer coming up with, in his opinion, a brilliant solution to our dilemma, and in mine, a bizarre one.'

He paused and Max said, 'Go on, Bubi.'

'It goes something like this. Colonel Kelso escapes, steals the Storch on the landing strip and flies back to Cold Harbour to a hero's welcome. Eisenhower will wish to see him. If not, he is certain to fly the General on some occasion, as he has before. At a suitable moment, he assassinates him.'

There was a profound silence then Harry laughed out loud. 'And how do I accomplish all this? I'm not getting crutches until the morning.'

'You don't understand,' Bubi told him. 'It wouldn't be you, it would be Max.'

Elsa said, 'Oh, my God.'

Max drank a little claret and put down the glass. 'And why would I do such a thing? I fly fighter planes, Bubi, that's what I do. Whatever else I am, I'm no assassin.'

Bubi came to the table and poured more wine, considerably

agitated. 'I'm just an errand boy. I've got Himmler's hand on my throat too. This is none of my doing.'

'All right,' Max said. 'Just tell us the worst.'

'The Baroness, regrettably, has enjoyed entirely the wrong circle of friends. Eighteen arrested, twelve executed, several of them generals, two women. It's called guilt by association. Let's put it this way. If you don't co-operate, you two, it will be very much the worse for her.'

Elsa tossed wine into his face. 'You bastard.'

Max jumped up and caught her arms. 'Don't be stupid, he's got just as much choice in this as we have.'

'To hell with that kind of talk,' Harry said. 'If you did this you'd need my co-operation, Max. My life in detail, my girl Molly, Munro, my friends at Cold Harbour, Eisenhower, Southwick House.' He shook his head. 'I won't do it.'

Bubi wiped his face and Max turned to him. 'Give us some time.'

'Tomorrow morning,' Bubi said. 'That's the best I can do. Sleep on it,' and he turned and went out.

Back in his room, he telephoned Himmler at Prinz Albrechtstrasse and found him still in his office. 'I thought I should bring you up to date, Reichsführer.' When he was finished, he said, 'What shall I do?'

'I've told you what to do, Colonel. Let them think it over. Not much sleep there, I think. Breakfast, everything nice and orderly. Then at, let's say ten o'clock, let the axe fall. I doubt if you'll have any further trouble.'

'Very well, Reichsführer.'

'I must go, Colonel, I'm needed in Paris. I intend a night flight. If you need me, I'll be at Gestapo Headquarters there.'

'As you say, Reichsführer.'

Bubi replaced the phone, imagining Himmler's personal JU 52

lifting into the night. If only an RAF Mosquito could appear on schedule and blow him out of the sky, but that, of course, would be expecting too much.

Elsa had retired, and the SS orderlies carried Harry back to his room and helped him on to the bed. After a while, the door opened and Max came in.

'Not one, but two sentries on the door. They are taking good care of you,' he spoke in English.

'I like the uniform,' Harry told him. 'Very handsome.'

Max crossed to the chair where Harry's tunic hung. He examined the medal ribbons. 'You're not doing too bad yourself.' He pulled a chair forward and took out his cigarette case. 'So, here we are, brother, together again.' He gave Harry a cigarette and a light. 'The only thing missing is Tarquin. How is the old boy?'

'Don't ask,' Harry said. 'Every mission I flew, he was there in his jump bag in the bottom of the cockpit. Right through the Battle. I jumped for it over the Isle of Wight and Tarquin went with me. Twice into the drink.'

'And what happened this time?'

'They shot me up real good, I clipped trees coming down.' Harry shrugged. 'The Lysander came apart, then flamed. I was dazed. I remember grabbing at the jump bag as I dived out, but my flying jacket was on fire. To give them their due, those SS guys came right in for me. As they dragged me away the Lysander blew up.'

'And Tarquin went with it?'

'So it would appear. He was my good luck, Max, and now he's gone.'

'Don't talk nonsense. You were your own good luck. A great pilot.' Max smiled. 'Almost as good as me.' He shrugged. 'Still, I'll ask Bubi to have some of his men search the area.'

'Speaking of Bubi, where exactly does he fit into all this?'

'Oh, we flew in France in the old days while he was in the Luftwaffe.' Max carried on and told him the story. As he concluded, he said, 'It's true what he said. He's just as much in Himmler's power as the rest of us.'

He went to the window and peered out and Harry said, 'What happens now?'

'I don't know. I'll hear what Bubi has to say in the morning. We'll see.'

'You mean you'd actually go through with this thing? Kill Eisenhower?'

Max turned. 'He's nothing to me, Harry, he's the other side. I've killed a lot of people and so have you. It's called war.'

'Okay, but there's still a difference. What if the shoe was on the other foot and they wanted me to assassinate Himmler, a Nazi bastard like that?'

'To people in America and England, I'm a Nazi bastard.'

'Like hell you are. The vast majority of the German people aren't members of the Nazi party. They got sucked in when Hitler took the country to war. They had no choice.'

'Oh, we all had a choice. It's just that we left it too late.' Max went to the door and turned. 'This young woman, the doctor? Do you love her?'

'She loves me. I don't really know what love is. I didn't seem to have the time. Mainly the odd one-night stand. You know how it is?'

'I'm afraid I do. Isn't life hell?' Max opened the door. 'I'll see you in the morning.'

At Lisbon airport, Joel Rodrigues waited as he'd been ordered at the main entrance. It was raining hard and he was thoroughly miserable after a flight from Berlin in an ME 110, a twin engine fighter often used now for courier work. He hadn't even been given the opportunity to see his family. He was not happy, not happy at all.

A black limousine drew up, a chauffeur got out and opened the rear door and a young man in a black overcoat approached. He had thin lips and dark, intense eyes. His name was Romão and he'd met Joel on his arrival.

'There you are, Rodrigues, the minister wants a word.'

Joel hurried after him, the rear window was wound down and Nunes da Silva looked out, his white hair silver in the lamplight, the eyes pale in a shrunken face.

'So you are Rodrigues?'

'Yes, Minister.'

'You know what you have to do?'

'Yes, Minister.'

'I know nothing of Reichsführer Himmler's instructions to you and I do not wish to. You proceed to London as an embassy courier and link up with your brother. Rodrigues, both of you, you're greedy little men. The fix you're in is of your own doing.'

'But how long do I stay, Minister?'

'Until I tell you otherwise.' Da Silva turned and said to Romão, 'What time is the flight?'

'One a.m., Minister, a TAP Dakota. They prefer to fly at night. The Germans are thorough, but even they can make mistakes.'

'You see, Rodrigues?' da Silva told him. 'You could end up going down in the Bay of Biscay and it'd serve you right. See him on his way, Romão, then join me at the apartment.' He wound up the window and the limousine drove away.

Rodrigues went back to the entrance and picked up his case. Romão said, 'Isn't he the original old bastard? Still, he's got a point. They recently shot down a passenger plane carrying Leslie Howard, of all people. You know, the film star.'

'Thanks very much.'

'If your luck is good, you'll be in London for breakfast. Wonderful city and they are winning the war.' He smiled. 'Of course, I'll always deny I said that.'

In any case, the flight was not good. There were thunderstorms over Biscay, the Dakota was crowded, every seat taken. Many people were airsick and the smell left a great deal to be desired. Somehow, Joel survived, helped by a half bottle of brandy he'd had the forethought to put in his pocket.

At Croydon airport, he waited in a queue to pass through customs and security, and was suddenly aware of his brother on the other side of the barrier, waving to him. Joel waved back and reached the head of the queue.

'Passport, sir,' the security officer said.

Joel passed it across. 'I have diplomatic immunity. I'm going to the Portuguese embassy here.'

'I see, sir,' and the officer examined the passport.

How often in life small things carry the seeds of disaster, for Joel Rodrigues had committed a serious blunder that others – Himmler, da Silva, Romão – should have foreseen. His passport carried arrival and departure stamps for Berlin.

Special Branch from Scotland Yard always had a presence at the airport. By chance that morning, Detective Chief Inspector Sean Riley was doing his weekly check and was standing not too far away – a tall, thin London Irishman with a scarred cheek from a broken bottle.

The security officer nodded and Riley stepped forward. He didn't take the passport, simply glanced at it, saw everything, looked up and smiled. 'Welcome to London, sir.'

Joel moved through and embraced his brother. 'I've got a car waiting,' Fernando said and picked up his brother's suitcase.

As they moved away, Riley beckoned to a young man in a shabby raincoat. 'Your chance to make sergeant, Lacey. You follow those two to the ends of the earth.'

'My pleasure, Chief Inspector,' and Lacey went after them.

The British secret intelligence services have always differed from other countries' in one major respect. Their agents have no powers of arrest. This is why they always work closely with Special Branch of Scotland Yard. As it happened, Riley regularly worked closely with Section D at SOE and Munro. It was eight-thirty when he phoned Baker Street and Jack Carter took the call.

Riley explained about Joel Rodrigues. 'The thing is,' he said, 'there was a Portuguese embassy car waiting and my lad Lacey heard the chauffeur call the other man Rodrigues too.'

'Really?' Jack Carter said. 'That is interesting. Anything else?'

'Yes, they stopped off at a flat near Kensington Gardens, Ennismore Mews, got rid of the suitcase, then carried on to the embassy. Lacey drove back and checked out the flat. It's in the name of a Fernando Rodrigues. I've already looked him up. He's Senior Commercial Attaché.'

Jack groaned. 'They always are, Sean, but I think this is a good one. Let me check with the Brigadier and I'll get back to you.'

Munro was in his office going through some files and signal flimsies. He looked up. 'There you are. We had another message from Jacaud. He can't help much. This SS outfit has Château Morlaix and the general area wrapped up tight. They did see a Storch land at the airstrip yesterday afternoon, but that's about it.'

'So, he could still be there, sir?'

'He could still be anything, Jack, alive, dead, wounded. Who the hell knows? Anyway, what have you got?'

Carter explained about the Rodrigues brothers. Munro listened and nodded. 'Riley's a good copper and he was right. The Berlin stamps in the passport, that's the thing.'

'So what do we do, sir?'

'Tell Riley full surveillance. I want details of who they meet, photos, the whole business.'

'I'll get right on to it, Brigadier.'

Breakfast at Morlaix was a private affair. Harry had managed to make it down the stairs, assisted by Schroeder's crutches, and sat at one end of the table. Elsa was on his left, Max on the right. Bubi sat at one end. They ate in silence, served by an SS orderly in a white jacket. Scrambled eggs and bacon, toast, excellent coffee.

'You do well, you gentlemen of the SS,' Elsa said.

'We aim to please.' His humour was forced. They heard the sound of a plane overhead and he got up and went to the window. 'Ah, the ME 109 from Fermanville.'

'Freiburg,' Max said.

Bubi turned and looked at his watch. 'Nine-thirty, I'll be back at ten. I'll expect your answer then,' and he went out.

'He can go to hell,' Elsa said and nodded to the orderly, who poured more coffee.

Max said, 'It isn't that simple.' They spoke in English.

'Remember who you are, Max. Baron von Halder, the Black Baron, possibly Germany's greatest ace. What can they do to you?'

He shook his head. 'You still don't see it, Mutti, do you? In the hands of people like Himmler we are nothing.' He turned to his brother. 'Tell her, Harry.'

Harry said, 'He's right. We're in one hell of a fix here.'

'You mean you'd go along with this ridiculous notion?'

'He certainly couldn't carry it off without my co-operation.'

'I despair of both of you.' She stood up.

Max said, 'Mutti, we have to think of you.'

She drew herself up. 'I am Elsa von Halder, Reichsmarschall Goering is my friend. They wouldn't touch me.'

She went out of the dining room like a ship under sail and the door banged behind her.

In the south sitting room Bubi supervised the setting up of a sixteen millimetre projection camera. He'd chosen the room because the end wall was plain white. He dismissed the orderly who'd helped him, took a reel of film from a tin can and carefully threaded it through the projector. Behind him, the door opened and Müller came in.

'Anything I can do?'

'Yes, bring them here now then wait outside. I'll send for you when I need you.'

Müller shrugged and went out.

'All right, Bubi, what is this?' Max demanded a few minutes later. He was standing by the window and Elsa and Harry occupied the couch.

'Early in the day for a film show, I'd have thought,' Elsa told him.

Bubi said, 'Before we start, let me say again that I'm only obeying orders. I have no choice in this matter.'

'Oh, get on with it,' Harry said. 'Let's hear the worst.'

At that moment, a plane roared overhead, obviously descending. Max looked out of the window. 'JU 52. Now what in the hell is it doing here?'

It couldn't be possible and yet, in his heart, Bubi knew it was. 'Wait here,' he said and went out.

Müller was walking along the corridor to the room he was using as an office. Bubi said, 'What do you think?'

'I'll phone through to the airstrip now. We'll soon know.'

They stood in the office, smoking cigarettes, and waited impatiently for the sergeant on the phone to come up with an answer. Finally, he said, 'I understand,' replaced the phone and turned, awe on his face.

'Reichsführer Himmler has just landed in the JU 52. He's on his way.'

It took all the strength that Bubi had to help him stay in control, then he said to Müller, 'Form an honour guard, of course, then bring him to the south sitting room. I think you'll find that's why he's here.'

'At your orders, Colonel,' and Müller hurried away, his eyes shining with excitement.

Bubi said to the sergeant, 'Would there be a little cognac available?'

The sergeant smiled. 'Not exactly the best, Colonel.' He opened a drawer and produced a half bottle.

Bubi drank deeply from the bottle itself. 'I see what you mean.' He handed the bottle back to the sergeant. 'It does hit the right spot though,' he said, and he turned and went out.

They were still waiting when he returned. Elsa said, 'Are we to sit here all morning?'

'I'm sorry. Things have taken a rather dramatic turn. Reichsführer Himmler will be here in a few moments. That was his plane.'

It was perhaps at that moment that the gravity of the situation really struck home to Elsa. She put a hand to her mouth and it was Max who said, 'That bad, Bubi?'

'I'm afraid so.'

It was ten minutes later that the door opened. Müller led the way in, turned and raised his arm in salute and Himmler walked in wearing black uniform and cap, his eyes glittering behind the steel-rimmed glasses.

'Ah, there you are, Hartmann. Is this matter resolved?'

'I'm afraid not, Reichsführer.'

'As I feared, which is why I decided to divert my plane, but I really don't have time to waste. I'm due in Paris as soon as possible, so let's get on with it.' He turned to Max, Harry and Elsa. 'Colonel Hartmann has told me that he has explained the purpose of your presence here. It would seem you are being difficult.'

Elsa, proud to the last and close to tears, said, 'You can't treat me like this. I'm Baroness von Halder and –'

'You are a traitor to the Reich,' Himmler said tranquilly. 'Many of your wretched associates have already paid the price for their treachery. If I'd had my way, you would have gone down the same road. However, you do serve a purpose.'

Max was on his feet. 'Damn you!'

Himmler said to Müller, 'Colonel, you will relieve this officer of his pistol.'

Müller drew his own weapon, went forward and complied. It was Harry who said, 'Look, let's get on with this farce. What is it you want?'

'Conspiracy against the Führer carries only a summary sentence. Death by hanging with piano wire, the execution to be filmed as a record to, shall we say, encourage the others.' He nodded to Müller. 'The curtain.'

Müller did as he was told and Bubi started the projector.

The film was absolutely horrific, one wretched victim after another brought in by SS guards, all rank insignia removed from their uniforms. With piano wire nooses around their necks, they were lifted up to be suspended from meathooks. Some defecated in death and the final convulsions were appalling to see. Particularly harrowing were the executions of two women, one who appeared to be at least seventy.

When the film ended, there was a stunned silence. Suddenly Elsa gagged, got to her feet and lurched to the fireplace and was sick. Müller went and pulled the curtains. It was Himmler who spoke first.

'I deplore violence of any sort, but when confronted with treachery, the Third Reich must protect itself. Men and women, all traitors must accept the same punishment.' He turned to Max and Harry. 'In your case, you have the chance to perform a great service. In return, your mother's life will be spared. If you persist in being difficult . . .' He shrugged. 'You've seen what happens. There is only one penalty. The Führer's express order.' Elsa lurched back to the couch, a handkerchief to her face, and Himmler turned to Max. 'You intend to be sensible, Baron, I trust.'

'Yes, damn you!' Max told him.

Himmler turned to Harry. 'And you, Colonel?'

Harry remained silent, his face white.

Himmler leaned in and spoke quietly. 'I need hardly point out that if your mother has to pay the ultimate penalty, then so shall Baron von Halder. Are you ready to sacrifice them *both*, Colonel?'

'You lousy little bastard,' Harry said, but Himmler saw that he had won.

'Excellent.' Himmler turned to Bubi. 'I'll be on my way again. I leave this matter in your capable hands, Colonel, and envy you your inevitable success.'

He nodded to Müller, who followed him out. Elsa sobbed

quietly, while Max lit a cigarette and Harry stared at the wall. 'Do you really think I can carry this off, Bubi?' Max asked.

'With your brother's assistance. You've got twenty-four hours to go over it together, then you go.'

'You swine,' Elsa said. 'How can you be a party to this?'

'I told you Himmler had me by the throat,' Bubi said. 'I'm part Jewish. I didn't think he knew, but that devil knows everything. It taints my family – my wife's dead, but there's my old father and his sister and that's just the beginning.'

Max said with genuine compassion, 'I'm truly sorry.'

'So am I. However, we're stuck now.' He took a deep breath. 'All right, first things first. Now that we've established that you're going, we must do something about your face.'

'My face?'

'Yes, your brother has a prominent scar on his left cheek. We'll have to take care of that.'

Max and Harry exchanged questioning looks.

'But how?'

'Schroeder's come up with an idea. I'll let him tell you.'

'Let's get on with it, then,' Max said and let Bubi lead the way. When the others had gone ahead, he put his hand on Harry's arm. 'We'll figure something out, brother.' Harry nodded grimly and left the room.

FOURTEEN

At noon Bubi led the way along a corridor to the room Schroeder had set up as a surgery. Harry followed on his crutches, Max at his side. Schroeder wore a white coat over his uniform. There was an assortment of medical equipment and an orderly also in a white coat.

Schroeder said, 'It's not exactly what I'm used to but we manage.' He nodded to Harry. 'If you would sit here.' Harry lowered himself down and Schroeder turned to Max. 'I've given you the easy chair, Colonel, it's the best I can do, but first please put on this white robe.'

The orderly helped him into it and Max sat on the large leather club chair. 'What happens now?'

Schroeder was charging a hypodermic. 'This is a local anaesthetic. It will freeze your face for a couple of hours. It works almost instantly.'

Max winced as the needle entered his cheek. After a moment or two, he grunted, 'Now what?'

Schroeder was examining Harry's left cheek. 'Good work and comparatively recent, am I right?'

'Yes.'

Schroeder turned to Max. 'Let's say you banged your face in the crash, leading to external bruising on the left side. As your brother's scar is only recent, it would be reasonable to assume that it would burst.'

'If you say so.' Suddenly Max couldn't feel his face.

'It would therefore be necessary to stitch it up again.' Schroeder nodded. 'Which is what I shall do.'

'But he doesn't have a scar,' Harry pointed out.

'True, but he soon will have.' Schroeder nodded to the orderly. 'Hold his head and you, Colonel, grip the arms of the chair.'

Max did as he was told. Schroeder moved to the table containing his surgical instruments, picked up a flat steel bar, turned and, without warning, struck Max across the left cheek. Max's head turned at the force of it in spite of the orderly's hold, but he felt nothing. Schroeder hit him twice more with much less force then dropped the bar into a bucket.

'Good, that should bruise nicely.'

He turned to Harry and took a small tape measure from his pocket. 'With your permission, Colonel?' He measured the scar carefully, then turned and held the tape against Max's cheek. 'Good.' He nodded to the orderly. 'Get ready.'

The man got out an enamel dish and cotton wool pads and stood waiting. Schroeder took a scalpel from the table and turned. 'You won't feel a thing, Colonel, trust me.'

'Just get on with it,' Max told him.

Very carefully, Schroeder drew the scalpel down Max's left cheek. Blood oozed and the orderly immediately sponged it with the pads. Schroeder dropped the scalpel into the bucket, reached on to the table and picked up a metal canister. He sprayed the wound twice.

'A new invention. It coagulates the blood instantly. Now comes the art work.'

'You're good, I'll say that for you,' Max said.

Harry, totally horrified, managed to get a cigarette out and lit it with hands that shook a little. 'For Christ's sake, ' he said.

Schroeder stitched the wound carefully and rapidly and when

he was finished, he covered it with a surgical plaster, swabbed the face and stood back.

'An interesting experience. I'm rather pleased with myself.'

'You know your business, I'll say that for you,' Max gasped.

Schroeder picked up a small box from the table as Max stood and the orderly removed the blood-spattered smock. 'You'll be in pain soon when the effect of the local wears off. These are morphine ampoules, a battle pack. Break the end off with your finger nails. A quick jab is all that's necessary.'

'You're too kind.' Max put the box in the map pocket of his baggy Luftwaffe pants. 'Now what?'

'Well, if you're up to it, lunch in the dining room – soft food for you, Colonel. Afterwards, I believe Colonel Hartmann has plans for you.'

Harry pushed himself up on his crutches and said, 'I need a drink after that.'

'*You* need a drink?' Max laughed lopsidedly and put an arm round him. 'You always were a selfish bastard.'

They had the dining room to themselves. Max, Harry, Elsa and Bubi. She was horrified at the sight of Max's face.

'What have they done to you?'

'It's necessary, Mutti. Harry has a scar, so I must have a scar.'

She was almost beside herself. 'But your beautiful face! And listen to me, I've thought of something. Even if this works, even if Max does what he set out to do . . . how does he get away?'

Harry, spooning potatoes onto his plate, said, 'An excellent point, Hartmann. What does he do?'

'Well, he has access to aircraft. He could conceivably fly back in one of the Lysanders.'

'And if that isn't possible?'

'We have agents in London at the Portuguese embassy. Portuguese boats still come into Liverpool and the Pool of London, and they are neutral, remember. We should be able to arrange a passage to Lisbon for Max.'

'Passage to Lisbon?' Harry snorted. 'With the whole country locked up tight after Eisenhower's death?'

There was a pause and Max said, 'Well, you can't have everything.'

Elsa glared at him. 'You mean you intend to go through with this madness?'

'I don't see that I have much choice, Mutti, not after seeing the film. I'm thinking of you.'

'No,' she cried. 'Don't put this one on me. I won't have it,' and she got up and ran out.

In her bedroom suite, Elsa sat on the window seat, smoked a cigarette nervously and told Rosa Stein everything.

'They're bastards, all of them. I'm expected to sympathize with Bubi Hartmann, but why should I? He's sending Max to certain death. The whole thing is beyond belief.'

Rosa said carefully, 'But with Reichsführer Himmler in total control, what can be done?'

'I'll go to Berlin. I'll appeal to the Führer.'

'Baroness, I must say this. In the first place we are prisoners here, so Berlin is out. In the second place, the Führer will listen to Himmler, not you.' She shook her head. 'Finally you learn, Baroness, what the Third Reich is all about.'

Elsa stared at her. 'There must be something I can do to save my sons from this insanity.'

Rosa gazed sadly at her, this woman she had served and loved for years in spite of her arrogance, petulance, selfishness and self-regard.

'No, Baroness, there is nothing to be done.'

A knock came at the door, she opened it and Bubi and Major Müller entered. Elsa stared at them coldly. 'I wish to see my sons.'

'That's not possible right now, Baroness,' Bubi told her. 'This operation has in effect begun and they have much to do. No interference can be tolerated.'

'I insist. I can't allow them to continue.'

Bubi had expected this. He'd realized that her attitude could well jeopardize the entire project. He took a deep breath. 'I regret to tell you that by direct order of Reichsführer Himmler, you may not see your sons again until this matter is concluded. If you will collect your things, you are to be transferred to the hunting lodge at the other end of the estate.'

'I refuse to go.' She stood there, defiant.

'Then my further instructions are to have you returned to Berlin, by force if necessary. If you wish to remain here, it's the hunting lodge and no further disruption.'

She seemed to age then and sat down. 'No, you win, I'll go, but may I please see my sons? Just once?'

'After Max has gone, you can see Harry. That's the best I can do.' Bubi turned to Müller. 'See to the Baroness for me, Major.'

'Of course, Colonel.'

Outside in the corridor, Bubi lit a cigarette, his hands shaking, his thoughts full of self-disgust. 'Dear God,' he whispered. 'Where does it all end?'

He walked to the small library, where Harry and Max were talking.

'Right,' Bubi said. 'Photographs first. Let's see what you've got, Harry.'

Harry reluctantly took out his wallet. 'That's me and Molly Sobel, at the entrance to the Savoy.'

'What were you doing there?'

'Dancing, in the River Room.'

'Name of the band?'

'Carrol Gibbons and the Savoy Orpheans.'

'Very good. She looks nice.'

Harry looked at Bubi, but said nothing for a moment, before continuing. 'This is Molly and me at Cold Harbour. Cold Harbour again: Zec Acland, the lifeboat cox you spoke to, Max. Julie Legrande, the housekeeper. Brigadier Munro and Major Jack Carter, his aide.'

Bubi was making notes. He said, 'I've got a file from Berlin. Photos of Munro and information on his organization. Let's see what we need. Details of the relationship with Doctor Sobel, Cold Harbour, Eisenhower, his headquarters at Southwick House, how the Courier Service works.'

He sighed. 'We've got a long day ahead of us, gentlemen. We'd better get started.'

Grimly, the brothers set to work.

The hunting lodge was comfortable enough. There was a log fire and beamed ceilings in the sitting room and the main bedroom had old-fashioned oak furniture, another log fire and an excellent bathroom. Rosa unpacked the suitcases and Elsa prowled from room to room, unable to be easy.

There was a drinks cabinet in the sitting room. She had a large brandy, but instead of calming her, it seemed to make her worse. She poured another and sat down. At last it was beginning to sink in. All her life she'd had position, power and, thanks to Abe Kelso, money. She went upstairs to the bedroom. Rosa was unpacking the smaller bags now, laying out jewellery on the dressing-table. She produced the Walther PPK.

'Where shall I put this, Baroness?'

Elsa held out her hand. 'I'll take care of it.'

She went back downstairs and put the Walther on the couch beside her. It was all over. Max was as good as dead and they'd finish off Harry afterwards and all because of her. It was the only reason her boys were doing this. If only she didn't exist, what a different situation it would be. It was then, of course, her brain clouded by the brandy, that she knew what she must do. She picked up the Walther, pulled back the slider, then put it down again.

She called, 'Rosa, come here.'

Rosa appeared a moment later. 'Yes, Baroness?'

'Phone through to the château. Ask Colonel Hartmann to come here at once.'

'Yes, Baroness.'

Bubi was informed of the call by the orderly sergeant while sitting in the room they were using as an officers' mess. Müller and Schroeder were with him.

'I can't take it,' he said. 'I've got enough on my hands.'

'We'll come with you,' Müller said and smiled to Schroeder. 'Good experience for you.'

The lodge had two men on the entrance and there were prowler guards in the vicinity. Elsa, peering out of the window, saw the *Kübelwagen* approach, went to the couch and sat down. She had secreted the Walther between the cushions and now she lit a cigarette. She had opened a bottle of champagne while waiting and called to Rosa.

'A glass of champagne.'

'Of course, Baroness.'

'After you've admitted them go to the kitchen and stay out of the way.'

'As you say, Baroness.'

The bell on the door rang. Rosa went and opened it and Bubi

entered, followed by Müller and Schroeder. 'There you are, Baroness, is there a problem?' he asked.

'Only the existence of you Nazi bastards,' she said. 'And the problem of my own existence. After all, without me, you've got no hold on my sons.'

Her hand came up clutching the Walther and Bubi, seeing it all and realizing what she intended, cried, 'No!'

He threw himself to one side and Müller, following him, took the first two bullets, which lifted him back as Bubi scrambled for the cover of the other couch. Schroeder, pulling open his pistol holster, found the Mauser it contained and instinctively fired three times, hammering Elsa, Baroness von Halder, into the back of the couch.

Bubi stood up and crouched over Müller. He looked up. 'Dead.'

Schroeder, leaning over Elsa, said, 'So is she.' He looked at the Mauser. 'I never killed anyone before.' He seemed dazed.

'It's not your fault, she wanted to die.'

There was hammering on the door and he opened it, admitting a sergeant and two men. They stood there, aghast.

'Colonel Müller and the Baroness are dead,' Bubi said and turned to Schroeder. 'I'm putting you in charge of this. Keep it all under wraps. Neither the Baron nor Colonel Kelso must know.'

Schroeder was baffled. 'But why not, Colonel?'

'The task the Baron is to perform, he accepted with reluctance and only to save his mother from the ultimate penalty for offences against the Reich. How would he react if he knew she was dead?'

'Ah, I see now.' Schroeder nodded. 'I'll get on with it.' He turned to the telephone and paused. 'What about the maid, Colonel?'

Bubi swore and went to the stairs on the run, but of Rosa

Stein there was no sign. He came down and went into the kitchen. He was out in the instant and spoke to the sergeant.

'There was another woman here, the maid. Tell the prowler guards to look for her.'

'At once, Colonel.' The sergeant nodded to his men and ran out.

Bubi took a deep breath, thinking of the Reichsführer in Paris, but that could wait. He lit a cigarette and drove back to the château in the *Kübelwagen*.

In the kitchen, the door partially open, Rosa had witnessed the whole appalling scene, had heard everything. Terrified out of her mind, her only thought was to get away. Grabbing an old raincoat from a peg, she pulled it on and opened the outside door.

It was then that she had her first piece of luck, for the prowler guards, attracted by the sound of gunfire, were running round to the front of the house. She waited until the last one had disappeared then hurried across the lawn to the gate in the brick wall. On the other side was a wood. She passed through it and found a stretch of the heath, what seemed to be a forest on the other side. She took a deep breath and ran for her life.

Max and Harry were still in the library when Bubi went in. He forced a smile. 'Still at it?'

'And then some,' Max told him. 'There seemed to be a lot of activity out there a little while ago. Guards all over the place when I looked out.'

'Yes, they thought there were intruders down in the wood. Possibly poachers. Are you feeling confident?'

'You must be joking,' Max told him. 'This is a hell of a thing to expect, Bubi. Do I kiss Molly, for example? Women are women. I may look the same to her, but I might not taste the same.'

Harry said, 'The state your face is in, she'll be afraid to touch you.'

Bubi lit a cigarette. 'Keep going over it. You could pull it off, Max.'

'And pigs might fly,' Max told him. 'Just remember, Bubi, I'm not doing this because I believe it's right and neither is Harry. It's solely because we can't bear to think of our mother on that meathook.'

'I know, I know, but with luck it could be over very quickly. You fly over to Cold Harbour, Munro brings you up to London at once. Eisenhower will want to see you – he's bound to. For God's sake, you're the hero of the hour. Hayes Lodge in London, Southwick House at Portsmouth – it makes no difference. You could be in and out, Max, a couple of days. These Portuguese diplomats I'm using, I've already given them instructions to check on shipping.'

'You'd better tell me who they are.'

Bubi explained about the Rodrigues brothers and Sarah Dixon and wrote down her address on a piece of paper.

'These people know what this is about?'

'In complete detail and they also know who you are. Eisenhower is nothing to them. The brothers are in this for the cash and Mrs Dixon is IRA.'

'Tell me more about her.'

Bubi opened a file and took out a sheet of paper. 'All there.'

Max nodded. 'There is, of course, one other solution to all this. It's probably also occurred to Harry. Twins, you know, enjoy a kind of telepathy. What do you think, brother?'

'Oh, you mean the glorious moment when you decide to die for the Führer and the Reich, draw your pistol in Eisenhower's office in front of everyone, shoot him down and die in a hail of bullets?'

'Exactly.' Max turned to Bubi. 'So simple and so convenient. Anyway, when do I go, Bubi?'

'I thought about four o'clock in the morning. You steal my Storch from the airstrip and it's not much more than an hour to Cold Harbour. The weather won't be marvellous, but it'll be dawn around five.'

'Sounds good to me. Best to get on with it.'

'A couple of bursts of machine-gunfire in the fuselage would be a nice touch,' Harry said, sarcastically.

'Actually, an excellent idea.' Bubi stood up. 'I'd go over it again if I were you. We could dine at nine if you like.'

'And say goodbye to Mutti,' Max said to Harry.

The lying began then. Bubi said, 'That's not possible, I'm afraid. Your mother has been difficult, to say the least. Himmler left explicit orders that the moment the operation began, she was to be held separately. She's staying at the hunting lodge at the other end of the estate. You can't see her, Max, and that's final.'

'Come on, Bubi,' Max said.

'Once you've gone, I'll let your brother visit her.' Bubi almost choked on the lie. 'That's the best I can do.'

There was a silence, then Max shrugged. 'Oh, what the hell, let's get on with it. Leave us to it, Bubi.'

Hartmann went out. Harry said, 'Time's running short, Max. Have you thought of anything yet?'

Gloomily, Max shook his head. 'We'll have to keep playing it out, see where it leads.'

'Christ.' Harry was silent for a moment, then: 'If it actually came down to it . . . if there were no way out . . . Do you really think you could do it?'

'You saw that film,' Max said. 'Those two women kicking on the wire, their eyes bulging, and you know what the worst thing was?'

Harry nodded. 'Their bowels opening.'

'Harry, I'd go to hell to get the devil himself before I'd let that happen to my mother.'

Around the same time in London, Fernando and Joel Rodrigues presented themselves at Sarah Dixon's flat. Lacey and an expert photographer, a constable named Parry from Scotland Yard, were in close pursuit and got pictures of them going in and more of them coming out. Lacey and Parry followed them along Westbourne Grove to the Italian restaurant Sarah and Fernando had used for years.

'There's something funny about this,' Lacey said. 'I've seen that woman before.'

'A lot of people live in those flats,' Parry told him.

'Brilliant. You're a truly great detective. Personally, I always believe in going for the throat. Take out the film and put a fresh roll in. I'm going to get it developed at once. I'll be back in a moment.'

He entered the restaurant, which was reasonably busy, stood at the end of the bar and ordered a glass of wine. As the head waiter passed, he pulled him over. He produced his warrant card.

'Read that.'

The head waiter's eyes rounded. 'Is there a problem, Detective Constable?'

'What's your name?'

'Franco.'

'Right, Franco, if you tell me what I want to know, I won't close you down. *Capisce?*' Franco nodded eagerly. 'The two men and the woman in the window? Who are they?'

'The lady is Mrs Dixon, Mrs Sarah Dixon. The taller one is Senhor Rodrigues from the Portuguese embassy. They've been coming here for years. She lives nearby.'

'And the other?'

'Never seen him before.'

Lacey patted his shoulder. 'Good man. Not a word, everything normal. Do you follow me?'

'Absolutely, officer.'

Lacey turned and went out and found Parry on the other side of the road. Parry gave him the film. 'Everything okay?'

'Fine. Stay here, follow them afterwards and phone in. I'll take this film to the Yard and get it processed.' He turned away, then paused and turned back. 'Jesus Christ, I've just remembered where I've seen her.'

In his flat at Haston Place, Munro sat by the fire enjoying a hot toddy, leafing through files from the office, when the phone rang. He picked it up.

'Munro.'

'Carter, sir.'

'Ten o'clock, Jack, I was going to get an early night. I want to be in the office at six.'

'We have a problem, Brigadier.'

It was a phrase they only used in the most extreme situations. Munro said, 'Bad?'

'Very bad, sir. Chief Inspector Riley and one of his henchmen are with me. I think you should see us.'

'Soon as you can, Jack.'

Over coffee at the restaurant, Sarah, Fernando and Joel discussed the situation in low voices. Fernando said to Sarah, 'Does this give you a problem?'

'Killing Eisenhower?' She shook her head. 'He's nothing to me. To be honest, when it looked as if Germany was going to invade in '40 it seemed as if every Irish dream was going to come true.'

'Sarah, I love you,' Fernando said. 'But if Hitler had occupied Britain he'd have sent the Panzers rolling down to Dublin, believe me.'

'Perhaps, but it doesn't alter the present situation. This German posing as his brother, we do everything we can to help him. You check on the presence of Portuguese shipping in the Pool of London. He'll need help to get away.'

'He isn't going to go anywhere,' Fernando said. 'If he kills Eisenhower, he dies. However, we don't know when he arrives.'

'Soon,' she said. 'Anyway, let's go. I'm on early shift tomorrow. Are you staying, Fernando?'

He leaned across and kissed her. 'Joel's first night. I'd better settle him in.'

He paid the bill, they left, walked up Westbourne Grove and escorted her to the block of flats. 'Good night, darling,' Sarah said. 'We'll speak soon.'

Parry, in a doorway, photographed all this with his special non-flash camera. Sarah went in and the brothers walked down Westbourne Grove.

'You like her, this woman?' Joel said as they walked up Queensway.

'Like her? I love her,' Fernando told him. 'I'd marry her tomorrow if things were different.'

'Marry her? She's got ten years on you.'

They went down the steps to Bayswater underground station and Fernando said, 'I've always liked the girls, lots of sex and sex with her is okay, but it's more than that. She's worth all the tarts I've been to bed with put together.'

'But you couldn't have children.'

They stood on the platform and Fernando said, 'You like men, Joel, that's your business, but the love I feel for this woman, that's my business.'

The train came, they stepped on board and Parry followed.

In the sitting room at Munro's flat, Sean Riley introduced Lacey. Jack Carter poured Scotch and sodas at the sideboard and brought them over on a tray.

'You're going to need one, Brigadier.'

'Oh, dear.' Munro took a glass. 'All right, let's hear it.'

Riley described the arrival of Joel Rodrigues at Croydon, the blunder of the Berlin stamps in the passport. He went into Lacey's involvement in detail and brought things right up to date. He snapped a finger and Lacey passed him a cardboard file, which Riley opened and extracted black and white prints.

'The Rodrigues brothers, Brigadier, and the lady.'

Jack Carter took over. 'Fernando has been here for most of the war, now Senior Commercial Attaché. His brother, Joel, Commercial Attaché in Berlin, mysteriously transferred to courier duties from Lisbon to London.'

'And the woman?'

Jack Carter hesitated then said, 'Detective Constable Lacey recognized her, sir. His duties with Special Branch take him into SOE headquarters frequently.'

'What in the hell are you saying?' Munro demanded.

'She's on the staff at Baker Street, sir,' Lacey said. 'As Major Carter says, I recognized her.'

'Dear God.' Munro got up, went to the sideboard and poured another whisky. 'Tell me the worst.'

Carter nodded to Sean Riley, who took over. 'This is just a fast appraisal, Brigadier. We'll be more thorough tomorrow. The lady is Mrs Sarah Dixon, widow of a George Dixon, who died of cancer. She was born in London, English father, Irish mother. Her maiden name was Brown. Her grandfather, Patrick Brown, was an IRA activist, the Easter Rising in 1916. He was executed by British forces. She was a clerk at the War Office for some time, then transferred to SOE headquarters the other year. Clerical work, secretarial, all low-grade.'

'Low-grade?' Munro looked as if he might have a fit. 'How in the hell can we be sure of that when she has the run of the place? And how did she get into SOE headquarters anyway? Didn't anybody screen this woman?'

Carter sighed. 'We're still checking into that, I'm afraid. She may simply have been . . . overlooked.'

'Dear God.'

Carter said, 'But Brigadier, none of this makes sense. We destroyed the Abwehr networks in Britain years ago, most agents were turned. There just hasn't been anyone active.'

Munro sipped his whisky, frowning. 'If memory serves me, Jack, we had a report many years ago, actually before your time. It came to our attention that before the war a Major Klein at SD headquarters in Berlin had broken all the rules and set up an English network.'

Carter said, 'I know about that, sir, but it was only a whisper, I've read the file. Nothing substantial there at all.'

'But what if there was? What if there were agents in deep cover? What if, Jack?'

Riley said, 'Shall we pull them in, Brigadier?'

'No, the Rodrigues brothers would claim diplomatic immunity. The worst we could do would be to deport them.'

'But the woman, sir?' Riley said.

Munro shook his head. 'Total surveillance will do for the moment, Chief Inspector. Every contact she has must be recorded.

Put your best men on it.' He turned to Carter. 'A careful check at Baker Street, Jack. Do one of your regular security checks on everybody. That will disguise our true motives.'

'Of course, sir.'

Munro stood. 'I need your best work, gentlemen. This could be serious.'

When Bubi went into the dining room to join the brothers for dinner, he received a shock. For a wild moment he thought it was Harry standing by the fire in American uniform then realized that Harry, seated next to him, crutches on the floor, was wearing the Luftwaffe *Fliegerbluse* with Knight's Cross, Oak Leaves and Swords.

'My God,' Bubi said. 'It's unbelievable.'

'You'd better believe it,' Max told him. 'Isn't Müller joining us?'

'No, he was called to St Malo and Schroeder is busy. A guard broke his leg.' He turned to the orderly by the door. 'Right, now we eat.'

'Yes, go to a good death, but do it on a full stomach.' Max sat down at the table. As Harry joined him, he said, 'Is there anything I've forgotten?'

'Just take it easy. There are still people you won't recognize. General Sobel, for example. Relax, let them come to you.'

'I'll do my best.' Max glanced at the window. 'Listen to that rain. Pity the poor sailors at sea on a night like this.'

'Pity the poor pilots, more like.' Harry picked up a glass of wine. 'I can't think of an appropriate toast.'

'What about God help us all?' Max said.

Rosa, trudging through the forest, was totally miserable and thoroughly soaked. It was so dark now that she blundered into trees. Lightning crackled in the sky and momentarily lit things up and suddenly there was a track and some sort of hut. She staggered towards it, found a large door and opened it. It actually seemed warm in there and when the lightning crackled again, she saw a great pile of logs and several stalls, although there were no animals in there. There were piles of hay and rain drifted in through high open windows and thundered on the roof. She took off her wet raincoat and hung it on a stall, then she lay on a pile of hay and covered herself with it. It smelled good. She closed her eyes and was instantly asleep.

Max took his leave of Harry at three o'clock and was driven to the airstrip through pouring rain by Bubi, who parked the *Kübelwagen* inside one of the hangars. The Storch stood outside in the rain and Max, a military raincoat over his shoulders, lit a cigarette as an SS sergeant major in black Panzer uniform approached.

'You know what to do,' Bubi said.

The sergeant major turned to one of his men and held out his hands. The man passed him a Schmeisser. The sergeant major stepped out into the rain and fired a burst into the Storch's fuselage, close to the tail, then another burst into the port wing. He came back.

'Excellent.' Bubi turned to Max. 'This is it, I suppose.'

'Moment of truth.' Max held out his hand. 'Give me your Walther, Bubi, and the spare clip.' Bubi frowned and Max said patiently, 'I took it from the guard I knocked out and then shot another.'

'I see.' Bubi nodded. 'Of course.'

He took the Walther from his holster and the spare clip and handed them over. Max fired twice in the air. 'That should do it.' He put the gun and the clip into a pocket of the raincoat.

'Off you go then.' Bubi held out his hand. 'I'm sorry.'

'Not your fault, Bubi. I'll be off.'

He walked to the plane, where the sergeant major waited to open the cabin door for him. Max threw the raincoat inside, turned and nodded to Bubi, then climbed in. The door closed. He switched on. A moment later the prop started to turn, then quickened. Rain hammered against the perspex, but as always, what he called the plane feeling enveloped him. This was what he'd been born to do. To fly.

The Storch moved forward and turned into the wind. There was only diffused light from the airstrip buildings, but it was enough. He roared down the runway, pulled back on the column and lifted into the darkness.

FIFTEEN

A headwind slowed him down, but the flight was no trouble at all. He kept radio silence for the first forty minutes and then called in.

'Cold Harbour, Cold Harbour, are you receiving me?'

There was an almost instant reply. 'This is Cold Harbour receiving you loud and clear. Who are you?'

'Colonel Harry Kelso getting the hell out of Brittany in a Luftwaffe Storch. ETA twenty minutes.'

'Stand by.'

The RAF corporal on radio duty that morning was considerably shocked, reached for his telephone and rang through to Julie Legrande's bedroom. She answered a moment later, her voice sleepy.

'What is it?'

'The radio room. I've got Colonel Kelso on the air. Apparently he's escaped from France in a Storch.'

'My God.' Julie was fully awake now. 'I'll be right down.'

She scrambled out of bed, pulled off her nightdress and reached for her track suit.

Dawn suffused the sky, the light very strange, a great blanket of grey cloud at 1000 feet. Max went down to 500, the dark sea angry and storm-tossed below him. He sat there, hands steady on the control column, enjoying every moment in a strange way, for this was flying, this was the only thing that had ever mattered to him.

He was totally exposed now in the grey dawn light, a perfect target for any wandering Spitfire or Hurricane. He wouldn't stand a chance. Blown out of the sky in seconds. He laughed. What an end that would be to the whole sorry business, but it wouldn't help his mother or Harry or even poor old Bubi, all still in Himmler's hands.

Julie spoke over the radio. 'Harry?'

'The coast's coming up. Yes, it's me, Julie.'

'It's a miracle!'

'I'll be with you in ten minutes,' he said. 'A trifle battered, but otherwise unbowed, as our British friends say.'

'I'll be waiting at the airstrip. I'll phone Munro in London.'

'Yes, wake the old bastard up. Over and out.'

The bedside phone brought Munro awake and bad-tempered. 'Who on earth is that at this time of the morning?'

'It's Julie. Something astonishing. We've had Harry Kelso on the radio. He's escaped from Brittany in a Storch. He'll be landing in ten minutes.'

Munro swung his legs to the floor. 'Good God, are you sure?'

'I've spoken to him myself, Brigadier.'

'How did he sound?'

'He said he was battered but unbowed.'

'Typical Harry. I'll arrange a Lysander from Croydon. I'll be with you as soon as possible.'

He sat there thinking about it, then went downstairs to the basement flat, went in and shook Jack Carter awake in bed and told him.

Carter said, 'I can't believe it.'

'Let's get moving, Jack. Phone the Courier Service at Croydon and book a Lysander.'

'I'll get right on it, Brigadier.' Carter sat up and reached for his false leg. 'Does Molly know?'

'Of course not. I'll tell her now, but there are more important things in life than young love, Jack.'

He went back upstairs, knocked on the door of her bedroom and went in. She'd been awake for some time, but then she'd slept badly since the news of the crash.

She sat up. 'Uncle Dougal? What is it?'

'Some rather astonishing news, my dear,' and he sat on the edge of the bed.

Max swept in from the sea and there it was below. Cold Harbour exactly as Harry had described, the lifeboat tied up at the quay, the pub, the cottages and finally, the manor and the lake. He skimmed over the pine trees and dropped down on the grass runway and taxied towards the hangar, where half a dozen ground crew waited, sheltering from the rain just inside. As he cut the engine and opened the door, they ran forward and it was with some irony that he noted the black Luftwaffe overalls and R A F sidecaps.

'Bloody marvellous, Colonel,' the flight sergeant said and they all crowded round, patting him on the back. 'Your face doesn't look too happy, sir.'

'Oh, I'll survive. Banged up when the Lysander went down.' Max pretended to examine the Storch's fuselage. 'You'll need some repair work here, Flight. I took off under fire, so to speak, but she flew well enough. You turned out pretty quickly.' He reached inside the Storch for the German military raincoat and draped it over his shoulders.

'Oh, that was Miss Legrande, sir. She said she'd be right down and here she is.'

Julie drove up in the Jeep, braked to a halt, got out and flung her arms around him. 'You'll never know how good it is to see you, Harry Kelso, but my God, your face.'

'Which is why I won't kiss you. It hurts.' He managed a grin. 'But I can still eat and you want to know something? I'm starving.'

'I'll take you down to the Hanged Man. A full English breakfast. Zec's always up early getting the fire going.' The rain increased its force. 'Come on, get in.'

He sat in the passenger seat. There was a packet of Senior Service cigarettes and a lighter in the glove compartment. 'You don't mind if I help myself?'

As he opened the pack, she said, 'I always thought you hated those things. I've only ever seen you smoke Players.'

He recovered quickly. 'Julie, my love, after what I've been through, I can smoke anything.'

She smiled. 'Yes, I can imagine,' and turned into the High Street.

Max, the first hurdle safely passed, leaned back, the adrenalin flowing, everything sharp and clear.

Zec Acland knelt at the fire, carefully placing more logs, then turned as the door opened and Julie stepped into the bar, followed by Max. Zec hadn't been so astonished in his entire life and stood up.

'Well, bless my soul, Colonel, and us thinking you were over there maybe dead and gone.'

'Almost, but not quite.'

'Your face is a mess.'

'Could be worse.'

'I heard a plane coming in.'

'That was me. I managed to steal a Storch and made a run for it.'

'And that couldn't have been easy.' Zec started to fill his pipe.

'I had to shoot one of the guards.' Max took the Walther from his raincoat pocket. 'The name of the game.'

Zec looked grim. 'The bloody war. Never stops. Still, not long now. D-Day soon, that's what we're calling it, so they tell me. I reckon you've earned a drink in spite of the hour.'

Julie said, 'I'll make some breakfast. I can hear you in the kitchen. I phoned Munro. He'll be flying down.'

Zec poured two whiskies and added a little water. Max said, 'Did he want the details?'

'No, but I couldn't have told him, I don't know them myself,' Julie called.

Zec leaned on the other side of the bar. 'What happened over there?'

Max stuck to the facts as closely as possible. The successful dropping of Jacaud, how he'd been bounced by the ME 109s. How the SS patrol had saved his bacon.

'I don't see any sign of Tarquin here,' Zec observed.

'Tarquin's gone, Zec, the Lysander fireballed just after I got out.'

'I'm truly sorry about that.'

Julie appeared in the kitchen door. 'That's terrible.'

'That's life,' Max continued. 'They took me to Château Mor-laix. My face was battered in the crash, the original scar had burst but they had a good doctor there. He stitched me up again. They didn't treat me too badly. It was just chance that an SS Panzer unit had moved in to the château.'

'Then what?' Julie asked.

'They had word that I was to be shipped out to Berlin. There's a Luftwaffe feeder station just outside the village and they were sending a plane.' He was warming to his story. 'I realized that once that happened, I was finished. The escape was just an absurd chance and very simple. I'd been dining late with the commandant and said I didn't feel very well, so the doctor gave me a box of morphine ampoules. There was a guard on my door, of course. I pretended to go to bed, lay there thinking about it and decided to make a break sometime after three. The bathroom was very old fashioned, with a French window leading to a terrace and steps down.'

'And no guard?' Zec asked.

'Prowler guards in the grounds, that's all. I simply went down the steps, turned the corner and there was a *Kübelwagen*, the driver standing beside it, smoking a cigarette. I picked up a half brick from the edge of a flower bed and struck him on the head from behind. That's where I got the Walther. I slipped on his military raincoat and sidecap and drove away.'

Julie brought in a dish of eggs, bacon and toast. She put it on one of the tables. 'Come and get it.' She sat down. 'What happened then?'

'I drove up to the airstrip at Morlaix. It's no big deal. Rather like Cold Harbour, but the runway's very long. You could get most things in.' He was eating now and enjoying the eggs and bacon. 'Anyway, there was an ME 109 in one of the hangars and a Storch parked on the apron. It was raining heavily, no sign of guards. I suppose they were all sheltering in the hangars. I drove up to the Storch, got out and opened the door. According to the fuel gauge, she was full. Then the sentry appeared, running across the apron, so I shot him. I got in, switched on and did the quickest take-off of my life. Two other sentries appeared and sprayed me with their Schmeissers, but no great harm and here I am.' He'd finished his breakfast and sat back. 'All I need now is a great cup of coffee.'

'Coffee?' Julie said as she stacked the plates on the way. 'I thought you'd switched to tea.'

Mistake number two.

Max grinned. 'All I've had since last Friday is coffee, Julie. The SS has never heard of tea, but you're right. Back to tea it is.'

Up at the manor, he played it very carefully and allowed himself to be taken by Julie to the room Harry had been using previously. He accomplished this by pretending not to feel so good.

'My face hurts like hell. I think I need an injection.'

She took his hand at the top of the stairs and led him straight to the bedroom. He put the military coat on the bed and got out the battle pack Schroeder had given him.

'Here, let me.' Julie snapped off the end of the ampoule. He took off his tunic and she jabbed it into his arm. 'Your slacks aren't too good,' she said. 'There's a twelve-inch rip in the left leg. Let's see what I've got in the supply room.'

Supply room. Yes, Harry had mentioned that.

Max said, 'I'll come with you.'

He was astonished by all the uniforms, the weaponry, but managed not to show it. Julie went through the stand and found a pair of khaki slacks.

'British Army, officers for the use of.' She handed them to him. 'They'll do until you get to Haston Place. You must have a spare uniform there.'

Haston Place. Number three. Basement flat with Carter downstairs. Munro's bedroom on the right at the top of the stairs, Molly next to him and Harry third door along by the windows. Sitting room opposite the head of the stairs. SOE headquarters ten minutes away in Baker Street.

Max said, 'Oh, I've got dozens. I'll go and change.'

'I'll see you in the library.'

He descended the broad stairs ten minutes later. Library to the left, dining room to the right, kitchen through green baize door. He found Julie by the fire, piling on logs. She had a look at him.

'That's better. How do you feel?'

'Much better. The morphine acts very quickly.'

'Not too much, we don't want you to end up like some Victorian poet, totally hooked.'

'I've only ever been addicted to one thing in my life, flying.'

'Yes, we all know that. I've got to go down to the pub and put the pies in the oven for the crew's lunch. I suppose you'd like to take it easy?'

'I've never taken it easy in my life, Julie, I'll come with you. I could do with a stroll to clear my head.'

'We'll drive down and walk on the beach later. You'll need your raincoat.'

'Yes, I'll go and get it.'

In the bedroom, he draped the coat over his shoulders, the Walther heavy in the right-hand pocket. He took it out and debated whether to leave it and yet there was something reassuring about the weight. He replaced it in his pocket and went downstairs. As he reached the bottom, Julie came out of the library, wearing an old raincoat and beret.

'You look very French this morning.'

'So I should. I've just had a call from Munro. He's just about to leave in a Lysander. He's got Jack with him. Molly wanted to come, but she has a heavy operating schedule this morning.'

Strange, the feeling of relief.

Max said, 'I'll see her soon enough.'

Julie took his arm. 'That's no way to be, Harry Kelso, you should be straining at the leash. Men.' She shrugged. 'I don't know. No romance at all. Come on, let's go.'

Zec and the crew were working in the lifeboat. Max stood

on the edge of the quay, looking down, and they called up to him. 'Great to have you back, Colonel,' cried one and another, huge and with tangled hair and beard, said, 'Sorry about Tarquin.'

Strange that. In the pub, he went behind the bar and helped himself to two packets of Players cigarettes. He lit one and leaned in the doorway watching Julie at work. She put a tray of pies in the oven and closed the door.

'That's it.' She turned. 'All right, let's have that walk.'

The tide was in, but there was plenty of sand at the foot of the cliffs and sand dunes by the headland tufted with coarse grass.

'How do you feel now?' she asked.

'Much better. Why do you ask?'

'Oh, you seem a little subdued, that's all.'

He managed a smile. 'I don't believe there is such a word, but I think we could say it was a subduing experience.'

'Silly of me.' She slipped her arm through his and they continued.

And he was grateful for this, the contact with this woman and the fact that she had accepted him and that Zec Acland and his men had. It gave him confidence, a chance to catch his breath. *And Eisenhower and the purpose of his being here?* He pushed that thought as far away as possible.

They sat on some decaying wood pilings. Julie said, 'Would you marry Molly, Harry?'

'If she'd have me, you mean?' He laughed.

'Oh, she'd have you all right.'

'I don't think people should marry when there's a war on, especially someone like me. That Lysander crash, for example. I was damn lucky to survive. In fact, I shouldn't have survived as long as I have. Flying's a hazardous sport, Julie.'

'Not for you, it isn't, not any more.'

'What do you mean?'

271

'I'd be amazed if they ever allow you to fly again. You're grounded, Harry. That's my opinion, anyway. As they tell prisoners, for you the war is over.'

He sat there thinking about it. 'It could be, I suppose, we'll see,' and then a Lysander swept in from the sea.

She jumped up. 'There goes Munro. We'd better get back.'

In the library beside the fire with Julie serving tea and sandwiches, Munro and Jack Carter sat opposite Max and listened intently as he told them the same story he'd given Julie and Zec.

When he was finished, Munro said, 'Amazing.'

Jack said, 'Jacaud told us in his first report about this SS Panzer unit arriving unexpectedly to take over the château.'

'Lucky for me they were there,' Max said. 'I'd have burned in that crash. Couldn't Jacaud come up with any more information?'

'Not possible,' Munro said. 'His report said the SS had the château, the village and the surrounding area wrapped up tight.'

'His second report did mention a JU 52 landing at the airstrip, if you recall, sir,' Jack reminded him. 'But no one could get close enough to see what was going on.'

'Oh, I can tell you that,' Max said. 'Major Müller, the commandant, told me they were dropping off replacement engines for two of his tanks.'

'Poor Müller,' Munro said. 'This isn't going to look good on his record at all. Anyway, finish your sandwiches and it's Croydon next stop. I rang Teddy West.'

Air Vice Marshal West and no photo.

'How is he?' Max asked.

'Ecstatic. He's flying up from Southwick House to join Eisenhower at Hayes Lodge. I've left it to him to break the good news to the Supreme Commander. I'm sure Ike will want to see you himself.'

'I look forward to it,' Max said.

Munro stood up. 'Great to have you back, Harry, even if you do look as if a truck's run over your face. Molly sends her love. I thought we'd dine at the River Room tonight, she'll be free then. We'll invite her father. Make a party of it. Celebrate your return from the dead.'

'Sounds good to me,' Max said.

'Right, then let's get moving.'

Rosa Stein had slept for at least twelve hours, the sleep of utter exhaustion. When she finally awakened, rain still thundered against the roof. She got up, went to the entrance and peered out. The forest was draped with mist, but the track, of course, was clearly visible. The trouble was she had no idea where she was, no sense of direction. She supposed she could stay where she was for a while – at least it was dry and warm. She cupped her hands to catch rainwater gushing from a spout, drank then bathed her face.

She couldn't get the memory of those dreadful events at the hunting lodge out of her mind. It was a nightmare. She started to weep uncontrollably, went back to the pile of hay and lay down. After a while she fell asleep again.

When they landed at Croydon, it was early afternoon and again Max was saved by chance for, as he assisted Jack Carter out of the Lysander, the major said, 'Air Vice Marshal West over there, sir.'

Max turned as Munro went to meet West. 'Well, here he is, Teddy. I'm afraid his face looks like one of the ruins that Cromwell knocked about a bit, but you can't have everything.'

West actually hugged Max. 'You young bastard, don't you ever frighten me like that again.'

'I'll do my best, sir,' Max replied.

'Dammit, we'll be running out of medals.'

Munro said, 'We're dining at the River Room tonight, Molly and her father, Jack and myself. Why not join us?'

'I'll do my best. Splendid idea, but for the moment I'll have to love you and leave you. I'm due to see Ike at Hayes Lodge. You can drop me off.'

'Our pleasure,' Munro said and led the way.

At Haston Place, Max found Harry's bedroom with no trouble. He dropped his military raincoat on the bed and checked the wardrobe. The extra uniforms hung neatly there, shirts and socks on the shelves, spare shoes.

There was a knock at the door and Carter looked in. 'The Brigadier's gone off to Baker Street, but he's asked me to drop you off at Guy's Hospital. He wants Molly to check you over. Frankly, he's horrified at the state of your face. He's right, Harry. You could have a hairline fracture or something.'

'When do we go?'

'It's got to be now. Molly's due in theatre at four-thirty. She'll make her own way to the River Room.'

'Fine, I'll have time to come back here and change into a fresh uniform later.'

'Bags of time, old chap.'

'Let's go then.'

Casualty at Guy's was as busy as usual. Jack led the way to the reception desk. 'Colonel Kelso for Doctor Sobel. He's expected.'

'That's right, Major.' The receptionist picked up the phone. 'Colonel Kelso's here.' She replaced it. 'That was X-ray. Someone will be along in a minute.'

And a minute it was. A young man in a white coat appeared, one eye obviously glass, the surrounding area badly damaged.

'Colonel Kelso? We are in a mess. This way, sir.' He smiled beautifully at Carter. 'You can come if you want, love.' He noticed the major's leg. 'Dear me, we are three crocks, aren't we? My name's Walker, by the way.'

'Where did you get yours?' Max asked.

'Lancaster over Berlin. I was a rear-gunner. Into my second tour and I got a shell splinter in the face. I tell you, love, I must have been mad.'

'Aren't we all.'

Walker looked at his medals. 'But you particularly, if you don't mind me saying so. In here,' and he opened a door.

Max lay on a table and did as he was told and Jack Carter sat in the corner. Walker took his pictures, whistling cheerfully, then vanished through another door. He was back in ten minutes, holding the X-rays.

'No fractures, Colonel, everything normal except for your face looking like a side of raw meat. I'll take you to Doctor Sobel now.' As they walked down the corridor, he said, 'I love your uniform and those RAF wings. You were a Yank in the RAF, weren't you?'

'That's right,' Max said.

'I saw the movie with Tyrone Power. A right load of old cobblers, but he was lovely, mind you.' Max tried not to laugh and Jack was obviously having similar difficulties. Walker opened a door. 'In here.'

Molly in a white coat, a stethoscope around her neck, sat behind a desk. She jumped up. 'My God, Harry.'

'Oh, so that's the way it is,' Walker said and put the X-rays on the desk. 'He's okay, Doc, no fracture. I didn't remove his plaster because I didn't need to.' He turned. 'All the best, gentlemen, but take my advice and stay out of Berlin airspace.'

He went out and Jack said, 'I'll go and wait at reception.'

'No need,' Max told him.

'No, I'd rather, old chap.'

Carter limped out and Max said, 'He loves you, I think.'

'And I love you, Harry Kelso.' She came round the desk and flung her arms around him.

'Careful, love. I'll have to go easy on the passion, I'm afraid. I'm in considerable pain unless I take morphine.'

'What strength?'

'I don't know. My SS surgeon gave me one of their battle packs. It's at Haston Place.'

'Don't take any more until I've checked it.' Suddenly she hammered at his chest with clenched fists. 'Don't you do that to me again. Never again. I've been in hell.'

He held her close and stroked her hair. 'I'm sorry.' He kissed her forehead gently.

She pulled away. 'What's this?' There was a slight frown on her face. 'Tenderness, romance from the great Harry Kelso?'

Max said smoothly, 'You know what they say in the movies? It was hell out there. Perhaps it's produced a new me.'

'I'll believe that when it happens.'

She got the X-rays, put them on the screen and switched on the light. After a while, she nodded. 'No fracture.' She turned. 'Tell me what happened.'

Which he did, sticking to the same story about the wound bursting on impact. She sat him down, turned the light of a desk lamp on his face. 'Just like last time, there's only one way, the quick way.'

She ripped the plaster away and Max sucked in his breath. '*Mein Gott!*' he said and in the same moment, realized his blunder. 'We always used to say that, me and Max, when we were kids, because Mutti thought it was blasphemous.'

She accepted it totally and inspected the stitching. 'This is good work.' *Which was exactly what Schroeder had said to Harry at Morlaix.*

Max said, 'I'm glad to hear it.'

'Just like last time, I don't want you to wear a plaster. I'll spray it again.' Which she did and mopped up the excess with cotton wool. 'Who's a good boy, then?'

'Only for you.'

'You'll have to go now. I've a rather tricky operation coming up. I'll see you later at the River Room. Good food and wine, Carrol Gibbons to dance to.' She hugged him fiercely. 'I never thought I'd have that again. The only trouble is I won't have time to go home and put on a decent frock.'

'Just bring yourself,' Max told her. 'That will do just fine.'

At six, back in his room, Max took a chance and rang Sarah Dixon's number. It seemed reasonable to assume that she would get home from the office round about now, but there was no reply. He changed into a fresh uniform and checked himself in the mirror.

'Very nice, Harry,' he murmured. 'Almost as good as ours.'

When he went into the sitting room, Jack Carter was pouring a whisky at the sideboard. 'Want one, Harry?'

Munro entered in full uniform. 'I'll have one of those. My God, Harry, that face of yours would frighten a regiment.' He took his whisky down in one swallow. 'Come on then, early meal tonight. I've a lot on tomorrow.'

At the River Room, they had a circular table at the window and Munro ordered champagne for himself, Harry, Carter and West, while they waited for Molly and her father.

'To you, Harry.' Munro raised his glass. 'I should think you've used up your nine lives.'

'We'll see,' Max said.

'No, we won't,' West told him. 'You're grounded by Ike's direct order. You're finished in the air.'

And Max didn't like that, just as Harry wouldn't have liked it.

'Is he going to see me?'

'Yes, but I'm not sure when. Tom Sobel will probably know. Ike's at Hayes Lodge now, but I'm flying him down to Southwick tomorrow morning.'

'You're flying him?' Max said.

'Well, there's life in the old dog yet and it keeps my hand in.'

At that moment, Molly and her father weaved their way between the tables. Max had no problems this time, for this had to be General Sobel and he was smiling broadly. He pumped Max's hand.

'I can't tell you what this means. Ike was thrilled.' He seated Molly. 'He wants to see you, Harry, but couldn't manage it tonight. He's up to his eyes. What he'd like you to do is join him at seven in the morning at Croydon. He told me Teddy here is doing the driving. I'm going with him and he'd like you to accompany us.'

'Sounds good to me.' Max reached for his glass, his hand steady and, yet, nothing but turmoil in his head.

Oh, God, so soon?

Finally, as light faded and the rain stopped, Rosa Stein left the hut and followed the track, her mind numb and the crazy thing was that within fifteen minutes she came to a farm. Smoke drifted from the chimney, cattle lowed from the barn. A young woman emerged with a pail of milk in each hand. It was Marie, Jacaud's radio operator and she paused, looking at Rosa.

'Who are you? What do you want?' she called in French.

Rosa stumbled towards her and burst into tears. 'Help me, please help me,' she cried in German.

Marie spoke no German and had only a smattering of English. It was their only link, for Rosa spoke no French, but did have a little broken English.

Marie said in English, 'Are you German?' Rosa nodded. 'Where are you from? Are you a Jew?'

Rosa shook her head. 'Château Morlaix.' Marie put down her pails. 'SS. My mistress dead.'

Great sobs racked her body and Marie picked up the pails. She gestured at the farm, turned to the door and Rosa followed.

SIXTEEN

Max and Molly danced on the crowded floor but he wasn't anywhere near as expert as his brother. In a sense, the fact that there were so many people on the floor helped. It provided an excuse for clumsiness.

After one bump too many he said, 'I'm sorry. I'm not doing too well.'

'That's all right. You've been through hell, Harry.' She held him close. 'Uncle Dougal told me that Julie mentioned you'd lost Tarquin.'

'I'm afraid so. He must have gone up with the Lysander in the crash. He fireballed. I'm lucky to be here. If it hadn't been for the SS . . .' He shrugged. 'I was saved by the devil, Molly.'

At that moment, the head waiter appeared on the edge of the floor and beckoned. Molly said, 'I don't believe this. Every time I come here with you, the same thing happens.' She pulled away, went and spoke to the head waiter and turned. 'Good old Guy's again. They can't do without me.'

'I'll wait up for you,' he said, as they went back to the table.

'I wouldn't bank on it. If it's after midnight I'll stay at the hospital.' They reached the table and she said, 'Guess what, everybody?'

Molly went off in Munro's staff car and West offered to drop off the others in his. Outside the Savoy entrance, Max said,

'Look, I feel like a walk, Brigadier. I don't know how to put it, but I'm kind of keyed up.'

'Perfectly understandable, dear boy,' Munro said. 'Have a saunter, enjoy yourself. You can always get a taxi. Americans are never refused by London cabbies these days. They overpay, you see. General Sobel won't mind me making the point.'

Sobel shook Max's hand. 'I'll see you in the morning at Croydon.'

'I'll be there.'

They all piled into West's staff car, which drove away. Max flagged down the first taxi that came along. 'Do you know Westbourne Grove, Bayswater?'

'I certainly do, guv.'

'Okay, take me there,' and Max climbed inside.

At the farm, Marie had sent for Jules, the farmer who was part of Jacaud's group. She explained the situation and Jules sat there listening and watching the German woman sitting at the end of the table with Marie's daughter on her knee. The bear sat on the table, the bear Jacaud had allowed Marie to have for her daughter.

'Whatever happened at the château is bad, but there's a limit to how much I can get out of her.'

Jules said, 'Jacaud speaks good German.'

'Yes, I know, but he went to Rennes to meet with people in the network there.'

'True, but he's coming back on the midnight train. He's asked me to pick him up at two a.m. at Beaulieu station in the *gazogène*.'

The *gazogène* was a truck operated by gas generated by a charcoal burner at the rear of the vehicle.

Marie nodded. 'All right, pick him up, but tell him to come straight here. I think this is trouble.'

★

The taxi dropped Max in Westbourne Grove. Max paid him off and found the side street leading to the block of flats with no trouble. He paused at the entrance, checked the names and pressed the buzzer. After a while, Sarah Dixon said, 'Yes?'

'Mrs Dixon? The day of reckoning is here.'

She said calmly, 'Come up. Second floor.'

He pushed open the door and went in. In the doorway opposite, Parry had caught him twice, one of forty-eight people he'd photographed that night. He was bored, he was cold and he was not pleased.

'Bloody Yank,' he said softly. 'Into some whore, I suppose. Lucky for some.'

Sarah Dixon admitted Max into her flat and led the way into the small sitting room. She opened a box of cigarettes and offered him one.

'You're here sooner than we expected.'

'So Joel Rodrigues made it all right?'

'Oh, yes. I know exactly who you are, Baron.'

'You tell Fernando Rodrigues to get a message through at his soonest to say I arrived safely. I'm meeting Eisenhower in the morning.'

'Will you kill him then?'

'It depends on the circumstances. Would you mind?'

'Frankly, I'm indifferent. I allied myself to your side a long time ago. That's a fact of life. Where are you staying?'

'At Haston Place, Brigadier Munro's flat. You can't reach me, so I'll have to keep in touch with you.'

'Fine. I can only wish you luck.' She opened the door for him. 'Good night.'

He let himself out of the front door. Parry said, 'That was quick,' and photographed him again.

Max turned into Westbourne Grove, moved towards Queens-way and hailed a taxi.

It was almost three o'clock in the morning, Max sleeping fitfully at Haston Place, Molly at Guy's and in Brittany the *gazogène*, driven by Jules, delivered Jacaud to Marie's farm. He banged on the door and she admitted him. He and Jules went into the kitchen and Jules stirred the fire.

'I'll make coffee,' Marie said and moved to the stove.

'Where is she?' Jacaud demanded.

'In bed.'

'Get her. Jules can make the coffee.'

Jacaud sat at the end of the table and lit a Gitane. Tarquin sat at the other end and Jacaud gazed at him morosely. 'It's all right for you.'

He'd once been a university professor of philosophy, but no one would have guessed it. The hard face, the unshaven chin, the dark eyes of a man who'd killed many times and whose notions of philosophy had gone out of the window. A man who didn't really believe in people any more. Jules took him milky coffee in a bowl and a moment later Marie brought Rosa into the room.

Jacaud spoke in good German. 'Sit down and listen to me. No one will hurt you if you tell the truth.'

Rosa, wearing a nightdress and robe Marie had given her, took a chair at the table.

Jacaud said, 'Tell me who you are and what this is all about.'

Fifteen minutes later, he sat there frowning as she finished. For a while he didn't speak and it was Marie who said, 'What did she say?'

So Jacaud told her and Jules in a few brief sentences.

Jules said, 'This is crazy. One brother impersonating another to kill Eisenhower? I can't believe it.'

'I've had a thought,' Jacaud said. 'We arranged for that friend of yours, Hélène, to screw the SS doctor, Schroeder.'

'That's right.'

'And she's still at it?'

'As far as I know.'

'You and Jules go round to her place now. If the German is there, bring him to me. He can confirm this woman's story.'

So it was that, twenty minutes later, Captain Schroeder, fast asleep and entwined with the delicious Hélène, awakened to find the barrel of a Colt automatic under his throat and Jules at the side of the bed.

'Get up and get dressed or I'll blow your brains out.' Hélène sat up in alarm and Jules grinned. 'Not you, darling, you've served France well. Go back to sleep.'

Schroeder, convinced that he was faced with death, was most co-operative. He sat at the end of the table and talked. 'You must understand, she wished to die. I only defended myself when she tried to kill Colonel Hartmann and did indeed kill Colonel Müller.'

'All right, go over it again, everything about the brothers – everything.'

When Schroeder was finished, Marie said in French, 'Was he any good?'

'Oh, yes,' Jacaud said. 'He doesn't know everything, but he does know enough to confirm what the woman says. I'll write a report. You must transmit it to SOE in Baker Street at once for the attention of Brigadier Munro.'

She shook her head. 'Not possible. They're not on channel for me until seven o'clock.'

'All right, seven then. Now let's have something to eat.'

'What about this SS bastard?' Jules asked. 'Shall I shoot him?'

'Good God, no,' Jacaud said. 'The invasion is in a matter of weeks. We'll need a doctor and he'll do just fine.'

At half past six, Air Vice Marshal West was on his way to Croydon in a staff car. It was raining and misty, although traffic was light. Suddenly, a delivery van came straight out of a side street without pause. There was little that West's driver could do. He tried to swerve, bounced off the van and mounted the pavement into a brick wall. West was thrown sideways and caught his head on the window column. The driver was in one piece, got out and opened the rear door. West joined him and stood there in the rain, mopping blood from his head with a handkerchief while his driver checked out the van and helped out the man in overalls, who was obviously in deep shock.

A moment later, a police Wolseley patrol car, which had been in the traffic behind, swerved in beside the staff car and an officer got out. Another stayed in the car and was already on the radio.

The police officer examined West's head. 'You'll need stitches there, sir. We're calling an ambulance now.'

'Never mind that, Constable. I'm Air Vice Marshal West. I'm due at Croydon at seven to fly to Portsmouth with General Eisenhower.'

The policeman was all attention. 'I don't think that's possible, sir, not in the state you're in.'

'Exactly. Get on to Croydon on your radio. Tell them what's happened. Message for Ike. I'm just knocked about a bit, but not fit to fly. Do it now, there's a good chap.'

'Of course, sir.'

The policeman turned to the car and spoke to his colleague. In the distance the bell of the approaching ambulance jangled

and West sat on the brick wall, cursing, the handkerchief held
to his head.

At Croydon, mist draping the airfield, Tom Sobel drank coffee
and looked out with some gloom at the weather. Max came in
from the Operations Room.

'It's fine at Southwick, no real problem landing there according
to the met report. Cloud and rain, but no wind to speak of. No
problem in taking off.'

'Well, that's a blessing, but where in the hell is Teddy West?'

At that moment, two things happened. A staff car drew up
outside and Eisenhower got out, then a flight lieutenant hurried
in from Operations with a signal flimsy, which he handed to
Sobel.

'Urgent, General.'

Sobel read it and looked up as Eisenhower came in, smiling.
'Bad news, General. Teddy West's staff car was in an accident
on the way here. Not too serious, but he needs hospital treatment.'

'Damn!' Eisenhower said. 'We have an important conference
at Southwick, Tom, as you know. Monty, the planning staff. It's
a critical meeting. Can you find another pilot fast?'

There was an inevitability about it, Max saw that. 'You've
got one, General. I'll fly you down.'

Eisenhower turned and held out his hand, that famous smile
in evidence. 'I'm truly glad to see you again, Colonel. What an
extraordinary happening. I look forward to hearing about it, but
are you really up to flying? Your face, if you'll excuse me, looks
terrible!'

Max held out his hands. 'Steady as a rock, General. No
problem.'

Ike glanced at Sobel. 'What do you think, Tom?'

'If Colonel Kelso says it's okay, that's fine by me, sir.'

Ike nodded. 'Right, Colonel, let's move it.'

'I'll check the Lysander, General,' Max said. 'But that shouldn't be a problem, it's out there ready to go.'

He went into the ante-room, took off his German military raincoat and helped himself to a flying jacket. He transferred the Walther and the spare clip to one of the pockets, his morphine ampoules to another, zipped up the flying jacket and went outside.

Munro and Jack decided to sign in early at SOE headquarters. There was always a good breakfast at the canteen. In deference to Jack's leg, Munro called his staff car and they drove through deserted streets, arriving in Baker Street at a quarter to seven.

'I'll check my desk, Jack,' Munro said. 'I'll see you at eight in the canteen.'

He went upstairs and Jack made his way to his own office, where he found Detective Constable Parry sitting on the bench outside.

'You're early.'

'Lacey told me to make sure you had each evening's surveillance photos on the Dixon woman for you first thing. I finished at midnight, then decided to use the photo lab here instead of going to the Yard. They let me have a bed.'

Jack led the way into his office. 'Anything interesting?'

'No sign of the Rodrigues brothers. The thing is, there are around forty flats in that block. The people going in could be calling on any one of them and a varied lot they are.'

Jack sat down. 'Let's see.'

Parry dropped one photo after another on the table. 'Pretty ordinary on the whole.' He laughed. 'Mind you, they've probably got their quota of whores living there. Here's a nice one of some American officer on the prod.'

Jack Carter looked at the photo, stunned, not wanting to

believe what he saw. 'Oh, my God!' he said and struggled to his feet. 'Get Sean Riley on the phone. Tell him I want him and Lacey here like yesterday.'

'You mean we've struck gold, Major?'

'Just do it,' Carter told him and went out.

Munro, absorbed in paperwork, looked up as Jack burst in.

'Why, Jack, you seem agitated.'

'I think you will be too, Brigadier.'

He placed the photo on the desk. Munro looked up, his face very calm. 'Explain.'

'Taken last night, Brigadier, timed at ten o'clock. That's the entrance to Sarah Dixon's apartment block.' He hesitated then added, 'After the Savoy, you see.'

'Yes, of course I see. But why, Jack? It doesn't make any kind of sense.'

There was a knock at the door and an ATS Signals Sergeant came in, a flimsy in one hand. 'Just received in the radio room from Jacaud in Brittany, Brigadier. Plain language, marked utmost priority.'

Munro read it, then looked at her. 'Who else knows?'

'No one, sir, I took the message myself.'

'Then keep it to yourself. You can go.'

She went out and Jack Carter said, 'Sir?'

'That isn't Harry Kelso, Jack. It's Max, his brother, and he's here to assassinate Ike. Read it for yourself.'

He reached for the phone. 'Get me Croydon.' A moment later, he was talking to Operations. 'General Eisenhower's flight? Has it left?' He listened, then replaced the phone.

Jack, looking stunned, passed the signal back. 'What do we do, sir?'

'Eisenhower's flight just took off, minus Teddy West who was in a road accident. The Supreme Commander, Tom Sobel

– and Oberstleutnant Max, Baron von Halder at the controls.'

'Oh, my God,' Jack said.

'No, let's keep a sense of proportion. Get on the other phone and book me a Lysander to Southwick. Utmost priority.'

'But Brigadier, what if . . .'

'What if he shoots Ike and Tom Sobel in mid-flight and flies off to France? We'll just have to hope he doesn't, because there's nothing we can do about it. I'll follow them down, now get on with it.'

Jack went into the next office and Munro rang Southwick House and asked for the head of security, a Royal Military Police major named Vereker. He was put through instantly.

'Vereker, we've known each other a long time, so trust me.'

'Naturally, Brigadier.'

'You'll get a Lysander in soon with Ike, General Sobel and Colonel Kelso as pilot.'

'We've already been notified.'

'This is difficult for you, but this is what you must do. As soon as they land, you arrest Kelso under the Defence of the Realm Act. I'm flying down myself and I'll have the warrant for you.'

Vereker, a policeman of one sort or another for many years had long since got past being surprised at anything. 'How discreet shall I be, sir?'

'Nothing public, I don't want the Supreme Commander to know at this stage. Tell him I'm on my way.'

'Leave it to me, Brigadier.'

'This is a bad one,' Munro said, thinking with dread of just how bad it could be.

'I understand, sir,' Vereker said and rang off.

Jack came back. 'Plane booked, sir, and car ready. Shall I come with you?'

'No, you hold the fort. Speak to the Portuguese embassy. Try to pull the Rodrigues brothers in, but I think the ambassador will plead diplomatic immunity and ship them home. Get Riley to pull the Dixon woman in. You've got plenty of blank warrants. Sign one for her.' He got up and reached for his cap. 'Acknowledge Jacaud's signal as received, no more. You can contact him again later when we know where we are.'

He adjusted his cap. Jack said, 'You noticed who's in charge at Château Morlaix, Brigadier? Bubi Hartmann, one of the best brains in the SD.'

'Of course I did, Jack, the man who took over Klein's department in Berlin. It all fits, but then these things usually do. By the way, you can tell the Dixon woman we don't intend to hang her, as long as she co-operates.'

He got the door open and Carter said, 'And Molly, sir?'

'For God's sake, Jack,' Munro said and went out.

In the Lysander, Max flew at 5000 feet through broken cloud. Ahead, it was even heavier, great dark banks of the stuff, and rain drifting in. Eisenhower and Sobel sat behind, shouting to each other above the roar of the engine.

Max was prey to conflicting emotions. He'd met the Supreme Commander, shaken hands, recognized the face, and yet the man himself meant nothing. It occurred to him then, as elsewhere Munro said to Carter, that it would be simple to draw his Walther, turn and shoot Eisenhower between the eyes, but that would mean Sobel as well, Molly's father, which would make her a victim also in this whole sorry mess. How would Harry feel if he flew into Morlaix with two dead bodies, one of them the father of the woman he loved? For he did love her, however he tried to avoid the fact: Max knew that now, having met her.

On the other hand, what about Mutti? This whole thing was

about her. If he didn't kill Eisenhower, she was dead, and Harry, too – he had no illusions about that.

So what should he do? Fly to Southwick and wait for another opportunity, one that would probably lead to his own death? Turn around now, get it done? Max had never felt this way in his entire life. He'd told Harry he would go to hell itself to save his mother – so why this strange paralysis?

The decision was taken out of his hands a moment later. There was a sudden roar, and the Lysander rocked in the slipstream of a black shadow that passed overhead and banked to port.

'My God, what is that?' Eisenhower demanded.

'A JU 88S nightfighter,' Max said. 'You still get a few over from France trawling around to see what they can find in the south country. He should have been home for breakfast by now. Hang on, gentlemen.'

Every pilot's instinct in Max's body was on full alert, as he dropped almost a thousand feet and the Junkers came in on his tail and fired, the cannon shell puncturing his left wing and shattering the windshield. The Junkers banked away in a wide circle.

Max yelled to the back, 'He's too fast for us. But on the other hand, we're too slow for him.' The Junkers was a quarter of a mile away, turning, and Max called over the radio, 'Lysander One *en route* for Southwick, under attack from JU 88S over South Downs.'

The Junkers came in again, Max banked steeply, and the stream of cannon fire missed. The flying took control of him then, so that he couldn't help reacting as he did.

'Right, you bastard, let's see what you're made of,' he said.

He went down, faster, 2000, 1000, the wooded slopes of the Downs looming below. The Junkers overshot, banked and came in again. Max took it to 600 and then, without warning, dropped his flaps, the old trick which he had used so many times before.

The Lysander almost lurched to a halt, and the pilot of the Junkers, banking frantically to avoid hitting him, lost control and went straight into the forest below. Flames mushroomed, as Max heaved back on the control column, climbed and levelled at 1000 feet.

He turned. 'Are we okay back there?' Eisenhower and Sobel looked stunned and suddenly Max knew: this was the time. He would never have a better chance. He could still pull his pistol, shoot them both and be off to France.

But he wasn't going to.

Something had changed over the last few minutes, a decision had been made without his even having to think about it. As the adrenalin of the air duel coursed through his blood, he knew it was just as he had told Bubi: he was a *pilot*. He was not an assassin.

He turned back and called Southwick. 'JU 88S down.' He gave the position. 'Be with you in fifteen minutes.'

A hundred yards from the Portuguese embassy, Jack Carter sat in the back of a staff car and waited. The grey-haired man in the blue suit, a raincoat draped over his shoulders as he hurried along the pavement, was a certain Colonel da Cunha, head of security at the embassy. Carter opened the door and da Cunha joined him.

'A long time, Jack. You said it was urgent.'

'It is. Fernando and Joel Rodrigues. They're in the pay of the Nazis in Berlin.' Da Cunha opened his mouth and Carter raised a hand. 'It's definite. I can give you all kinds of proof.'

The colonel took a cigarette from his case and lit it. 'They'll claim diplomatic immunity, Jack.'

'You mean you will? Fair enough. We know all there is to know about them. They're of no further use to us. Get them on tonight's TAP Dakota to Lisbon and tell them not to come back, ever.'

'Thank you, Jack, you're very kind.'

'I can afford to be, we're winning the war. Oh, and tell Fernando Rodrigues we've got his girlfriend. She isn't Portuguese.'

'Will she be executed?'

'What would be the point?'

Jack reached over and opened the door and da Cunha got out and walked away rapidly.

When Jack got back to the office, Sarah Dixon was signing a statement sheet, Sean Riley seated beside her, Lacey by the window.

'Have you got everything?'

Riley nodded. 'It's the German twin all right. She's admitted it, but I've got even more dramatic news for you. There was a phone call. Apparently when he was flying Ike down to Southwick, they were bounced by a Jerry plane. It seems he did some fancy flying and made the Jerry crash.'

Carter felt no sense of surprise. 'Well, he is one of the Luft-waffe's greatest aces and it wasn't his sort of thing, all this. You read that report from France I left you?'

'Yes, poor sod, and at the end all for nothing. I mean the bastards shot his mother.'

'And still have his brother.'

Sarah Dixon said, 'What happens now, a trial?'

'Good God, no,' Carter said. 'You're no longer important. We'll put you in detention, of course. As for after the war, we'll see. I left a message for Rodrigues, by the way. Told him we had you. He and his brother are being flown out to Lisbon tonight.'

'That was good of you.' She smiled. 'Can I go now?'

Riley and Lacey took her out between them and Jack sat down, thinking about it, then wrote a signal for Jacaud, bringing him up to date. He thought about it again, then added procedure instructions. He rang for a messenger, sat back, frowning, then picked up the phone again.

'Major Carter. I need a car to take me to Guy's Hospital. Yes, five minutes.'

At Southwick at the airstrip, the Lysander rolled to a halt and a large group ran forward, officers of the General Staff and RAF personnel. Eisenhower raised his arms and waved them back.

'I'm fine and so is General Sobel, thanks to the finest bit of flying I've ever known.' He turned to Max and motioned for silence. 'Colonel Harry Kelso, by the authority vested in me as Supreme Commander, I intend an immediate award of the Distinguished Service Cross.' He shook Max's hand and turned to Tom Sobel. 'We'd better get moving. We have a lot to do.'

Sobel put an arm around Max's shoulders. 'I'm proud of you, son, and Molly will be even prouder. Look, we've got a hell of a lot to get through this morning. Why don't you get something to eat in the officers' mess? Just take it easy. I'm sure Ike will want to catch up with you later.'

'Fine,' Max said. 'I might just do that.'

Sobel moved away, following Eisenhower and the others, and the RAF ground crew started to inspect the Lysander. Max lit a cigarette, his hands shaking. What happened now to Elsa, to Harry? But even as he stood there, the germ of an idea began to form. Rain started to fall, and a Royal Military Police major moved to his side and raised an umbrella.

'Got to keep you dry, Colonel, for Brigadier Munro. He'll be arriving soon.'

In that single moment, Max knew they were on to him. 'What is this?'

'My name's Vereker and I'm in charge of security here. The two corporals over there are my men.' Max looked across and saw them, large and wearing the distinctive red cap of the Royal Military Police. 'I don't know what's going on here, but I've been ordered to arrest you under the Defence of the Realm Act.'

'Sounds interesting,' Max said.

'I know you're carrying a weapon, Colonel. If you could just pass it over discreetly, I'd be obliged.'

'Oh, I'm always discreet.' Max took the Walther and the spare clip out of one of the pockets in his flying jacket and passed it over. 'There you go.'

Vereker slipped the Walther into his pocket. 'Very sensible, Colonel.'

'I've never done a sensible thing in my life,' Max said. 'What happens now?'

'Well, you haven't kicked up a fuss or got on your high horse.'

'And what's that tell you?'

'As I've been a policeman for twenty years, both at Scotland Yard and in the Army, I'd say it means you're as guilty as hell of whatever they think you've done, but that's not for me to decide. That's for Brigadier Munro.'

'So what do we do until he gets here?'

'How about a drink in the mess?'

'You think you can trust me?'

'Oh, I think so. After all, where do you have to go?'

'You never said a truer word, Major.' Max smiled. 'So just lead on.'

In fact, Vereker left him to his own devices, stood at the bar himself with a whisky and *The Times* newspaper, while Max sat in a window seat, also enjoying a whisky and a cigarette, and thought things over. What was it Munro had discovered and how? Not that it mattered. It was all over and God help his mother and Harry, unless . . . His face was hurting like hell, so he got out his battle pack and extracted an ampoule. Vereker was over in a flash.

'What's this?'

'Morphine,' Max said. 'For my face. It's kind of recent and very painful. Here, you do it for me.'

Vereker examined the pack. 'German?'

'SS, actually. Only the best.'

Vereker hesitated, then snapped the end of the ampoule and jabbed Max's wrist when he extended it. 'I wish to God I knew what all this meant.'

'So do I.'

Dougal Munro entered the mess, hesitated, then came towards them. 'Brigadier,' Max said cheerfully.

Munro ignored him. 'Major, from this moment you are bound by the Official Secrets Act. We'll use your office.'

Moments later, Munro sat behind Vereker's desk and took a folded document from his pocket. 'Your warrant for this arrest, Major, under the provision of the Defence of the Realm Act.'

Vereker examined it and looked up, bewildered. 'But this is in the name of Oberstleutnant Baron Max von Halder.'

'Quite right. It seems Colonel Harry Kelso crash-landed in Brittany last week and escaped after a few days to fly back in triumph in a stolen Luftwaffe Storch – only it wasn't Harry Kelso, it was his twin brother.'

Vereker was dumbfounded. He had heard of Kelso's brother, but – 'But why?'

'To assassinate General Eisenhower.'

'But that's crazy, Brigadier, he's just saved Ike's life with the most stupendous piece of flying anyone's ever heard of.'

'Yes, bizarre, isn't it?' Munro turned to Max. 'When it came to it, you couldn't do it, could you?'

'Oh, I was thinking about it, just turning round and shooting him, but that would have meant shooting Sobel too and I couldn't do that, not to Molly's father. Harry loves her, you see.' Max lit a cigarette. 'And then the Junkers turned up. Strange that. If I was a fatalist, I'd have just let it happen and the three of us would have gone down together, a perfect solution.'

'But you're not a fatalist?'

'Never have been. I'll always kick and struggle even at the end and when that bastard came in on my tail . . .' He shrugged again. 'I'm a fighter pilot. I did what came naturally.' He laughed. 'And that's finally what did it for me. When that Junkers went down, I sat there at my controls and I said: this is what you are, Max. You're a pilot, you're not an assassin. You may be a killer, but you're not *that* kind of killer.' He laughed again. 'Incidentally, three hundred and nine was my official score. Now it's three hundred and ten.'

'I think I understand.'

'Which leaves my mother and Harry in deep, deep trouble.' He frowned. 'But wait a minute, Brigadier. You haven't told me how you caught me.'

'We were shadowing the Rodrigues brothers, and don't tell me you don't know who they are. It led us to Sarah Dixon, who unfortunately is employed at SOE headquarters. We had a police cameraman checking everyone calling at her block of flats and there you were. Foolish, that.'

'Well, I'm just an amateur at this kind of thing.'

'And then we had a report from my chief agent in the Morlaix area and now I know everything: Himmler, Bubi Hartmann. Oh, yes, we know all about Bubi, your mother, Harry, the dreadful dilemma Himmler put you both in.'

'How could you know all this? I was transferred to the château secretly, and my mother was flown down from Berlin secretly.'

'Your mother's maid, Rosa Stein, was found wandering in the woods and, thank God, fell into the hands of my agent. What she told him arrived on my desk earlier this morning.'

'Rosa? Wandering in the woods? What on earth are you talking about?'

So Munro told him.

Max sat there, haggard and drawn. Vereker opened a cupboard, poured brandy into a glass and handed it to him. Max gulped it down and, sitting there, looked up at Vereker, a dreadful smile on his face.

'So now you know what you're fighting for.'

'I'm sorry, Colonel.'

'Just make sure the good guys win, and give me another.' He held out his glass and Vereker poured more brandy.

'I'm sorry, too, Max,' Munro said.

'Our own fault. All I thought of was flying, all my mother thought of was the von Halder name and our position in society. Hitler took over and we sat back and went with the flow.' He turned to Vereker. 'We weren't Nazis, Major, we kept telling ourselves that, only I ended up shooting down over three hundred planes for the Third Reich.'

There was nothing anybody could say to that and Vereker went and put the brandy bottle back in the cupboard.

'And what really hurts is that it isn't over. The bastards have still got Harry.'

'And Bubi Hartmann lied to you.'

'Yes, Bubi lied. But I think I understand him a bit. He's part Jewish, you see, and Himmler found out. Bubi was as much under the thumb as the rest of us. They threatened his father, his aunt. You know what they do? They hang you with piano wire, men and women – very even-handed, the Reichs-führer.'

'My God,' Vereker said. 'The bloody swine.'

'Spoken like a true Englishman.' Max took out a cigarette, his hands shaking, and Vereker gave him a light. 'What happens now, the Tower of London?'

'Cold Harbour,' Munro said. 'This has gone on long enough and I want you out of here before Ike sends for you. We'll fly out in the Lysander I arrived in.'

'Do you want me to come with you, Brigadier?' Vereker asked.

'No need, not now. Tell Ike that I needed to inspect the remains of that Junkers and that I needed Colonel Kelso's expertise. You don't mind lying for me?'

'No, sir.'

'Good man, and remember the Official Secrets Act. This never happened.'

'If you say so, Brigadier.'

The Lysander pilot was a flying officer named Hare, very young and in terrible awe of Max. His flying wasn't brilliant, but good enough to get them there and it was early afternoon when they drifted across Cold Harbour and bounced down rather uncomfortably.

'Terribly sorry, Colonel,' Hare said. 'Rotten landing.'

'We all make them,' Max told him and followed Munro out.

Julie drove up in the Jeep and got out. 'Nice to see you back. There's still time for lunch. The boat's gone out on a practice run, but Zec's around and there are still some pies left.'

Munro said, 'Why not?' He turned to Max. 'That suit you, Max?'

Max said, 'As you say, why not?'

Julie said, 'Max? What is this?'

'Let's get into the Jeep out of this damned rain and get down to the Hanged Man and I'll tell you.'

Zec was the only person in the bar, sitting by the fire reading a book of some sort. He looked up and smiled. 'Good to have you back.'

Munro said, 'Let me introduce you. Oberstleutnant Baron Max von Halder, Harry Kelso's brother.'

'Dear God,' Zec Acland said.

Max went behind the bar and helped himself to a pack of Players cigarettes. He lit one and gave a tired smile as he came back.

'Get it over with, Brigadier. I'll go for a walk if that's all right with you. Mind you, I could do with some sustenance. I'll eat later.'

The door closed behind him and Munro turned to them. 'It's a rotten story, but here goes.'

When he had finished, Julie said, 'Truly dreadful. His poor mother.'

'I never heard the like,' Zec observed. 'But what are you playing at here, Brigadier? By rights you should have taken him to London. You haven't even told General Eisenhower about this.'

'True, and the answer is that I don't know what I'm playing at. I've no bloody idea.' Munro sighed. 'This job I do does make one such a liar. I can't help feeling that there is some way we can use this, though, but I'll let that bubble around for a while.'

The door opened and Max came in. There was more colour now to the unbruised section of his face. 'I could murder one of those pies right now. I'm starving.'

'And a pint of ale,' Zec said. 'I'll join you.'

'And me,' Munro added. 'An active morning, to put it mildly, and I didn't catch breakfast.'

Julie produced steak and kidney pies and potatoes and they worked their way through them, mainly in silence. It was Zec who said, 'One thing I can't get over. If Eisenhower gave you the DSC for saving his life, can he take it back 'cause you be on the other side?'

'A neat point,' Munro said. 'And I doubt whether it's been raised before.' At that moment, they heard a roaring overhead. 'What on earth is that?'

Julie went to the door and looked out. 'Lysander,' she said.

'Now who would that be?'

'Shall I drive up and see?'

'No, finish your lunch. Whoever it is will show themselves soon,' and Munro returned to his food.

It was perhaps fifteen minutes later that they heard the sound of a Jeep outside. A moment later the door opened and Jack Carter limped in, followed by Molly.

'Don't blame Jack, Uncle Dougal, I made him bring me,' Molly said.

'I've sent the Lysander straight back, sir,' Carter told him.

'I should think so. We'll be running out of them.'

'There was a signal from Southwick, sir. General Eisenhower trying to find you.'

'Well, I didn't receive it and for the moment I stay lost.'

Jack turned to Max. 'That was one hell of a thing you did this morning.'

'Runs in the family,' Max told him. 'Just like Harry. The only thing we do well is fly.'

Molly said, 'I'd like to talk to you. Is that all right, Uncle Dougal?'

'I think we could stretch a point.'

She went out and Max followed her. They walked to the end of the quay and she sat on a bench and he leaned on the railings. There was a strange intimacy between them.

'Jack told me everything about the whole rotten business. I'm so sorry about your mother.'

'So am I. I'm also sorry about Harry, still stuck over there.'

'Tell me how he was.'

'You love him a lot, don't you?'

'Oh, yes.'

'Nothing but grief there for you. I know, because there's nothing but grief there where I'm concerned.'

'It doesn't matter. Love doesn't look for reason. Love is beyond reason. So tell me.'

'He was in fair condition. A badly smashed left ankle, but Captain Schroeder did a good job there, just like he did on my face.'

'Schroeder was the doctor?'

'An SS doctor, so he was damn good.'

'What did he do to your face?'

'Gave me a local anaesthetic, beat me with an iron bar, sliced me open with a scalpel. Harry sat there watching. He was distinctly unhappy.'

'Terrible, the whole thing.' She shook her head. 'But to kill Eisenhower . . .'

'If you'd seen the film Himmler made us watch of the executions of so-called traitors. Piano wire slicing into their necks, faeces trickling down their legs. To see the men was bad enough, but the women?' He shook his head. 'It was past belief. It was a joint enterprise, had to be. I needed Harry's expertise if I was to stand any chance of getting away with it.'

'I understand, I really do. The irony is that if anyone else had been piloting Eisenhower's plane the General would probably be dead by now.' She stood up. 'There must be something we could do.'

'Send in the commandos?' Max shook his head. 'Things like that take time to organize. The Rodrigues brothers will be back in Portugal fast, enjoying their diplomatic immunity. They'll report into Prinz Albrechtstrasse eventually from Lisbon, if only in the hope of a little extra cash. God knows what will happen to Harry. The least Himmler will do is pull him out to Berlin.'

They walked along the quay and the lifeboat moved in. Someone called and waved from the stern and Max waved back.

'This is terrible,' she said, tears in her eyes. 'I feel so helpless and there's nothing to be done.'

Max put an arm around her shoulders. 'Oh, I don't know. I've been thinking. Molly – what if I became the pride of the Luftwaffe again? Changed into the right uniform in Julie's supply room, sneaked up to the airstrip under cover of darkness? There are two Storchs there. I'd be at Morlaix in an hour, land at the airstrip and play it by ear.'

'It's madness,' she said. 'Certain death for you.'

'Certain death for Harry now. At least we'd be together.'

'So if you could, you'd fly him back?'

'I'd have to. He couldn't fly himself.'

'It's fantasy, it's not possible.'

As they reached the pub, Jack Carter came out with Julie. 'I've got orders to run you up to the house, old son. Lock you in, barred windows, all that sort of thing.'

'Why not,' Max told him. 'I've nowhere else to go.' He climbed into the rear of the Jeep, Carter got in beside Julie and she drove away.

Munro was leaning on the bar, talking to Zec over a whisky, when Molly got back. The brigadier turned to Molly. 'Are you all right?'

'I'm not sure. We talked, he explained a great deal and he's concerned about Harry. Tell me, why did you bring him here?'

'Too much had happened too soon. I thought it best to get him out of the way until the dust settles.'

'So you've no ideas about how to help Harry?'

'No, it's impossible.'

'Max doesn't think so.'

'Doesn't he then?' Zec Acland put in.

Munro was frowning. 'Tell me,' he said, which she did.

SEVENTEEN

Max spent the afternoon brooding in the bedroom Carter had shown him to. It was comfortable enough, if old-fashioned in furnishings, and the important feature was the barred windows. The rain fell relentlessly, drumming against the windows. There was nothing to do except think, and he'd had enough of that. He found a few novels on a shelf, and selected a copy of Daphne du Maurier's *Rebecca* because the Cornish scenario seemed appropriate. He managed an hour, lying on the bed, but it had been a hard day and, finally, he drifted into sleep.

It was six-thirty when Jack Carter came for him. 'Time for dinner, old son. We didn't like to leave you on your own.'

'That's very civil of you,' Max said and followed him downstairs to the library, where he found Munro with Zec Acland and Molly seated by the fire.

'There you are,' Munro said. 'What's your pleasure, whisky?'

'Actually a brandy and soda would go down nicely.'

Carter got it for him and Molly stood up. 'Let me check your face,' which she did and nodded. 'It could be worse. Does it hurt?'

'Not too much. It feels numb more than anything.'

'Then don't use any more morphine. Dangerous stuff.'

'Thanks for the consultation, Doctor.' Max took the brandy and soda Carter handed him. 'So what now?'

'I'm not sure,' Munro told him.

'I asked you if the Tower of London was the next stop. I always thought that was *de rigueur* for people like me.'

'My dear boy, there's never been anyone quite like you.' Munro was exasperated. 'Damn you, Max, I keep thinking you're Harry.'

'Inconvenient, isn't it? What does Eisenhower have to say?'

'He doesn't know yet. This whole affair is dynamite stuff as our American friends would say. To be frank, I don't quite know how to handle it and publicity is the last thing we need, not with the invasion due in a matter of weeks.'

Julie looked in. 'Dinner on the table.'

Zec was the first to stand up. 'I always think better on a full stomach myself,' and he led the way out.

They sat round the table and enjoyed Julie's carrot soup, Dover sole, sauté potatoes and a salad. Conversation was sporadic.

Finally Munro said to Julie, 'You're a credit to France, my dear.'

'Well, don't get too worked up, Brigadier, we're fresh out of coffee. Tea for everyone.'

'Spoken like a true Englishwoman. Let's adjourn to the library.'

'Not until we've cleared the table, surely.' Max smiled. 'If I may, Julie?' and he started to stack the plates.

'Not really your job, Baron,' Munro said.

'Yes, but it is a gentleman's,' Julie told him tartly, as she helped Max.

'That's put you in your place, Brigadier,' Zec said. 'I'd come and have a brandy if I were you.'

Gathered in the library again, with Julie pouring tea, the atmosphere was more strained than before. Finally, Molly said, 'Nobody's saying a thing. It's ridiculous, like one of those Agatha Christie novels where Hercule Poirot gets everybody to meet in the library to tell them who the murderer is.'

Max laughed. 'A perfect description, only we know who the murderer is. It's me.'

'Nonsense.' Zec was filling his pipe. 'I've seen some of those plays. It's usually the butler who did it, or the vicar.'

'True,' Munro agreed. 'But in this case, the Baron it is.'

'Quite right, but frankly, I've had enough.' Max stood. 'When you decide what to do with me, let me know, but I think I'll go back to my room. Jack?'

Carter stood up and reached for his stick. 'Certainly, old boy.'

When Jack returned they were all sitting quietly, not a word spoken. He went to the sideboard and poured a whisky. He raised his glass. 'Cheers everybody and if you'll excuse me saying this, Brigadier, he's an absolutely smashing fella and I don't give a damn if he's an ace of the Luftwaffe.'

'Good heavens, man, they took your leg at Dunkirk,' Munro reminded him.

'Quite right and I'd like to have it back, but war is war, a bloody stupid game over which we have no control.'

'But this is just an episode of war,' Molly said. 'And we do have control.' She turned to Munro. 'What do you intend to do, Uncle Dougal?'

'All right, I'm defeated. Give me another brandy, Jack, and I'll tell you about a rather interesting conversation Molly had with Max von Halder earlier.'

When he was finished, there was a silence. It was Carter who said, 'And you believe that, sir, that he would fly to Morlaix and try to save his brother?'

'For God's sake, Jack, use that fine brain of yours,' Molly exploded. 'This is a great man, a fine man who had everything, so much that it's meaningless. Medals?' She shrugged. 'What the hell do they mean at the end of the day? They blackmailed him and his brother into attempting a terrible act. Then they butchered his mother.'

Munro said, 'According to Rosa Stein, she sought death.'

It was Zec who said, 'Yes, but from what I've been told, that was a futile attempt to get her sons off the hook.'

'Which Hartmann kept silent about,' Molly said. 'The ultimate betrayal, whatever his own fears.'

'And now there is Harry at that damned château awaiting the outcome,' Julie put in. 'An outcome already ordained. Himmler will have him executed without a second's thought. You are talking evil walking the earth here.'

'While we sit and do nothing,' Molly said.

There was silence while Munro brooded. It was Zec who spoke, quite calm, with no emotion. 'They're good boys, Brigadier. They deserve a chance, both of them.'

Munro nodded. 'You're right, of course, all of you. I'm not making excuses, but I'd like to think that, in my heart, I've known it all along, the reason I brought Max down here instead of taking him back to London.'

'So what do we do, sir?' Carter asked. 'Will you tell him?'

'Good God, no, that's far too simple for my complicated mind. We'll let him escape.' He turned to Julie. 'I'd like you to organize it for me. Will you?'

'Of course, Brigadier.'

Munro turned to Molly. 'Not you, my dear. There's too much of the heart in this for you.'

At Château Morlaix, Bubi Hartmann, young Freiburg, the 109 pilot and Harry were finishing dinner. Harry wore a Luftwaffe uniform. No one had said a great deal. Bubi was preoccupied, still waiting for news of what had happened in England and also concerned at the disappearance of Schroeder. Freiburg was, as always, overawed by the rank of the two colonels. As someone who had flown with Max, it had been necessary for Bubi to explain the connection; that Harry was the Baron's brother, a fact self-evident, but what Max was up to, that was still a secret.

They finished the meal with coffee and cognac and finally Harry reached for his crutches. 'I'll go back to my room.'

'I'll see you up,' Bubi said.

They mounted the stairs and Bubi nodded to the SS guard who unlocked the door. Harry said, 'What about my mother, Bubi, when do I see her?'

'Tomorrow, Harry, I think I can promise that.'

'For some reason, I don't believe you.'

'I'm sorry you feel that way.'

Bubi turned and Harry went in the room. He felt strangely uneasy, went and peered out through the barred windows, wondering about Max and what was happening to him. Finally, he sat on the edge of the bed and took off his right shoe. His left was bare, the toes sticking out of the plaster cast. He didn't bother taking off the flying blouse because it was rather chilly. He lay back on the bed, looked up at the ceiling and, after a while, slept.

Bubi sat in a corner of the sitting room, drinking more brandy than was good for him and Freiburg, in another corner, leafed through a magazine nervously. Finally, he stood. 'I think I'll get an early night, Colonel.'

'Well, good for you,' Bubi told him. 'I'll see you in the morning.'

Freiburg retired and as Bubi reached for the bottle of cognac, the phone rang. He checked his watch, frowning. *Ten o'clock.* Who could it be?

He picked up the phone and the operator said, 'I've got a call for you, Standartenführer.'

'Who is it?'

'Well, he's obviously French, though his German's good. He insists on speaking to you personally. Says he has vital information.'

'Put him on.'

Jacaud said, 'Colonel Hartmann?'

'Who is this?'

'Oh, I run what you call your opposition in this area of Brittany. A friend of mine, a Brigadier Munro, who I think you know, has been in touch with me by radio, not once, but twice.'

Bubi almost choked. 'What do you want?'

'Nothing,' Jacaud said. 'I'm simply here to impart information. I understand the following names will mean something to you. The Rodrigues brothers, who claimed diplomatic immunity when lifted, are winging their way back to Lisbon. Mrs Sarah Dixon is in custody and so is Baron von Halder. Here's a good one for you. The Baron was actually flying Eisenhower down to Southwick when a wandering JU88 bounced them. Would you believe the Baron made the bastard crash? He saved Eisenhower's life.'

'Damn you!' Bubi groaned.

'You're the one who's damned. The great day's coming soon. Oh, by the way, thanks for Schroeder. We'll need a decent doctor when the real fighting starts.'

He rang off. Bubi sat there clutching the phone then slowly put it down, horror on his face as the full implication of what he'd been told sank in. It was all over. He was finished. He had no illusions about the price of failure over this business.

He got up, lit a cigarette nervously and paced the floor. Max in British hands and his brother upstairs. He thought about that particularly, but what was he supposed to do? Go and knock on the door and say, 'They've arrested your brother and, sorry, we lied to you, your mother was shot to death before Max flew to Cornwall'? On the other hand, there was something he could do. At least he had a priority line to Berlin. With any luck, Trudi would be overnighting at Prinz Albrechtstrasse.

Which she was, lying on a narrow camp bed in the corner of her office, reading a magazine. She picked up the phone and recognized his voice instantly.

'It's me, Trudi.'

'Colonel, what is it?'

'Just listen. The whole thing's a failure, the Rodrigues brothers, the Dixon woman and Max, all arrested. You know what that will mean.'

'Oh, my God!'

'Get out of there, Trudi, use your authority as my secretary while it's still worth something and run for it. That's the best I can do. If you could warn my father, I'd appreciate it.'

She was in tears. 'This is so terrible. What will the Reichsführer say?'

'It's what he'd do that's important.'

'I saw him an hour ago at his corner table in the canteen.'

'You mean he's there?'

'Oh, yes, the bombing started early tonight. He's stayed over.'

Bubi felt a strange kind of relief. 'What the hell, let's get it over with. Put me through to his office, and Trudi –'

'Yes, Bubi.'

'Run like hell, my love.'

A few moments later, Himmler said, 'So, Standartenführer, you have good news for me?'

Bubi, suddenly past caring, said, 'On the contrary, Reichsführer, all bad.'

There was a pause, then Himmler said, 'Tell me.'

Which Bubi did, experiencing a perverse enjoyment by going into the finer details, such as Max actually saving Eisenhower's life in the encounter with the Junkers. When he was finished, there was a silence.

Finally, Himmler said, 'An ill-judged venture from the start, Colonel, but I must confess to having been carried along, in spite of my better judgement, by your own enthusiasm for the project. The death of the wretched Baroness showed a deplorable lack of leadership on your part and now we have the embarrassment of Baron von Halder in British hands.'

What Bubi wanted to say was: Go and stuff yourself, you rotten little bastard. Instead, he said, 'Have you any further instructions, Reichsführer? What do I do with Colonel Kelso?'

'You will do nothing. I will contact Gestapo headquarters in Paris. You'll have a plane there tomorrow with Standartenführer Fassbinder on board. He'll take Kelso in charge and bring him to Berlin.'

'And myself, Reichsführer?'

'You might as well come with them. I'll see you then and we'll discuss the future.'

He rang off and Bubi put down the phone. He'd just received his death sentence and so had Harry Kelso. The coffin lid had closed. He picked up the brandy bottle and went upstairs to his room. He shouldn't, of course, but to hell with it. He drank another large one, took off his belt and holster. He withdrew the Mauser, lifted it in one hand and grinned. Standartenführer Fassbinder could be in for a surprise. Bubi had never liked the swine and it was much better to go down fighting. He lay back and plunged into a drunken sleep.

Max was lying on the bed and smoking a cigarette when the door creaked open. He glanced at his watch. It was two o'clock.

'Max, it's me.' Julie switched on the light and Max sat up. 'What is it?'

She sat on the edge of his bed. 'It's a bloody mess. No one seems to know what to do. Except Molly.'

'What are you talking about?'

'After you'd gone, we were talking in the library and Molly told us what you'd said to her on the quay. About stealing the Storch and flying off to Brittany to get Harry.'

'And what did Munro say?'

'He thought it crazy.' She shrugged. 'But I don't.'

'Why, Julie?'

'I fought the Nazis in the Resistance. What happened ruined my husband's life. We got out, but he died and Munro found this job for me. I don't like them, Max, but God help me, I like you and I'm probably a little bit in love with Harry, though don't tell Molly that.'

'She's a woman, she'll know it already,' Max told her.

'Anyway, you deserve a chance, you and Harry. If you're mad enough to go, I'll help you. I checked that Storch you came over in and the tank is full. They've been expecting someone from the Enemy Aircraft Flight to pick it up.'

'Is there a guard on the field?'

'No need. The ground crew are all in bed, but I'd say you're wearing the wrong uniform to do what you have to.'

'Definitely.'

'Let's go then.'

In the supply room, he changed into Luftwaffe uniform. She even found him a Knight's Cross to hang at his neck. 'Sorry we don't have the oak leaves and swords.'

'A mere detail.' He walked to the weaponry table. 'Can I help myself?'

He selected a Walther. 'Do you recommend this?'

'Especially with this silencer. It was developed for the SS.'

'Only the best.' He slipped a magazine into the butt, and screwed the silencer on the end. 'Loaded for bear, that's what my grandfather used to say to Harry and me when we were on camping holidays as boys. I'll take a spare magazine.' He slipped it with the weapon into the large map pocket in the Luftwaffe pants, picked up a *Schiff*, placed it carefully on the straw-blond hair and looked at himself in the mirror. 'There you go. Pride of the Luftwaffe.'

'If you're ready, I'll take you up there. Let's use the back stairs.'

He followed her down to the hall outside the kitchen. She opened the back door and they went out and across the yard to the gate in the wall. The Jeep was on the other side. She got behind the wheel and Max joined her.

As she switched on and drove away he said, 'Touch of fog in the air and low cloud.'

'I've checked the met report. You'll find it like that on your way across, but from about four, it's due to clear and you'll have a full moon up there.'

As they approached the airstrip, he said, 'This is the second time in a week that I've taken on an impossible task. My mother thought the Eisenhower thing was madness, that I was going to my death.'

'You're still here.'

'Only just. Is this madness, Julie?'

'God help me, but I don't know.'

He lit a cigarette. 'Okay, an hour to get there, bluff my way at Morlaix airstrip, ten minutes' drive to the château. Get Harry, back to the airstrip, an hour's flight back. I could be here by five, but that's if it works and if the guard at the airstrip, the duty controller, accepts the famous Black Baron. They never knew what I was up to, you see.'

'Let's hope they haven't found out.'

'I think I stand a chance on that, as long as Bubi has kept the lid on things.'

The Storch was on the apron. She pulled up and they got out and walked towards it. All was quiet. Max opened the door, reached for a parachute and put it on. 'Not that it matters, but old habits die hard.' He kissed her on the cheek. 'God bless you, Julie.'

'God bless you, Max.'

He got into the pilot's seat, turned and smiled. 'Where's Munro, by the way?'

She was taken by surprise. 'I don't really know.'

'Come on, Julie.' He smiled, closed and locked the door. He switched on and taxied to the end of the runway. A moment later, he lifted into the night.

In the Hanged Man Zec stirred the fire into life. Jack Carter and Molly sat in the inglenook and Munro stood at the bar. The lifeboat crew were scattered around the room. One of them spoke for all.

'What's it all about, Zec? You said something special.'

At that moment, there was the sound of the Storch passing overhead and moving out to sea. Another man said, 'What in the hell was that?'

Zec looked at Munro, who nodded. Zec said, 'That was Colonel Kelso on his way to France to attempt a pick-up.'

There was the sound of the Jeep drawing up outside and a moment later, Julie came in and went to Munro. They conversed in low voices. Finally, Munro nodded and turned.

'This is probably the most hazardous mission ever undertaken from Cold Harbour. Positively suicidal. If he's successful, we may see him at around five. On the other hand, he may need assistance at sea. I don't know.'

'Which is why I want you buggers on hand,' Zec said. 'Any objections?'

One of the men laughed. 'For God's sake, Zec, build up the fire, shut up and let's get the cards out.' He turned to Julie. 'And a pie or two wouldn't go down too badly.'

She smiled. 'You've got it. Would you mind giving me a hand, Molly?'

'Of course not.'

Molly followed her into the kitchen and Zec said, 'Anyone wants a drink, have it now. One pint each and that's it.' He turned to Munro and took a pack of cards from his pocket. 'What's your pleasure, Brigadier?'

'Poker,' Munro told him. 'I've always had a weakness for stud poker. Unfortunately, I only play for money.'

There was a roar of laughter, someone joined two tables together and everyone crowded around.

Max left his contact with Morlaix until he was five miles out. His trip across from Cornwall to Brittany had been made at 500 feet, his hands tight on the control column. He felt calm, totally in charge, no fear at all.

'I'm coming to get you, Harry,' he murmured softly. 'I'm coming.'

At the château, Harry stirred, came awake as from a dream, stared up at the ceiling and then the dream receded, its content already fading. He lay there, for some reason very alert and excited and reached for a cigarette.

The duty controller at Morlaix was a Sergeant Greiser. There was nothing to do, no traffic, but regulations demanded that someone be on the radio. He sat there, yawning, when at three-thirty Max's voice sounded over the air.

'Come in, Morlaix, are you receiving me?'

Greiser reached for the mike. 'Loud and clear. Who are you?'

'Baron von Halder on special assignment. I'll be with you in five minutes. You will notify no one of my arrival. I act directly under the orders of Reichsführer Himmler. Over and out.'

Greiser, incredibly excited, switched on the landing lights, went out of the hut and ran through a light rain to the hangar which housed Freiburg's M E 109. A young sentry sheltered there, his Schmeisser slung over one shoulder.

'What's the flap?' he asked.

'Storch coming in.'

'At this time in the morning? Who is it?'

'Mind your own business,' Greiser told him.

The Storch made a perfect landing, taxied towards them and halted. Max switched off, got out and approached. 'You are?' he asked.

'Greiser, Herr Baron.' The sergeant got his heels together. 'A great honour.'

Max took out a cigarette and Greiser offered his lighter. 'I'll take you into my confidence, Greiser. This is a special duties flight. I'm due at the château to pick up a passenger. Have you a vehicle I can use?'

'The duty *Kübelwagen*, Herr Baron. I'll drive you myself.'

'Not necessary, I need you here. I'll be back within thirty minutes. Show me.' Greiser led him to the second hangar and there was the *Kübelwagen*. Max slid behind the wheel and switched on. 'You're a good man, Greiser, and I'll say so in my report to Reichsführer Himmler.'

'My thanks, Herr Baron.' Greiser saluted and Max drove away.

At the château, the young S S sentry huddled from the rain in the sentry box. Max pulled up at the swing bar. 'For God's sake,

317

get this thing raised. It's Baron von Halder. I've just flown in and I'm tired.'

The boy never even queried him. He took in the Luftwaffe uniform, the Oberstleutnant's tabs, the Knight's Cross, stumbled to the bar and raised it. Max drove through, moved along the drive, stopped at the main entrance and switched off. There was a sentry under the portico at the main door.

Max said, 'Baron von Halder. I'm expected.'

This one was older and harder, a different proposition. 'Your pass, Herr Baron.'

'Certainly.' Max took the silenced Walther from his map pocket and shot him between the eyes.

He dragged the corpse into the shadows, then opened the front door and stepped inside. A young SS corporal sat at a table. He glanced up and Max shot him twice in the heart, driving him back so that the chair tilted.

It was very quiet. He stood there for a moment then mounted the stairs. It was strangely dreamlike, not happening at all and yet it was. He had never felt so purposeful, so strong in his life. He moved with total certainty, almost like a cat, his feet quiet as he drifted along the carpeted corridor towards his brother's room. The sentry was seated, reading a book, his Schmeisser on the floor. He looked up at the last moment and Max put the silencer against his forehead and fired and blood and fragmented bone spattered the wall as the sentry fell out of the chair. The key was in the door. Max turned it and opened. He moved inside.

'Harry, it's me.'

Harry, lying on the bed, couldn't believe it. He sat up. 'Max? What the hell is happening here?'

'Just listen. I got to England and they all accepted me, Zec, Munro and Carter, even Molly. Then it went wrong. They were on to the Rodrigues brothers and Sarah Dixon and that led them to me. I was arrested at Southwick and Munro took me to Cold Harbour.'

'But how come you're here?'

'I stole the Storch and flew over. I'm going to take you back. Do you think I could have left you here? To Himmler?'

'But what about Mutti?'

'Mutti's dead. She was shot to death before I left. They lied to us, Harry. Bubi lied.'

'Oh, God, no!' Harry moaned.

'Time to grieve later. Let's go.'

Harry pulled on his right shoe, picked up his crutches and pushed up. He struggled after Max, his mind in a turmoil and then the unexpected happened. They had reached the head of the stairs when a bathroom door opened and Freiburg came out, sleepy in his pyjamas. He paused, looking at them.

'My God, Max, it's you.'

Max could have shot him. Instead he struck him twice across the side of the head and Freiburg went down like a stone.

'Come on,' Max said to Harry and they descended the stairs.

At the bottom, Harry took in the body of the corporal, but Max already had the door open and the feet of the dead sentry were sticking out of the shadows. 'You don't take prisoners, Max.'

'Not tonight,' Max told him. 'Now let's get the hell out of here.'

He helped Harry in, slid behind the wheel and drove away. At the gate, the sentry was out in a flash and raised the barrier. They passed through and Max increased speed and drove back to the airstrip.

He pulled in beside the Storch and helped Harry out. 'Just dump the crutches, okay?'

'If you say so, brother.'

Max helped him into the Storch, closed the door and went round to the pilot's side. As he climbed in, Greiser ran across the apron. 'Is there anything I can do, Herr Baron?'

'No, thanks, you've done splendidly,' Max told him.

He taxied to the far end, turned into the wind and thundered down the runway. A moment later the Storch lifted and faded into the dark.

At the château, Bubi came awake to a frenzied knocking. He got out of bed, opened the door and Freiburg staggered in, blood on his face.

'For God's sake, what is it?' Bubi demanded.

'He was here, the Baron, with his brother.'

'You're mad,' Bubi told him.

'No, I swear it. I saw Max von Halder in Luftwaffe uniform and his brother on his crutches at the head of the stairs. I needed the toilet, I'd gone to the bathroom. I came out and they were there. The Baron clubbed me with a pistol and the sentry that was outside Kelso's room is dead.'

Bubi flung him to one side, ran along the corridor to the head of the stairs, looked down and saw the dead corporal. It was enough. He made it back to his room, got his uniform from the wardrobe and threw it on the bed.

As he took his pyjama jacket off, he said to Freiburg, 'Raise the alarm and have my staff car brought to the front entrance.'

Five minutes later, he rushed down the steps past the SS personnel already busy with the corpses and jumped into the back of the staff car. 'The airstrip,' he told the driver.

It had to be the airstrip, the only way Max could have got here. My God, both of them together once again. Enough to make even Himmler happy. It could change everything.

He leaned over and struck the driver on the shoulder. 'Faster, damn you, faster.'

Zec threw down his cards. 'That's it, Brigadier, I reckon you've cost us ten quid.'

'I can't help superior play,' Munro told him.

'Yes, and I can't help my nose. Out there at sea I smell things, Brigadier, things on the wind, but I smell something different now. I can't sit here. I've a feeling we could be needed and, if that's true, we're better fifteen or twenty miles out there and waiting.'

Munro didn't even hesitate. 'I bow to your superior judgement.'

'We'll leave now.' Zec turned to the crew. 'Move it!'

They all crowded out and Molly stood up, her medical bag in one hand. 'You might need me, Zec.'

'Good girl.'

'Dammit, I won't be left out.' Munro stood up. 'Hold the fort, Jack.'

Carter said, 'You don't want me out there, Brigadier. A Watson type lifeboat is no place for a false leg.' He turned to Molly and kissed her cheek. 'Good luck, love.'

She didn't say a word, simply turned and followed everyone out. It was quiet now, only Jack and Julie at the bar. She said, 'Time for prayer, I think.'

'Yes, well, a large whisky would assist,' Jack said. 'So, if you don't mind.'

At the airstrip, Bubi jumped out of the staff car and ran across the apron. He opened the door of the radio hut and Greiser turned in his chair, surprise on his face.

'Standartenführer.'

'Baron von Halder, he was here?'

'Why yes, Standartenführer. He landed in a Storch, told me he was here on a mission for Reichsführer Himmler and borrowed a *Kübelwagen*. He came back twenty minutes ago with a passenger and took off again.'

'You imbecile.' Bubi turned, and ran towards the ME 109 in the hangar. The Storch was slow, the 109, the latest model, was very fast indeed. All he had to do was catch up, threaten to blow them out of the sky unless they turned back. He could still retrieve the situation.

He clambered into the cockpit, not bothering with a parachute, pulled on the flying helmet with the radio mike and switched on. The roaring of the ME's engine seemed to make the hangar vibrate. He taxied out, moved to the end of the strip, turned into the wind and took off.

Julie's met report proved totally accurate for, as the Storch moved out over the sea, the cloud cover cleared and the moon appeared, clear and bright, a hard white light. Max turned and spoke to Harry, who was wearing the spare headphones and mike. 'You okay?'

'I've never felt better.'

Max smiled. 'We made it, brother. I'm sorry for Bubi, but I'd love to see Himmler's face.'

'So would I.' Harry checked the instruments. 'ETA thirty minutes, I'd say.'

There was a sudden roaring and the Storch rocked in turbulence as the ME 109 passed overhead and banked to take station to starboard. Bubi's voice crackled on the headphones.

'Turn back, Max, the jig's up. I can't let you do this. It's a death sentence for me and those close to me.'

'What about our mother, Bubi? You lied.'

'That wasn't my fault, I swear it.'

'Too bad,' Max told him. 'But it's a fact of life. Come on, Bubi, you seriously want me to turn round and fly back to Morlaix?'

'If you don't, I'll shoot you down.'

'Bubi, I always liked you, but you were never very good in the old days over France before the Battle. What do you say, brother?'

'Tell him to go and fuck himself,' Harry Kelso said.

'You heard, Bubi. If you fancy trying to blow us away, go for it. It's a lot quicker than dangling in a wire noose from a meathook.'

He went down fast and, at 1500 feet, Bubi came in on the Storch's tail. Pieces flew from the fuselage and wings. Max kept on going down and Harry said, 'Not that old trick?'

'It saved Eisenhower the other day. Remind me to tell you about it some time.'

At 700 feet, Bubi came in again, the Storch staggered and Max groaned at a hammer blow in the back. He dropped the flaps, the Storch almost stopped dead and Bubi Hartmann, with nowhere to go, ploughed into the sea.

'It never fails,' Max gasped. 'Don't you find that?'

'Takes me back to Rocky and those first lessons,' Harry said. 'Where would we have been without him?'

'Long gone.' Max choked and blood poured out of his mouth.

'Jesus!' Harry said.

'Call Cold Harbour,' Max told him, 'because I'm losing power fast. We're not going to make it.'

Harry called. 'Cold Harbour, come in. Colonel Kelso here, plus brother, in one badly damaged Storch.'

It was the lifeboat that answered. 'Zec here, Colonel, we're twenty miles out in the *Lively Jane*. Give me your position.'

Harry did as he was asked. 'My brother's been hit. It's not good and the engine's failing.'

'We'll be there, boy, no more than three miles away.'

The Storch descended, clear in the bright moonlight, the sea black below and yet dawn was touching the sky to the east. On the *Lively Jane* it was as if all the crew saw the plane at the same moment and there was a general chorus. Molly, in the stern cockpit, leaned on the rail with Munro, as the boat raced on over a strong sea, lifting over the waves. The Storch was clearly visible now, a mile to port, smoke trailing.

At 400 feet the engine died and the propeller stopped. There was silence, only the sound of the wind, and Max coughed again. 'Get your lifebelt on.'

Harry did as he was told then pulled another from under the seat. 'Now you, Max.'

'No point. I'm drowning in my own blood.'

A hundred feet now, and then lower, skimming the wave tops and Max swung the Storch to port and landed parallel to the crests. The Storch settled, water pouring in. Harry opened the door and unfastened his seat-belt. The Storch was already sinking. He tried to unfasten Max's belt but it seemed jammed.

Max coughed, another gush of blood erupting from his mouth. 'Daft bastard. I'm finished. Get out of here.'

'Max,' Harry cried. 'For God's sake!'

Baron Max von Halder summoned up every last atom of strength and punched him in the mouth. Harry went backwards through the open door, a wave caught him and pulled him away. Behind him the *Lively Jane* swerved in broadside, but Harry only had eyes for the Storch, the port wing under the water, the aircraft tilting slightly, a last glimpse of his brother in the cockpit, only a shadow and then it went under the waves, disappeared for ever.

*

The two crew members who came over the side for Harry towed him in and willing hands reached down and pulled him over. Harry slumped to the deck and someone draped a blanket over his shoulders.

'Harry, it is you, isn't it?' Munro demanded.

'Look at my bloody face, damn you.'

'What happened?'

'Max got me out, Bubi Hartmann chased us in an ME 109. Shot us up good. Max took a cannon shell in the back, then he made Bubi crash back there. End of story.'

'Good God.'

Molly had an arm around him. 'Come below, let me check you over.'

'What for, to tell me I should be dead? I've known that for years. I believe my brother knew the same. Now he's gone.' Harry's face was like stone. 'You know what, Molly, my love? My luck ran out with Tarquin. I'm a dead man walking,' and he stood up and went below.

COLD HARBOUR

1998

EIGHTEEN

It was almost a year to the day when Denise and I returned to Cold Harbour, and what a year. My hunt for the truth about Harry and Max Kelso had taken me to many places. Files at the Pentagon, the Public Records Office in London, Luftwaffe files in Germany, Portugal and Madeira. Of course, I'd been greatly helped by my cousin, Konrad Strasser, the old Gestapo hand. What he'd managed to dig out before he died was incredible. I stood in the rain at his burial in a Hamburg cemetery and regretted his passing more than most.

The Public Records Office has strict regulations on the disgorging of highly secret information. Thirty-year holds, fifty and even one hundred are common. On the other hand, if you know the right people, it's surprising what comes out. For example, I traced a wonderful old American of eighty-three who'd flown with the RAF, had ended the war as a colonel in the US Air Force and after a successful international business career had retired to England. He'd known Harry Kelso well and, like him, had flown for the Courier Service. His information was invaluable, more what he'd had to say about the man than anything else.

The prime movers were all dead, needless to say. Brigadier Dougal Munro; Jack Carter, who'd ended the war as a full colonel; Teddy West, who became an air marshal and received a knight-hood. General Eisenhower was long gone and so was Major

General Tom Sobel, who disappeared over the English Channel in a Dakota *en route* for Normandy two weeks after D-Day.

One incredible piece of luck concerned a certain Major Vereker of the Royal Military Police. He'd died of cancer in 1953, but I discovered his daughter, a widow living in Falmouth. She was kind enough to see me and I told her what I knew. She sat there in her cosy sitting room, thinking about it, then went to a desk and took out a buff envelope.

'I found this amongst my father's effects all those years ago. I don't suppose it matters now. You can read it if you like.'

Which I did and discovered a meticulous account of the events of that day at Southwick when he'd arrested Max on Dougal Munro's orders.

Why the island of Madeira? Simple enough. Fernando and Joel Rodrigues were finished with the Portuguese diplomatic service. They opened a bar in Alfama, the old quarter in Lisbon, another in Estoril. With the end of the war in Europe, Sarah Dixon was released from detention. A happy ending for someone. She went to Portugal and married Fernando. In 1950 they moved to Madeira and opened a bar and restaurant.

She was long gone when I visited that beautiful island, but not Fernando, still around at eighty-nine, incredibly active, still in charge of a mini empire of restaurants and bars, much in control of his extended family.

He listened to what I had to say and laughed when I'd finished. 'I read your books in Portuguese, do you know that and this is a good plot.'

'Just like my other good plots?' I asked.

'Except that this one is true.' He laughed again. 'What the hell, I've one foot in the grave. Who cares any more, so let me put you straight on a few points.'

Which he proceeded to do and died a few months later.

★

The plane Denise hired at Goodwood Aero Club was an Archer, a single-engine job. The reason for the trip was simple. I'd sent a typescript of the story to Zec Acland at Cold Harbour. It wasn't perfect, there were still some puzzling gaps, but I wanted to get his opinion. I'd had a phone call the previous day at the house in Chichester, asking if we could come down.

So, here we were, flying west, Southampton, the Isle of Wight, the sky dull, a hint of rain and immersed in the facts of the book, as I had been for so long, I thought of 1940, the Luftwaffe flying in, the RAF rising to meet them, the Battle of Britain, Harry and Max, the brave young men on both sides, more than fifty per cent of whom had died. It was a depressing thought, all those planes on the bottom of the English Channel and in one of them were the remains of Oberstleutnant Baron Max von Halder.

Thunder rumbled on the horizon as Denise banked and took us from the sea to Cold Harbour. The village was spread below, the Hanged Man, the cottages, the lifeboat, the *Lady Carter* tied up at the quay. We drifted over the manor, the lake, the trees and dropped down on that grass runway. Denise taxied towards the wartime hangars, where an old Land Rover waited, Zec Acland leaning against it. She switched off and we got out.

Zec came forward and she kissed him on the cheek. 'You don't look any older.'

'You have a way with the words, girl. You've got Tarquin in there, I suppose?'

'Oh, yes,' she said.

'Bring him along. We'll take a run down to the Hanged Man, have a sandwich and a drink. We need to talk.'

'Fine by us,' I said.

He got behind the wheel of the Land Rover and we joined him, Tarquin in his new waterproof jump bag, and set off.

As we drove down the High Street the *Lady Carter* moved away from the quay and started out to sea.

'What's that?' I asked. 'An emergency call?'

'No, just an exercise. They have to keep up to scratch. Simeon's a hard driver.'

He pulled up outside the pub and we got out and went in. There was no one else there, but then it was only eleven o'clock. The fire burned brightly though and I was filled with a strange sense of déjà vu, not just because Denise and I had been here before in dramatic circumstances. It was everything that had happened here. Dougal Munro, Jack Carter and Molly, Julie Legrande and Max and Harry.

'Betsy?' Zec called.

She came in from the kitchen. 'Hello, there.'

'We're ready. Let's be having you.' He turned to Denise. 'Can we have a look at him?'

'Of course.' She unzipped the bag, took Tarquin out and sat him on the bar.

Zec sat down and stared for a long moment and I suddenly realized there were tears in his eyes. 'You wonderful little bugger,' he said.

Denise put an arm around his shoulders. 'It's all right, Zec, don't get upset.'

'You're right, no sense in that.'

Betsy came in with a huge mound of sandwiches on a server and a mass of salad. 'The bread's our own baking and the ham is home cured and off the bone. What about a drink?'

'Tea for me,' Denise told him. 'I'm flying.'

Zec said, 'He likes his champagne, this one, so open that bottle I put in the fridge and I'll have some too.'

We tucked into the sandwiches, which were delicious. I said, 'The typescript I sent you. What did you think?'

'All right as far as it went.' He suddenly guffawed. 'No, dammit, it was bloody fascinating. A few gaps though.'

'Such as?'

'No mention of Julie Legrande at the end of things.'

'I couldn't trace what happened to her.'

'I can tell you. She went back to France after the war, died of leukaemia in Paris. I went to her funeral.'

'I see.' I drank some champagne. 'You said a few gaps? What would the others be?'

'I'll let Lady Carter fill you in on those. She's expecting us at the manor at noon.'

Denise stopped eating. 'Lady Carter? But that's what the lifeboat's called.'

'It would be. Her husband paid for a new boat ten years ago just before he died. The RNLI named it after her.'

'Lady Carter?' I asked.

'Jack Carter's wife. Sir Jack Carter after his father died. Ended the war a colonel, Jack did. Came down here and bought Grancester Manor.'

'And Lady Carter?' I asked although I think I already knew the answer.

'Lady Molly, people call her round here, Molly Sobel as was. She was the doctor in these parts for years. A saint.'

Denise looked at me, a query in her eyes, then turned back to Zec. 'Were there any children?'

'God bless you, no. Jack was blown up at Dunkirk and lost his leg, but he was damaged, if you follow me. No, a family wasn't possible. Not that it mattered, not after Harry.'

'What happened?' I said.

'I'll let her tell you that.' He stood up and checked his watch. 'Let's be off then. She'll be waiting, and bring Tarquin.'

★

333

At Grancester Manor, he didn't bother with the front door but led the way round a corner, a light rain falling, and followed a terrace above a wonderful rose garden. French windows stood open and, as rain spattered the flagstones, he led the way in to what was obviously the library. There she was, sitting on the couch by the fire.

She was eighty years old, her white hair a halo, the face still young, good cheekbones, the frock simple but elegant. She looked up from the typescript, my typescript, and put it to one side.

'My third reading. I recognize you from those photos on the backs of books.'

'Lady Molly.' I took her outstretched hand. 'My wife, Denise.'

She pulled Denise down beside her. 'What a remarkable escape, my dear, but they tell me you're an excellent pilot.'

'Thank you,' Denise said.

'You probably walk on water. That's what Harry used to say.' She patted Denise's hand. 'But I've been fascinated by the book. So many things I never knew.' She hesitated. 'Could I see Tarquin?'

Denise unzipped the bag, took him out and offered him. Lady Molly gazed at him, enraptured. 'Oh, Tarquin.' She held him close and there were tears in her eyes. 'Where did you get him? Harry thought he was destroyed in the Lysander crash in France.'

'Apparently Munro made some enquiries of his agent, Jacaud, in Brittany at the end of the war,' I said. 'Jacaud told him they'd found Tarquin at the scene of the crash and his radio operator, a woman called Marie, took him for her daughter.'

'And then?'

'Marie was killed fighting with the Resistance after D-Day.

The child was adopted by relations and that was the last heard of Tarquin.'

'Until we found him on the top shelf of an antique shop in Brighton,' Denise said. 'How he got there we'll never know. His name had travelled with him though.'

There was a pause. I said, with some diffidence, 'There's one gap. Exactly what happened to Harry afterwards? I had difficulties there, and I ran into roadblocks.'

She smiled. 'Well, Eisenhower had to be told. It was decided to put Top Secret on the whole thing. I mean, the idea that the Supreme Commander had been in hazard before D-Day was unthinkable. They carried on as if nothing had happened. Harry kept Max's DSC and continued to do courier work and the occasional job for Munro.

'He wouldn't have it, always had to go back for more, even after they made him a full colonel. After the Channel crash and what happened to Max, he was never the same. He said he was a dead man walking. I think he wanted to prove it. I think he wanted to be with Max. They were one, you see, interchangeable in a way you don't appreciate. Was Max Harry or was Harry Max?'

It was Denise who took her hand and said gently, 'What happened?'

'So stupid, so bloody stupid. Almost the end of the war. My uncle had this thing going with some German general on the wrong side of the Rhine. Harry volunteered to make the flight from here in an Arado wearing Luftwaffe insignia. He landed, picked the man up, flew back across France. They were attacked by an RAF Mosquito and badly shot up.'

'And went into the Channel?' I asked.

'Oh, no, the weather was lousy and he went down and lost the Mosquito and he made it to Cold Harbour. I was here with my uncle, Jack and Julie. It was raining and misty and the Arado rolled to a halt and the engine was switched off. When we opened the door, the German general was gibbering in the back seat and Harry was dead at the controls.'

She stared into the past, anguish on her face and Denise hugged her, Tarquin between them. Finally Lady Molly pulled herself together. 'It means so much to see Tarquin again.'

'He's come home,' Denise said. 'It's you he rightfully belongs to.'

'Oh, no, I'm very grateful.' Lady Molly hesitated. 'If I could borrow him. Would that be all right? Temporary loan only?'

'Of course,' Denise said.

Molly nodded. 'I'm so grateful.' She stood. 'Now I'd like you to come with me. There's something you should see.'

She put a raincoat over her shoulders and cradled Tarquin in her left arm and Zec came with us. He took two umbrellas from the stand in the hall, gave us one and walked to one side, holding the other over Lady Molly, for that light rain was drifting down again. Denise and I followed and she gripped my arm lightly.

There was a flintstone wall, an old grey stone church on the other side, cypress trees and a clump of beech trees. Zec opened a gate and we passed through into the usual kind of country church graveyard. It was very peaceful and then rooks lifted out of the beech trees, calling angrily.

'Noisy buggers,' Zec said.

We followed a narrow path between gravestones, many obviously very ancient, here and there the odd Angel of Death or Gothic monument. Finally we stopped in the far corner under a cypress tree. The grave there was well tended, there were fresh flowers, the grass carefully cut. The headstone was a slab of Cornish slate and the inscription cut into its face was stamped in gold. It looked as if it had recently been freshened.

'Here we are.' She smiled and held Tarquin tightly.

It said, '*March 1945. In loving memory of Colonel Harry Kelso and his brother, Oberstleutnant Baron Max von Halder. Together at last. Brothers in Arms.*'

The rain increased and Zec moved close, holding the umbrella over her, something indomitable about him as he stood there, an arm about her. Denise and I huddled under our own umbrella and she was fighting to hold back the tears.

Lady Molly turned. 'Don't be sorry, my dear. It was a long, long time ago and now that it doesn't matter, I'm going to tell you something that even dear Zec here never knew.'

Zec frowned, puzzled, and we stood there in the rain, heavy now, and waited.

'As you discovered, back in 1930 when their father died and the boys were twelve, Elsa struck a bargain with Abe Kelso that she would return to Germany with her eldest son, Max the Baron, and Harry would stay with his grandfather.'

'That's right,' I said.

'Harry gave me a different version. He told me just before he died. I've always felt he saw death coming. He often told me he'd no idea what he'd do with himself without a war.'

'What on earth are you talking about?' I asked.

And yet Denise, with her woman's intuition, had already seen it, gave a dry sob and clutched my arm fiercely.

Lady Molly carried on. 'When the decision was put to the boys, there was a problem. They didn't like the idea and there was a further problem. Tarquin, the bear, who'd flown in France with their father. Who got Tarquin? All this was between the boys. Abe and their mother knew nothing of it.'

'What did they do?' I asked.

'Decided that Tarquin must stay in America in the house their father had been born in, had returned to after the war. Then they tossed a coin to see who would go to Germany with their mother.'

Zec looked stunned and Denise said, 'Oh, my God.'

'Yes, my dear,' Molly said. 'Harry Kelso was Baron von Halder and Max was Harry Kelso.'

It was the most astonishing thing I'd ever heard in my life, it took my breath away. It was Denise who said, 'Together at last – but in a way, they always were.'

'Exactly.' Lady Molly smiled. 'We'll go back now,' and she walked ahead of us, Zec holding the umbrella over her.

At the house, she offered us tea, which we declined. 'The weather's taken a turn for the worse,' Denise told her. 'We'd best be off.'

We said our goodbyes, walked back to the Land Rover and Zec drove us to the airstrip. When we got out, he shook hands and kissed Denise on the cheek.

'Take care, girl.'

'A shock for you,' I said. 'Hearing that.'

'Not really. At the final end of things, what did it matter?'

We got into the Archer, Denise sat on the left-hand side and I locked the door. As she switched on and the engine rumbled, rain lashed across and there was mist out there on the sea.

'We'd better move it,' she said. 'It'll get worse before it gets better.'

We roared down the runway and lifted into the grey sky, climbed to a thousand feet and then suddenly she banked to port.

'What are you doing?' I asked.

'I just want a last look.'

But as we turned over the sea and moved back to the land, the mist had already rolled in. Of Cold Harbour, there was no sign. It was as if it had never been.